THE BROKEN AIR

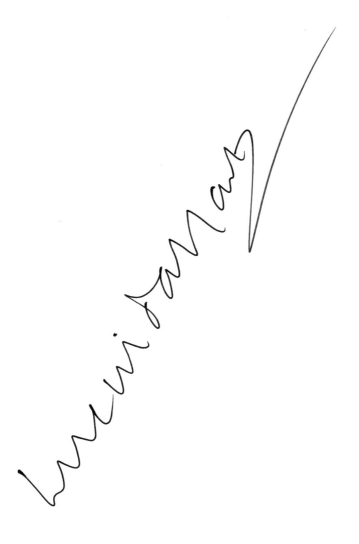

THE BROKEN AIR

Lucinda Hart

PRESS

Published by Vulpine Press in the United Kingdom in 2022

ISBN: 978-1-83919-208-1

www.vulpine-press.com

For Caroline Matthews

.

Author's Note

As a child growing up in Mullion, I was obsessed with the wonderful foghorn at the Lizard lighthouse. If the wind was in the right direction, we could hear it in Mullion, some miles up the coast. The sound was a deep, mournful call, a sound from the depths of the earth, the sound of forever. I was heartbroken when it was changed for an electric hooter. After the change, the old foghorn remained connected and was occasionally sounded for special occasions, but I heard now from my friend and Lizard lighthouse guide, Andrew Read, that it has been completely dismantled. This is a huge loss. You can hear it on this YouTube video: lizard Lighthouse, "Sounding" for fog. 1997 – YouTube

Kynance is a real beach just north of Lizard village. The geology there is extraordinary. The beach is only accessible at low tide when the strand is clear of water, and you can walk across to Asparagus Island. Bishop's Cove and the Buttress are figments of my imagination, but there are several rugged crags on the cliffs of the Lizard.

The solar eclipse of 11 August 1999 truly was a once-in-a-lifetime event. I was lucky enough to live in the path of totality. On the morning of the eclipse, the sky was heavy and overcast. Just moments before totality, a ragged hole appeared in the clouds, and I saw the black sun and the diamond ring from my garden. I will never forget the sudden sweeping darkness and the cheers from those watching on the cliff.

I hope you have enjoyed the book; if you have, I would really appreciate a review. Please join my Facebook page *Lucinda Hart - Author* where I share news, competitions, and short fiction.

PROLOGUE

11 a.m., 11 August 1999
The Lizard, Cornwall

It happens in seconds. The darkness rolls in over the mercury sea, like a giant silk curtain unfurling. The air is still. There is no birdsong. Nature holds her breath. In the unnatural dusk, I sense the pulse of the lighthouse over my shoulder, but, for once, just this once, I am not turning to that light. Instead, I'm staring up, like the hundreds of others gathered here at the end of the world. There is a cry, a cheer, a roar from those on the very edge of the cliffs, and the filmy cloud overhead at last tears apart. There it is: a black disc where the sun should hang, circled with a pale, flaring corona.

Totality.

Silence falls. Just a ragged hole in the clouds where the sun and moon fuse together. Light and dark. The lighthouse blinks and blinks in this daytime night. There are people around me, but I feel I am alone. Through my eclipse glasses, the corona turns a strange gold. The moon slides on, and there's the luminous glow of the diamond ring. I have seen pictures of it in books, but here it is, sparkling for me, in the sky.

Light bleeds from the edges of the moon. Voices rise again. Heads drop. People are laughing, shouting, crying. The noise after the silence makes me dizzy. Still, the lighthouse shines on. Straggles of silver cloud creep over the sun and moon.

"Emily, Emily."

Someone's talking to me.

I shake my head and turn to her.

"Wasn't that amazing?" Rachel says, her eyes wet with tears.

"It was … I don't have the words."

I don't. What I've just seen is ancient, cosmic. I feel like I, too, have been swallowed by the moon.

Gary and Sonia have their arms round each other. Sonia's dropped her eclipse glasses on the ground. I cannot hear what they are saying.

Rachel's miserable because she doesn't have anyone special – a man – to share the eclipse with, but I don't care that I'm alone.

It's something I will tell my children about, I think suddenly. *I'll share it with them.*

Gary, Sonia, and Rachel are my friends from university in Bath. We all came down together in Gary's car. They are staying with me. Gary and Sonia have one of the caravans; Rachel's in the house, in the spare room. They will be going back to Bath at the end of the week, but I'll stay on a while longer. It is the summer holidays, and though I have a new life in the city now, new friends, and new places to go, the end of the world still calls me home.

A large wave breaks over the Man of War rocks south of the headland. The oldest rocks on the Lizard. We are standing in the scrubby car park by the lighthouse. The dry grass and hard mud have been churned up underfoot. Some people are walking back to their cars.

Gary's asking what are we going to do now? Walk back to the Lizard village and on to the holiday park, or hang out here for a bit?

The sky's gradually lightening. A seagull soars across the headland. The daisies by my feet are unfolding their petals, turning their pale faces back to the growing sun.

I scan the crowds. I am surprised I haven't seen anyone I know. But then I do, and my heart rate shoots so high that I can hardly breathe.

She is only ten, fifteen yards away. Dark-brown shiny hair, cut shorter. She's pregnant, very pregnant. She's holding a little girl by the hand. The girl must be about four. She has curly hair, a lighter brown. She's wearing a pink-and-green flowered dress. Pink trainers.

"What are we doing?" Gary asks again.

"Give me a moment."

I am already walking to her.

She looks up and stares at me. The little girl tugs on her arm, but she ignores her.

"Mummy," I hear the girl say.

"Zoe," I say.

I haven't seen her for almost seven years. Not since that day.

"Emily?" She makes it a question, but she knows who I am.

"Who is it?" the girl asks.

Zoe's eyes don't leave my face. "It's someone I was at school with."

"What happened?" It rushes from my mouth. I know I shouldn't ask, not here, in front of her daughter, but it may be the only chance I have.

"I can't talk about it now." She looks round at the long bank of cars parked on the dirty grass. Looking for someone.

"Please," I say. "We tried to find you. We wanted to know what was happening, that you were OK, but they wouldn't tell us anything – where you were, what you were doing."

"I'm sorry. It was so difficult." She starts to pull the child away.

"You're expecting again, then?" I ask, needlessly, and it sounds accusing.

"Another four weeks. Are you living here still?"

3

"I live in Bath now. I'm at uni. Down with some friends. My parents are still here."

"I'll write to you," Zoe says. "I'll explain everything. I'll send it to your parents' place. We must go now. My husband ..."

She wheels her daughter around firmly towards the row of cars.

I stand, watching, waiting to see her husband. The child peers once over her shoulder. I'll follow them if I have to, to see this husband. But no. I don't have to. Zoe lets go of her daughter's hand by a silver Ford estate car. The boot is up, and a man's head appears round the side. He looks about forty, with brown hair and glasses. Zoe's talking to him, leaning on the side of the car. Zoe and her happy family. Husband and daughter. Another on the way.

Does she ever stop and think about before? I wonder. *Does she have regrets?*

It wasn't that long ago – only a few years.

I'm just about to walk away, to find my friends, when another child runs round from the back of the car. A boy. He's got dark hair and wearing jeans and a bright T-shirt.

"Emily, come on." It's Gary, grabbing me by the arm. "We're going to the pub. You OK?"

"I'm fine," I lie.

We walk back up the lane to the Lizard village. The sky lightens moment by moment. I want to turn round, run back to the car park, and march up to that silver car. But I can't. Zoe said she would write. I wonder if I should tell my parents that I've seen her.

No. It would be too unkind. Too cruel.

Mum still struggles with the aftermath of that August afternoon.

I grunt a reply to whatever Sonia has said. We pull in to the hedge to let a couple of cars go by and then straggle out across the road behind them.

"Another car," Gary says, and I move aside.

4

Silver. A silver estate car. It crawls past. I see the old guy at the wheel and Zoe in the passenger seat. I see the boy and his sister in the back. Then, the car has gone, and I'm staring only at the metal fish sign stuck below the rear window.

PART ONE

February 1992

Kynance Holiday Park, the sign shouted in black lettering, and underneath was a stylised depiction of the jagged stacks and islets under a golden summer sun.

It wasn't sunny this afternoon, Emily's sixteenth birthday. The wind was cold, roaring over the low-lying clifftop, and the sky was the colour of gunmetal.

"So, this is where I live," Emily started awkwardly.

It was the first time Zoe had come to her house; in fact, it was the first time in ages she had brought a friend home. Sometimes the boys from the Lizard would straggle into the clubhouse to play pool, and Richard's older friends might come – to check out the girls staying in the caravans – but Emily couldn't remember when she'd last invited anyone back. She had, in the early days, when she was still new to Cornwall. One by one, the girls from Mullion or the Lizard or Ruan Minor thought they wanted to be best friends with her because she was from "elsewhere". Because her mother had been an actress. Because her father had met big names in music back in the seventies. Because she lived in a caravan park on the edge of the cliff, or whatever. And, one by one, she had brought these girls back. Then, a week or so later, she would go to their houses, and the girls would stop sitting next to her in class. They went back to their old cronies, and sometimes Emily heard them whisper her name, so she knew they were bitching, but she was never sure what about. Her history, her parents, the holiday camp, her rust-coloured hair? It could have been any or all of these things, or maybe something else entirely.

"You haven't got people staying in caravans at this time of year?" Zoe asked.

"Not many. We close for December and January, and we've only just reopened."

"They look very cold." Zoe stared at the field of caravans, white with lime green trim, in the field beyond the bungalow and clubhouse.

"They are cold." Emily shrugged. "But warmer than a tent. That small field over there is for tents." She gestured to the right.

The field was empty, just churned up mud and wintery grass.

Emily's mother, Cheryl, was waiting for them in the kitchen when they came in.

"Hello, Zoe," Cheryl said.

"Hello, Mrs Knight," Zoe said.

Emily didn't bother to tell Zoe that her mother never used her married name. Zoe wouldn't understand that. They were so different. How had they ended up friends? Why had she suddenly found in Zoe someone she could talk to, someone who listened to her and didn't run off and bitch to other girls? Someone who didn't snigger or groan at her when she missed a catch in netball but rather rolled her eyes and grinned sympathetically when she went to root the grubby ball out of the bushes behind the goal post.

Zoe lived in Gunwalloe, further round Mount's Bay. She was in Emily's year at school but in a different form. Although Emily had known the willowy girl with the straight, shiny brown hair was called Zoe Cassidy, they'd never spoken to each other until they sat together in RE the first week of their fourth year …

10

Emily had chosen RE because it was either that or history – and history was boring as it was bound to be the bloody war again or, failing that, the Reformation. She walked into the RE room and glanced quickly at the rows. Now that everyone had chosen their GCSE subjects, they were, at last, mixing with people from other forms who they might have only met in games and assemblies. The RE group was small. There were two girls from Emily's class. One of them had – a long time ago – come to tea at Emily's. They were sitting together under the window. The others were from other classes, sitting in twos and threes, except for one girl with brown hair, sitting alone in the back row by the door.

"Hi, can I sit here?" Emily asked.

Zoe Cassidy half-smiled and moved her bag from the tabletop to the floor.

In that first lesson, the teacher asked the class their thoughts on God. The two bitches by the window laughed and said they didn't believe in God, and so did most of the others. Some said they didn't know.

"The Bible's interesting," Emily said, evading the question.

Someone made a snoring noise.

Before her family moved to Cornwall, Emily had been to a church school, where they had sung hymns every morning and repeated prayers throughout the day. At Christmas and Easter, the children went to church, and some read from the Bible. Emily read every time; she could still remember the passages written in black felt pen on pieces of card to hold.

"I'm a Christian. I was created by God," Zoe said.

Emily realised this was why Zoe, too, was an outcast. She was a real Christian; she and her family went to church, and she'd been confirmed.

"What have you got after break?" Zoe asked as they slid their new textbooks into their bags.

"French. Mr Finlay," Emily said.

"Yeah, me, too. Come with me to my locker to get my French stuff?"

They walked through the enclosed quad with its muddy grass and brick-edged pond to the bank of lockers by the art department.

"I don't know why that lot are doing RE," Zoe said as she fished out her key. "They obviously don't believe in God."

Probably because they think it's an easy option, Emily thought.

That was what her father had said to her when she said there was no way she was doing history any longer.

"*RE?*" Terry Knight had echoed. "*You're far too clever for that. That's what the dumbos take.*"

He was right, Emily realised quickly – *except for Zoe and me, that is.*

There was a pile of envelopes on the kitchen table for Emily: white envelopes, one pink, and one cream. She tore the first open. A cheque dropped out of the card.

"My grandparents," she told Zoe. "On Dad's side. I think this one's from my other set." She lifted the pink envelope. A small brown one was stuck to the back of it. **Ms Cheryl Ross** was typed above the address. "This is for you, Mum."

"I must have missed it," Cheryl called from the utility room. "Cake in ten minutes."

"I'll just show Zoe the bathroom."

While Zoe washed, Emily waited in the corridor.

The front door opened, and her father and brother came in, headed straight for the kitchen.

"Fabulous cake, Mum," she heard Richard say. "Here, use my lighter."

"Birthday tea," Terry shouted.

Back in the kitchen, four pink-and-white-striped candles wavered on top of a frosted pink cake.

"I went for the square root for safety," Cheryl said.

"Zoe, hi, Terry Knight." Her father offered his hand, which Zoe shook shyly. "And this is Richard. You might remember him from school?"

"Um, I'm sorry …" Zoe said.

"Come on, make a wish," Cheryl cried.

"Happy birthday, beautiful girl." Terry dropped a kiss on Emily's copper-haired head as she bent to blow the candles.

They expired with four tiny plumes of smoke and the faintest scent.

Cheryl cut the cake. Inside, under the pink icing, was soft sponge and layers of raspberry jam and buttercream.

Emily and Zoe carried their plates to Emily's room.

Emily heeled off her black lace-ups and sat cross-legged on her purple bean bag.

"Shall we have some music?" Zoe rattled a forefinger through the rows of tapes on Emily's shelf. "Madonna? Queen? Michael Jackson?"

"You choose." Emily forked up the cake. "This is yummy. Mum studied catering when she stopped acting. She makes wonderful cakes."

Zoe slid a Madonna cassette into the machine and hit 'play'. She glanced over her shoulder to the door.

"Are your parents married?" she asked Emily as she picked up her plate.

"Yes, why?"

"Oh. It's just … I saw that letter for her. She's not called Knight. And she doesn't wear a wedding ring … so I just wondered if they were."

13

"She doesn't use her married name at all now. She only used it for a while when she was having me. The hospitals and that – they weren't very open-minded then. And when they were adopting Rich, of course. They had to be ultra-conservative for that."

"Richard's adopted? You never said."

"Sorry. I don't really think about it. He's my brother. That's all. But yes, he's adopted."

"He doesn't look much like you or your parents. That explains it."

"No, he doesn't at all." Emily laughed and started taking books out of her rucksack. "I don't think we could ever pass him off as one of us."

Both Emily's parents were fair, though Terry's hair had faded to a silver-sand colour. Emily was auburn, but Richard was completely different, with shaggy black hair and peppermint-green eyes. Once people knew he was adopted, it seemed so obvious.

"Does he know his real parents? I mean his *biological* parents?"

"Not yet. He's nineteen, so he could look for them. I guess he probably will sometime."

"Your present." Zoe reached for her bag and unzipped it. "I know you said you wanted to keep your birthday quiet at school." She withdrew a long squashy parcel and handed it to Emily. "And here's your card. Sorry, it's a bit bent."

Emily unwrapped the parcel. It was a frilly lavender-and-cream make-up bag with a paper sachet of lavender inside.

"Thank you," she said.

"Show me what else you got, then."

Emily crawled off the bean bag towards the pile of presents in the corner. She showed Zoe the tapes, the videos, the watercolour box she'd chosen for herself in the art shop, the furry slippers, and the earrings. It felt odd – sitting on her bedroom floor at five o'clock in the evening, still wearing her creased school skirt and tights that had somehow become all skewed so that her feet weren't in the right place. It felt odd – having another girl in her room after all this time. Emily felt like she didn't even know how to behave in front of Zoe.

Perhaps Zoe will go the way of all the other girls?

No.

Emily realised she didn't want that. However different they were, she liked Zoe and wanted her around. She should have asked her over before this – they'd been sitting together in RE and French for eighteen months.

When the cassette finished, they went back to the kitchen for Pepsi and more cake.

Richard was sitting at the breakfast bar, smoking and drinking pale lager from a bottle.

"You coming to the bar?" he asked, grinding out his cigarette in a Heineken ashtray that he'd nicked from the clubhouse. "Play you both at pool?"

Emily glanced at Zoe, expecting her to shake her head.

"Why not?" Zoe licked buttercream off her fingers.

Richard checked his watch and slid off the stool. "OK, see you there soon."

When the girls wandered up the lane shortly afterwards, it was dark, and the mist had rolled in from the sea. Emily could hear the waves breaking on the rocks below. Beyond the five-barred gate at the end of the caravan field was the giant crag called the Buttress. She wouldn't take Zoe there. They had no torch, and it was slippery and treacherous in the dark.

The clubhouse was on the left, with a large gravelled area for parking. There were no cars, and when they stepped inside, the bar was empty except for Terry behind the bar and Richard shooting balls on one of the pool tables with a hollow *clack*.

15

It was always cold in the bar in winter. Terry lifted the bar flap and turned on a portable gas fire by the fruit machine. The walls of the bar were painted pale green, and the settles and stools were covered in a darker shade. On the walls were framed music posters from the seventies and eighties, and a mirror ran the length of the bar behind the optics, reflecting the golds and bronze of the spirits. The only sound was the *clack, clack, clack* of the pool balls and Richard's "Fuck it" as the white shot into the corner pocket behind the black. The long light over the table died.

"Play you two now," Richard said as he crouched down and fed coins into the table.

The balls were released with a loud *rumble*. The light flared again under its frayed green shade.

Emily unhooked the triangle and scooped the coloured balls from the hole.

"I've never played," Zoe said.

"It's easy enough." Emily racked the balls and replaced the triangle on the light. "If he can do it, anyone can."

"I play for the team, Zoe."

"You have a team?"

"Yeah, we play on Thursdays."

He broke off; the triangle of balls scattered, and a red slid into a pocket. He missed the next.

Emily helped herself to a cue from the rack, held it to her eye to check it wasn't too bent, and slammed the cue ball to the far corner. It knocked into a yellow, which trembled in the jaws but didn't sink. She lifted her arm and looked up. Zoe was leaning across the second darkened table. Richard was behind her, holding her arms in position for cueing.

"I get it," Zoe said.

Emily jumped as her father turned on some music.

The front door opened, and two of the regulars from the Lizard came in.

Terry called out a greeting.

Richard peeled away from Zoe, taking his cue from her hands. He sunk two more reds and said something to Zoe that Emily didn't catch.

Zoe giggled.

March 1992

Emily unlocked the cubicle and knocked on the neighbouring door.

"It's safe now," she said.

At the sink, she ran tepid water over her hands. Although she had only touched the door, she felt dirty.

In the mirror, she watched Zoe coming out of the middle cubicle. She'd had her hair permed over the weekend, and it tumbled in spirals round her ears.

Emily glared at her own flat hair. Over the months, she had tried sprays, mousse, and curlers, but nothing gave her the look she wanted: an effortless, tousled mop, neither lank nor frizzled. She envied Zoe's new waves but knew she would never get hers permed because someone would make a bitchy remark about it.

"They'll have gone," Zoe agreed and quietly opened the door onto the corridor.

The lavatories were by the library, hardly used, and about as far from the changing rooms as possible. There was no one about as they sneaked out, past the rows of lockers, and through the side door. The other girls were playing hockey on the upper field, where the wind blew cold. If they stayed on the other side of the school, they should be OK. After all, it wasn't like it was the first time they had bunked off.

"You know the geography trip next Wednesday?" Zoe began, trying to shove her wild hair into her jacket collar.

"Yeah. Kynance," Emily said without enthusiasm.

"Could I, well … You won't be coming back to school after, will you? So, could I come over to yours?"

"After the trip? Yeah, why not? I'm sure that'd be OK. I'll ask to-night."

"Great, thanks. That'd be lovely."

"What are you doing for your birthday?" Emily asked.

Zoe was only a few weeks younger than Emily. Her birthday was the following Sunday. Emily had wondered if she might be invited to Gunwalloe, but Zoe hadn't said anything.

"Well, it's Sunday, so church. Then Amanda's coming over for the afternoon."

"That'll be nice."

So Zoe was having a family party with her parents and sister, who was twenty-something, a nurse, and lived in Penzance. Obviously, she – Emily – wasn't included. She was surprised at how much it hurt.

"I'll keep you a piece of cake and bring it in on Monday," Zoe offered.

Zoe's birthday cake wasn't anywhere near as good as the one Cheryl had made. Emily ate it out of its scrunched-up foil as she stood by Zoe's open locker. The cake tasted rather stale, but perhaps that was because it'd been in Zoe's locker all morning. The icing was brittle and too sweet; Emily wished she had a toothbrush.

There were only a couple of vehicles in the cliff car park at Kynance.

Emily and Zoe filed off the bus and jumped down onto the gravel. It was a misty day, the air pale and clotted, damp and salty to inhale. The foghorn's mournful boom sounded twice. They trudged behind Mr Clarke to the viewpoint, and when they arrived on the cliff edge, the offshore islets were hardly visible.

Emily turned her head southwards to the sound of the horn. Just along the cliff path was the Buttress, somewhere in the murk. She couldn't discern its dark outline; neither could she pick out the field of caravans behind it nor the outlying bungalows of the Lizard village.

Emily knew Kynance. She had grown up with it, but she'd never liked it. Below the caravan site, below the monstrous Buttress, was the stony Bishop's Cove with tiny shells and pebbles like coloured sweets. She liked Bishop's Cove and happily went there alone. She would never go to Kynance alone.

For her art project, she was drawing rock formations and cliff strata. She had drawn the Buttress in powerful charcoal strokes and painted it against a flaming winter sunset. To inspire her palette, she'd scrambled down the path to Bishop's Cove and collected pebbles and sea glass – blue-and-green, milky white, and amber. One cold Sunday, she'd borrowed her father's Pentax camera and walked with Richard to Kynance. He had pointed out the streaky tremolite, bastite, and striped gneiss for her. But she had snapped quickly and couldn't wait to leave.

Even standing in a brightly coloured group of students with vivid raincoats and rucksacks, she still could not feel anything for the beach below except some undefined dread, made more potent because she could not properly see the three islands across the exposed sand strip.

The holiday park's brochure boasted that Kynance was one of the most beautiful beaches in the country.

Overwhelming, yes. Sinister, yes. But beautiful? No way, Emily thought.

"Come on," she said to Zoe.

She didn't want to be left at the back as the group scrambled down the cliff. The way down was steep and uneven, slippery underfoot with the damp. There were slugs on the grasses beside the path.

20

As they descended down the cliff path, the foghorn grew fainter, and instead, they could hear the *shushing* of gentle waves on the rocks below. The massive shoulder of Asparagus Island appeared out of the fog, and behind it, Gull Rock's vicious tooth and the round hump of the Bishop. The track disappeared into large rocks at the cliff base.

The beach at Kynance was the wrong way round. The sand stretched from the cliff to Asparagus Island, scattered with rocky outcrops and stacks. There were pools left by the receding sea, deep and triangular against the barnacled rocks.

Emily looked up at the black cliff above her, tracing back the way they had come, and at the mist that sucked at Asparagus Island's grassy summit. The mist was like a soluble aspirin, white and gritty, bitter on the tongue. Gulls cried from the stacks, and the waves unfurled on both sides of the sand bridge. The spray moistened the pages of Emily's notebook when she tried to write.

Standing at the back of the group, she didn't always hear everything Mr Clarke said. Her hair was damp and limp. Zoe's new curls still bounced, with tiny droplets of water sparkling on them. Emily glanced over her shoulder towards the offshore islands. The tide had crept in a little. At high water, the sand would be awash with the roiling ocean and their jumbled footsteps not even be a memory.

They went into the caves, slimy and dark, and some of the boys tried to climb the lower flanks of Asparagus Island.

Emily pocketed a few small pebbles: a sharp point of tremolite, a speckled slice of schist, and a humbug of banded gneiss with swirls of charcoal and cream.

A wave broke on a previously dry outcrop of serpentine.

The teachers called everyone together. Two of the boys had soaked jeans from running into the shallows. Girls shared the tiny shells they'd collected. The stream across the sand seemed to have swelled from a narrow trickle to a wide, shallow lake, and when Emily splashed through it, the wet sand sucked at her feet. Larger waves thrashed and broke on the rocks, and one of the smaller stacks was now flooded with seawater.

Emily had always feared Kynance. It was more than the overpowering cliffs, more than the incoming water. It was almost a premonition.

She climbed quickly over the boulders at the foot of the cliff until she felt sweat under her clothes. Halfway up, she stopped.

Zoe bumped into her. "You all right?"

"Just looking."

We stood there, we walked there, Emily thought, watching the rushing water.

The sky was clearer, and the islands no longer looked like they'd been rubbed out. A few steps higher and Emily saw the jutting face of the Buttress. There was a small figure standing on it. Someone in red. Richard had a red jacket.

Is it him?

He often went there on his own. He liked to sit on the cold serpentine and watch the waves breaking on the rocks. At dusk, he liked to watch the lighthouses across the bay: Tater Du and Wolf Rock.

Emily stared at the little red figure on the Buttress.

Yes, I'm sure that's Richard.

"Come on. I want my lunch," Zoe said, giving her a shove.

Emily climbed on, watching her trainers, ignoring the jagged drop to the right, the heaving green water, and the dirty froth that marked the swirl of currents. She suddenly noticed the forlorn blare of the foghorn had gone.

They ate on the bus, where the windows quickly steamed up.

"Was Richard adopted as a baby?" Zoe opened a bag of crisps with a *bang*.

"Yes. Well, not like the day he was born, but a baby, yes."

"But you're not?"

"I'm not. You know that."

"But then you came along."

"It sometimes happens. Mum told me. People adopt a child and then suddenly have one of their own soon after. It's like they're more relaxed or something."

"Did he resent you when you were born?"

"I don't remember, do I? I don't think so. He was only little himself then. We get on really well. I'll miss him."

"What do you mean, 'miss him'?"

"When he goes to uni in the autumn. I'll miss him."

"I thought he worked at your place?"

"He does at the moment. He did his A levels a year ago and deferred his degree."

"So, where's he going?"

"Exeter. Geology."

"What, you mean rocks and stuff?"

Emily slid her hand into her pocket. She could just feel the jagged lines on the banded gneiss.

"Rocks and stuff. I'll show you the Buttress. That's a rock. His favourite place."

When they stepped outside again, the last of the sea mist had evaporated, revealing a colourless sky. They split into two groups and spent the afternoon looking at the tiny plants that survived on the windswept moorland and the uneven bumps and troughs of the Bronze Age settlement. Emily had seen it all before, with Richard, with her father. She rolled the serpentine, the schist, and the gneiss together in her pocket and felt the loose grains of sand that had fallen from them. The sand grit got under her nail and stung; when she sucked her finger, the skin tasted of salt and iron, the taste of the rocks, the taste of blood, of forever.

At last, everyone else climbed back onto the bus.

Emily and Zoe waved to the lads on the back seat as the bus *hissed* and *grunted* out of the car park and along the narrow road back to school.

"We'll go back along the cliff," Emily said.

She led Zoe to the southwards cliff path. There was the Buttress, huge and ravaged, looming over them as they walked.

"That's where Rich likes to sit. You can see all round the bay – Wolf Rock Lighthouse, boats at sea, the sun going down."

"How lovely. Do you own it?"

"No, it's on the cliff path. This is our gate." Emily started to un-latch the five-barred gate into the caravan park.

"Let's go and see the rock. What's it called?"

"The Buttress."

Emily *clicked* the gate back.

Zoe was already striding along the path, up the gentle rise towards the crag.

"Be careful," Emily called. "I'll show you how to climb up."

They squashed together on the ledge, looking north to Kynance. The sea had flooded much of the sand. Waves rose and broke against the rocks of Asparagus Island, where the boys had tried to scramble up.

Emily pointed out the hut circles of the prehistoric village.

Richard had left nothing to give away his presence on the rocks. He smoked on the Buttress, but he always took the dog ends home.

"What sort of rock is this then?" Zoe asked.

"Serpentine. Kynance is where serpentine and schist meet. And there's gneiss, too."

Emily had been about to pull the stones from her pocket to show Zoe but stopped. They were her stones, warm from her hand. Instead, she stood, a little unsteadily, as there wasn't much room with two people on the Buttress.

"Nice?" Zoe echoed. "What do you mean?"

"Gneiss, with a G. It's a kind of rock."

Emily stood on the bottom rail of the gate, riding it as it swung inwards. The caravan field was quiet. Cars were parked outside a couple of vans, but no one was around. The clubhouse was shut.

As they came to the bungalow, the front door opened, and her father came out, sliding his wallet into his pocket.

"Hi, girls. Good day at the beach? Your mum's inside, Emily. I'm just off to Helston."

Her mother was on the phone, explaining to the caller that dogs were allowed in some caravans, but it was advisable to book early just in case. She waved and mouthed a silent *Hello*.

Emily took an apple from the fruit bowl, and Zoe scuttled into the bathroom.

Cheryl hung up and filled the kettle for tea.

"Is Zoe having a bath in there?" she whispered.

Emily shrugged. They hadn't worn their school uniform to Kynance, so she didn't think Zoe was getting changed.

Zoe came back into the kitchen. She'd brushed her curls and even changed her top. At Kynance, she had worn a plain long-sleeved T-shirt under her jacket; now, she had a flowery smock.

"That's pretty," Emily said, knowing she looked ghastly with her wind-torn hair and stained jeans.

She was suddenly irritated with Zoe for changing and showing her up in her own house.

They sat at the kitchen table and drank tea with Cheryl and talked about the trip.

Emily had hung her coat up, and the pebbles were still in its pockets. She had nothing to roll between her fingers.

"Is Rich around?" she asked, taking another chocolate biscuit.

"Somewhere. He said he'd do the tyres on my car for me."

"He wasn't out there when we arrived," Zoe said.

"Do you need a hand with the geology stuff?" Cheryl asked.

"Emily says Richard's going to study geology."

"That's right. He's off to Exeter this autumn. Are you going on to do A levels at Helston, Zoe?"

"Yes, but I'm not sure what in, except RE—"

The front door *slammed*.

Richard came in. "Done your tyres, Mum. Em. Hi, Zoe." He helped himself to a couple of biscuits. "I think I saw you lot trudging up the cliff."

"Saw you, too," Emily said.

"Where were you?" Zoe asked.

"On the Buttress. Out there." He gestured over his shoulder.

"Emily showed me the Buttress. It's serpentine, right?"

"Yes." Richard sounded surprised.

"She said you often go there to think."

Cheryl scraped her chair back. "I must see to the washing."

Emily heard the *click* of the washing machine opening in the utility room and then the soft falling sound of heavy wet material falling onto more heavy wet material.

"Shall we go to my room?" Emily finished her tea and stood.

"Pool later?" Richard asked.

"Definitely," Zoe said.

Emily worked her tongue round stuck biscuit crumbs in her mouth as she walked. She was angry. Zoe was making a play for Richard.

It's so embarrassing. He's nineteen for God's sake. "It's serpentine, right?" How long had she known that? Half an hour?

26

"Let's have some music." Zoe closed the bedroom door.

Emily threw herself down on the bed. She couldn't say anything. She didn't know how to. And anyway, Zoe was her friend. The only decent friend she'd had.

Does it really matter if she likes Rich? It's not like anything will come of it.

"Music?" Zoe said again. "Hey, you OK?"

"Yeah, sorry, tired. Shit, just remembered. I haven't done the RE for tomorrow. You done yours?"

"Yes, all done. I did abortion."

"What did you say about it?" Emily sat up again and tugged her RE folder off the shelf.

"That it's wrong. We have no right to end anyone's life, even if they're not born. I used lots of quotes from the Bible to illustrate it. What are you going to write about?"

"What was the choice? Abortion, euthanasia … What were the other two?"

"Contraception and test-tube babies."

"Oh yes, that's right."

"You going to do it now? Are you doing abortion, too?"

"I'll do it later tonight. Not going to write while you're here."

"We could talk about it. You don't believe in abortion, do you?"

"Well, only in extreme cases, you know – like rape or … maybe if the mother's life was in danger or something. I think you have to look at each case individually. But, no, no, not as a routine thing. I don't think that's right."

"Good. What about euthanasia?"

"I don't know anything about it," Emily confessed.

"It's the same as abortion. It's still killing. Only God can choose when and how we die."

"Is contraception the same as killing? I mean, you're stopping a life from happening, but if you stop it, it's not a life yet, is it?"

"I don't think that's the same. If a baby hasn't been made, you can't kill it."

"They're all negative, though, aren't they? Killing or stopping life. IVF – that's the only one about making life, not stopping it or ending it?"

"But maybe God decided some people shouldn't be parents. Maybe He knows they shouldn't have children. It's still going against His decisions, don't you think?"

"Did God decide my parents shouldn't be parents, then? When they were trying for a child before Rich?"

"He couldn't have, could He?" Zoe said quickly. "Because after they adopted Richard, you came along. They were definitely meant to be parents."

Emily closed her folder and pushed it to the end of the bed.

"Thank you for the lift, Mrs Knight." Zoe *clicked* off her seatbelt and turned round to Emily in the back seat. "See you tomorrow. Don't forget the RE."

Emily watched Zoe walk up the path to her front door.

I could run after her … Say "Hello" to her parents?

But if Zoe had wanted that, she'd have asked her to – *Wouldn't she?*

"You getting in the front?" Cheryl asked.

As Emily *slammed* the rear door, Zoe turned and waved and then put a key to the lock. Her front door opened, revealing a slice of light and something – *A table? A shelf?* – in the hall.

"She's a funny one." Cheryl turned the car on a patch of scrubby grass. "But you two get on well, don't you? I'm glad you've got a nice friend now."

"Yeah, she's nice," Emily said as they drove out of Gunwalloe. "She's just a bit, well, you know, religious. I think that's why other people don't like her. I don't know why they don't like me."

"I'm sure they would if you gave them a chance. You're so prickly."

"I am not." Emily's fingers found the ridges of banded gneiss in her pocket again.

"Are."

"I don't like people, you know that. Anyway, we're leaving school in a couple of months."

"Zoe's doing A levels, too."

"We probably won't do the same subjects."

When they got home, Richard and Terry were both in the clubhouse. There were quite a few cars parked outside. Emily could hear music when they got out of the car.

"I'll just run up and see what's going on," Cheryl said. "Coming?"

"I'll get a bath."

Emily borrowed her mother's key and let herself into the bungalow. She took the three stones out of her pocket, leaving behind only a gritty drizzle of sand, and ran them under the kitchen tap, washing away the scent of iron. The cold water brought out the green-and-red veins in the tremolite. She placed them on her bedroom windowsill with the rest of her treasures.

Emily forgot to do the RE homework, but Mr Williams was so nice that it didn't matter.

The boys in the group had written about euthanasia, but all the girls had chosen abortion, and soon the classroom was noisy with sharp voices. The bitch by the window – who had come to tea at Emily's – said her older sister had an abortion recently, so did that make her a slut? Emily remembered the sister, remembered the rumours about her but said nothing.

"*Thou shalt not kill,*" Zoe replied. "Exodus Twenty. And Jesus re-iterated it on the Mount."

The other bitch started yelling something about women's rights and choices.

Emily had no stones to roll between her fingers, so she doodled in her margin.

Zoe was arguing again about Deuteronomy and Jeremiah.

"*Choose life,*" she cried. "*And both thou and thy seed may live.*"

Emily stopped doodling and listened. She had never heard Zoe so fierce and determined. The rest of the class shouting her down did nothing to crumble her.

She draws strength from it, Emily realised, *because of the power of her convictions.*

Emily hadn't thought much about abortion before; she found it sad and cruel, the thought of a tiny bundle of cells being flushed out in blood before it even had a chance.

I will never have an abortion, she vowed as Zoe jabbed the air with a pen, yelling "*Jeremiah!*" like it was a battle cry.

Emily and Richard walked together through the caravan field. One of the vans had the door open, and there were voices inside.

"Knock, knock," Richard called as he leapt up the steps. "Is the shower OK now?"

Emily looked at the many coloured stickers slapped on the nearby car while Richard talked to the man inside, saying something about Mullion. The showerhead kept coming loose when they'd arrived the night before. Richard had gone out to tighten it up for them. He was good with things like that – mending things, doing things with cars.

When did he learn? Emily wondered.

He just seemed to know how lots of things worked. He'd passed his driving test on the first go. He was so capable.

He came bounding down the steps, and they trudged on along the gravel path to the gate.

Emily shifted her drawing pad from one hand to the other. Her fingers had gone stiff from holding it.

Through the gate, they turned left where the path climbed up to the Buttress and then dipped down again towards the shore. The sea was silver, and the horizon blurred. In Bishop's Cove, the waves curled and died quietly.

Richard went first down the narrow muddy track, leaping over jutting protrusions of serpentine and granite. The tide was out, exposing the scattered rocks, the sand at the cliff base, and then the deep band of pebbles and tangled weed.

Emily looked up at the giant crag overhead. From the cove, she couldn't see the hollow where she'd sat with Zoe. This southern face of the Buttress was almost sheer: mottled green serpentine blasted by the sea winds and the wild spray thrown over the cliff.

They were alone on the beach. Richard jumped from boulder to boulder, under the cliff, stopping and bending, picking up a stone, maybe pocketing it, sometimes discarding it.

Emily weighed down her drawing book with a heavy chunk of rock and tugged off her trainers. The tiny shells and pebbles *crunched* under her feet as she walked to the water. It was cold when it sucked at her toes. She let the waves break round her ankles. A frond of weed slapped her foot. She ran out of the sea, her legs stinging from its bite.

Richard was standing on a flat-topped black rock beneath the overhang of the Buttress. A wave rose and broke, splattering him. His red jacket looked very bright against the dark rocks.

April 1992

Thou shalt not bear false witness against thy neighbour, the Bible said.

In other words, lying, but Zoe had lied. Not huge lies, really, more like omissions. She hadn't told her parents everything about Emily and the caravan site. She'd only said that Emily's parents – Mr and Mrs Knight, as far as she was concerned – owned a small caravan park near the Lizard. She didn't mention the licenced clubhouse or how she'd played pool with Richard – who was on the team on Thursday evenings. Her parents didn't read the sports section of the *West Briton*, though, so they were unlikely to see anything about the league matches. When they'd finished with the paper, Zoe turned to the back, where the pool column was, and looked up Kynance Holiday Park.

Zoe knew that, even with the little she had told her parents, they weren't keen on her going to Emily's. Luckily, they didn't go to the Lizard, so there was no danger of them wanting her to point out the caravan site or call in unexpectedly to say "Hello". No, that wasn't likely to happen. Her parents wouldn't want to mix with the Knights.

"What do you know about her family?" her mother had asked her once.

"Not much. Her mum was an actress in London. Her dad did something with music, clubs or whatever. Anyway, that was ages ago. They've worked at holiday camps for years. Before Emily moved here, they were up north somewhere."

Zoe stopped. Running holiday camps wasn't much better than acting or music to her mother.

"Mrs Knight qualified in catering," she added. That seemed safe.

Zoe didn't want to ask Emily back to her house. She knew what would happen. Emily would never ask her back to Kynance again. This was what had happened before when Zoe had invited girls over. Unused to saying Grace before eating, disturbed by her parents' religious pictures and icons, the girls backed off. Zoe didn't want Emily to see this side of her life, didn't want her to back off, didn't want her to say anything about it to Richard.

Richard Knight is gorgeous, Zoe thought. He had thick dark hair and green eyes. Zoe had never met anyone with real green eyes before. *Richard's eyes are the colour of the sea at Kynance.*

He'd been at school a few years ago, but she didn't remember him. Probably because she kept her head down and didn't look at – or speak to – the older kids. And, no doubt, he had grown up since then. He was a man now. She wondered again if he had a girlfriend. Emily hadn't mentioned one. Hadn't said anything like "*His girlfriend will miss him when he goes away*" or, worse, "*His girlfriend is moving to Exeter with him.*"

Zoe couldn't think of a discreet way to ask about it. He'd been so attentive to her, showing her how to hold the cue, how hitting the white in different ways made it do different things on the baize. She found that she wasn't shy with him like she was with the boys at school. She would just have to ask Emily, casually, in conversation.

It was still chilly in the clubhouse in the evenings. The windows faced north, and the spring sunshine never warmed the inside of the buildings. Emily needed a jumper to stop the gooseflesh rising on her arms. It was the Easter holidays, and most of the caravans were occupied. Richard opened the bar at lunchtimes. Terry was there every night with a guy from the Lizard to help. There was a new chef in the kitchen, and many of the caravanners came up night after night to eat burgers, toasties, and scampi. The place smelt of fried food and cigarette smoke.

Emily sat sideways in the window seat. The glass was grimy and needed a wipe. There was a crack running across one of the small panes.

How did that happen? she wondered. *A flying pool ball?*

She drank the last of her Pepsi, which had gone watery with dissolving ice, and turned back to the pool table.

Richard sent the black into the centre left. There were still four of Zoe's reds on the table. When Zoe came to the club, it was no longer her and Emily playing Richard: it was Zoe playing Richard by herself.

"*You have lots of opportunities to play,*" Zoe once said to Emily. "*I don't. My parents would go ape if they thought I was in a club playing pool.*"

"*They're very strict, aren't they?*" Emily said.

In other words, the complete opposite of her parents, who were easy-going and tolerant. Emily never had to lie to her parents because telling the truth didn't matter.

"*Very,*" Zoe agreed.

"*Don't they want to meet me?*"

Emily wished she could gulp back the words. It sounded rude, like *Why haven't you asked me to yours?* If Zoe didn't want her to visit, there must be a reason.

"*They don't like me having people over,*" Zoe said, but Emily wasn't wholly convinced.

Now Richard took Zoe's cue off her and slotted it into the rack. He swigged down the last of his beer.

"I got stuff to do," he said. "See you later, Em. Zoe, will you be here in an hour or so?"

"I'm going in about twenty minutes."

"Right. See you soon, yeah?"

"Definitely."

Emily watched Zoe watching Richard leave the club. A moment later, he walked past the window where she was sitting, heading for the caravans.

Zoe *clacked* the remaining balls together on the table until a large woman with meaty tattooed arms shoved some money in.

"Shall we go home?" Emily asked.

They waved goodbye to Terry at the bar and went out into the milky mauve evening. Some kids were yelling in the nearest caravan.

Zoe looked over her shoulder. "Emily … does, um, Richard … does he, er … does he have a girlfriend?"

"Not now."

"He used to, you mean?"

"There were a couple when he was at the sixth form. I only met one of them. She was called Vicky. She was okay."

"I see. I just wondered."

Emily stopped walking. They were almost at the bungalow. She wanted to say something, but she didn't know what. She already knew Zoe was after Richard. He seemed to quite like Zoe, too, which Emily hadn't expected. She didn't want them to get together but couldn't say why. Maybe because Richard was going away to university in a few months, and she didn't want anything or anyone to screw up his plans. Maybe it was because there was something odd about Zoe's background and how she kept her parents so secret. Maybe it was because Zoe was the only girl she'd got on with at school, so if she hooked up with Richard, she – Emily – would be the gooseberry, the wallflower, the odd one out. Or maybe it was all or none of these.

Emily felt her heart rate jump at the thought of it, as much as it had jumped when she started down the cliff path to Kynance. It was a feeling she couldn't define but sinister nonetheless.

"I know why you're asking," she said at last.

Zoe blushed. "Is it obvious?"

"To me," Emily said quickly. "Rich isn't very observant."

"He's so lovely. And he's got green eyes."

"Spare me. I don't want the details."

They went round the side of the bungalow and let themselves into the back door. In the utility room, the washing machine door hung open. The laundry basket was in the middle of the kitchen. One of Richard's socks had fallen on the floor. Emily picked it up.

"Mum?" she called.

"In here."

Cheryl was on the sofa in the living room. She'd kicked off her shoes.

"You all right?" Emily asked.

It wasn't like her mum to just abandon the washing.

"I came over really dizzy when I was doing the washing. I thought I was going to faint. I wondered if Rich could drive you back, Zoe. I will if he can't or if he's drunk too much or whatever."

"He only had one beer in the club." Emily squatted down to look at her mother's face. "You do look pale. Shall I get you anything?"

"Some water would be nice."

"Sure."

Zoe was standing by the bookcase, her head sideways, reading the titles on the spines.

Or pretending to, Emily thought when she came back with a glass of water.

She tapped Zoe on the shoulder. "You stay with Mum and make sure she doesn't do anything silly. I'll go and find Rich."

Emily ran through the kitchen, past the basket of damp clothes. She knocked shut the washing machine door.

Zoe must be delighted to be going home with Rich. But what do I do? Emily wondered. *Do I go with them or not?*

She didn't know. If she went, too, Zoe would be pissed off, but if Emily stayed at home, she would be making herself that wallflower. Once again, she felt a flutter of foreboding.

She found Richard behind the clubhouse, chucking swollen black sacks into the wheelie bin.

I'll ask him, watch his reaction, and then choose what to do, Emily decided.

"Mum's not well."

"She all right?"

"She came over all faint. She said to ask if you would please take Zoe home tonight as she doesn't want to drive."

"Take Zoe home?" he repeated. "Yeah, absolutely. Let me just finish here and get a wash. I'll be about ten minutes."

He wants to take her home.

Emily trudged round the clubhouse building. She heard the sound of something hard *clunking* into the wheelie bin, and then its lid falling down. Footsteps *crunching* through gravel. She glanced in the club window. Two blokes playing pool.

When she got back to the house, Zoe was sitting on the other sofa. Cheryl was drinking small mouthfuls of water.

"I told her to stay put and not move," Zoe said, avoiding Emily's eyes.

"Rich'll be here in a few minutes."

"I'll just use the bathroom then." Zoe jumped up.

The back door *slammed*. Richard coming in. The sound of running water at the kitchen sink.

"I'll stay here with you," Emily said to Cheryl. "Look after you."

"I'm fine. You go with them."

Emily shook her head. "I'm feeling a bit headachy myself."

She turned, and there was Zoe, pink and breathless. Behind her, Richard was tossing the car keys in the air and catching them, tossing and catching.

"See you, Zoe. I'm going to stay here with Mum," Emily said.

"Of course. Good idea," Zoe said quickly. "I hope you feel better, Mrs Knight. I mean, Cheryl."

"I'll sort out the washing," Emily offered when she heard the *screech* of tyres leaving.

She unfolded the drying rack, shook out the shirts and jeans, unballed the socks, and paused.

Maybe I should have gone with them after all ...

The light was draining from the sky. To the east, the clouds were dark as an ink stain; to the west, the last flares from the sun turned the sky pink over the moor.

Zoe kept her bag on her knees. It gave her something to hold, something to do, something to stop her hands fluttering and to stop her biting her nails.

Richard reached over to the radio dial. It was set on Radio 2.

"Mum likes the golden oldies." He tuned it to a new station, Pirate FM. "We have bands some Fridays and Saturdays in the summer. You should come then. Roadkill, Oxygen Rock ... you know them?"

"I don't, sorry," Zoe said. "I'd love to come. I'll have more time once our exams are over."

"Shit, yes, not long to go. You feeling okay about them?"

"I'm not thinking about them." She lifted her eyes from the canvas bag on her knees and looked at Richard.

His hair was unkempt. Her father would say it was far too long and messy. She couldn't see the green of his eyes in the half-light, but she saw his long, thin fingers on the gear stick, just inches from hers. There was an old scab on the back of his left hand.

I wonder how that happened?

He moved his hand onto the wheel, and she looked once more out of the windscreen at the darkened hedges that sometimes whipped the car with stray tendrils.

Zoe was glad it was dark.

This lift home is a gift from God.

It was just her and Richard, but the car was gobbling up the miles from the Lizard to Gunwalloe, and this might have been the only chance she would ever have to be alone with him.

The headlights lit something white stuck to a tree trunk. A notice. She saw the first words in capitals.

"Are you going to Flora Day? You and Emily?" she asked.

"Probably. Don't know if Em'll be going. She sometimes does."

"My parents don't like crowds," Zoe started tentatively. "So, we don't always go."

"Go with friends."

"I've never wanted to go with anyone from school."

Because I've never been invited.

"Well, go with Em. I expect I'll be there for some of it."

"Great. That'd be ... great."

Why couldn't she be like other girls? Why didn't she know how to toss her hair or stick out her boobs or whatever it was they did that got them noticed by boys?

Like those two in RE, the ones from Emily's form. They have boys sniffing round all the time, and why? One is a slut – her sister had an abortion – and the other is spotty. But—

Zoe stopped herself.

No, I don't want to be a slut like that, but it would be lovely, so lovely, if some nice boy, some older boy – well, Richard – thought I was pretty, or funny, or sexy or something.

Just because she was a Christian, just because she had values, didn't mean she was some sort of nun. She didn't really know when girls actually had sex with boys. Some of the ones from school had probably done it – with boys from school or a friend's brother. She was pretty sure Emily hadn't.

Emily doesn't seem that interested, that bothered. She's more concerned with handing in coursework on time and doing her paintings of rocks.

"What will you do with a geology degree? I mean, do you know what sort of job you'll be looking for?" Zoe asked Richard.

"Not sure yet. Something environmental, I think. Hydrology maybe. I might even do teaching. I don't even know where I want to live. Cornwall, somewhere else, abroad … I'd love to take a year out abroad. I fancy somewhere like Greenland or the Faroe Islands. That'd be awesome."

Time was trickling away so fast. The amber and white lights of Culdrose air station ahead stained the sky iodine-brown. There was the turning for Gunwalloe on the left.

Richard flicked on the indicator and turned into the narrow lane.

Zoe felt like crying. She hadn't been able to tell Richard she liked him, that she really liked him. She just couldn't. It was too embarrassing. And she could never ask Emily to say anything – *Oh, by the way, Rich, Zoe fancies you* – so he would never know. There was no way she would be able to tell him. She twisted the strap of her bag round her wrist.

"It's here. On the left." Her voice sounded loud. "Where that car's parked."

When Richard stopped, he left the headlights on and the engine running. He wanted to get away quickly.

"Thanks for the lift. I hope your mum feels better." She unclipped her seatbelt. "I'll … er … see you some time then."

"You're not disappearing, are you?"

"Not … What d'you mean?" She had her hand on the door.

"It sounded like you weren't coming over for a while."

"No, I'd love to. I really like it at yours."

"Remember to come when the bands are on."

"Yes … Well, thanks. Bye, then."

His hand was on the gear lever again, waiting to go.

When Zoe opened the door, the interior light came on, hard and white. She saw that scab again.

Then, with a *slam*, he was in darkness once more.

Richard roared up the lane towards the main road. In his rear-view mirror, he saw the last pink-mauve over the western horizon. Ahead were the amber lights of Culdrose. He was thinking about Zoe. He knew that Emily had never been invited to her house or to meet her family anywhere. He also knew that to start with, Emily thought Zoe was ashamed of her or embarrassed about her or something. In fact, he was the one who had suggested that possibly it was the other way round, and Zoe was embarrassed about her parents, who did sound a bit weird.

Anyway, she obviously likes coming up to Kynance.

Richard braked at the junction, looked left and right. He was pretty sure he was one of the reasons she liked visiting, not that he'd tell Emily that. Not yet anyway. Right from the first time – when he'd stood behind Zoe and slid her arm back and forth with the pool cue – he knew she fancied him. He'd heard her tell Emily that she never had any other chances to play pool, so would Emily mind sitting it out? Sometimes he played badly so Zoe could pot a few balls. Sometimes he even set up shots for her – once, he even let her win. And she was always watching him. If he was helping out behind the bar, or just having a smoke in the kitchen, or whatever.

He was about to light up but remembered that his mother didn't like him smoking in her car. So, he rolled the window down, allowing the cool air to rush inside.

He turned up the volume on the radio.

So. Zoe Cassidy. Emily's friend. A girl of sixteen.

He knew she was sixteen because Emily had told him about a rather dry and oversweet birthday cake.

But so what?

Louise was a sixteen-year-old Helston girl he had first gone out with during A levels. They'd met when he moved to the sixth form and was put in the same tutor group as Louise. She was fluffy, blonde, wore silver eye shadow, and was the first girl he'd had sex with. They had stumbled through it together one Saturday afternoon in her house when her parents were out. A few months later came Vicky, the quiet, dark-haired girl in his biology and chemistry groups. He was almost hurt that Louise didn't seem to care that he left her, didn't even mind it when she came round a corner and found him kissing Vicky outside the library. His parents liked Vicky. She came over quite often. She complimented Emily on her hair colour. And then, suddenly, just after their A level exams, she ended it. She was going to medical school; she wanted to be a surgeon.

"*I have to focus on my career, Rich,*" she'd said.

Richard told people he had deferred his university place because he wasn't ready to go away – he wanted a year's break – but Vicky was also a factor, though only his family knew that.

As the months passed, Richard had thought less and less of Vicky, and now, over the last few weeks, he'd found himself thinking more and more about Zoe. He was sure she was a virgin.

Would she be willing to relinquish that to me?

Most people he knew found their virginity a cumbersome load to be dumped at the first opportunity, but Zoe could be different. Emily might know the answers to these questions, but he was buggered if he would ask her.

He had other things on his mind as well – obviously, the geology degree. His A levels were good, and he knew a lot about his subject, so he wasn't apprehensive about university. But he'd come to love the rugged coastline of the Lizard, the serpentine crags, the *sucking* and *crashing* waves, the twin heartbeats of Tater Du and Wolf Rock.

It'll be odd to be away from the sea.

There was the other thing, too. He was nineteen now. He could try to find his birth parents. Of course, the subject had come up at home several times, and he was quick to refuse every time. Cheryl and Terry were his parents, and Emily was his sister, and that was that. But there were other people out there. Not just his parents, whose genes he carried, but maybe brothers and sisters, grandparents, cousins. A whole host of people who shared his blood. Richard didn't know what to do. His parents would be stressed if he started investigating, but they wouldn't stand in his way. It was his right to discover all the missing pieces of his jigsaw.

Maybe make some initial enquiries in Exeter?

Yet even if he did find his birth mother or father and spoke to them, he wouldn't have to say anything to his parents.

He swore aloud.

Of course I would.

He loved them; he couldn't deceive them.

But what can of worms would I be opening?

Once opened, he would never be able to close it again.

Past the holiday camp by Mullion, the land flattened out into scrubby moorland. On the right, on the seaward side, were a few red lights from the lonely airfield at Predannack, and off to his left, Richard saw the flash of a helicopter circling over the downs. The road twisted on, and there were the scattered lights of the Lizard looking, as always, like the very last outpost.

He eased off the gas at the turning to Kynance Cove and took the next right to the holiday camp. Lights shone out from the bungalow, the clubhouse, and several caravans. His home. His family.

He parked on the gravel beside his father's car, quickly glanced at the passenger seat in case Zoe had deliberately dropped an earring or something he could return to her in person – she hadn't – and sprung out of the car. He could hear Emily and his mother in the kitchen.

Cheryl was standing at the stove now, stirring a pan of spaghetti.

"Just in time for dinner, Rich," she said.

"Are you better?" he asked.

"Much better. Don't know what came over me."

Emily glanced up from the cheese she was grating, looked at the clock on the wall, and then at him, her face both open and guarded.

He felt strangely uncomfortable as he dropped the car keys in the saucer on the dresser.

"Rich?" Emily tapped on Richard's bedroom door.

Inside, the light was off; there was only the blue-white flare from the TV. He was lying on top of the duvet, still in his jeans and T-shirt. He picked up the remote from the bedside drawers and turned the sound down.

Emily watched the neon-green bars disappearing across the bottom of the screen. It was some blokey film with men running through city streets, the flash of gunfire, silent fireballs of orange flames.

"Can't sleep?" he asked.

Emily shrugged.

The clock beside his bed said nearly three a.m. Richard had taken his meal into his room, and Emily ate with her mother in the living room in front of the TV. She'd heard Richard bring his plate back into the kitchen, heard the *clatter* of his fork as he set it down. Then he'd disappeared out to the club again and not come home until late.

She perched on the end of his bed, suddenly cold in her T-shirt and bare legs.

"What happened tonight? In the car, with Zoe?" she asked.

"Nothing," he said, watching her.

"Didn't she come on to you or anything?"

"Sadly not." Richard grinned.

"So, you like her as well, then?"

"Yeah, I think so. Wish we knew what the story was with her parents. She never asked me in."

"Well, why should she when she hasn't asked me?"

"You've never even set eyes on them?"

"No. I got her dad on the phone once, and he handed it over straight away. I don't ring her often. She rings me."

"How did she get here today? Didn't they bring her over?"

"She got the bus."

Richard fiddled with the remote and watched the silent figures shouting muted abuse on the screen.

"Would it really bother you if I asked her out?" he said at last.

Emily watched the figures, too; one guy's mouth was frozen open in a scream. It was unfair to say "Yes." She knew Richard had been cut up about Vicky last year.

Would it hurt me so badly?

"I mean, she'd still be your friend," he added.

"Yeah, I know. Sure, do whatever. But I'm not being your go-between. And don't think for a moment her parents will think you're suitable." She slid off the bed to go but then stopped. "But you're going away in the autumn."

"Months away. Anyway, she might say no, and I'll feel a right twat."

"She won't." Emily opened the door. "You'll have to wait a while, though – they're off to see her grandparents for the rest of Easter."

She padded back into her room. The bedside lamp cast a small, pale glow on the pink wall. Once the exams were over, they had the whole summer, but now Richard and Zoe would be doing everything together, and she would be the lemon – *As predicted.* Then, come September, Richard would leave for Exeter, and Zoe would be devastated.

Emily banged her duvet into shape.

Great. He'll take my friend, hurt her, and leave me to pick up the pieces.

Across the corridor, she heard the muffled sound of Richard's film again.

May 1992

Flora Day in Helston. Coloured flags hung from upstairs windows, zigzagging across the streets. The shop doorways were decorated with garlands of laurel, bluebells, and gorse.

Emily and Richard stumbled through the crowds in Meneage Street towards the Guildhall where they were meeting Zoe. The marching band was somewhere close.

Emily checked her watch. *It's time for the children's dance.*

A balloon seller stood by the Guildhall with a sparkly cloud of jewelled fish, dragons, moons, stars, and birds.

Emily kept her hand tight on her rucksack strap as they pushed between people, a baby's buggy, and a whippet.

"There she is," Richard said.

Emily glanced up at the stone face of the Guildhall, draped in flags and clusters of bluebells. There was Zoe, in pale blue jeans and a white jacket that Emily hadn't seen before. Two other people were beside her.

"Must be her parents," Emily muttered.

But Richard, ahead of her, didn't seem to hear. He was already waving, and Zoe waved back at him.

"This is my friend, Emily," Zoe said to her parents. "And her brother, Richard," she added breathlessly. "He's off to uni this autumn. To study geology."

"Hello, Emily," Zoe's father said.

"It's nice to meet you," her mother added.

Emily suddenly wondered if they might have liked to meet her before, but it was Zoe who wouldn't allow it to happen.

Zoe's mother was short, with dark hair cut in a straight bob. Emily saw the glint of a gold cross at her throat. Her father was taller and broad, going bald.

They don't look that odd. They just look ordinary.

"Are your parents at Flora Day?" Zoe's mother asked.

"Dad's in the bar," Richard explained. "And Mum's doing stuff at home."

"In the bar?"

"Yeah, the clubhouse at ours."

Emily saw Zoe's face, saw the imperceptible shake of her head.

"Are we going to the fair?" Emily interjected.

Obviously, Zoe hadn't said anything about the clubhouse and playing pool, and Richard had put his foot right in it.

"I'll see you back here at two," Zoe told her parents.

"How are you two getting home then?" Zoe's mother asked. "Did you drive in, Richard?"

"Mum dropped us off. She's picking Em up later. I'm staying on to see some friends."

Emily watched Zoe's parents start off down the hill towards the market.

"The fair then," Zoe said and skipped off after them.

Emily trailed behind Zoe and Richard, stopping to look at some of the market stalls. She saw Zoe's parents pulling out trays of bedding plants and hurried past them. Ahead, Richard was pointing at something, and Zoe was laughing. There were so many people, and the sun beat down on Emily's head. She lowered her rucksack and pulled off her cardigan. She shoved it into the rucksack, which made it bulge uncomfortably on her back. When she looked down the hill for the other two, she couldn't see them anywhere.

On her left was a stall of tie-dyed fabric and clothing, incense sticks wrapped in twists of foil, and handmade soaps cut in slices of pink, lime, and mauve. She unhooked a smock from the rail, found the price ticket, put it back, and looked again down the road. She saw the white denim of Zoe's jacket under another metallic drift of helium balloons. She slid through the crowd towards her.

"There you are. We thought we'd lost you," Zoe said.

"You know, I'm not that bothered about the fair. You two go on. I'm going to look at the market. I'll come down later and look for you."

Emily turned back up the hill before she had to see their faces and know that they were pleased to be rid of her. Her new jealousy was uncomfortable. Didn't fit her. She had always thought of herself as easy-going like her parents, but Richard and Zoe being together was so wrong in so many ways.

She marched up the centre of the road, against the flood of pedestrians, counting the reasons with her heartbeat.

One, I'll lose my brother. Two, I'll lose my friend. It's no good Rich saying things won't change – of course they will! Three, Rich is going away in the autumn. Four, Zoe's parents will go ape. Five, my parents will probably think it stupid as Richard finally has his future sorted out. Six, Zoe – the strange, quiet girl, the outcast – will have a boyfriend before me and probably have sex before me … Oh God!

Emily tried to push that last image from her mind. Her marching had brought her back to the tie-dye stall again.

Perhaps I'll find Mum a present: some earrings, or a decorated box, or something.

The neighbouring stall was a cart with a yellow awning overhead and ropes of twined chillies and garlic. There were shallow wooden bowls of green and black olives, blood-red sundried tomatoes, and slices of feta drizzled with thick gold oil. Emily fancied buying a carton of the cheese. She was about to reach into her rucksack for money when she realised the woman taking a plastic pot of stuffed olives was Zoe's mother. Quickly, Emily darted back to the hippie clothes and incense and huddled into a corner, sorting through embroidered wallets.

She bought a pair of earrings for her mother – made from shards of turquoise glass – and a tub of feta, which she ate with a plastic fork as she wandered through the market. There were second-hand books and videos, painted ceramics – she bought her dad an ashtray – rainbow-coloured towels, homemade biscuits and cakes, pewter jewellery, household hardware, leather belts, handbags, windchimes, and mirrored sunglasses on twirling stands.

The two bitches from RE came stalking past with another girl from school and an unattractive carroty boy Emily didn't know. She turned away, inhaling the hot breath of the burger stand rather than speaking to them.

At last, she reached the bottom of town and the boating lake. The crowd was thinner because everyone was now hauling back uphill for the start of the midday street dance. Beyond the boating lake, Emily saw the spindly Big Wheel and the striped pepperpot Helter Skelter. Yet another balloon seller stood at the entrance to the fairground. Her mouth tasted salty from the feta, and she wished she had a drink on her. The ground underfoot was as dry and dusty as her mouth. Thick black cables snaked across the way. The air was hot from so many giant machines.

She glanced round for Richard and Zoe. A couple of boys from school were squabbling over some food in a greasy bag. The monstrous centrifuge reared up, the riders tiny Lowry figures. Beside her, spinning teacups striped in blue and pink whirled shrieking children round, and beyond them, a tiny space rocket was filling up with small passengers.

Emily trudged past a stall of cheap-looking teddies and candy floss. She felt like a prat wandering round the fair on her own. She came round the side of the Waltzers, and there was a huge golden carousel. The painted horses flew past, up and down, and up and down, and suddenly Emily saw that white denim jacket again. Zoe was riding a black horse, decorated in red and gold, with her curls bouncing on her shoulders. And there, on the horse beside her, a white one with emerald trim, was Richard.

Zoe held her balloon on her lap in the back of the car. It was a fish with metallic green-and-blue scales, and it bobbed impatiently on her knees, wanting to shoot up to the car roof. She hadn't told her parents Richard had bought it for her when she and he had walked back up the hill towards the Guildhall.

"I didn't know they had a pub at that holiday camp," her mother said.

"It's not a pub. It's a club. They do meals for the visitors. You know, burgers, pizzas – that sort of thing. They've got pool tables and darts, I think."

"I hope you don't spend all your time in there."

"Of course not," Zoe lied. "We're in Emily's room – listening to music, doing homework, and that."

Neither of her parents said anything.

The car rumbled along past Culdrose naval station.

"Do you like her?" Zoe asked at last. "Emily?"

"I don't know her," her mother said. "She seems all right, but they're not really my kind of people."

How do you know that if you don't know them? Zoe thought, but her disloyalty burnt her because she knew what her mother meant.

She and Emily were friends because no one else wanted to know them. They'd been crushed together and had now stuck. But everything happens for a reason, and, through Emily, she had met Richard, who'd bought her the sparkly fish and laid his hand on her shoulder to say goodbye outside the Angel. She could still feel the imprint of his palm now.

"*I'll make my own way home,*" he'd said to Emily and slid inside the pub.

Zoe had inhaled the sharp scent of beer and heard raised voices and music. She'd tried to look through the windows into the cool, dark room inside but hadn't seen anything. Then, Emily had tugged on her arm.

Zoe twiddled the balloon string round her fingers as she had done with the strap of her bag in the car with Richard. They were almost home. Beside her on the seat were some flimsy market carrier bags, some plain, some striped – green towels in one, tubs of olives and feta in another. Zoe opened a third and saw a handful of paperback books.

She wondered if Richard was still in the Angel with his friends from Helston or whether they had moved on somewhere else and whether he was thinking about her, wishing she were there, too.

Cheryl was waiting at the entrance to the car park. Emily ran the last few yards, her lumpy rucksack bouncing on her back. The car park was still packed; two cars rolled slowly round, waiting for spaces. Emily flung open the passenger door and dumped her rucksack between her feet.

"Did you have fun?" her mum asked.

"It was OK. I got you a present. I'll show you at home. Rich says he'll make his own way back. Bus, I suppose. Unless he's got something better to do."

"Have you two fallen out?" Cheryl turned left onto the bypass.

Cars were parked on the grass verges, and some were even on the central reservation. A family was walking up the hill, a golden sun balloon tied to a little girl's wrist. It reminded Emily of the fish Richard bought for Zoe. He didn't even ask if she wanted a balloon, but Zoe only had to flutter her eyelashes at him, and there was the string in her fingers.

"Have you fallen out?" Cheryl asked again. "You and Rich? Or you and Zoe?"

Emily raked her hair. It was sticky and tangly. She must wash it.

"Not really. It's just … well … it's all Rich and Zoe now."

"What? I didn't know."

"Oh, no one's said anything. But I know Zoe likes him, and he says he likes her. They went off today down to the fair. He even bought her a bloody balloon."

"They went off without you?"

"I told them to. I knew they didn't want me there, and I wanted to look at the market. They weren't horrible. It's just I never wanted this to happen. It's not fair. Rich is my brother. Zoe's my friend. They'd never have met without me. I don't have anyone of my own."

"You will one day."

"And don't say that crap. You know I don't like people, and people don't like me. Then, as soon as I thought I had a friend, she goes off after Rich."

"She never seemed the sort of friend you'd pick."

"You don't like her, do you?"

"I don't dislike her," Cheryl said evenly. "She's friendly, she's polite, you two get on. I can't explain it. She's just a strange choice."

"I didn't choose her. We started sitting together, you know, and neither of us had any decent friends. She's not awful, Mum."

"No, no, I know she's not awful."

"And I feel like a bitch. I talked to Rich about it, and he said Zoe would still be my friend, but it doesn't feel like it."

"Right now, your exams are the most important thing. Just get through that, and don't let anyone upset you. After that, you don't ever have to see Zoe again if you don't want to."

"Of course I'll see her. We're both doing A levels."

"There will be new people there."

"And if she and Rich get together, she'll still want to come to ours. And anyway, I don't want to not see her. I don't know."

"It may never come to anything, or it may fizzle out. In any case, Rich is going to Exeter in the autumn, so he can't commit himself too much, can he?"

"I suppose not."

"Is she with him now in Helston?"

"No, he went to the pub, and she met up with her folks. I think they were going home. I met them today. They just seemed … well … boring."

"More boring than me?"

"Much more." Emily smiled.

Maybe she was making a big deal of it. She spent so much time thinking about Richard and Zoe, and maybe it didn't matter. Richard would always be her brother. Whatever happened to Zoe, he'd be there for the rest of her life. And her mother was right. There would be new people at the sixth form. People from Helston, people from other villages. She and Zoe would be taking different subjects so, of course, they would both meet new faces. By then, Richard would have gone, and summer would have ended. Whatever happened in the next few months would all change with the end of summer.

Emily stood back from the tiny section of wall allocated for her work.

Shit, the one on the right isn't straight.

Luckily, she'd only tacked the paintings up with Blu-Tack until she was sure. She was exhibiting her rock strata paintings. In the centre was a wild charcoal drawing of the Buttress, all angry scrawls and sudden dashes of white. Around it, she'd stuck colour studies of serpentine – the tiny flecks picked out in translucent watercolour – a photo collage of the pebbles and sea glass in Bishop's Cove, and pencil sketches of seaweed over stone. At the bottom was a mixed-media collage: a close-up of banded gneiss with torn strips of tissue paper and dripped Indian ink.

Emily adjusted the lopsided sketch and stood back again. *No, the banded gneiss should go in the middle and the Buttress beneath it.* She took them down, swapped them, looked again. *Or should they be like they were?*

Emily didn't want to ask the boy next to her, who was sticking up a boring painting of a pair of trainers, laces trailing. Instead, she turned to the other side of the hall, where the textiles students were assembling their exhibition. Zoe was standing on her tiptoes, trying to drape a length of fabric over a screen. Emily had never seen Zoe's textiles properly. There was a lot of pink in it, and mauve.

"Could you look at something for me, please?" Emily asked.

"Of course," Zoe said. "Would you help me with this? You're a bit taller than me."

Emily held out her hands, palms up. There were charcoal smears on her skin.

"Ah. Best not then." Zoe folded the filmy material over her arm and dropped it back into a cardboard box beside her.

Emily glanced at the clock. They had been given the last period to arrange their artwork, and time was running out.

"Just come and look at this for me, then I'll wash my hands and help with yours." Emily indicated the two pictures. "The Buttress and the gneiss. I don't know which way round they should go."

"The Buttress should be in the middle. It's the most powerful. You want people to see that first."

"That's how I had it first. But I really like the ink and paper …"

"No, definitely the Buttress there. I think so anyway."

"OK, thanks." Emily changed the pictures again, glanced quickly at them, and zipped her portfolio shut. "I'll run and wash."

When she came back to the hall, Zoe had found a chair and was standing on it, draping the fabric across the top of her screen. She'd put up squares of quilting, embroidery, and a screen-printed runner. They were all pink, lavender, and fuchsia: sweet, delicate, flowery.

"Up a bit on the left," Emily said.

Everyone else was packing up, closing portfolios, wrapping Blu-Tack, gathering together spare sketches and fabric swatches. It was nearly time to go home.

Zoe jumped off the chair. "I think that's OK," she said breathlessly. "I've taped it on, so it should stay."

Emily moved the chair into a corner.

Zoe propped up her portfolio, so it was ready for the examiners' visit the next day.

"Do you need to go to your locker?" Emily asked.

"No, I've got everything here."

"Yeah, me, too. Shall we go?"

Emily glanced at her work – last on the left on the front wall – as they left the hall. She still wasn't sure if it was right.

Too late now.

"See you tomorrow then," Zoe said, stopping by the Gunwalloe minibus.

Emily hesitated. "I'm not here tomorrow."

"Oh? What are you doing?"

"We're going to Truro. Mum's going to help me look for a prom dress, and Dad's got stuff to do, too."

"On a Tuesday? Why don't you go on a Saturday?"

"Because Saturdays are difficult. It's the changeover day. Tuesdays are quieter. Easier for us. Rich can hold the fort and open the bar at lunchtime."

"So, you won't be back for the afternoon then?"

"No, I'm taking the whole day off. Keep it quiet, though. Please."

"Of course. I won't say anything. If anyone asks, I'll say I don't know, and you must be ill."

"Thanks. OK, I'll see you Wednesday then."

Zoe got onto the minibus and waved.

Emily walked on towards the elderly red double-decker with *The Lizard* on its forehead. She shouldn't have told Zoe that she was taking the day off. She would have to tell the teachers that she had a migraine or felt sick or something. Zoe would know she was lying, and Emily didn't like that. She shouldn't have said anything to Zoe.

Zoe was first on the minibus and went to her favourite seat, the one in front of the long bench at the back. Emily and her parents were going to Truro the next day. All day. Or at least until the afternoon because Richard would be opening the bar. He would be on his own up there. Emily had said so.

A few more people got onto the bus. After Gunwalloe, it went on to Helston, but it was never that full, and Zoe usually kept her double seat. The driver fired the ignition and let the bus idle with the door open, waiting for the last stragglers.

The idea was so outrageous she could barely talk herself through it.

The next morning Zoe put on clean black trousers and a newly ironed white shirt. She would have preferred to wear a skirt, but that looked more school uniform than trousers. She brushed her hair, untangling a knot in one of the curls, and slid her makeup into her school bag.

She felt sick and could hardly swallow the toast her mother gave her, but she had to, or it would look strange.

I don't have to do this, she repeated silently as the bus chugged closer to Mullion.

She had her schoolbooks in her bag. She could just walk into the building and registration, and from there, into the lessons, and no one would ever know the thoughts, the plans she'd made.

The bus pulled into the car park. She shouldered her bag and stood up. The other buses were arriving. There was the awful-looking Lizard bus. Zoe loitered on the edge of the staff car park, watching who got off. Emily was quite easy to see from afar because of her hair. No, she wasn't there.

Decision time.

Once she went into school, there was no going back.

What time will Emily and her parents leave home?

She hadn't been able to ask that the previous day. She looked at her watch, but she knew the time anyway.

Not yet nine. They won't have gone yet. She was sure of it.

The buses were starting to *hiss* away again.

Zoe glanced round. No one seemed to be watching her. She ran onto the upper field. In the far corner, there were some bushes. She could wait there, screened from the school and the road, until everyone was safely in morning registration.

She heard the bell, distant and tinny. A couple of kids were running across the other end of the field, but soon they, too, had gone. There were daisies under her feet, tiny and white, edged with pink, and dandelions as well. It was already a warm day, and the sky was a clear blue. A helicopter *ticked* overhead. A dog barked somewhere. A car sped up the road just behind her.

Zoe looked at her watch again. *Five past nine.*

Carefully she crept out of the tiny copse where she'd been hiding. There was a low wooden fence and then the footpath and road leading into the village. She climbed over the fence, careful of splinters and rough wood, and jumped down onto the narrow path. A car came past, followed by a van going the other way. No one paid her any attention. She smoothed down her shirt and started walking. Her fingers felt in her pocket for the scrap of paper with the bus times on, which she'd copied from the timetable on the hall bookshelf. She drew it out, but she knew the times already. The first bus to the Lizard was at 9.30 a.m.

It wasn't easy trying to do her face on the bus. It was another ancient lurching double-decker. Zoe was afraid she'd stick her mascara wand in her eye. She did smear a black streak across her nose, and she had to spit on a tissue to wipe it off. She was sitting on the upper deck so that when the bus went past the entrance to Emily's, she would be able to see if any cars were parked outside the bungalow.

From this height, Zoe saw the field of caravans, a couple of bright tents in the camping field, and, far away on the cliff edge, the charcoal crag of the Buttress. There were the clubhouse and bungalow, too. She saw Mrs Knight's small red car parked outside and – *Oh no* – Mr Knight's silver Volvo beside it. The bus lumbered on, and suddenly, the Volvo reversed and swept away. As the bus passed the camp, the Volvo was just turning left. Zoe could see someone in the passenger seat, but she couldn't tell if it was Emily or her mother, and she wasn't able to see if anyone was in the back.

The bus stopped at the Lizard green, and she went down the stairs on shaky legs. She stood on the green, waiting, wondering what to do. If she got to the Knights' house and Emily and her parents were there, she could just say that she knew Emily was going shopping for a prom dress and she really didn't want to be at school, and could she come, too? No, she had seen the Volvo leaving. Emily was buying a dress, and she would want her mother to help with that, and her father had "stuff to do", so they would all be going to Truro. They were already on the way. They'd almost be at Helston by now while she loitered on the green.

The Lizard village was quiet. There were a few holidaymakers, a couple of people walking dogs, and a woman with a pram. Zoe saw the Ladies across the green and jogged over. She'd only had two cups of tea at breakfast, but she was very nervous.

When she came out, she turned her back on the strange, straggly village and started walking back along the main road. The land was low-lying, and she could see the roof of the Knights' bungalow from the back. At the entrance to the drive, she stopped and checked. Just the one red car, the one Richard took her home in. She walked up the drive and rang the front doorbell.

No one came. No shadows moved behind the frosted glass.

Perhaps Richard is in the club or sorting out a problem with the cara-vans?

Zoe stood back from the door and glanced behind her. Still just the one car.

She *crunched* up the track to the clubhouse. The doors were shut, with the windows dark. She stood aside as a car came *bumping* out of the caravan field. Richard was definitely here because Emily said he would be opening the bar at lunchtime.

She ran back down to the bungalow and rang the bell again and, suddenly, through the milky pane, was a dark figure. She couldn't run away now. As she had seen him, he had seen her.

"Zoe." Richard was wearing jeans and a T-shirt. His feet were bare and his hair damp and wild. "You weren't supposed to be going with them, were you? They've gone. Sorry, did you ring a moment ago? I was in the shower. I—"

"I thought I must have missed them," Zoe said.

"They never said anything about you."

"I just … said I might. They had to go. They've got lots to do."

"Well, don't just stand there. Come in."

Zoe stepped into the hall and dropped her bag on the floor. Richard smelt vaguely of citrus.

"Would you like a coffee? Tea? Cold drink?"

"Some water, please."

She sat down at the kitchen table. Richard filled a chunky glass with water and set it down in front of her. She watched him *flick* on the kettle and spoon coffee into a mug.

She drank some water, but he still didn't turn round; he just stared out of the window at the straggly garden beyond.

"They're having lunch in Truro," he said finally, bringing his drink to the table. "So I'm on my own all day."

"I guess you're not on your own now …"

He grinned. "I guess not."

"I'll have to get the bus home from school."

"That's ages away. I'll take you back to Mullion when I've shut the bar. I'll have to open up at twelve."

"Do you want to walk up to the Buttress?"

"No, I want to kiss you."

Richard watched Zoe. He watched the stain flush her cheeks, watched the way her gaze drifted away from his face. He had planned to kiss her on Flora Day when they jumped off the carousel, but there was Emily with a grumpy face, so he couldn't. Instead, they'd all wandered round the fair and gazed up at the huge arcing arms of the rides, all agreeing they'd puke if they went on them. Then, Zoe had said she should head back to the Guildhall to meet her parents, and as they left the fairground, there was a balloon seller, and he'd bought her a fish.

"Richard," she started, her hand on the water glass.

"Zoe." He peeled her fingers away; they were cold in his. "You know I really like you, and I thought you liked me."

"I do." She gulped, looking at their entwined fingers. "I'm just … I mean … I've never … I've never kissed anyone before."

"Oh, that's good." He smiled. "That's very good. Excellent."

"I do like you, Richard. Very much. You're … I mean, you see, I was hoping you'd be here. Emily said you would be, and I wanted to see you on your own. Are you shocked? That I lied and came up here when I knew everyone else would be out?"

"I'm not shocked." Richard traced the lines on her palm.

He stood, pulling her up with him. She turned her face to his. When he kissed her, he saw her close those blue, dark-lashed eyes. He sensed her hands fluttering at her sides and then felt them, as hesitant as two butterflies on his back.

Zoe stood at the basin and rinsed her hands with the cube of lime-green soap in the metal dish. She rinsed and rinsed, keeping her eyes down. At last, she raised her face to its twin in the mirror. Her hair was scruffy, and she could feel a tangled lump behind her ear. Her eyelashes had smudged black grit into her skin. And then there was the rest. The changes inside that she could never undo. When she set off on the Lizard bus, she'd never really imagined that *this* would happen. She wasn't sure what she had hoped for. That maybe Richard would be in, and they might talk or play pool or even, yes, that he might kiss her, but she hadn't thought he would be so determined and that she would be so weak.

Is it weakness? Or is it a strength to make that choice?

She had made a choice. She could have said no at any time.

Or could I?

She didn't want to say no, and she hadn't.

He'd given her a T-shirt of his to put on. Underneath, she had nothing but her skin. Quietly she unlocked the bathroom door and padded back to his room. He was dressed again in jeans and a patterned shirt this time. He shoved his feet into red Converse boots.

Zoe stopped in the doorway, embarrassed at her bare legs, the huge T-shirt, everything.

"Hey, it wasn't that bad, was it?"

"Where are you going?" she asked.

"The club. I have to open up. Dennis – he's the cook – will be there now. I must get the bar open. Are you coming?"

She sat on the edge of the rumpled bed and found her clothes before tugging off the T-shirt. She was shy with him now.

He kissed her forehead as she flapped out her school trousers. Then, he ran down to the bathroom, leaving her alone.

Zoe got dressed and tugged feebly at the tangle of hair.

Emily bent to look in the black carrier bag on the floor. The waiter had taken their order, and a glass of white wine and jug of iced water with two tumblers had come to the table. Emily and Cheryl had looked briefly in the usual shops, the high street shops, and found nothing but a few taffeta dresses in neon pink and bright blue.

Where do people get dresses for these bloody things? Emily wondered.

Just before they were due to meet Terry at the restaurant, they'd wandered into a tiny, dark shop in one of the backstreets. Tea lights had burned in glass dishes, and amethyst, rose quartz, and agate tumble stones lay scattered amongst jars of incense and joss sticks. In the window, crystals caught the sunlight in their sharp facets, and wind chimes rang softly when anyone came in. At the back of the shop had been another room of clothes: soft cottons scented with patchouli, tie-dyed, and sewn with tiny mirrors. In that cool, fragrant cavern, Emily had unhooked a long, slim dress of copper-and-sludgy-green. She'd

63

taken it into the poky changing room under the angle of the staircase, tugged across a faded Indian curtain, and tried it on. She hadn't even bothered to remove her jeans and shoes. It was the one. No one else would have anything like it. In the same shop, Cheryl had bought her a pair of green-amber earrings to wear with it.

After lunch, they would look for some shoes. Emily didn't think there would be any shoes in the whole of Truro that would work with this dress. She almost wanted to go barefoot to the leavers' prom.

It was quiet in the clubhouse; one family of caravanners were eating pizza; two guys were playing pool; and an older couple were drinking beer and eating crisps whilst flicking through a Cornwall holiday guide.

Zoe was drinking Coke on a bar stool. Richard had offered her a beer, but she'd refused it.

"You must be hungry," he said. "Can't I get Dennis to make you a toastie before we close up? Chips? Pizza?"

"The crisps were fine. I'm not hungry."

Richard reached for her hand across the bar. "When will I see you again?"

"I ... I don't know. I'm sure I'll come up to see Emily sometime soon."

"You don't have to wait for Em. I'm asking you. I thought, after today ..."

"Oh. Yes. Of course."

"You don't regret it?"

"No." Zoe felt another flush blooming on her cheeks. Why did her skin always betray her? "Of course I want to see you. It's just Emily – what on earth am I going to tell her?"

"She's not that fierce."

Zoe drank the Coke through her straw until she sucked up the air around the ice cubes.

"Does she need to know?"

"She needs to know you're my girlfriend, yes."

"Am I your girlfriend?"

"I'm not in the habit of doing *that* with anyone, you know." He glanced round. The family were standing up, leaving. "Dennis!" he called.

Dennis came shambling out of the kitchen, a big, florid man with greying sandy hair.

"Could you close up for me? Please? I need to … give Zoe a lift."

Dennis squinted at Zoe, and she went hot again.

Richard lifted the bar flap and put his arm round her as they walked to the door.

Outside, the sunlight was warm after the unearthly chill of the club.

Richard stopped as the door banged and kissed her, there in the gritty car park, with the caravan family shoving past. As they peeled apart, Zoe saw one of the caravan boys gawping over his shoulder at her.

"My bag's in the house," she said.

Richard grinned. "We've got over an hour until I have to take you back."

"You can take me now if you like."

"I don't like. I want to be with you."

"But what if they come back?"

Zoe's stomach was surging. It was partly because she'd only eaten a packet of crisps since breakfast, and because of what had happened, and because she was now nauseous with fear that Emily and her parents would return early from Truro.

"They won't yet. I told you they're having lunch out. Come on. Please."

This time she knew what to expect.

The flimsy rubber thing Richard took from his drawer made her think again of a slice of flayed skin. Still, she was ready for the momentary discomfort. She only thought about the taste of Richard's mouth. The vivid green of his eyes when he said, "Look at me."

And then, she was scrabbling for her clothes because the clock had bitten off huge mouthfuls of the afternoon. She had to get away. She had to be back in Mullion for the bus. She had to be gone before the others came back and found her in Richard's bed.

As they drove back in Cheryl's car, she slid low in the seat, watching the oncoming cars for a silver Volvo.

"It's not time yet," Richard said as they approached the school. "You'd do better to wait in the village and walk up nearer the time."

"Yes."

"Can I ring you at home this evening?" He slid the car into a parking space by the churchyard gate.

"What for?"

"Just a chat. I want to know you."

"I don't know. It's not you. It's my parents."

"They don't think I'm good enough."

"They wouldn't want me to have … anyone at the moment. Not with the exams coming up. What are you going to say to Emily?"

"I don't know." For a moment, Richard looked uncertain. "I'll think about it."

"But if you tell her what happened, she'll know I came up."

"Does it matter?"

"I think so."

"I'll say I came down to Mullion to buy something and saw you in the village because you didn't want to go to school and—"

"No, that's just rubbish. Let me tell her. Please don't say anything tonight. Let me think about how to do it."

"OK then. Don't worry about it. Everything will be fine. Come up soon, won't you? I can collect you, take you back, whatever. I really want to see you again, Zoe."

"You will," she said.

"What have you been up to?" Emily asked.

Richard shrugged. "Nothing. Bar was quiet at lunchtime."

"You look shifty."

"I do not."

He does, Emily thought.

But she couldn't think why. The house looked OK. He hadn't obviously spilt something on the carpet or broken a window or anything.

"Aren't you going to ask me what I got?"

"Oh, yeah. Well, a dress. That's what you were going for."

Emily scooped the dress out of its dark carrier. The material fell soft and light, still scented with incense.

"Very nice. Yes. You'll look great."

"I've got earrings, too, and some shoes. Cream ones. Oh, what the hell would you know?"

"Not much," Richard agreed cheerfully.

Emily watched him swagger out of the room.

Something's up.

He'd done something or not done something he should have done. Oh well, she'd got her dress and her shoes and some lovely new earrings. It wasn't her problem.

Emily jumped off the old Lizard double-decker. The small Gunwalloe minibus was just coming into the school car park. She waited for the crowds to disperse and then crossed over to meet Zoe as she stepped onto the tarmac.

"Emily? Hello."

"You sound surprised to see me," Emily said. "I said I'd be back today. What did I miss? Yesterday?"

"Yesterday?"

"When I was away."

"Oh. Nothing."

"Can you show me your notes later?"

Zoe checked her watch. "Come on. The bell will go in a minute. Did you get a dress? Did you have a nice day?"

"I got a lovely dress."

Emily glanced at Zoe. She had her head down, watching her feet as she walked.

"What happened in French?"

"Oh. Not a lot. Just speaking practice. I made up a three with Jake and Tim."

"Is everything OK?" Emily asked as they reached the side door to the school.

"Fine," Zoe said.

Emily left Zoe at the lockers and went to registration with her tutor group. She had a note in her pocket from her mother saying she'd had an upset stomach the previous day.

There's something wrong with Zoe, Emily thought as she went into the woodwork room and inhaled the familiar dry, dusty air.

Everything was dusty in there: the workbenches, the stools, the windowsills. A fine pale powder covered everything. It made the air taste of wood chippings. She sat in her usual place on a wooden stool and gazed out of the window at the spun-sugar-like streaks of cloud. A tiny black helicopter *buzzed* below them, and a Painted Lady butterfly buffeted the glass three times and flew away.

She felt like her head was thick. Like she'd missed something everyone else could see.

The first lesson was maths. She and Zoe were in different groups. Emily hated maths – even more now that the exams were looming. Zoe was being weird, and Richard had been weird last night. Was it something she'd said?

It must be.

At morning break, Zoe wasn't at the lockers. Emily saw one of the girls from Zoe's tutor group and asked her if she'd seen Zoe anywhere. The girl shrugged.

The bell rang for the end of break. Emily gathered up her English stuff and cut through the quadrangle with its silted-up pond. Zoe had English, too, but again they were in different groups.

In English, Emily sat with three girls from her own tutor group. They weren't unfriendly, but she wasn't one of them. She didn't listen to what the teacher was saying about Wilfred Owen; she was thinking.

It wasn't something she'd said. It was something she didn't know. Something about Richard and Zoe. Whatever it was, it hadn't happened two days ago – when she told Zoe she was going to Truro. But today, Zoe was evasive about what had happened at school and didn't want to talk to her. At home, Richard was grinning and cocky. Something had happened when she was in Truro. She didn't know what.

Did Richard go down to the school to perv on Zoe?

After English, Emily loitered in the corridor outside Zoe's classroom.

At last, the door opened.

"Hey, I looked for you at break. Where were you?" she asked Zoe.

"I had some books to take back to the library."

"Are you coming for lunch now?"

"Sure."

They collected their food from their lockers, went out into the quad, and sat on one of the low concrete walls.

"What's going on?" Emily asked. "It's not just you. It's Rich as well. What's happening?"

"Rich? What's he said?" Zoe stabbed a straw through a juice carton and avoided Emily's eyes.

"Nothing."

"Well, then, there's nothing, is there?"

"I thought we were friends. Perhaps you don't want to come up to ours anymore?"

"I do. Of course I do." Zoe put the juice carton down on the wall.

"Zoe?"

"I said that I would tell you. I told him not to."

"Tell me what?" Emily felt suddenly sick. She hadn't imagined it.

"Yesterday. I saw Richard up at yours. I went up there. When you were out."

"You went up there? How? I thought you were here?"

"No. I came to school, then went into Mullion and got the bus to yours."

"You knew we were out."

"Yes, you'd said. And I wanted to see Richard, and you said he would be there, so I went. I'm sorry."

That was it then. Zoe had bunked off school and gone up to the caravan park to see Rich.

"Was he pleased to see you?"

Zoe blushed. "Yes. He ... We ... He says I'm his girlfriend now." She met Emily's gaze. "Please don't say anything to my parents. I don't want them to know."

"Because he's not good enough?" Emily snapped. The nausea had swelled and died. Now, she was plain angry.

Rich is quite good enough for anyone.

70

"That's what he said. It's not that. It's just you know what my parents are like. I don't want them to know. Not yet anyway. They'll say I can't see him. Or you."

"I'm not likely to tell them anything, am I? I don't see them."

Emily bit into her banana. It was too soft and sweet.

Yuck.

Beside her, Zoe was fiddling with her juice carton again, pulling the straw up and down. There was something else she'd missed, something else Zoe wanted to say.

"You haven't …? You didn't …?" Emily asked at last.

"Yes," Zoe said quietly. "Twice."

"Oh Jesus," Emily said, even though Zoe hated it when she said that.

"Why didn't you tell me last night?"

Emily scrambled up the lower flank of the Buttress.

Richard turned at the sound of her voice. He was sitting in his usual spot, looking up the coast to Kynance, where the sea gushed white at the bases of the islands. He had a cigarette in his hand, and she could smell the sweet raisiny smoke.

"Tell you what?"

"Tell me what? About Zoe. About what happened yesterday?"

"Why should I?"

"You should have told me. I knew you were up to something."

"She wanted to tell you herself."

"She bloody didn't. She avoided me and avoided me, and I had to force it out of her."

"She was worried about telling you. She thought you'd be upset."

Richard turned back to the sea, to the waves, and the high pale clouds.

71

Emily started to speak. Closed her mouth. She was hot and sticky, still in her school uniform. Perhaps she shouldn't have come racing straight out to the Buttress to confront him.

She left him there and stumbled off the rocks, to the gate, which she had left swinging ajar, and into the caravan field. Her father came round the side of the bungalow. She called to him, and he waited for her.

"Where's Mum?" She indicated the empty parking space.

"Helston. You OK?"

"Fine. Just been talking to Rich."

"Sounds heavy."

"I'll leave him to tell you."

"What?"

"Ask Rich," she snapped as she opened the door to the bungalow and stooped to pick up her bag where she'd flung it earlier.

It isn't the same. Of course it isn't the same. Nothing will be the same again.

Zoe caught the bus to the Lizard on Saturday afternoon, and Richard walked down to the green to meet her. He didn't ask Emily to come, and she wouldn't have in any case. While he was gone, she welcomed two new families with her mother and showed them to their caravans. One of the women asked her about beaches, and she described Kynance and Bishop's Cove. She went back to the bungalow. There was no sign of Richard and Zoe, though the bus should have arrived ages ago. Richard's bedroom door was open, and the room was empty. Emily felt twitchy. She realised she didn't know what to say to Zoe when she saw her. Zoe had asked her on the Friday at school if she could come up. Her parents mustn't know about Richard, she'd said again. As far as they were concerned, she was coming to see Emily.

I'm nothing but an excuse now. A cover story, a lie.

When she'd marched up the street in Helston on Flora Day, counting the reasons why she didn't want Zoe to hook up with her brother, she hadn't thought of that one, and it was the one that hurt the most.

Cheryl was gardening out the back.

Probably to avoid them when they arrive, Emily thought.

She filled a glass with Pepsi and stood at the sink, watching her mother bend and straighten over the tangled flower bed. There were early foxgloves now, dark violet and pale pink, and fat hairy buds on the Oriental poppies. One was just starting to split, and a razor line of blood-red showed through the green.

Cheryl straightened again and pushed at her hair with the back of her hand. Her gloves were stained with earth.

Suddenly the front door opened. Richard and Zoe. Their voices in the hall.

"Emily," Zoe called.

"In here." Emily didn't move from the window.

"There you are." Her voice was high and babbly. Guilty.

Emily turned. It had been only twenty-four hours since she'd seen Zoe by the school buses, but in that time, the ground they stood on had torn open. Zoe was wearing her white denim jacket over a short, straight dress. There was a stain on the denim, Emily noticed. Grass or lichen or something.

"We came along the coast path," Zoe said. "And we sat on the Buttress for a while."

Richard poured two drinks and handed one to Zoe.

Emily hovered by the sink. She didn't know what to say. She didn't know whether to stay and talk with them, go to her room alone, or what. If she didn't live at the end of the world, she'd probably go out, but there was only the Buttress, or the cove, or the Lizard, and she couldn't hide all day.

In the end, she left her dirty glass in the sink and went to her room.

A moment later, she heard the others pass her door. It sounded like Richard was tugging Zoe, and she was pretending to protest. Emily snatched a tape at random from her shelf and clamped her Walkman into her ears. She really didn't want to hear anything.

That evening there was a band playing in the clubhouse. There were caravanners and locals from the Lizard, and the bar was thick with noise, smoke, and the smell of fried food. Cheryl was in the kitchen with Dennis, and Terry was behind the bar.

Emily sat on a high bar stool with her back against the wall. It was cool through her T-shirt. She drank juice and nibbled at a cheese toastie, but it tasted fatty and made her hands greasy. She left most of it on the plate, under a scrunched up sticky paper napkin.

The band was playing beyond the pool tables. Richard and Zoe were huddled into the window seat, the one by the cracked pane, where Emily had once sat, watching them play pool. Richard had his arm round Zoe. She said something into his ear, and he laughed and stroked her hair. Emily wondered what her parents really thought about Richard and Zoe. If they weren't that keen on her being a friend of Emily's, then surely they would be even less keen on her hooking up with Richard? Maybe her mother was right, and it would burn itself out by the end of summer when everything would change anyway. Richard was going to university. Nothing, no one, would stop that. Emily was pretty sure of that now. He wanted to go away. He wanted to study. Not even a girl could affect that. And yet, it was a girl who had stopped him going twelve months earlier. Perhaps she should ask him what would happen when he left. Or maybe she should just stop getting so stressed about it and let them get on with it and sort out their own problems. They wouldn't welcome her opinion.

Someone tapped her arm. A young man with spiky fair hair and a beer in his hand. One of Richard's friends from the Lizard.

"Who's the bird?" he asked, gesturing with his drink to Richard and Zoe.

"Zoe Cassidy," Emily said. "She's at school with me."

He leaned against the wall beside her, and she felt him trying to slide his arm round her.

"Leave me." She slithered off the bar stool.

"Oh, Emily, I—"

"I said *leave me*." She waved at her father, who was handing over two whiskies. "I'm going home."

She didn't bother to speak to the two in the window. She let the glass door *clunk* behind her. It softened the noise of the band, and she shook her head to clear her ears. The sky was darkening in the east, and the day's heat had burnt off. She started across the car park. Behind her, she heard the door open and a bout of applause and shouting as a song finished. She turned, but it wasn't that idiot from the Lizard; it was just a couple from one of the caravans.

As she drew level with the two cars outside the bungalow, she heard her name. Richard was running towards her, tugging Zoe by the hand.

"We saw you going," Zoe said. "Are you OK?"

"I'm fine. Just had enough."

"I'm taking Zoe home now," Richard said.

Emily eyed Zoe. "I'll see you next week, then."

"Emily doesn't like me," Zoe said.

"Don't be daft. Course she does." Richard re-tuned the radio in Cheryl's car.

She doesn't, Zoe thought.

But she didn't say it again. It sounded childish and silly, even though it was true. Did the truth often sound stupid? She wasn't sure. She hadn't been truthful for a long while. Her parents didn't know she had bunked off school and had sex with Richard last week. They

75

didn't know she had again today. Emily could probably say something like that to her parents, and they wouldn't care, but Zoe knew she could never, ever, let on to hers. Especially now, with the exams. Richard would have to be her guilty secret. She was lucky that he was Emily's brother because she always had a perfect alibi.

But for how long will Rich put up with being a secret?

Zoe was afraid to think forward to the end of summer. There was too much to fear. Richard was leaving for university in September. What would happen then? She couldn't bring it up. It was some months away. Maybe he wouldn't even want to be with her that long. Sometimes, when she couldn't sleep, she wondered if he'd just wanted to take her virginity, to prove he could, but then she thought about his kisses and the laughs they'd shared, and she didn't believe that. But, however much he liked her, he was still going away.

"Sorry?" she said.

"I said *you're quiet*. Everything all right?"

"Of course." Tentatively, she placed her hand over his on the gear lever.

"Well, here we are." He pulled up outside her house. The lights were on behind drawn curtains.

"Thank you. I'll see you soon."

Richard kissed her, and she thought he might be about to ask if he could come in, say hello to her parents, assure them his intentions were honourable.

"Bye, Richard," she said and slid out of the car.

Zoe felt him watching her all the way to the front door before he turned the car round and roared off.

June 1992

There was half an hour to go. Emily had read through her paper twice. She tapped the loose sheets together and shoved them to the side of the desk. It was a rickety single table on wobbly legs. The RE exam was in the gym. There weren't many people taking it, so all the tables were at the front. Behind Emily were four or five rows of empty desks. Zoe sat directly in front of her, still writing, her head cradled in her left hand. Richard had given Zoe a googly-eyed cow's head to stick on the top of her pen for good luck. Zoe called it Moo-Moo. Emily could hear the faint tiny *rattle* of its eyes as Zoe wrote.

People aren't always as you imagine, Emily thought once again.

Zoe the Christian, Zoe the girl with morals and all that, but she was lying to her parents all the time and bonking Rich up at the caravan park. She wouldn't tell her parents because they'd go bananas at the thought of anyone doing that to their precious daughter, especially someone from a holiday camp who was probably little better than a traveller in their eyes. And yet, Rich was the one who was quite happy to be open about it and meet them, let them see he was OK. Emily fiddled with her pens. Maybe Zoe's parents had every idea about what was going on and chose to ignore it. Perhaps they knew they couldn't stop it. Or did they really think she just came up to see Emily and revise with her, play music, and whatever? The truth was, though, that Emily hardly saw Zoe now when she came up to Kynance.

"Fifteen minutes," the invigilator said.

Zoe had stopped writing at last and was reading her papers. Moo-Moo was lying on its side on the desk, its eyes rolling. Zoe reached out for it and gently waggled it over her shoulder at Emily.

Stupid bloody thing.

It was Richard who asked if Zoe could stay over the night after the school prom.

Cheryl and Terry looked at each other, and Emily looked at no one.

"I'd have to ring and ask her parents," Cheryl said.

"Don't say anything about me," Richard said. "You know they can't know."

"But you've just asked her to stay."

"Yes, but it'd be Em who invites her, as far as they're concerned."

"You're asking us all to deceive them. They may be really square, or odd, or whatever, but I don't like that. The exams are over. If Zoe wants a boyfriend, she should tell them. If it was you, Emily, I'd rather know who you were with than have you lie."

"I'm not doing anything."

"I know, love, but you understand what I mean."

"I don't understand her parents at all." Terry lit a fresh cigarette and offered the packet to Richard. "OK, they don't like the sound of us, but they let her come up here all the time. You would think, at least, they'd ask Emily over there."

"They're not interested in her," Richard suggested. "But they wouldn't want her having a man, either."

"That doesn't make sense." Cheryl scowled as Richard dropped ash. "If they don't care about her, why can't she do what she likes?"

Emily had a headache. She was tired of thinking about Zoe's parents and why Richard wasn't good enough.

"I'll ask her if she wants to stay after the prom," she said.

"Cheers, Em."

Cheryl looked uneasy. "I'll have to ring her parents and check it's OK."

"Yeah, well, Em's invited her, not me."

"This is getting out of hand," Cheryl said to Terry after Richard left the room.

Terry stubbed out his fag and shrugged. "If Emily's happy to invite her, just go with it. Don't look for trouble, Cheryl. There's obviously something with her folks. I don't want any shit."

Richard was collecting them at eleven, and Emily knew Zoe couldn't wait. There was a disco in the school hall with swooping pink and green lights. The DJ was some guy who'd left school a few years ago, but Emily didn't know him. At the back of the hall, where Emily had hung her artwork, were tables laid with juice, water, Coke, sandwiches, crisps, sausage rolls, and so on. In the disco's half-light, it was hard to see what the food was; Emily bit into a vol au vent with something sloppy like chicken soup inside it and hastily gulped Coke.

The boys wore suits and waistcoats, and many of the girls were in those bright taffeta dresses Emily had rejected in Truro. Zoe wore a long, flowered dress with shell-pink court shoes. No one was wearing anything like Emily. The green ambers her mother had bought for her were in her ears, and she had a chain of copper-coloured bells round one ankle.

Later, she and Zoe followed the crowd to the photographer in the courtyard. The queue moved forwards, group by group, pair by pair.

"I wish Richard was here, too," Zoe whispered as the photographer gestured for them to move closer together. She draped her arm around Emily's shoulders, and the shutter *clicked*. "We'll have that forever."

At eleven o'clock, the night was heady with the scent of honey-suckle. Moths were gliding round the flower beds at the edge of the car park.

"There he is." Emily pointed to Cheryl's car, bleached in the darkness, waiting where the Lizard bus used to stop in the car park.

Zoe scooped up her skirt and ran across the tarmac, her heels *clicking*. Emily's ankle bells tinkled as she walked more slowly. Zoe opened the front door, and a wedge of light lit Richard's face. She slid in beside him and kissed him.

"All right, Em?" Richard asked as Emily got in the back.

Emily kicked the duvet off. It was a hot night again. She would have liked the window open, but creepy crawlies might get in. She had her Walkman on again, plugged tight into her ears, but the batteries were fading. Rod Stewart's voice sounded like the voice of someone in a fairground mirror, long and bendy in the wrong places. She yanked out the earphones and pressed *stop*.

Cheryl had gone to bed almost as soon as they'd arrived home. Probably to avoid any embarrassment about where Zoe would be sleeping. There was a sleeping bag rolled up on the sofa, should she wish to bed down on Emily's floor, but not long after Cheryl had gone to bed, Richard tugged Zoe off down the corridor, whispering and giggling, and Emily was left alone in the kitchen, in her lovely tie-dyed dress and the tinny ankle bracelet and gritty mascara.

She ejected the tape from her Walkman and wound the wires together. She couldn't hear anything from Richard's room, but she could hear the sound of the kettle in the kitchen. Her dad was back from the clubhouse. She drank from her glass of water until it was empty and then scrabbled her feet into her slippers and padded down to the kitchen to refill it. She saw a chink of light under Richard's door.

Zoe could feel the sweat on her back and under her hair before she woke. Her back ached, and she found she couldn't move because someone else was there. *Richard.* She was waking in Richard's narrow bed. She was on the outside, between him and the bedside drawers, and she couldn't move without disturbing him. The curtains were half-open. The dawn sky was pale, and there was a steady splash of rain. The room smelt of cigarettes, though Richard didn't smoke round her as he knew she didn't like it. For a moment, Zoe lay there, quite still, listening to the rain and Richard's breathing. She had spent the night in his bed. If her parents knew … No, they didn't, and they wouldn't. Richard had told her his parents wouldn't say anything. But God knew. She couldn't hide it from Him. And He knew she had lied to her parents and that she would lie again and say she slept in a sleeping bag on Emily's floor. And she would lie again and again and come up here whenever she could, but now it would be to see Richard, not Emily. And she also felt guilty about Emily. Emily didn't like her anymore.

When I'm at Helston, when I'm doing my A levels, I'll come clean, Zoe thought, as she had thought many times before. *When Richard's at university, and I only see him some weekends, and at half term, or whatever they have, then I'll tell my parents.*

What would really happen when Richard went to university? It was only Exeter. Would he come back some weekends to see her? Or would that be the end? She would have to talk to him, but not yet. There was the whole summer to enjoy. A summer without school, without exams.

She kicked feebly at the duvet, but it wouldn't dislodge. Slowly she disentangled herself from Richard. He stirred and muttered, but that was all. She tugged the quilt free, slid off the bed, and reached for his discarded T-shirt. At the window, she watched the rain splash into the open faces of the poppies and felt the sweat cool on her back and behind her knees.

She moved away from the pane and padded to his bookcase. Mostly non-fiction: geology, geography, meteorology. There were several books on Northumberland, and she pulled out a hard-backed volume on the coastline.

"Hey." Richard turned over in bed, watching her.

"Sorry, I was being nosy."

"That's OK. What are you looking at?"

Zoe checked the title. "*Northumbrian Coast*. There are some lovely pictures."

"We used to live there. We went up when I was about eight."

"From London?"

"Yes. My parents managed a holiday park in Seahouses. Mum did the catering, and Dad was the manager, but we came here so we could have a place of our own."

Zoe replaced the book. "Which place do you prefer?"

Richard sat up. "I like them both. I'd love to go back. I did think about applying to Newcastle University."

"I'm glad you didn't."

"Well, yes, it was just too far."

Zoe hesitated. Now was the time to say it.

"I'm glad you're at Exeter," she reaffirmed. "It's only a couple of hours away."

"Something like that."

"So … what's going to happen then? I mean, will you come back at weekends or what?" She spun round to the window; she didn't want to see his face.

"Oh, fuck, I don't know. Sometimes, I guess, but I might be on field trips and that."

"Oh, yes. Of course."

She heard the *rustle* of the quilt falling and then Richard's foot-steps. He came up behind and put his arms round her.

"Don't fuss," he said. "It'll all be fine. Somehow."

"I'm not fussing. I just wondered how we might see each other."

"You could come up for a weekend and stay in my room."

"I couldn't—"

"I know, I know." He withdrew his arms. "Your parents. I'm going for a piss."

He tugged on a pair of shorts and swung the door open. He left it gaping, and she ran to push it closed. They didn't understand. None of them did. Not Richard, nor Emily, nor Mr and Mrs Knight. They didn't know how she had been brought up. It was not OK to lie, to be deceitful, to her parents or to God.

If it's so wrong, though, then why are you doing it?

Emily watched Zoe and Richard through the rainy window. Zoe was wearing stonewashed jeans and a patterned T-shirt with the court shoes she'd worn the night before. Her prom dress was stuffed into her overnight bag. Richard held the passenger door open for her.

Emily was alone in the house. Her father had gone into Mullion for some bits and pieces; Cheryl was out with the cleaners. It was a Saturday morning in June: changeover day. Richard drove off, with the last holidaymakers leaving behind him in a rusty estate car with surfboards on the roof rack.

Emily snatched her jacket and pulled the hood up. Outside, the air tasted bitter with rain and mist. The monstrous voice of the Lizard foghorn cried over the moorland. She *crunched* past the clubhouse and through the gate into the caravan field. The rain brought out gold and pink in the gravel beneath her feet. She could hear one of the cleaners shouting from an open caravan. The smell of bacon frying came from another, where the visitors were staying another week.

Emily unlatched the gate onto the cliff path. The snails were out on the grasses and leaves. The foghorn sounded once more. She stopped and looked up at the Buttress through the grey-green fret. Beyond the crag, she couldn't see the horizon or the Land's End peninsula, just a steely, white sea blurring into steely, white clouds somewhere offshore.

She was too hot in her jacket. Her hood had fallen off, and her hair was wet and clammy. She stamped through the undergrowth to the Buttress and climbed up. The rocks were slimy from the rain and the moisture in the air. Her trainer sole slipped a fraction.

Up the coast, the stacks at Kynance were hardly visible, just darker patches in the mist. She could hear the rush and suck of the breakers in Bishop's Cove to the south. Again, the dreadful foghorn.

It's a horrible sound, Emily thought. *It's a lonely sound. It's trapped here at the end of the world, and it's lonely ...* She jumped down from the crag. *Just like me.*

"I wasn't expecting you." Richard put his arms round Zoe and kissed her.

"I wanted to surprise you," she said.

"Like that first time."

Zoe flushed and looked at the ground. "My parents are at work, and I'd rather be with you than at home."

"And guess what? I'm on my own again."

"Even better."

His mother and Emily were shopping in Helston. His father was in the clubhouse, supervising a delivery. He drew her into the hall and shut the front door. He hadn't been expecting her, and his room was a tip. The duvet was heaped on the floor where he'd kicked it off in the night; there was a dirty ashtray on the bedside cupboard and a stale smell of cigarettes; the sheet was stained with spilt coffee. He stooped and threw the quilt onto the bed to hide the stain.

Zoe slipped off her shoes and unbuttoned her shirt. He pulled her down beside him, her shirt half-open. Zoe was always up for it, which had surprised him after that first time. She never drank alcohol, never accepted his offer of a cigarette, never swore, but she was always happy to jump into bed with him. Either she disagreed with her God over that, or she didn't care anymore, or she was wracked with daily guilt. He didn't ask her; she didn't tell him. It didn't matter. She was pretty, sexy, fun. He liked her a lot, and she brightened the long summer, but he didn't for a moment think it was forever. When he went to Exeter, that would be it, at least until the holidays. If she still wanted to see him, that would be good, but he suspected she'd not forgive him for going away and leaving her with no promises.

He fumbled in his bedside drawer and pulled out the small packet.

"Shit," he said.

It was empty. He hadn't realised he was out. He was sure there were a couple in there. They must have slipped out.

"Hang on," he said to her and sat up.

Keys, torch, pens, a few coins, chewing gum, some cigarette papers from when he rolled his own. No foil squares.

"I haven't got any," he said. "I'm sorry. I didn't realise."

"It's OK." Zoe drew him back down to kiss her. "It's fine. It'll be fine."

"What d'you mean? Are you taking anything?"

"No. But it's fine this week. Really."

"You're sure?" he asked uncertainly. "I mean, I could just come out of you and do it."

"No, not that. It's all right. I promise."

That night, back at home, Zoe could not sleep. She hugged one of her pillows to her chest. The bedroom window was open a crack, and the curtains were drawn back. She watched the lights of a helicopter cross the strip of violet sky and tasted the breath of the sea. She heard her parents coming up the stairs, the bathroom door lock, water running, footsteps on the landing. The stair light went out. She wondered if Richard were in bed or sitting up late in the kitchen, smoking and drinking beer. He had offered her drinks and cigarettes, and she'd always turned them down. She didn't drink or smoke, she'd explained to him, and he'd shrug and put away his lighter.

That day, for the first time, she had felt Richard inside her, skin to skin, the hot burst of tiny seeds flooding her. She didn't know if it was a safe week or not; she just could not have said no to him. But that would be a chance missed, a time they could have been together, been close, which wouldn't have happened because of her. And she found, when she was with him, that she couldn't say no, couldn't refuse him. She needed him to want her and desire her above anyone else. Anyway, it wouldn't happen to her. She couldn't be pregnant.

What are the chances it could happen just that once?

It couldn't. Her parents would – Well, she couldn't even imagine what they'd say or do. They didn't even know about her and Richard. And yet, she couldn't help thinking how lovely a baby would be, someone to bind her to Richard once he'd gone to Exeter. He'd have to come back to her then, wouldn't he? She fast-forwarded the film in her head: her parents, at last, reconciled to her being a mother, she and Richard getting married – quickly before her bump was visible – and joined before God.

She sighed. *It will never be like that.*

Richard would make sure what happened today never happened again. She'd never feel that urgent heat again, never have to tell her parents the worst news they could imagine, would never stand beside Richard in church.

The house was quiet. The night breeze gently stirred the curtains. Zoe turned on her side, still hugging the pillow.

The following evening, Zoe's mother knocked on her bedroom door. Zoe just heard the tap over the sound of the radio through her Walkman earphones. She was listening to Pirate; it reminded her of being in Cheryl's car with Richard. Zoe turned off the radio. Her mother came in and sat on the bed beside her. Zoe's heart rate soared a second. No, her mother didn't look angry, just anxious, as she fingered the gold cross at her neck.

"Zoe, about your friend, Emily," she began.

She'd left the bedroom door open. Moss, their tabby, stalked in, tail held high.

"What about her?"

"You're always going up there. To that … caravan park. And we've never had a chance to meet Emily."

"You met her at Flora Day."

"That hardly counts. I know she's not the sort of girl I'd want for your friend, but you seem to like her a lot."

"Yes, yes, I do." Zoe twiddled the Walkman wires.

"I think you should invite her over. For dinner one evening."

"But you've always said you didn't like her, didn't like her background. It's better I go to see her up there. Like you said, she isn't your sort of person."

"I know, I know, but maybe I shouldn't judge her so harshly."

Moss jumped up onto Zoe's desk chair.

"The thing is, well, Emily doesn't like people to know, but she has terrible asthma. I don't think she could be in a house with cats. She gets ever so poorly with fur and stuff."

87

Another lie, Zoe thought miserably as her mother left the room, followed by Moss padding silently behind her. A boy in Zoe's tutor group had very bad asthma, and he'd said his parents had to get their cats re-homed. Some people were like that, so her mother had believed it. Tell one lie, and another followed, and another, like waves breaking on the shore. Whatever happened to *thou shalt not bear false witness against thy neighbour?*

Zoe didn't want Emily coming over. They didn't get on at all now – because of Richard. It would all be false, and Emily might accidentally say something about her brother – or on purpose. And Zoe couldn't bring Emily into her bedroom, where her walls were covered in Bible posters. And she couldn't sit at the dining table with her while her father said Grace. Emily wouldn't get it. She wouldn't understand the way Zoe had been brought up. She'd go home and tell Richard, and she might tell other people from school if she bumped into them in Helston or something because Zoe knew Emily felt no loyalty towards her now. She knew she was different, that her parents were different, but her religion had always been a huge part of her life. It formed the structure of her days. After her A levels, she wanted to train as an RE teacher and help bring the Word of God into the lives of other young people. That was her, what she'd always been, what she would always be, but other people didn't understand. Emily certainly wouldn't, once she saw it for real, and as for Richard …

July 1992

It only took Emily a few minutes to walk to the Lizard village. There were cars parked on the green; in the spaces between them, the grass was dry and coarse, yellowed by the sun. Outside the gift shops were swinging signboards, spinning racks of postcards, and fluorescent footballs in net bags. Traffic through the village was slow as holidaymakers meandered on and off the pavements, licking ice creams, fanning through guidebooks.

Emily was already hot. She was wearing an old pair of jeans cut off above the knees and a T-shirt. She'd slapped sunblock onto her pale, freckled skin; even so, her arms were prickly. The sky pressed down onto the low scattered buildings of the Lizard like it was crushing the land with its shimmering blue heat.

Emily walked on, through the village, past the restaurant, and down to where the road narrowed and twisted on towards the lighthouse. She was angry that she'd been forced out. The day before, Zoe had phoned and asked if she could come over for the afternoon.

"I'll be out," Emily said. "I'll get Rich for you." She dropped the receiver and yelled for Richard before Zoe could ask her where she would be.

"I've just had enough," Emily told Cheryl afterwards. "She doesn't want to see me anyway. I'm just a bloody gooseberry. I'm not going to be here when she comes. I doubt she'll notice."

"Well, where will you go? I've got to be here to make that cake for Sandra's daughter."

"I dunno. I'll just go out somewhere. Do some drawing. Be on my own. The lighthouse probably."

The lane was narrow. A few dusty foxgloves straggled through the weeds in the hedgerow. A dark butterfly swooped in front of her. *A red admiral*, Emily thought, from the size and wing shape, but it had gone in a heartbeat. Across the green-gold fields, she could see the two white towers of the lighthouse and the row of houses between them. She squeezed in tight to the hedge to let another car by. She had a small sketchbook and pencils in her rucksack, but she didn't feel much like drawing. It was too hot for drawing. It was too hot to be walking to the end of the world.

At last, the final turn. The lighthouse towers were close now, tall and luminous in the heat. The sea was an inky dark blue, the land faded green and khaki. There were cars and people in the car park. A dog chased a ball on the straggly grass. Offshore were the great black fangs of the Man of War gneiss, foam gushing down their ragged flanks. "*The oldest rocks on the Lizard*," Richard had said. Five hundred million years old.

Impossible to imagine.

Emily swung down her rucksack and took out her pad. Though the day was hot and heavy, there was still a breeze here on the Point, and she shoved her hair down the back of her T-shirt so it was out of the way. She sketched the lighthouse towers with the low dwellings in between; the Man of Wars; the gentle sloping field with the five-barred gate; and even a couple sitting on folding chairs outside their camper van. It was hot, and she was tired, and her legs ached, and she had to walk back, uphill all the way, and when she got there, Zoe would be there, or she'd hear muffled giggles from behind Richard's door.

Emily scowled and stashed away her book and pencils. The couple from the camper van stood up. The woman took off her sunglasses and stretched her arms; the man folded their chairs, collected their cups.

Emily shook her hair free and started walking. The houses of the Lizard village were a long way off. She didn't want to get home, but she didn't want to stay out in the heat, either. One foot in front of the other, up the narrow lane with the high hedges of foxgloves, poppies, and cow parsley.

She was sweating when she reached the green. Her rucksack had rubbed a raw strip on her shoulder. She wanted a cool bath and a change of clothes.

"Hey, Emily."

She turned to the voice. Two girls from school, Jane and Beth.

"What you doing?" Beth asked.

"Been down the lighthouse drawing. It's boiling."

"We're just going back to Jane's. D'you want to come?"

"My folks are at work," Jane said.

Emily was hot and sticky and tired, but she only hesitated a second. "That'd be great." She hoisted her bag onto her other shoulder and flapped her T-shirt to cool her skin.

They walked away from the crowded green into one of the side streets. Houses on the left, the football field on the right.

"What you been up to then?" Jane asked Emily. "Haven't seen you since the prom."

"Not a lot," Emily said.

She didn't know Jane or Beth very well. They weren't in her tutor group or Zoe's. Beth had done art with her, and Jane maths, but they'd never really spoken to each other.

They've never been bitchy to me, either, Emily conceded.

Jane swung open a gate. Her house had a tiny garden in the front and a glass porch. They trooped in. A black cat wound itself round Emily's legs.

"You still hang out with Zoe Cassidy?" Beth asked, kicking off her shoes.

"I guess."

"Like that, huh? Thought you two were friends?"

"We were. She's going out with Rich now."

Both girls gaped at Emily.

"Your brother?" Jane shook her head in astonishment.

"The same."

"Richard and Zoe? But isn't she, like, religious? Isn't she going to be a nun or something?"

"No." Emily laughed. "An RE teacher."

"Yeah, but she'd never go with a guy, would she? She'd want to be a virgin bride."

"Not anymore." Emily felt sudden disloyalty, but she was so pissed off with the situation with Zoe and Richard.

Jane handed her a Coke. "She's not done it with him, has she?"

"She has. They're probably at it right now. She's at home with him. She's always coming up. I've had enough of it. I don't want to be there."

"You can always give me a ring," Jane offered. "I'm at a loose end. If you want to hang out."

"I've got a job in the café," Beth said. "Come and have a cream tea."

In the living room, Jane put *Dirty Dancing* in the video recorder and threw herself in an armchair. Emily and Beth took the sofa. The cat padded in and out again.

Emily relaxed with the film. She didn't have to stay at home and listen to Rich and Zoe shagging; she could come out and make friends of her own. Maybe it was because they were done with school, but Jane and Beth were fun. Or maybe they always had been, but Emily hadn't given them a chance, thinking Beth was thick and Jane boring.

"I must go," she said at the end of the film. "I've been gone ages. They'll worry."

"Call round. Any time," Jane said.

She did. She called round at Jane's, and went to the café, which was run by Beth's aunt, and ate a large triangle of lemon cake. It wasn't as good as her mother's cakes, but so what? Whenever she and Zoe met at the house, Zoe was nervous and formal, and her eyes darted away from Emily's.

One evening, Beth came to the clubhouse and played pool with Emily, and they shared a pizza and a large basket of chips.

"What really pisses me off," Emily said, "is that Zoe refuses to tell her parents she's going out with Rich. She tells them she comes up to see me, but she's always in bed with him. They won't think he's good enough, so she won't tell them."

"And the God thing, too," Beth suggested.

"Yeah, and that."

"She's a fucking hypocrite," Beth muttered as Richard came into the bar and gave them a wave. "Spouting all that God shite, then shagging your brother and lying to her olds. Who does she think she is? He should watch out."

Emily walked with Beth to the main road. It would only take Beth a few moments to get home, and it was still light. As Emily started back to the bungalow, she saw Richard leap down the steps from the club and head through the gate into the caravan field. Emily sucked the salty remains of chips from her teeth and walked on past the bungalow, trailing behind Richard. His hands were in the pockets of his jeans, and he seemed to be watching his feet, one red Converse after the other, striding towards the gate and the cliff path. Emily *crunched* through the field behind him. Through the open curtains of one of the caravans, she saw the flicker of the TV; voices shouted from another; music pulsed from a third, something in the charts, but she couldn't remember the song or the artist.

Richard swung open the gate and *clicked* it shut by touch alone. He still hadn't seen her. She slowed at the gate, watching him climb the Buttress. He stood for a moment, only holding on with the palm of his left hand, gazing at the streaky pink sunset and the sparkle of lights that marked Penzance across Mount's Bay. Emily opened the gate onto the cliff path. A couple of small pale moths drifted up from the grasses.

Richard hunkered down on the crag, felt inside his pockets. Cigarettes and lighter.

Emily *swished* through the grass.

Grey gulls soared towards the offshore islands at Kynance.

"Rich," she said quietly. She didn't want to startle him.

"Hi." He turned and patted the rock next to him.

She squatted down beside him. If she looked out across the bay to the horizon, to the three white pulses of Tater Du, and further out, alone in the ocean, the flash of Wolf Rock, she was all right. She only felt dizzy if she looked down at the churning currents below the Buttress.

"I know you're pissed off with me. I'm sorry," Richard said.

"It doesn't matter. Are you happy? With Zoe?"

He didn't answer. He smoked.

Emily waited.

"Rich?" she asked at last. "Are you happy? You shouldn't have to think about it."

"I really like her. It's just ... there's something not right, isn't there? The way I'm her dirty little secret."

"Maybe her parents have worked it out for themselves but are pretending they don't know. Surely they don't think she wants to come here all the time on those shitty buses just to see me?"

"I don't know."

"What's going to happen? When you go away?"

"I'll be going away."

"I meant with Zoe."

"Yeah. I'll be going away. I told her she could come and stay with me for a weekend, and she just said *no* without even considering it. I don't think there's any future in this really."

"Did you ever?"

"I dunno. I was living for the moment. I liked her. She liked me. It doesn't have to be forever, does it?"

"What the hell are you going to say to her?"

"Nothing at the moment. But if she won't be honest about me, there's no future in it. I don't want to be someone's dirty secret. I still want to see her until I go, but after that … who knows? Maybe she'd like to see me again at Christmas. Maybe she'll have missed me."

"Maybe you'll have met someone at uni. Someone who likes geology. Someone who isn't … weird."

"Perhaps I will." He stubbed out his cigarette on the rocks, took out the packet, and slipped the dog end inside. "I never intended to marry her and have it be all happily ever after."

"No, no, course not."

That would be ridiculous, Emily knew that. Was there even such a thing as happily ever after?

August 1992

Time. Time was passing. Time was running away. Time was flying by. Time was doing all those clichés people said about it. Not in geological time, obviously. In geological time this summer was nothing, not even a heartbeat. Richard's life was nothing in geological time, either. He wasn't even a dot on the planet.

It was Saturday evening. He had been to see a friend in Helston. He couldn't stay on drinking into the evening because of driving home, and in any case, he wanted to get away. He'd had an idea.

Why the fuck hadn't it come to me before? he wondered.

He'd been gazing down into the well in the bar of the Angel. There were tiny lights fixed into the well's walls, casting a weird yellow light onto the damp stones. He knew where Zoe lived. He'd taken her back enough times.

Why don't I just call in on the way home?

It wasn't that far out of his way. Then she would have to introduce him to her parents. He felt giddy, looking back up from the well, giddy and a little sick.

"Same again?"

"Yeah, OK. Just the one. I'm driving."

And I want a clear head. I don't want to look drunk.

He had some chewing gum in his pocket. That should get rid of the smell of beer. He lifted the fresh glass.

Maybe it's not such a good idea …

Not when he'd been drinking.

Another day then – no, today.

His mind was made up.

He indicated right for Gunwalloe. It only took a few moments to reach Zoe's house. Richard spat out the chewing gum and quickly checked his face in the driving mirror.

Should have brought her some flowers or something.

Quickly, he got out and locked the car. A few strides took him to the front door. He rang the bell.

Zoe's mother answered. She stared at him a moment, as though trying to place him.

"Hello, Mrs Cassidy," Richard said. "I'm Richard Knight. Emily's brother. We met at Flora Day."

"Oh yes," she said. "Is Emily with you? I can put the cats outside—"

"Richard." Zoe shot out of a doorway to the left.

"Hi, Zoe," he said, though he wondered why her mother had been going on about cats. "Em's not with me," he added, confused.

"Well, come in and have a cup of tea. Or coffee. What are you doing in Gunwalloe?"

"I'm going home from Helston." Richard glanced at Zoe. "I wanted to see Zoe."

He heard a noise from Zoe – a cry, a gasp, he wasn't sure.

"How is Emily?" Zoe's mother asked, leading him into the living room. "I'm sorry she hasn't been able to come over. A terrible thing, asthma."

Richard stood in the centre of the room gazing round. There was a Bible out on the coffee table. There were hideous cross stitch samplers framed on the wall: Bible quotes they looked like.

Asthma? What the fuck?

"Please sit down, Geoff – my husband – he's not here at the moment. Let me make you a drink. Coffee?"

"Thanks." Richard sat on the pale green sofa and smiled up at Zoe. "Come here." He patted the cushion beside him.

"What on earth are you playing at?" Zoe hissed, sliding down on the sofa.

"Sssh." He took her hands and kissed her on the mouth.

She wrenched back. "No. What are you doing here?"

He leaned back, suddenly angry with her. "I came to see you. I thought you were my girlfriend. I thought you might like to see me. Obviously not."

He could hear a cupboard slamming in the kitchen, the rush of tap water, the clink of mugs.

"Of course I want to see you," she said more gently. "But not here. It's … difficult."

"I don't see why. OK, so I'm nineteen, but I'm not forty-five. I may not be religious, but I don't have a problem with you being a Christian and that. My family know about us. It's time yours did. You're not being fair to them."

"You don't understand. We've … had sex." The word was hardly audible, just a whisper of air.

He laughed. "It's not written across your forehead."

"Sssh."

Mrs Cassidy came back with a tray of three mugs and a plate of biscuits.

Richard helped himself to a chocolate digestive.

"How is Emily then?" Mrs Cassidy settled herself in an armchair.

"Yeah, she's fine."

"Not long until the girls get their GCSE results."

"A week on Thursday," Zoe said quietly.

"Zoe says Emily will be going to Helston to do A levels, too."

"That's her plan."

Richard drank coffee. It was clear Zoe's mother wasn't going to move, wasn't going to let him speak to Zoe in private. He thought about his home and his parents. It was so different. Jesus gazed down at him from a painting on the wall. Jesus, nailed to the cross, with hooded eyes, a thorny crown on his head. Richard looked away.

"Is it a good year at your holiday camp, Richard?"

"Pretty good," he said. "We have quite a lot of locals as well who come to the … club."

He glanced at Zoe. She was sitting very still, picking her nail. He wanted to take her hand. He wanted to kiss her and say to her mother, *I've fucked your daughter, and God hasn't cut us down.* But he couldn't. Each time he tried to say something, the words dried in his mouth with the coffee. Zoe hadn't touched hers.

This is pointless. A complete waste of time.

He stood up. "I should be off. Thanks for the drink and biscuits, Mrs Cassidy."

"Don't you want yours, Zoe?" her mother asked.

"I told you. I've gone off coffee." Zoe scrambled up from the sofa. "I'll see you out, Richard."

Richard stopped, surprised. She was probably only going to give him a bollocking.

Zoe trailed down to the car behind Richard. He looked back at the house. Mrs Cassidy had gone from the open front door, but no doubt she was hiding behind the curtains or something. Zoe looked wretched.

"I'm sorry," Richard said. "I didn't mean to upset you. I was passing, and I wanted to see you. That's all."

She smiled then. He thought she looked pale.

"Will I see you soon?" he asked.

"I'll come up."

"When?"

"I don't know. I may have to do something one day this week."

"OK. Can I kiss you?"

"Better not."

Richard unlocked the car and got in. He wound down the window and reached out to catch her hand.

"See you soon," he said.

She nodded.

Something's wrong, he thought as he drove back to the main road. *She's pissed off at me for turning up. What did I even achieve from that visit? Fuck all.*

But there was something else as well.

Is she about to dump me?

She didn't sound very keen about coming to Kynance. But that could have been because she knew her mother was watching at the window.

Richard turned right for the Lizard. Time was passing, tapering. Months had become weeks. Soon he would be leaving, and summer would be at its end. Already the hedges were looking tired, the mornings were sometimes misty, and after it rained, the slugs came out. Autumn was rusting the edges off the long days of summer.

"Knock knock."

"Yeah?" Emily called.

It was Richard. He always said *knock knock* when he wanted to come into her room. The door opened. He came in and shut it again.

Emily was lying on her bed reading. She marked her place with an old postcard of the Farne Islands from their days in Seahouses.

Richard threw himself sideways onto the end of her bed.

"I went to Zoe's," he said.

"What? Did she ask you?"

"Nope. I called in just now. It's weird all right. Bibles and Jesus everywhere. Her mother creeping about, watching her every move. And what's all this about you having asthma?"

"I don't know what you're talking about. Asthma?"

"Her mum thinks you've got asthma. She was going on about putting the cats out and saying what an awful disease or something."

"I never said I've got asthma."

"I didn't think you would."

Emily flicked through the pages of her paperback. Words jumped out of the typeface at her.

"I don't know," she said at last. "I don't understand. Did you come clean to her mum?"

"I didn't know how to. Zoe wouldn't let me touch her. Her mum was sitting there like a pudding all the time. I just didn't have the words. Sounds a bit bloody feeble, doesn't it?"

"You said the other day this isn't forever. You'll be off soon. I don't see any point in saying anything now. You'll only piss off Zoe."

"I wish I hadn't gone. If she gave a fuck about me, she'd have said something to her mum when I was there. She was really odd."

"The mum?"

"I actually meant Zoe. Like something was wrong. Something else."

"Did you ask her?"

"Well, not really. I asked if she'd be coming up to see me, and she was kind of vague."

"She'll come, Rich. Don't worry about it."

Emily was surprised that Richard had heard nothing from Zoe. She wondered if Zoe had a huge row with her parents, and they'd forbidden her from coming to the caravan site. She even wondered whether to ring Zoe herself, but after Richard's visit, she was apprehensive. And anyway, she and Zoe were hardly friends anymore. She'd talked more to Jane and Beth lately. She wouldn't really know what to say.

Zoe's Richard's problem now.

On Tuesday afternoon, Emily was in the kitchen talking to Cheryl, who was making an anniversary cake for a couple in Mullion.

The phone rang.

"Could you get it, please?" Cheryl waved her sticky hands.

Emily slid off the stool and picked up the receiver just as the answerphone was about to kick in.

"Emily. It's Zoe."

"Oh, hello. D'you want Rich? I'm not sure where—"

"No. I need your help. Please."

"What's happened?"

"Can you meet me in Helston tomorrow? I can get a bus in for about eleven. I know we haven't, you know, spoken that much lately, and I'm sorry, it's all been so full-on and that, but I really need to see you. Please, Emily."

"Are you OK?"

"Can you? Can you come tomorrow?"

"Wouldn't you rather see Rich?"

"No," Zoe yelped. "Don't say anything to him. That's really important."

"Mum's going to Helston tomorrow morning. I'll come with her. Let me talk to her, and I'll call you back."

"Not after five. My parents will be home."

Emily wandered into the kitchen with the phone in her hand.

"That was Zoe. She wants to see me tomorrow. Urgently. In Helston. Are you still going in?"

"Yes, I need some shopping. We'll go about half ten."

"OK, I'll call her back."

"What's so urgent that she suddenly needs you again?"

"I don't know," Emily said. "I don't know what's going on."

"I'll be about an hour." Cheryl dropped Emily at the top of Meneage Street. "I'll pick you up in the car park."

"That's fine. She said she only wants me for a short time."

Cheryl rolled her eyes.

Emily slammed the door. Those were Zoe's exact words.

She wants me, Emily thought, starting down the street towards the Guildhall. *She wants me to do something. That's the only reason she spoke to me.*

It was not quite eleven when Emily arrived at the Guildhall. She loitered on the steps. This was where she and Richard had met Zoe's parents on Flora Day. A minibus hissed round the corner and into Coinagehall Street. Someone was waving from the window.

Zoe.

The bus stop was near the bottom of the hill.

Better walk down and meet her there, Emily thought, *as she's already seen me.*

The minibus indicated left with a muddy orange signal.

Zoe and Emily faced each other on opposite sides of the road.

"Come here," Zoe called.

"Yes, sir," Emily muttered as she ran across the street.

She stopped, taken aback. Zoe didn't look well at all. Her perm had long since grown out, and though her hair was longer, it looked straggly and messy. She was pale, and it looked like she'd lost weight.

"Thanks for coming," Zoe said. "I really, really need you."

"Yeah, I figured it wasn't because you wanted to see me and catch up."

"Emily, please don't be like that. I said I'm sorry. It's just ... Everything's so awful. I need your help."

"Because Rich came to yours?"

"No, but he shouldn't have done that. And everything's worse now."

"I haven't got long. What d'you want?"

"It won't take long." Zoe pulled a twenty-pound note out of her jeans pocket. "Please, would you go to Boots for me?"

Emily didn't take the money. "You want me to buy Durex for you?"

"No," Zoe sobbed.

"Hey, don't cry. What then?"

"I ... I think I'm pregnant," Zoe said at last.

"Jesus. You what? Didn't Rich ... Oh, for fuck's sake. Are you sure? When were you due?"

"It's the second I've missed."

"Oh."

"I thought maybe it was stress and that the first time, but you see, there was this time when Rich, when we, when he didn't have any, and we did it anyway. I didn't think it could happen, even though part of me would have liked it to. I know, stupid. And I don't feel well. And my parents will ... I don't know what."

"Come on." Emily took Zoe's arm and spun her round. "Boots is this way."

"I can't go in. Mum's friend works there."

"Superdrug then."

"I can't. Someone might see. Please, you get it." She held out the note again.

"Because I look like the sort of girl who'd need to buy a pregnancy test," Emily snapped, taking the money.

"It's nothing to do with that. I just can't have anyone seeing. I'll wait right outside. You'll know better what to get anyway."

Why should I? Emily thought. *I haven't even had sex with anyone.*

She glanced at her watch.

Will Zoe want to do the test then and there in the ladies behind the Guildhall? And if it's positive, what next?

"Would they make you get rid of it?"

"No, no, they don't believe in abortion. And I wouldn't want that. I don't believe in it."

"No, of course not." Emily vaguely recalled a conversation in her bedroom. Something about abortions and euthanasia. Stuff for RE.

"Would it have to be adopted?"

"I don't know. I don't know. I want to keep it. If it's there."

"Rich has no idea."

"No."

"He'll have to know. He has an opinion, too."

"What would he say?"

Fucking hell, that's what he'll say. Fuck, shit, bollocks.

"He won't want it." Zoe rubbed her eyes. She was really crying,

"I can't answer for him. Let's just get this. You wait here. I don't know anything about these things, you know."

Emily went into Boots with the twenty crumpled in her palm. She wondered if the woman on the till was Zoe's mother's friend or whether that was a load of crap. Like the asthma thing. She'd never asked Zoe about that, and she didn't know how she could now.

Makeup, hair dye, deodorant, false nails, toothpaste. Where the bloody hell? By the sanitary towels? No. Oh fuck, I don't have to ask, do I?

At last: a small display of Durex. Emily felt her face flame under her freckles. She had no idea there were so many sorts. She glanced over the slim white boxes on the neighbouring shelf. She didn't know which was the right one to buy or how accurate they really were. She selected what she thought would be a good choice and took it to the till. She could see Zoe standing on the street outside. As the man in the queue ahead of her flicked a note out of his wallet, she studied Zoe's profile.

She might well be, Emily thought.

Zoe looked grim.

But shouldn't she have gained weight rather than lost it?

Maybe Zoe had some virus or something that had made her periods stop.

The man moved on.

Emily placed the box down and flattened out the twenty-pound note. When the woman slipped the receipt into the plastic bag and handed it back to her, Emily exhaled with relief.

"Here you are." She handed the bag and change to Zoe.

Zoe peered into the bag. "Thank you. Thank you so much. I just couldn't have done that. You're amazing. Thank you. If I can ever do anything for you—"

"Are you doing it now?"

"No, I'll do it at home. I'll hide it. I can't do it now. I just can't. Anyway, you might have to do it first thing or last thing or something."

"Will you ring me? Let me know?"

"Of course. I'll do it tomorrow. I promise. I'll ring when my parents are at work. And Emily—"

"I know, don't tell Rich. There's nothing to tell him until you do the test. But if you are, you'll have to tell him, especially if you're going to keep the baby."

"I'll have to tell my parents," Zoe whispered.

"Tell Rich first, and he could tell them with you."

"No. That'd be worse. I don't know how to tell them."

"Could you talk to your priest or vicar or whatever you call him? Could he help you?"

"I couldn't do that."

"Or your doctor?"

"You don't get it. It's different for you. If you were pregnant, your parents wouldn't care."

"They would care!"

"You know what I mean."

Their families were different. Anyone could see that. But Emily's parents would care. They wouldn't be happy because they had high hopes for her future: university, a career. But they would accept it, and support her, whatever she chose to do. And Emily would choose the same as Zoe. She couldn't kill a baby.

Emily checked her watch. "I have to go. I'm meeting Mum."

"What will you tell her we did?"

"Had a catch up."

"OK." Zoe put the Boots bag into her rucksack.

"What are you going to do?"

"Wait for the bus home."

"Oh, come with me. I'm sure Mum will give you a lift."

"No. I don't want to see her today. Not with this hanging over me. And she'd tell Richard she saw me. I'll get the bus."

They walked together to the alley leading to the car park.

Zoe could be pregnant, Emily thought. *There could be a bundle of life inside her. Rich would be a father. I'd be an aunt. Auntie Em, like in* The Wizard of Oz.

She tried it out quietly with an American accent before swallowing a bubble of hysterical laughter.

"Ring me," she insisted. "As soon as you can."

"I will," Zoe said.

Zoe was asleep when her alarm beeped at six. She woke instantly – because she'd really only been dozing, counting down the night hours – and clicked it off. She held her breath, but the house was quiet. Her parents' alarm went off at six forty-five. She had three-quarters of an hour.

When she got home from Helston the day before, she'd read and read the instructions on the pregnancy testing kit. It should be done first thing in the morning because hormone levels were highest then. She'd shoved the instructions and the stick back into their box, put the box into the carrier, the carrier into her shoulder bag, and stashed that at the back of her wardrobe and dumped shoes all around it. She didn't think her parents would go through her things, but if they did, there was nowhere to hide.

I could say I got it for Emily, but what if it's positive? Then I'll have to tell them anyway.

She felt nauseous once more at that. Maybe she wasn't. Maybe she was just overstressed, worrying about her secret affair with Richard and his imminent departure for Exeter. That could just as easily be it.

But I've never been late before, she said to herself, over and over.

It was August, but she was chilly and tugged on a dressing gown. She crouched down in front of the wardrobe and moved aside her trainers, sandals, and the heels she'd worn at the school prom. The bag was still there, still rustling with its inner secret. Zoe slid out the white test stick and the instructions and stuffed them in her dressing gown pocket. She opened her door and padded softly across the landing. She could hear her father snoring. She locked the bathroom door, unfolded the paper, and read the instructions one more time. Either way, this was a moment she'd remember forever.

Urine trickled warm onto her hand as she held the stick in the stream. When it was suitably covered, she sat down.

Stupid girl – she'd forgotten to take her watch into the bathroom. *Count the seconds slowly, don't rush it, don't look down.*

The stick was wet and dribbled onto her bare knees, where her robe was scrunched up. She tore off a handful of paper. She would have to get rid of the stick somehow. She hadn't thought of that. She could keep it wrapped in her room, and when her parents had gone out, she could walk down to the litter bin.

The time must be up now.

"I'll get it," Emily said when the phone rang at ten o'clock.

She'd been up since nine, wondering, waiting for Zoe to ring.

"You expecting someone?" Cheryl called from the kitchen.

Emily didn't answer but swiped up the receiver.

"Hello," she said quietly, walking away from the kitchen door and towards her room.

"It's me."

Emily closed her bedroom door behind her. "Have you done it?"

"I've done it," Zoe said.

Emily knew instantly that the test was positive, that Zoe was expecting a baby, that she was the first person to know, and what the fuck would happen when Zoe told her parents, who didn't know she'd as much as kissed Richard.

"It's a yes, then?" she managed.

"It's a yes. I knew it would be."

"When are you going to … You need to see Rich … He must know."

"I don't want to be on my own today," Zoe whimpered.

"Come up then." Emily sighed. "We'll talk about it. Rich isn't up yet. I'll tell him you're coming, and you need to talk to him, and it's important."

"No, don't say that. Let me do it my way."

"You must do it. It's not fair otherwise. How can he support you if he doesn't know?"

"I'll see you soon," Zoe snuffled and hung up without saying goodbye.

Emily padded back down the corridor and replaced the receiver with a *click*.

"That was Zoe, I take it?" Cheryl's voice behind her.

"Er … yes."

"What does Rich need to know?"

"Nothing."

"I went past your door. I heard you. What does Rich need to know?"

"Oh God, Mum."

"She's up the duff, isn't she?"

"You can't be," Richard said.

She's lying. Must be.

"I've done a test," Zoe said. "I did it this morning. I've missed two periods."

"But we've always used condoms." He was about to say, *Who else have you been shagging?* but he choked back the words.

"Not every time." She wouldn't meet his eyes. "*That time* you hadn't got any."

"You said it was a safe week!" Shit, he never meant to shout, not with his mother and Emily just down the corridor in the kitchen. "I asked you, and you said it was OK."

"I thought it was. It was. It must have been then. Or maybe one tore. That happens, doesn't it?"

"It's never happened to me," he said, suddenly wanting to remind her that he'd had other girls before her, other girls who hadn't let this happen.

"I'm sorry," she said.

"So am I."

He sounded bitter, and he was. He knew, without asking, that if there was a baby, she would keep it. It couldn't have come at a worse time. People said that all the time, but it was true; it really was true for him right now. In a month, he was moving to Exeter to start his career in geology, which he hoped would take him around the world, to deserts, volcanoes, and the Arctic.

I can't give that up.

It was what he'd always wanted. He had to go.

Zoe hadn't spoken. She was crying into a wet, screwed up tissue.

"You're sure then?" he asked lamely.

She nodded.

"When … when is it due?"

"I don't know. I think it must be about April."

"You'll need to see a doctor."

"Yes."

"And what about your parents? You'll have to tell them. You'll have to tell them about me now."

"I don't know how. They'll … They might disown me. They'll see it as a disgrace. Sex is only for people who are married before God."

"Bollocks."

"That's what they believe."

"Then they need to wise up. That's not how the world works."

Richard stood and the bed exhaled. The room was hot and enclosed, and he felt light-headed. He stalked to the window and forced it open. A cooler breath of air kissed his cheek.

"Would they rather you got rid of it?"

"No, that's wrong."

Richard picked up a spiky chunk of amethyst from the windowsill and turned it over and over in his hand.

"So, they think you're a disgrace for having a baby and a disgrace for having an abortion. Jesus."

"We should never have done it," Zoe sobbed.

"You wanted to. You came here. You bunked off school and came up here when you knew the others were out." He was shouting again; he checked himself.

"What am I going to do?" she cried.

He put the amethyst down, turned to face her with folded arms.

"If you have an abortion, you might be able to do it without your parents knowing. I don't know. But, you know, I've been pretty pissed off lately about the way you won't tell them about us, like I'm not worthy of you or something. If you're going to keep it, you have to tell them. End of."

"I can't have an abortion."

"Why not? It's not a person yet."

"It is."

"I don't think so."

"Is that what you want me to do? It's part of you. Imagine if your mother had had an abortion instead of having you adopted. You wouldn't be here."

"That's stupid."

"It's not. It's the same."

"You don't know anything about my birth mother or what she did."

"Do you want me to have an abortion?" Zoe demanded, shredding the tissue all over his bed.

He opened his mouth and stopped.

Do I?

He wasn't sure. It didn't seem fair, really, to kill this kid. It didn't ask to be created. It was his fault and Zoe's. Zoe's for lying about it being a safe week; his for believing her instead of saying no. But it wasn't this baby's fault. What Zoe said about his birth mother had stung him.

"No," he muttered at last. "I don't."

"Because I'm not. And I'm not having it adopted, either. It's mine. And if my parents won't have me at home, I'll go and live with Amanda."

"I'm sure your parents will have you at home. It won't be as bad as you think, telling them. I'm sure. They may not like it, but they'll have to accept it. If it really is true."

"It's true. I told you. I did a test. I'd have brought the stick up to show you, but I dumped it in the litter bin by the bus stop because I didn't want anyone to find it."

"Emily knows, doesn't she?"

"She bought the kit for me. I was too embarrassed. I told her not to tell you."

"She didn't," he said truthfully. "She was a bit odd, but that's Em. Jesus, she's going to be an aunt. This is madness."

It could work, couldn't it? he thought desperately.

Just because Zoe was having his child didn't mean he and she were tied together forever. He would have nearly finished his first year before it was born. He'd have to send Zoe some money to help her. He could get a job in Exeter. Bar work or shop work or something. He'd see the child during the holidays. He'd make sure it knew who he was, but he would also have his own life. Other people did this, and it was OK.

It can work, can't it?

"Let's do it tonight," he said suddenly.

"Do what?"

"I'll drive you back, and we'll tell your parents. We'll do it together."

"I don't know."

"Yes," he said firmly and sat down beside her again. "We'll tell them today.

Adrenaline surged through Richard's body as he drove. He knew he was driving carelessly, swooping through the wooded bends, at times careering over the white line. Beside him, Zoe sat stiffly. The radio fizzed between them. He felt queasy, afraid. In half an hour – no, less than that – everything would be out in the open.

"*Richard, don't do anything,*" his mother had whispered urgently to him before he left. "*Wait and talk to me and Dad first.*"

But he'd shaken his head, and then Zoe had appeared in her white denim jacket and drawn face, and he rattled the car keys and opened the front door. He knew his mother didn't want him to talk to Zoe's parents, but he had to; it was his responsibility. He was a man now. The notion made him light-headed.

"Don't," Zoe said as he braked too sharply.

"Sorry." He glanced at her and quickly squeezed her hand.

This must have been the first time they had met and not had sex. In fact, they'd hardly touched. Afraid, embarrassed, edging round each other, aware of the silent glances between his mother and Emily.

Too soon, there was the turn-off for Gunwalloe. Richard braked more gently and swung round.

"We don't have to tell them today." Zoe's voice was sudden in the quiet.

"It's not going to go away. We must tell them as soon as possible. Give them plenty of time to get used to it."

"I feel sick."

"That's kind of normal, isn't it?"

"I mean about telling them. Oh no."

"No, what?"

There was a blue hatchback in the space where Richard usually parked. He pulled in tight behind it.

"It's the Jacksons."

"The Jacksons? What, all five of them?"

"No, no, the Jacksons. Barry and Elaine. From church. That's their car."

"That blue one?"

"They must have come to see Mum and Dad."

"I suppose that means …"

"No way. No way at all." Zoe released the door.

"Shall I come in and see? They might be leaving any minute."

"No." She leaned towards him, and he grazed her mouth with his. Her eyes looked hurt for a second.

"I thought I wasn't allowed to kiss you here."

"They'll all be talking."

This time, he wrapped his arms round her. "OK, not today then. Don't worry. It'll all be all right."

He watched her trudge up to the front door. Her relief at seeing the blue car had almost overwhelmed her. He was relieved, too, but frustrated. He was ready to tell them, he wanted to tell them, and at the same time, his heart rate had steadied.

Let off the hook. A stay of execution.

They were all in the living room talking.

Zoe hesitated in the doorway.

Her mother looked up. "Ah, there you are. Did you have a nice day?" She turned to the visitors. "Zoe has some friends who run a caravan site at the Lizard. She goes up on the bus a lot these days."

"Yes, fine, thanks," Zoe said.

"I've asked Barry and Elaine to stay for dinner. I'll do some pasta. Would you give me a hand with a salad in about half an hour?"

"Of course. I'll just go and get changed."

Zoe fled into the kitchen and poured a glass of water. Her note was still on the table, her note from the morning: **Gone to Emily's**. She screwed it into a ball and threw it in the direction of the bin. It fell short. She left it there on the tiles and climbed upstairs, tugging off her denim jacket.

With the bathroom door locked, she peeled off the rest of her clothes and studied herself.

I don't look very well, she thought. *Aren't pregnant women supposed to bloom or something?*

She certainly wasn't. Her skin looked waxy, and her hair messy. If anything, she thought she had lost some weight, but she couldn't weigh herself because her mother refused to have scales in the house after Amanda's anorexia. Zoe placed her hand on her stomach, but it didn't feel any different. She knew nothing about pregnancy – when she would start to show, how much weight she'd put on, what other changes might happen. As for the birth itself, she knew nothing about that, either, except that it would be painful beyond imagination without intervention, but there were drugs and anaesthetics nowadays. She did know that much.

When she turned off the taps, she heard Barry Jackson's loud guffaw from below.

I can't do it. I can't tell them. I can't even tell Amanda. I can't tell anyone.

She lowered herself into the bubbles. She'd tied her hair up on top, but it was starting to fall down, and a long straggle clung wetly to her back.

I don't have to tell them. I could just go away.

Richard was leaving soon for Exeter. He wanted to stand by her and the baby; he'd said that. She could go with him. They could rent a small flat or bedsit. He must have some sort of grant or bank loan, whatever university students had. The baby would be due about April, so she could get a job until then. When the baby was born, she would get benefits or find a job that fitted round Richard's degree. If she worked in the evenings, as a waitress maybe, Richard could look after the little one.

Zoe had never been in a bedsit before. She tried to visualise it.

A double bed with a bright, patterned throw on it. Posters on the walls – not Bible ones. Fine art prints, music posters. A pot plant on the windowsill. A kettle and maybe a hand basin. Richard would need somewhere to do his work. A small desk with a bookshelf. And a table lamp that cast a warm pool of light on autumn evenings.

And later, in the spring, a cot pushed against the wall and, wrapped in soft blankets, a tiny baby. Our baby.

Zoe hoped it would have Richard's green eyes. The three of them would lie on the bed, and Richard would tickle the baby's feet. Then she would open her shirt and guide its mouth to her nipple, and Richard would put his arms round her as she held the baby, and they'd all be together.

"Zoe!" her mother called up the stairs.

The salad. The Jacksons.

"Five minutes." Zoe hauled herself up, and water splashed over the rim.

She was still terrified at the thought of telling her parents that she would be moving to Exeter with Richard, but at least she wouldn't have to tell them about the baby. She could even say they were engaged. That might make it easier.

Besides, we will be one day, won't we?

Richard didn't go straight home. His mother thought he was going to be speaking to the God Squad, so she wouldn't expect him for a while. When he got home, there would be "The Conversation" with his parents, too.

How could you have been so careless? etc. etc.

Soon the hedges fell back to reveal the scrubby moorland of Goonhilly Downs and huge white satellite dishes pointing to the clouds. Messages beamed around the globe: secrets spoken, dreams escaping.

He drove faster with the Earth Station on the right. The road spooled out ahead of him towards the crossroads in the middle of the downs. A heat haze fragmented the tarmac. At the crossroads, he turned right until he saw the dried-up dew pond of Croft Pascoe Pool. He swerved across the road and braked in the rutted layby.

In winter, the pool was a glassy sheet of water spiked with jagged reeds. Now there were only a few small muddy puddles, churned up grasses, and litter. He opened the door and stepped out. One of the dishes was pointing straight at him. He couldn't hear the hum, but he fancied he could sense it in the hot air. Traffic noises soared and died on the road. Richard stood on the edge of the dew pond, staring at the distant antennae.

I must be nuts. It can't possibly work.

Going back to Zoe's house had reminded him of that weird visit he'd made before: the Bibles, the God stuff. Even their friends were in the God Squad. What chance would the child have in that environment without Richard there to protect it? And he couldn't be there for it, not all the time. He had his own life to lead. And if he wasn't there all the time, would the Cassidy family even let him see his child?

He scuffed at a stubby mound of grass with his toe. The choice was stark; he could see it now. They would want him to marry Zoe, join the church, bring up the child like one of them. Or he could just fuck off and have nothing to do with it, and the poor little bastard would be brought up like Zoe had, whether or not it wanted to be, and would no doubt be condemned for being illegitimate. He couldn't let it happen. It would never end happily, not for him, not for Zoe, and not for the baby.

She has to have an abortion.

She wouldn't ever need to tell her parents. He would take her to the doctor or a clinic or wherever girls had to go. She'd see it was for the best. Not in an ideal world, no, but, realistically, the child was only a handful of cells.

It's the only answer.

"The Conversation" didn't happen until late when his father came back from the club.

"How could you have let this happen?" Terry said, snapping his lighter at a cigarette. "Now, of all times? Honestly, Rich, I thought you had more sense. And with her, of all people."

"That's nice," Richard said.

"You know what her background's like. Do you want your kid being brought up like that? Can't do this, can't do that, can't have friends round. Because make no mistake about it, that's what's in store for it, and you'll be lucky to see it a couple of times a year."

"It's not going to happen. She's not keeping it."

"What?" Cheryl gasped. "Is that what her parents said?"

"I told you. I didn't see them."

"I thought you might have spoken to her on the phone since. When did she say she's not keeping it?"

"She hasn't," Richard muttered. "But she can't. It's stupid, ridiculous. It won't work. I want her to … get rid of it."

"Get rid of it? This is a child, Richard. Your child. A human being. My grandchild."

"Not genetically."

"That's enough," Terry said.

"I'm sorry. I just meant – it's not your flesh and blood."

"It's still my grandchild. Your baby." Cheryl's eyes were glassy with tears.

"I wouldn't have thought Zoe would agree with abortions." Terry tapped ash carelessly on the side of the ashtray.

Richard wished he had a cigarette, something to do with his hands. He hadn't meant to say that – *not genetically* – to his mother. It was unkind. He felt guilty. He had a headache.

"I'll talk to her," he said at last. "She's terrified about telling her parents. This way, she won't have to."

"Having an abortion isn't just like having a tetanus shot," Cheryl said, eyes flared. "Of course she'll have to tell her parents."

"She's over sixteen."

"She'd want her mother with her, for God's sake."

"She wouldn't. Not her mother. I'd be with her."

"Some comfort that'd be."

"Well, perhaps you could come, too."

"She wouldn't want me. The whole thing's … just wrong."

"It's wrong because her family's fucking nuts. If they were like us, there wouldn't be a problem. Well, not quite like this."

"You knew they were nuts before you picked up with her," Terry said. "Emily had told us from the start they were … different. You should have been a damn sight more careful."

"Knock knock."

"Come in."

Emily was awake, with her book discarded on the floor. She'd overheard most of the conversation in the kitchen. She sat up in bed as Richard came in. He looked tired and ravaged and was holding a can of lager.

"Want one?" he offered. "I can bring you one."

"No thanks."

Emily watched him just standing there in the middle of the room.

"You can't do that to her, Rich."

"Do what?" He threw himself down on the beanbag, and lager slopped out of the can.

"You can't make her have an abortion. It's not right. It's not what she wants. It's wrong. It's evil. I don't believe in it."

"It's not a baby yet."

"It is."

"It's not. And if she has it, it'll have a shitty fucking life with that lot."

"It's up to you, then, to make sure that doesn't happen. You're its father."

"And what could I do against them? They'll want me to give up uni, marry her, in the bloody church, join the bloody church, spend my life on my bloody knees." He gulped the lager. "I'm so fucking stupid. I should never have believed her."

"About what?"

"She said it was a safe week. I believed her. I didn't know she was a liar."

"She probably wasn't lying. She probably didn't know. I wouldn't know," Emily confessed.

"If you didn't know, you wouldn't have said it. She was trying to trick me. She knew she'd get pregnant. Did you tell her I wanted to end it when I go away?"

"Of course not."

"She probably sussed it, though."

"Have you broken up now?"

Richard gazed at her with the can hanging from his finger and thumb. He started to laugh. "I don't know … I don't know what's going on."

"You must talk to her."

"Yeah. I must tell her to have an abortion."

"Rich, you don't just tell people to have abortions. You can suggest it, if that's what you think, but it's her choice, it's her body. And I know she'll keep it. She told me she was going to."

"She might think an abortion is less awful than telling her parents about it."

"I doubt that. I guess there'll be a lot of yelling and praying, and then her parents will be pleased they're going to be grandparents." Emily stopped. "What do Mum and Dad want? Really?"

"Didn't you hear?"

"I heard Mum getting upset. I think she wants Zoe to keep it."

"She does."

"She wanted babies for so long before they adopted you."

"Dad … I don't know. He's just pissed off at me for getting into this bloody mess."

This poor baby, Emily thought. *Everyone thinks it's a mess. It's a tiny human.*

She suddenly felt a strange ache of protection for it, this niece or nephew of hers. She almost said, *I'll look after it*, but that was stupid. Richard was watching her.

"D'you want kids?" he asked.

"I think so. Not yet. Not for a while. I can't really imagine it. I can't imagine you or Zoe as parents. Not right now."

"God, I should have gone away a year ago. Then none of this would have happened."

Emily twiddled her earring, which had come loose. The green amber. The earrings her mother had bought to go with her prom dress that day in Truro. That day when it all began.

"Everyone thinks she's Little Miss Innocent," he said. "And she's not. She knew what she was doing all right. Trapping me."

"If that's right," Emily said, "you walked right in."

"Zoe for you." Cheryl held the phone out to Richard.

He was still in the shorts and T-shirt he'd slept in. His throat was thick with stale lager and cigarettes from the night before, when he'd lain awake in his room, watching the ungainly flight of a crane fly juddering around the ceiling.

He pulled a desperate face at his mother, but she simply held out the phone. He didn't want this conversation at this time of day, not right now.

Not ever.

"Zoe, hi, how are you?" He walked the phone back to his room.

"I want to come with you," she started.

"Come with me?" He didn't understand. He was tired.

What the hell is she on about?

"When you go to Exeter. Listen, I've thought it all through. We can rent a flat or something, and I can get a job until the baby's born, and then you can help look after it in the evenings, and I can go back to work as soon as I can. And I won't have to tell them about the baby because we'll go before it shows and then it'll be too late, but if we're living together, that'll make it better. I know I'll still have to tell them about us and that I'm going with you, but Amanda had a boyfriend when she was eighteen, so they can't complain too much, can they?"

Richard's throat was too dry, and he was too tired and pissed off to even speak. He'd hardly heard anything after *Exeter*.

"Richard? What do you think? Say something. Are you there?"

"I'm here," he managed at last.

"It's a good idea, isn't it? I worked it all out last night after you'd gone. We won't tell them I'm going until the last possible moment. When are you leaving?"

"No," he said.

"No?"

"No, Zoe. It's not a good idea. It's a fucking shit idea. You're not coming to Exeter with me. What planet are you on? I'm going to university. I'm not getting tied down with a family. You've got no idea about finances or anything. It's absolute shit, and I don't want to hear any more about it."

"What?"

Oh Jesus.

The tears were coming. He could hear them.

"I said you're not coming to Exeter with me. That's it."

"Don't you want to be with me?"

He didn't say anything.

"Richard?"

"Not like that. I don't want commitments."

"A baby's a commitment."

"Yeah, well, I was thinking, too, last night, and I see now it would be better if you had an abortion."

"No. Never."

"You won't have to tell your parents. It'll all be cleared up, I can go away, and you can get on with your life and A levels and that."

"I said *no*. I'm never having an abortion. Never. And you can't make me."

"I can't, but I've changed my mind. I don't want to be a father. Not yet. So, if you go ahead with this, count me out."

"I love you, Richard."

"You don't. Not really."

"Don't patronise me."

"I wasn't. I was just saying I don't think—"

"No, you don't think, do you?"

"I've done nothing but think," he shouted. "I don't want to be a father. Not now. Not with you."

"You have to support me. There's a law."

Richard hesitated. He wasn't sure how that worked.

"That's just money," he bluffed. "I mean, I don't want to *be there* for the kid. I don't want to change nappies and take it to school and that. It's not what I want."

"I do. And you should be with me when I tell my parents. It is yours."

"Zoe, I have to go. I don't want to talk about this anymore. I feel ill with it."

"How do you think I feel?"

"Please. Just back off. Give me some space for a few days."

Richard hesitated. He knew he was being unkind to her and the child, but it was for the best.

It really is.

If she wouldn't have an abortion, he didn't want to stand by impotently while his child's life was wrecked. Better to have no part in it whatsoever.

"Look," he said. "We'll talk next week sometime. But please, please, just give me some space."

"Are you leaving me?" Zoe cried.

"I don't know. I need to think. Look after yourself. Bye, Zoe."

He ended the call. He expected the phone to ring straight away, but it didn't. Like with the satellite dishes on Goonhilly, he thought he could sense the hum of it in the stale air.

He sat on the bed, holding the receiver for five minutes. Then he opened the door quietly and padded back to the hall.

In the afternoon, Emily phoned Zoe. The answering machine came on. Emily started speaking, and Zoe picked up.

"Do what he says," Emily said when Zoe had choked and gabbled what Richard had said, how he'd shouted about abortions, and how he didn't want to share his life with her and the baby.

"I'm not killing it!"

"I mean, give him some space. Let him cool off. Don't come up for a while. There's no rush, is there, if you're keeping the baby?"

"He's going soon."

"A few days won't hurt. Really."

Emily sighed.

Over the summer, she'd distanced herself from Zoe and made other friends. Now, she was flung back to Zoe's side because she felt sorry for her and hated how Richard was treating her. But Emily knew Zoe's parents would like her even less once they knew she'd covered for Zoe and Richard, bought the pregnancy test, and kept Zoe's secret.

"What are you doing on Thursday?" she asked.

"Thursday?"

"Results day."

"Oh. I'll go on the bus, I suppose. Mum and Dad'll be at work."

"On your own?"

"Well, yes. What about you?"

"Mum's coming with me. I'm sure we could pick you up. It'd be nicer if we went together, wouldn't it?"

She hadn't asked Jane and Beth what they were doing. They might suggest they all went together or something, but she would have to say no. Zoe needed support now, despite how pissed off Emily had felt before.

"Just you and your mum?"

"Yes. It'll be OK."

"Isn't she angry with me?"

"She's angrier at Rich. She was really upset when he was going on about … When he was shouting the odds."

"She wants me to keep the baby, too?"

"It's her grandchild, she said. Then Rich said *not genetically* or *bio-logically* or something shitty, and that made her upset, and Dad was furious."

"Oh," Zoe whispered. Then, "OK, yes, it'd be much better to go with you."

"We'll sort it out nearer the time. And do you know what I'd do? I wouldn't get in touch with Rich before then. If he calls you, that's different."

"He won't. He hates me."

"He doesn't. He's fucked up. All his plans have gone up in smoke."

"He hates me."

"No, he doesn't." Emily didn't think Richard hated Zoe.

Not really. Not forever.

"That's nearly a week," Zoe said.

"I know. Give him space. That's what he wants."

"But it's so awful. I'm here on my own. And then when my parents are here, it's worse, and I cry all the time, and I'm frightened, so frightened, and I have to pretend everything's OK."

"Could you talk to your sister? Could you go over and see her and tell her first? She's a nurse. She must have seen things like this."

"She a paediatric nurse."

"Couldn't she help?"

"I don't think so. She's ten years older than me. She moved out ages ago."

Emily was running out of ideas. Zoe should see a doctor, get herself checked out, make sure the baby was all right. She was over sixteen.

Surely she can see her doctor without her parents' knowledge. This stress can't be doing her any good. Some time and space away from Richard can't hurt.

Besides, he might begin to miss Zoe and see what a shit he was being, and change his mind again, and ring her up and say, yes, he would stand beside her when she told her family and when she raised the child.

Maybe.

"Promise me," Emily said. "Don't try to speak to him until we've got the results."

"It's ages away."

"Let him miss you."

Emily had no idea at all if Richard would miss Zoe. She didn't know if he planned to speak to her again or if he was just going to set her adrift. No, their parents would never allow that.

How will it end? Emily wondered. *Will Richard bully Zoe into having the abortion? Or will she have the child as she wants to? Or will her parents make her give it up for adoption like Rich's mother did with him?*

Whatever happened, it would be a child growing up without knowing its father because Richard was never going to jack in his university course and stay in Cornwall, bringing up an accidental baby with a girl he barely knew.

Poor baby, Emily thought again. *It doesn't deserve any of this.*

Emily hardly saw Richard over the weekend. He went to see some friends in Helston on Saturday afternoon. He caught the bus, so Emily knew he was planning on drinking; otherwise, he would have asked to use Cheryl's car.

That evening, Emily was alone in the house. Her parents were both in the club. There was a big party from Ruan Minor in there, a birthday or something. The phone rang. It wouldn't be Zoe at the weekend. No, it was Richard. There was a lot of noise, pub noise: braying voices, a snatch of music, clinking, sudden laughter.

"I'm staying at Hugh's tonight," he said.

"When are you coming back?" Emily asked, suddenly imagining him running away, hitching a lift on a lorry to nowhere.

"Tomorrow. Some time. Can you tell them for me? Hang on, there are the pips. Cheers, Em."

On Monday, Emily escaped to Bishop's Cove. The house was an unhappy place. On Sunday afternoon, Richard had turned up late, stinking of beer and sweat. There had been a God-awful row between him and Cheryl about Zoe, his drinking, and his attitude. Emily had heard Richard shouting something about Cheryl not being his *real mother*. Then Emily had shoved her Walkman on and stayed in her room, only creeping out to get some food. She found Cheryl sitting at the kitchen table, her head on her arms, hardly moving.

In Bishop's Cove, Emily sat on one of her favourite boulders. There were streamers of seaweed caught round its base and barnacles stuck to its flanks. Some kids were paddling in the ripples – she recognised them from one of the caravans. Their parents had set up camp at the cliff base, where it was sandier, with a windshield and rug. One of the kids ran back up the beach, holding something in her cupped hands.

Shells, maybe, or a crab.

There were other people on the beach, fiddling at the tide line, scrambling over the rocks under the Buttress. Emily wanted to escape, but it wasn't far enough. She couldn't meet Jane or Beth because it would be impossible not to tell them about Zoe's baby. She couldn't talk to Rich because he slammed himself in his room or strode off down the cliff path. She couldn't talk to Zoe because she had no words for her – no words of advice or comfort.

It felt like the sky and the cliffs and the Buttress were squeezing down on her, crushing her.

Zoe cried. As soon as her parents left in the morning, she cried. She cried for the tiny life inside her. She cried for her lost love. She cried for herself. Soon, the tears had no cohesion or meaning; they just ran unchecked from her eyes. Emily told her to stay away from Richard.

Well, I am.

She wouldn't ring Emily either. If she was going to be on her own, she could start now.

Except I'm not on my own, she thought, placing her palm over her abdomen, where she believed the baby might be. *I'll never be alone now.*

Half an hour before her parents were due back, she stopped crying. She washed her face with cold water and put Nivea on her eyelids. There was a time to cry and a time not to cry.

She had another person to think about now.

"Emily," Zoe cried. "What's happening?"

"We'll pick you up tomorrow. About half ten. OK?"

"Tomorrow?"

"Exam results."

"Oh yes. Of course. I meant, how's Richard?"

Emily had dreaded making this phone call. She was surprised that Zoe had kept to her word and not been in touch with anyone at Kynance. Emily had found the silence unnerving.

"He's been out a lot."

"Who with?"

"Friends. Guys. In Helston, and some at the Lizard last night." That creepy bloke who'd tried to snake his arm round her in the club.

"Is he all right? Is he still angry?"

"He told Mum and Dad you were having some time apart. Mum said you must get yourself checked out if you're going to have the baby. He said he didn't know what you were going to do."

"I'm keeping it."

"What about your mum and dad?"

"I'm not telling them anything. I'm not saying anything until I get fat, and it'll be obvious, and they'll have to ask me."

Emily didn't know what to say.

"Look, try to not worry about that tomorrow. We've got enough to worry about with the exams."

"You'll have done brilliantly, Emily. You know that."

"I don't know anything. I'm sure I screwed up the French oral. And maths, obviously. Mum said you could come back with us afterwards if you wanted to?" She turned it into a question.

"Will he be there?"

"No. He asked Mum for the car so he could go to Truro, and she said no as she was taking me to the school – she didn't mention you – and he said he'd get the bus then."

"I'll think about it," Zoe said.

Emily woke early with a fluttering stomach.

Results day.

The curtains didn't meet, and a thin white light had slid into the room. She reached up and opened them further and knelt on the bed to look out. Moisture drops on the plants and windowsill. There was a snail on one of the paving slabs, stretching and pulling, stretching and pulling. The garden looked clammy and damp, and suddenly, through the glass, came the plunging drone of the foghorn.

She and Cheryl left just after ten. The air tasted gritty and salty from the sea mist. Emily felt the first stirring of a headache, but there wasn't time to go back and take any painkillers. It was just stress, worrying about Zoe and the GCSEs, the oppressive weather, and the constant boom of the foghorn. She was glad when her mother fired the ignition, and the roar of the engine swallowed the mournful call.

Zoe was waiting outside her house.

"Poor kid," Cheryl muttered. "She should have her mother's support at this time. She must feel so alone."

"Hello, Emily, hello, Cheryl," Zoe said, sliding into the back seat.

"How are you?" Cheryl asked.

"I'm OK."

"Are you coming back to ours?" Emily turned round to look at Zoe. "He's not there. He got the bus before we left."

"What's he doing in Truro?" Zoe asked.

"Getting some stuff for uni, I think. I don't know. He doesn't talk much to any of us."

"Because of me."

"It's not your fault," Cheryl said. "Accidents happen, yes, but it's how you deal with them that matters, and I don't like how he's dealing with it at all. Let's get today over with these exam results, and then we need to work out what is happening with your family, Zoe, and with Richard. It's your choice, whatever you do. Do not let yourself be bullied by him into doing anything you don't want to do. I'll stand by you."

Emily looked from her mother to Zoe and saw a tear wobbling in Zoe's eye.

Strange. Mum didn't like Zoe before, but now she seems almost fond of her. She wants to be a grandmother so much.

Emily wondered if she would ever make her mother a grandmother.

In the school car park, kids were loitering in twos and threes, each holding slips of paper.

Emily felt sick. She looked again at Zoe, who hadn't spoken for ages. She was pale and sad-looking.

"I'm sure you'll want to have a chat with a few people," Cheryl said. "I need to get a few bits in Mullion. Let's meet at the Old Inn and have a drink and some lunch. I'll wait there for you."

132

"OK." Emily wrenched open the car door.

"And good luck, both of you." Cheryl gave them a thumbs-up and drove off.

Zoe turned to Emily. "Would you get mine for me? I don't feel good."

"What d'you mean?" Emily felt a flare of panic.

"Nothing. I just feel a bit light-headed."

"I don't think they'd let me. Come on, let's just do it, then we can sit somewhere before we meet Mum. Don't you feel like lunch at the pub?"

"Not really."

Emily took Zoe's arm and steered her down the path towards the main doors. A couple of boys from their French group were coming the other way. One was whooping and punching the air, the other just gazing at the scrap of paper in his hands.

Emily went first to the office hatch. The secretary fiddled with papers and ticked her name off. As Emily took the results, she glanced at Zoe beside her. She didn't look well. She looked wretched. Her parents obviously never really looked at her or talked to her, or they would have seen the difference in her. Emily knew Cheryl would have seen it straight away if it were her, and she felt a rush of love for her parents for being the people they were.

Zoe's fingers curled round the paper. She didn't want to open it. She didn't want to know. She didn't want anything more to worry about. She wanted to lie down.

"Can we go out?" she asked.

"I didn't!" Emily cried. "I didn't bugger up the French oral." She was grinning, laughing, gesturing at her results slip.

"What did you get?" Zoe managed to ask.

"A's for everything but sciences and maths. I got a C for maths. I thought I'd fail it." Her voice seemed to spiral away from Zoe.

"I have to go." Zoe stumbled towards the door.

"Hey, what's up?" Emily grabbed her by the shoulder.

"Emily, Zoe!" Jane from the Lizard was coming into the hall.

Beth was just behind her. "How did you do?"

Zoe pushed past Beth and stepped outside. Her legs were wavering, and she felt sick. She knew she was crunching up the paper in her hand. She heard the other girls' voices behind her and more voices drifting down from the car park.

"Zoe's not well."

She heard that clearly before Emily's arm was round her.

The slabs beneath their feet shifted like crazy paving, and then Zoe's guts contracted, and she heaved into the bushes. She felt Emily whip the results from her hand. She hadn't even looked at them.

"Zoe, Zoe." Emily didn't know what to say.

It's normal, though, isn't it? To throw up when you're pregnant? Especially on a day like this.

Some boys were making stupid comments behind them.

"Just fuck off," Emily shouted. "She's ill."

At last, Zoe stopped retching and straightened up.

"I'm so sorry," she said.

"I got an A for art!" Beth shrieked.

Oh shit.

Beth and Jane were back with their papers.

"Zoe, what's wrong?" Jane asked.

"I'm fine," Zoe said.

"Here's a tissue. It's clean." Beth handed over a scrap of pink.

"I'd better look at them, then." Zoe took her slip off Emily.

134

"What did you get?" Jane demanded, trying to look over Zoe's shoulder.

"Here, have a look. I'm going to get a drink." Zoe handed it back to Emily.

Emily glanced down and saw a D for maths.

Oh no, Zoe needed a C to train as a teacher. She'll have to retake it. No, she won't be training as a teacher. Not yet. She probably won't even be doing A levels.

"Is she OK?" Beth asked. "She got a bug?"

"I think so," Emily said. "Did you two get the bus?"

"Mum brought us. She's in the car. D'you want a lift?"

"No, Zoe and I are meeting Mum in Mullion."

"Zoe still with your Richard?" Jane asked.

Emily hesitated, and then Zoe was back. A wet strand of hair hung over her shoulder. She must have washed her face.

"Here, have a Polo." Jane offered a tube.

Zoe shook her head.

"Better now?" Emily asked.

"I think so. Just ... so stressful today."

"You've done all right," Beth said. "Only one D. I got D for maths, too, and history, and E for French."

"Heard you were going out with Emily's brother." Jane crunched her Polo and looked at Zoe.

"Oh, well ..." Zoe floundered.

"Has he dumped you?"

"I don't know."

"What d'you mean?" Beth asked. "What's he said?"

"Oh, I don't know," Zoe said again.

"Rich is being a bastard at the moment," Emily started. She vaguely recalled some of the bitchy things she'd said about Rich and Zoe to the other girls.

"Isn't he going to uni?"

"Yeah. Exeter."

"That's why he's dumped you, Zoe? Charming."

"He hasn't dumped me," Zoe said, and suddenly she was crying, great heaving sobs that shook her shoulders. She flailed her arms towards Emily and dropped her flimsy paper.

Beth crouched down and picked it up.

Emily held Zoe and saw the other two look at each other.

"He's not worth it," Jane said. "Whatever's going on, just tell him to fuck off to Exeter. You don't need that kind of aggro."

"Is it your folks?" Beth asked. "Emily said they were really strict. They don't like him."

"They don't know," Zoe muttered.

Beth gasped. "They still don't know."

Emily scowled at Beth, but Zoe didn't pick anything up or didn't care.

She freed herself from Emily and rubbed her eyes with the heels of her hands.

Some more kids came running down the path towards the front door. Beth waved at them. Jane called something to one of the boys. Emily ignored them all.

"I can't tell them," Zoe said. "I can't tell them any of it."

"Why not? What's wrong with Richard?"

"You're not, like, um …" Jane trailed off. "I mean, you've thrown up. You're not pregnant, are you?"

Zoe said nothing.

Emily said nothing.

"Oh my God," Beth said.

"You are," Jane said. "Is it Richard's?"

"Of course it's Richard's."

"And your folks don't know? Oh shit, Zoe Cassidy. What are you going to do?" This time Jane ignored the boys on their way out. She stared at Zoe and Emily. "Are you keeping it?"

"Yes."

"What does Richard think? Is he still going to uni? You'll have to come clean. Do your parents know, Emily?"

"Yeah, they know. Rich is being a shit. He wants Zoe to have an abortion."

"No."

"I'm not. I don't believe in it. That's it. I just don't know how I can do this."

"My cousin in Redruth, she had a baby at sixteen." Beth patted Zoe on the arm. "No one batted an eyelid. He's coming on for three now. Cute little thing. Don't know what happened to the dad. He buggered off."

"It's not that simple," Zoe faltered.

"D'you still like Richard?"

"Of course."

"Even after the way he's been to you?"

"Yes. I love him."

"D'you want to be with him?"

"Yes, him and the baby. I suggested going to Exeter with him, us having the baby up there, and he yelled at me and said he didn't want it."

"You put him on the spot," Emily said, but she didn't think Richard would ever have wanted it. He saw his future travelling the globe, exploring rock strata and caves, divining the birth of the planet.

"What would your folks say if you and he got married?" Jane asked, peeling the wrapper down the tube of Polos and shoving two in her mouth.

A sudden image surfaced in Emily's memory: a boy in her tutor group trying to see how many Polos he could eat at one time.

"That would be better," Zoe admitted. "We could get married in a church, and that'd make them feel better, I think, and then the baby would be legitimate, wouldn't it?"

"No one cares about all that now."

"My family does."

"Right," Jane said. "You must tell him you want to be with him and want to have this kid with him. He should marry you. I mean, he got you in this mess."

"When's it due?" Beth asked.

"April, I think. I don't know. I haven't seen a doctor or anything."

"You're pretending it's not happening. You've got to face up to it."

"I know, but I wasn't going to tell my parents until it became obvious."

"Would they make you get rid of it, too?"

"No. They wouldn't want that."

"What would they want?" Emily asked abruptly. "You're having the baby. It's not ideal for them, but it's happening. It can't be changed. How would they want you to deal with it?"

"They'd want us to be married," Zoe said.

"How can he marry her if he's going away?" Beth asked.

"I could go with him. Or even if I stayed down here. At least then we'd be married, and the baby would have both its parents." Zoe turned to Emily. "You don't think he'd ... postpone going to uni, do you? If we were getting married?"

"I don't know," Emily lied.

"I've given him space just like he wanted."

"Then it's time he started doing what you wanted," Jane said. "You've let him have his tizzy, now go and tell him he's got a duty to look after you and his child. It's his child, remember? Two to tango and all that."

"We'd better go." Beth nodded up the path to where her mother was standing, making exaggerated stares at her watch. "You take care, Zoe. Good luck."

"You *bloody* tell him," Jane emphasised. "See you some time, Emily."

It wasn't as misty in Mullion, but there was still a thickness to the air that made it seem hard to breathe. Emily's hair felt damp and flat, and she was sweating under her clothes. They were sitting at a picnic bench on the raised terrace garden of the Old Inn. Zoe had insisted she couldn't eat anything, but Cheryl had told her she would feel better if she did and ordered her a sandwich anyway. There was a large basket of chips in the middle for them all to share. Zoe did look better, having eaten half a ham and salad sandwich and some chips.

"Can you ring your mum or dad from ours?" Cheryl asked. "I'm sure they'd want to know how you got on."

"I can ring Mum at work," Zoe said, taking another chip.

"If Rich comes back, you need to speak to him," Emily said.

Zoe winced.

"I'm so sorry he's being like this. His only excuse is he has a lot on his mind right now with university. I understand this has come as a shock to him, but that's no reason to be so unkind. It'll sort out, Zoe. Things do."

When they got back to the holiday park, Cheryl and Zoe went inside the bungalow, so Zoe could ring her mother, and Emily ran on up to the club to see her father. He was behind the bar because Richard was out, but Emily knew he was doing more and more of Richard's jobs the last week or so. Terry gave her a hug when he saw her exam results.

"Rich not back then?" Emily asked.

"Not that I know of."

"Zoe's here. She wants to talk to him when he does show up."

The clubhouse smelled of beer, damp air, fried food, and sweat. Emily knew she would always think of that as the smell of home, the smell of the Lizard. In years to come, even if her family left the holiday camp, left Cornwall, that smell would bring her right back.

She let the door swing behind her and walked back to the house. The foghorn sounded again from the Lizard. It was foggy here; she could see the end of the drive, but she could see little beyond the tangled hedge on the opposite side of the main road. That sound, the foghorn, that was the sound of the Lizard.

It seemed so long since she and Zoe had been in her bedroom together. Back in those days, they'd talked about school and homework and laughed and played music, and then everything had changed, and Zoe was in Richard's room, and Emily was left alone, embarrassed, feeling like an outsider in her own home.

Zoe was curled up on the bean bag as Emily lay on the bed. She needed to clean her teeth. She could taste onion from the sandwich and chips.

"What time do you think he'll be back?"

Emily turned her head to look at Zoe. "I don't know when the buses are. This afternoon I expect. I don't think he has any special friends in Truro."

Zoe didn't answer.

"Is it true what you said earlier?" Emily asked. "That your parents would want Richard to marry you?"

"They would think it was the best outcome."

"That's not enough of a reason to marry someone. What do you want?"

"I want to be with him. I love him. I want him to bring up our baby with me. A proper family. You'd be my sister-in-law."

"And an auntie."

"Are you looking forward to being an auntie?"

"I don't think I know much about it." Emily swung her legs down. "I'm going to clean my teeth. Put some music on."

When she came out of the bathroom, Cheryl intercepted her in the corridor. She had changed into old jeans and a tatty paint-stained shirt.

"I'm going up to the club to give your dad a hand painting the lavs when he's shut."

"Right," Emily said. "OK."

It was also probably an excuse for Cheryl to be out of the house when Richard came back, to give Zoe a chance to talk to him. Emily wondered if she should go to the club, too, when he came home or whether Zoe would want her to stay.

She trailed back into her room. Zoe was flicking through the rows of tapes, not really looking at them. Emily didn't care what they listened to; she just wanted something other than the breathing of the house while they waited for Richard. Zoe grabbed a home-recorded cassette, stuff that Emily had taped off the radio, off the Top Forty probably. Emily closed the door as Zoe slid the tape into the deck.

They sat, hardly speaking, listening to the jumble of songs. There were missed intros, DJs' voices, and radio static. The music ran out halfway through the A-side, but neither of them got up to change it, and the tape spooled on with its quiet noise.

And then, the *bang* of the front door.

Zoe's head snapped up.

Emily put her finger to her lips. Footsteps on the corridor, the *swish* of a couple of carrier bags, Richard's bedroom door *creaking* open, more footsteps, and then the *click* of the bathroom lock.

Richard didn't knock or call out to Emily; instead, he went to the kitchen.

Emily heard a glass or cup on the worktop and some rustling.

"Come on." She snapped the cassette player off at last. "Rich, that you?" she called.

"Kitchen, Em."

He was gulping lager from a bottle. He'd got the bread out and some cheese.

"Hi, Richard. How are you?" Zoe asked.

"Oh. Zoe. Hi." He hacked at the cheese, watched the knife.

"Good time in Truro?" Emily asked.

Richard shrugged and chewed cheese. "OK. Didn't get much. Had a few beers in a pub. Don't like the bus. Takes forever."

"Well, we needed the car."

"Oh, yeah. GCSE results. Good, bad, ugly?"

"Good," Emily said.

Thanks so much for asking.

"Zoe?"

"Much as I expected. I failed maths."

"A D isn't a fail exactly," Emily said.

Richard *plonked* lumps of cheese on a slice of bread.

"What?" he said, glaring at the girls.

"Zoe wants to talk to you," Emily began. "Please, Rich, just talk to her. She's given you some space."

"I'm eating." He took another lager out of the fridge and wrenched the lid off with a bottle opener. The lid skidded across the floor.

"Come and sit at the table," Emily said. "And just listen to what Zoe has to say."

"I've given you some time to think," Zoe began. "And I've done lots of thinking, too." She pulled out a chair.

Emily sat opposite her, watching Richard.

142

He shoved bread into his mouth and stayed behind the kitchen worktop.

"So, what are you thinking, then?" he asked at last. "Are you thinking the same as me?"

"I'm having this baby. It's part of me. Part of you, too."

"How can you have a baby, Zoe? You won't even tell your parents you've been shagging me. What is this? An immaculate conception?"

"Rich," Emily snapped.

"This is crazy. Just get rid of it. It's not a person yet. Honestly, it isn't."

"Every day, it becomes more of a person."

"Only because you've been wasting time. If it was me, I'd have had the abortion by now."

"What's happened to you?" Zoe cried. "At the beginning, you said you'd be there for me, for us. If the Jacksons hadn't been at ours that night, we'd have told Mum and Dad then."

"I'm glad they were there. It gave me time to see what a twat I'd been. Of course I couldn't *be there* for you. I don't know what I was thinking."

"Why are you being so cruel?" Emily asked Richard. "You don't have to be. Why do you want to upset her more and more?"

"I don't want to upset her. It's just she won't listen to reason. Why the hell does she want to have this kid if I'm not going to do it with her?"

"*She's* here, too," Zoe cried. "Why can't we do this together? I thought you liked me. You said you liked me lots."

"I did. But I don't want this."

"Why not?"

"Oh, come on." Richard drank from the bottle and threw the pale heel of cheese into the fridge. "I'm going to university. You knew that from the start."

"You never said I was only for the summer."

He shrugged. "I wouldn't put it like that."

"What if there was no baby? If I wasn't pregnant? Would you still be so horrible to me?"

"I'm not horrible. I'm realistic."

"You're completely selfish," Emily said.

He stared at her with cold green eyes. "I'm not the selfish one. She is. She wants to tie me up, financially and emotionally, for the rest of my life. Just when I'm about to start getting somewhere. That's selfish. She wants to go ahead with something that'll piss off her family. That's selfish. She wants to bring a child up with no father. That's selfish."

"It doesn't have to be without a father," Zoe said. "Please, can't we start again over this? Can't we talk properly?"

"I'm sick of talking. You're not interested in what I say."

"And you're not interested in what I say."

"Then we're never going to find common ground, are we?"

"I asked Zoe what would be the best answer for everyone," Emily said. "And she said it'd be if you and she got married."

Richard spat out beer. "You what? For fuck's sake. No chance."

"It'd be easiest for her with her parents. They'd find that more acceptable."

"A shotgun wedding? From what I hear, I don't think they'd find that acceptable. In fact, they sound like complete and utter arseholes. I couldn't give a shit what they think."

Zoe gulped.

"That's not on," Emily shouted.

"Yeah? Well, I've been there. God, God, God everywhere. But, of course, you haven't been there, have you? Zoe's never asked you over. Why's that? Because she's ashamed of you, of us. I'd never have got in if I hadn't just turned up. We were never good enough for Zoe's parents. That's why she never asked you over. Either that or she was so

144

embarrassed about all the God stuff and didn't want you to know. Whatever."

Emily came round the table to Zoe and put her arm round her. Zoe was crying. Not the wrenching sobs she'd choked out at school, just silent tears running down her cheeks like rain.

"You really are a shit," Emily told Richard. "I shall tell Mum and Dad what you've said. They hate what you're like now, too."

"They're not my real mum and dad. I'm going to find my real family when I go away."

"They are your real mum and dad. They chose you. They love you, though God knows why right now. Your *real* parents dumped you. They didn't want you. Mum and Dad did."

"If we got married, you could still go to university," Zoe whispered. "I don't have to come with you. I could stay here, but we'd be together, and you'd come back in the holidays, and the baby would have us both."

"For the last time – I'm not marrying you. I don't want to marry you. I don't want this child with you. If you'd only do what's sensible, we could all forget it, and maybe things would be OK again."

"I don't know why Zoe would even want to marry you. She's better off without you, and so's her baby."

"Fine. Get on with it then. But, Zoe, don't come up here again. I don't want to see you. I don't want to hear about the kid. I don't want to know what it is or anything. I don't want to know what your parents say because I'm bored of it all. I'm bored of you."

He threw the empty lager bottle into the bin. It hit something – the other bottle – with a cold *clink*.

"You can't just walk away like that," Emily yelled. "You can't walk away from Zoe, whatever you think. She's the mother of your child. Come back here."

The front door slammed.

"Let's get Mum. Come on. He must be drunk. Don't think about what he said. He's just being a shit again."

"He hates me," Zoe cried. "He really hates me. Is it because of the baby, or does he hate me anyway?"

"Who cares? I hate him."

Emily tugged Zoe to her feet. She stumbled. Emily steadied her, afraid she might faint or be sick again.

"They're in the club. Both of them. Come with me."

She half dragged Zoe to the door and wrenched it open. She blinked in the hard, white light. The fog had clotted into damp whorls. The foghorn sounded again from the lighthouse to the south. She could just make out a dark, hunched figure marching between the caravans.

"Don't tell them," Zoe pleaded as Emily tried to steer her towards the club.

The doors were shut and blank as the fog.

"Let me talk to him again."

"What's the point?" Emily cried, hands on hips, wishing one of her parents would come out of the clubhouse.

"He'll never talk to me after today. I don't want him to go off hating me."

Zoe started running into the caravan field.

Emily put her hands to the club windows, but she couldn't see anyone there. They must be out the back decorating.

Zoe was vanishing into the mist. Emily raced after her. She saw a family locking their caravan and getting into the car. She heard the ignition firing. Zoe was almost at the gate when Emily caught her.

The Buttress. That's where Richard is. Where he always goes.

The rocks loomed darkly through the mist. The foghorn again. A figure on the crag, where the land fell into milky nothingness.

146

"Richard!" Zoe called, pushing through the spiky grasses towards the Buttress.

He was standing on the ledge, gazing into the white.

Emily caught Zoe's arm. Damp grasses snagged on her jeans. They were at the foot of the crag. The rocks looked slimy with damp and mist.

Richard shouted something out to sea.

"Please come down." Zoe put her foot on the lowest ledge.

Richard turned. "Leave me alone." A ghost voice.

"Rich," Emily said, and her voice, too, sounded strange, distorted.

His foot – his red Converse boot, that bright slash of colour – slid on the serpentine. He swore as his hand reached out and clawed the white air. He slithered again, and the foghorn howled. Then there was nothing but the rocks and the mist and the second dreadful cry of the foghorn and Zoe screaming.

"No, no," Emily shouted as Zoe struggled onto the crag.

"He's there, he's there, he fell." Zoe lashed out at Emily.

Emily ran back to the stony cliff path. She was crying.

Serpentine, serpentine, serpentine, slippery.

At the gate, she turned. Zoe had fallen to the ground and was curled over, scratching at the wet grass.

Emily ran on.

The foghorn cried.

PART TWO

May 2012

I saw him just that once at the eclipse. Zoe's son. Richard's son. My nephew. If he had not come running round from the back of the car, I might never have seen him, never have known. Zoe said she would write. She never did. I never spoke about this to anyone. Not my parents. Not the friends I was with that day.

I am here again, at the end of the world.

The Buttress rises from a mauve drift of bluebells. The air is scented with wild garlic. It is evening, but still, the insects hover over the petals. There are three early foxgloves, bright in the falling light. A grey moth glides in front of me. I scramble onto the crag and hunker down against its ravaged shoulder. Below, the waves rise and break lazily on the jagged skerries. I hear the cries of gulls flying to roost on the stacks at Kynance. Twilight chases the curve of the earth to the western horizon, where the sun gilds the cloud edges with pink. Across the gaping mouth of Mount's Bay, the lights of Penzance blur into a shifting gold sparkle. The three white pulses of the Tater Du lighthouse swell and die, swell and die, swell and die, and then, beyond the distant snake's head of dark land, far out in the Atlantic, Wolf Rock answers with its single flash.

I lost three people that long ago foggy afternoon: my brother, friend, and nephew. Zoe never came here again. Mum and I went to her house to tell her about Richard's cremation. Dad said we were fools, should stay away. Her mother met us at the front door and barred the way. She said Zoe was no longer living there. She would not be able to pass on any information.

150

"Move on and forget it," she said – as Zoe would be doing.

There would be no baby in our lives. We drove to the nearest layby and cried.

I started at Helston, doing my A levels. Zoe wasn't there. People asked me what had happened that day. It had been in the papers, on the news. After only a couple of weeks, I left the sixth form.

I phoned Zoe's house several times, and her parents hung up. Mum rang the hospital in Penzance, trying to track down Amanda. Another nurse, who answered the phone in the children's ward, said she would give Amanda our number and ask her to call us back, but the line remained silent. Mum tried again and spoke to Amanda, who hung up on her.

We scattered Richard's ashes at Kynance. Not at the Buttress.

Why do I come here?

I'm crouching where Richard's foot slipped. He flung out his hand to grasp the rock beside my head. I reach up and rub my palm over it. Rough lichen on smooth, cool serpentine. From here, I can just see the sharp slope of the cliff face falling away below, stubby grass and soil becoming dark rocks, slapped by the waves.

Accidental death.

That was what the inquest said. I didn't need to wait all those months for an inquest. I know. I was there. I saw what happened.

I turn my back on the Buttress and the bay and the lighthouses. The eastern sky is amethyst dark. I crunch along the coast path to the gate. There are soft scuffles in the undergrowth. Rabbits, perhaps, or shrews. The gate swings shut behind me, and I am in our field. It's different now. The caravans are mostly long-term lets. Single people, people between houses, people looking for anonymity. There are lights on in several of the vans, turning the drawn curtains into glowing colours. I hear the sounds of TVs through the thin walls. Kids' voices.

151

The lights are on in the clubhouse. It has become a bar for locals, a place to drink beer, play pool and darts. I open the door. Flashing lights on the fruit machine. The rumble of pool balls escaping, then the *clack* of them being racked in the triangle. Motown on the stereo; I can't think of the singer. The breath of beer. The usual crowd in – young guys from the Lizard at the pool table, some of the residents at the bar, faces I know, and a few I don't. Mum's serving plates of scampi and chips to a couple at one of the tables. Dad's behind the bar, with a glass under an optic. I hover there in the doorway for a moment. Then, I step out again into the soft spring night.

Later. I'm in my room. The same room I had as a child. The pink walls are now turquoise. The books on the shelves are no longer Enid Blyton and Penelope Lively, but I have kept the Robert Westalls. I have a double bed with white covers. I sit cross-legged on the bed and unfold my laptop. Open up Facebook. I type *Zoe Cassidy* into the search. A list of profiles comes up; none of them is her. I know this. I've looked so many times. Not one of my friends is friends with her. And she won't be called Cassidy now. She'll have changed her name when she got married. And the boy, my nephew: no doubt he will have the same name as her. I flick through a few friends' profiles. Beth has changed her picture to a puppy. She lives somewhere in the southeast now. She's married with four kids; one of her daughters has some medical problem. Jane's divorced with a son, living in North Cornwall. I start to type another name, *Jamie Eddy.* My first boyfriend from Helston. I met him at the sixth form when I returned a year later. He was in my art group, a year younger than me. Well, seven months, really. I open his profile. Married, with two boys. His wife's expecting again. He's posted a comment about her due date, which is in a few weeks.

Losing Richard sent me even further apart from other people. I don't know anyone else who lost a brother of nineteen. And now, this drives me still further away. I'm friends with a lot of people from school on Facebook. People who never liked me. Girls who bitched about me and didn't return my invitations. Suddenly, behind the safety of a screen, they all wanted to be friends, and I accepted because I didn't care. That was truly it: I didn't care. But time stretches on, and all I see on here are pictures and comments about children, babies, schools, health visitors, pregnancy. The girls I knew are all mothers, and I am not. I have lived away, been to university, worked in another city, but here I am, at thirty-six, living at home once more. No husband or lover (I never had the former, and I've not had the latter since I left Bath last year) and – more cutting, more acute – no child of my own.

I look at the photographs on Facebook and watch these kids grow up: babies becoming toddlers, toddlers growing into school uniforms, and, in some cases, school kids turning into teenagers. The people I knew when I was younger are shooting away from me into another world, an adult world, and here I am, back where I started with no one to call my own.

What would have happened if Richard hadn't died that day? If he hadn't stormed out of the kitchen? If Zoe and I had only stopped him?

That was all that played in my head for so long afterwards. It was our fault – my fault – that he slipped. If we – I – hadn't aggravated him. He had been drinking; he was angry, careless. It was damp and foggy.

Did he hear that dreadful foghorn as he fell? Did the sound end before he hit the rocks? Did he really hate us all?

Mum likes to imagine that Richard would have gone with Zoe to tell her parents. He would go to university but still be the child's father, watch it grow up, sharing its life. Dad knows Zoe and her family would have shut us out, never let Richard near the baby. I'd sit there with my parents, listening to them talking round and round, listening to Mum's sobs, and all I'd see is a jagged mosaic of those moments:

153

Richard's red shoe sliding, the slimy grey of the serpentine, Zoe crumpled on the wet grass, the stones of the cliff path under my feet as I ran, and all I'd hear is my heart and the foghorn.

Always the foghorn.

Sometimes in books, characters dream about traumatic events. In dreams, moments are distorted, changed, abstracted. I don't dream about that day. I live it, over and over, in the present tense.

I stumbled through the field of caravans. Two boys were playing, chasing each other; one was hiding behind the tall red gas cylinder, and the other waving a neon beach spade. I saw them, and they must have seen me running, stumbling, crying, shouting. Shouting for Mum, for Dad, for Richard, for Zoe. I don't know what I shouted. The clubhouse windows were dark. The door was unlocked. I slammed it open, shouting still, crying still. The sudden cold, the smell of paint, the chatter of the radio. Then we were running, all three of us, back through the field, back past the kids.

Dad saying, "*What happened?*"

Mum crying Richard's name.

The relentless foghorn, moisture drops in the air, the clotted white mist, Zoe on her knees in the mud and grass.

My laptop screen has gone black. It's humming quietly on the bed. I don't know how long I've sat there thinking, remembering. It happens often. I'll just be there again, that day, smelling the sea and the paint on my parents' clothes, hearing the screaming and the foghorn.

I reach out and turn off the computer. There are no answers there. If Richard had died now, his friends would have set up a memorial page on Facebook. There would be pictures of him drunk in the Angel, playing pool in the club, doing stupid things. People would type comments about how he would be missed, how he was taken too young. People who had never met him would somehow hit on the page and see his grin and green eyes and wonder about this young man snuffed out in a moment of carelessness and anger. But Richard has nothing. Not even a headstone. His ashes drifted onto rocks and waves. I don't know where they might be now, or if they have broken down into carbon atoms or what. Sometimes it's like he never lived.

Dad up on the Buttress, his hand on the rock, leaning over.

Mum screaming.

Dad bellowing, "*Richard!*"

The only reply was the foghorn.

The police called an ambulance for Zoe. Mum stammered that Zoe was pregnant. We were in the house again. The women. Dad on the cliff. It was impossible to reach Richard from above. His body would be retrieved by boat. The police called Zoe's parents and told them to go to the hospital in Penzance to meet the ambulance. Zoe, sobbing, tearing at her eyes, limp as a crushed flower.

That was the last I saw of her, being lifted into the ambulance – until the eclipse.

I have a secret. I have kept it to myself, beside my heart, for nearly fifteen years. I have a nephew. No, he may have no shared blood with me, but Richard was my brother, and this boy is my nephew. My parents have a grandson, and they don't know.

I couldn't tell them that day. The caravans were full; the camping field was crowded with bright tents. There was an eclipse party in the bar that night. My friends were down from Bath. I couldn't say it. Luckily, after a few drinks, Rachel, Sonia, and Gary had all but forgotten the brunette with the little girl I'd spoken to at the Lizard. And then the chance had gone. I had to speak that day or not at all. I wonder if I made the right choice. If Zoe had written, I could have told them then, but I think I knew, that strange dark-light morning she wouldn't.

I read something once about a kind of surgical implant, artificial bone or something that tissues adhere to, so the prosthesis and the flesh eventually become one, inseparable. That's me and my first secret.

I don't want secrets. Not from my parents. I will talk to them tomorrow about my second secret.

"I want to have a baby," I say.

Since that day, time has distorted, run differently for us than for other people. I'm thirty-six, but neither my parents nor I really believe it. We have not noticed the years spinning past. I watch their faces, and I know they, like me, are thinking of another baby, another grandchild. A grandchild who must be almost an adult now. A lifetime lost.

Dad's drinking tea. He no longer smokes. At times like this, his hands are restless, needing something to hold. He picks up his mug again, looks to Mum to answer. This is women's stuff.

"Have you got a boyfriend?" Mum asks.

I laugh. They know I don't have a boyfriend. I hardly ever go out. I drive into Helston to the jobcentre or to pick up some bits and pieces in Tesco. I don't see people. I'm almost a recluse. Perhaps she means someone living in one of the caravans. Swiftly, I run through them in my head.

Jesus.

"No. I want to do this on my own. I don't want to wait for a boyfriend. I can't wait for a boyfriend. I'm thirty-six," I say with some amazement.

Just where have the last twenty years gone? Wasted. That's what's happened to them.

I stayed in Bath after I left university. My friends moved away, but I stayed, beguiled by the crumbling haunted city. I moved a lot: I lived in a damp basement, a gabled attic, a tiny bedsit in the Royal Crescent. I drank too much sometimes, cried a lot, slept with married men, alcoholics, bastards. I worked in shops, I temped in offices, I delivered magazines. I never saw Richard's ghost in the amber haze of the street lamps or leaning out of an upper window. Sometimes I came home, back here, and roamed the cliffs, but I did not find him there, either.

"So, what are you going to do?" Dad asks at last.

"I keep telling you to join a dating agency," Mum says. "It won't be like Bath here."

A married man who forgot to tell me he had a wife; a creep who wanted to take me swinging; a fantasist who pretended he worked in Whitehall.

"I don't want to join a dating agency," I say. "I want to do this on my own. I've looked into it. When I was in Bath. I kept thinking about doing it, but …" I shrugged.

"What do you mean?" Dad asks. "Do you mean you're just going to go to a club and—"

"Christ, of course not. I want to use a sperm donor."

I've said it. It's out. One of my secrets has spilt out of me. It's not a secret any longer.

"Who?" Mum asks. "Someone here? What would it mean? Would he have rights?"

"Not someone here, not someone I know. I'm going to do this by myself. An IVF baby – with a donor from one of the sperm clinics."

"But how would you know who it was?" Dad asks. "It could be anyone, some lunatic. Genes pass on, you know."

"They don't just take anyone. They couldn't. It's all monitored."

Mum and Dad look at each other.

Dad picks up his mug, realises it's empty, drops it with a clunk.

"You're not that old, Emily," he says. "You could wait a year or so and see if you can find some nice guy."

"Dad, I don't do nice guys."

He smiles. "That's true."

157

"And there's no one here. And I don't want to do this with anyone. I want to do it for myself. And for you two. I've wanted a baby for so long."

Since Zoe found herself pregnant, I amend silently.

"But what would it mean for the child?" Mum asks. "How do you know the man would be suitable?"

"I would pick him. The baby won't know him until it's eighteen. It's like … being adopted."

There are other people I think about, too, in my dark times. People I have never met. Richard's birth parents and the rest of his family. Zoe's boy is a blood relative of theirs, and they will never know about him, and they'll never know what happened that day, almost twenty years ago. Zoe's parents must know my nephew, and, at that point, I have to stop, go and do something else, anything else, because if it weren't for them and their monstrous intolerance, none of this would have happened. Richard would be alive, and we would all know his son. And Richard would have had the chance to find his roots.

When we were arranging the cremation, Mum said something about his birth parents. Something like: *"Should we try to find them?"* Dad said we wouldn't be allowed to and, anyway, Richard wasn't in touch with them, and if they had thought anything of him, they would never have abandoned him in the first place. I didn't say it then, because the days were a raw haze of undertakers, newspaper headlines, and white and silver sympathy cards, but later, after the cremation, I told my parents what Richard had told me: that he was planning to find his family once he'd moved away.

"He didn't want to hurt you by doing it here," I said, but then wished I had never spoken because Mum started crying again, and Dad just sat there smoking, and at last, I slid out of the kitchen and hid in my room.

I wonder if somewhere there is a woman with dark hair and green eyes who cries because the son she gave up nearly forty years ago has never tried to find her. Does she think about him all the time? Does she look at the faces of men in the street in case one is him? Does she regret her choice – the one that led him to us, and to Zoe, and to the Buttress?

I call Mum into my room. The laptop's already on, *buzzing* quietly. I pat the duvet next to me, and she sits down.

"It's not something that I've just thought of," I explain. "It's been in my head for a few years."

"Why now?" she asks me.

I shrug. "It never seemed to be the right time to do it. I didn't want to bring a child up in the city, so far from you, but I couldn't get my head sorted out about what I was going to do. I wanted to be in Bath because I love it, but I knew I couldn't stay there forever. First, I had to make a decision to leave. And that was hard enough."

"I know. I don't know why, though. I can't see there was anything there for you, really."

It's hard to answer that one. It always is. There wasn't anything except the place. My friends from uni had moved away: Rachel back to South Wales, Gary and Sonia to London. I couldn't get a decent job, even with my degree. I met men either on dating sites or through the crappy jobs I did. I never met anyone I wanted to share my life with. I never met anyone I loved.

"I love the city," I said. "I always will."

And that's true.

I dream about Bath every few nights. The tall, cream houses, stained dark with rain; windows above windows; spindly balconies; amber street lamps. I love that city of stairs and windows.

"That's where I want to do it." I hand the booklet to Mum.

It's a bit tatty round the edges now, as I have had it a couple of years. I collected it one lunchtime. A hot day. June, I think, or July …

I was working at the hospital as a typist. Eight hours a day shut in a tiny office with two other girls. I mostly typed for ENT and oral surgery, but it could be anything. The porters would bring the heavy bags of notes, with the tapes for dictation sellotaped inside brown envelopes. These were the overspill clinics, the ones the consultants' secretaries couldn't – or wouldn't – type. The bags would pile up in the office, so we could hardly walk through the gaps between desks, filing cabinets, and doors. By lunchtime, my ears were sore from the hard buds of my headset. I would always get out for a walk, whatever the weather. I even walked in a snowstorm, my shoes sliding on the icy paths.

This hot day, June or July, I deleted the tape I had been working on and slid it into the cassette tray on the windowsill. I thought I was lucky because my desk was nearest to the window, but there were no blinds, and it only opened a few inches, and in summer, the little room heated like an oven, and my skin blotched pink. As I walked out of the office, I tugged my skirt down where it had risen up. My tights had stuck to my legs, making my skin sore. The corridor stank of hospital food, that grey-brown smell you get used to when you're there day in, day out. I ran down the four flights of stairs to the ground floor. There was a gentle flutter inside me, like a newly emerged moth stretching damp wings. This was the first step.

The corridors were busy: porters pushing linen trolleys and oxygen cylinders, theatre staff in blues, a secretary in noisy heels with a folder of notes held against her chest. There were patients, too, peering at the signs on the walls, checking the details on appointment letters in their hands, one in a gown, wheeling a drip beside him.

I passed the labour ward on the right. I always felt strange when I saw that sign. I was terrified of labour, of that prolonged, uncontrolled

160

pain, but I wanted to be there, holding my own tiny child, its head still bloodied, eyes screwed shut.

Electric doors opened, and I was out in the sunshine. My own eyes squinted. I knew where I was going. I had walked there two or three times before and stopped when I came to the building, afraid to go in, afraid to ask. But not today; today was the day.

It was a small scruffy building across the car park. The signs were discreet. A path led to the glass doors through an overgrown walled garden. It was a blurry Impressionist haze of pastel flowers. Lavender brushed my legs, and a couple of white butterflies soared up as I passed. Through the glass door, I could see the waiting room beyond: squashy chairs, a low table with a fan of magazines, a water machine. There didn't seem to be anyone there except the receptionist behind her window. I pulled open the door …

"Have a look." I give the booklet to Mum. "It doesn't tell you everything. They said I would need to be referred first of all, and then it goes from there."

"You mean referred by the doctor?"

"Yes."

She flicks through. There are pages for couples, pages for lesbians, then pages for single women.

"I didn't know it was available like this," she says. "Or only at special clinics in London."

"It's becoming popular. The clinic at Bath is very good. They have excellent success rates. I've looked at the website a lot. I can show you." I tug the laptop towards me.

"It'll be expensive." Mum lays the booklet down.

I stare at the mother and child on the cover. I want that. I want it so much. I want it more than money, or sex, or success. I want to be a mother with my child in my arms.

"I know. Several thousand. I've got Grandma's money."

Dad's widowed mother. She died a few years ago. Dad was her only child. Without Richard, I was her only grandchild.

"She'd like this idea," I say.

Mum smiles. "Yes, she would. But we'll help, too. Dad and I." She *clicks* on the mouse pad, and the screen changes.

"What?"

"We'll help," she says again.

"You don't have to. I'm sure—"

"I want to." She scrolls down, but I can see she's not really looking.

"Mum."

She puts the computer aside on my pillows. "It won't be easy. I'm sure the things you'll have to do won't be nice. The procedures, and so on. And it might not work. It's not magic. It doesn't work for everyone."

"I know. I understand that. But I think I'm healthy. I don't see why it wouldn't work. Maybe not the first time, but I think I have as good a chance as anyone."

"You'll be a great mother." She reaches out to hug me. "And I'd love to be a grandmother." She stiffens a moment in my arms.

The eclipse. The boy. Her grandson.

Richard's room.

I don't often come in here. We still call it Richard's room. We have another spare room if we need it, so this one remains Richard's. The same white carpet. The single bed was stripped ages ago. It's just a mattress now, piled with bin bags of stuff. I can just see the blue stripes between the black sacks. Blue stripes faded in some places to grey. Mattresses look so cold without bedding.

I push the door behind me. His bedside cupboard, his bookcases. They're all still there, though his things have gone. Into boxes in the

162

loft, into the black bin bags. Mum took a lot of his clothes to the charity shops. Later, she said she wished she hadn't. The only things of his still out are the stones on the windowsill.

I walk over to the window, pick up a dusty chunk of amethyst. There's a pale shape on the sill marking where it sat. I spit on my finger and wipe some of the dust off the stone. It will need to soak in water to get the grime out from all the crevices. I replace it on the brighter spot of the windowsill. Idly I touch the other crystals: rose quartz, tiger eye, turquoise, citrine. There is a golden lozenge of amber. There are rocks, too, their stripes and whorls hidden under dirt and dust: serpentine, gneiss, granite, schist. I still know the names.

I turn away from the window and open one of his drawers. There's a screw rolling around and a torn flap of cellophane.

I can't smell him in the air.

It smells vaguely stale: the smell of things that have been wrapped up too long. There are Blu Tack marks on the walls from where Richard stuck his posters; like scars, they have gone brown and crusty.

It's been twenty years.

This room would be a lovely nursery. I imagine it cleaned out, repainted in pink or blue or peppermint green. A white cot, a joyful mobile of animals or flowers. Cuddly toys. Tiny clothes folded in drawers. And, above all, the essence of another person.

A new person, one who will help us all to heal.

They have been a long time coming, but the time is right now.

Someone for us all to love.

This time when I walk out of the room, I leave the door open.

I ring the surgery in Mullion to book an appointment with my GP. There is a branch surgery at the Lizard, a small building just off the green. He has a clinic there, and there has been a cancellation for two days' time. I give my name, imagining the receptionist typing it into the blank space on the screen.

I have known my doctor since we moved to the Lizard. He lived in Cadgwith.

I think he still does.

Then, he was young, new to the practice, new to the area like us. I remember seeing him in Helston one weekend with his wife, and she was very pregnant. Now both his kids have been to university. The younger one, the boy, went to Bath. I remember that now. I would never have known his face if I'd passed him in the crowds of Milsom Street or caught his glance across the displays in Waterstones.

The Lizard surgery is very small. There are only a few chairs in the waiting room. Sitting on one of them is a friend of Richard's from long ago. He used to come to the club to play pool. Once, he slithered an arm round me at the bar. His hair has thinned; he has grown jowls. There is a tattoo curling round his bull neck and another sliding out from his sleeve. He smells. He looks down at his dirty trainers, and I look away. I don't know if he remembers me. I don't think I have changed much since then. Time stood still for me.

When he is called in, I watch those trainers lumbering across the room. The smell stays in the atmosphere. Sweat, beer, unwashed clothes. He came to the cremation, wearing black jeans and a heavy metal T-shirt turned inside out, and the jagged writing was faintly visible through the material.

But he came.

Mum and I saw Dr Redfern when Richard died. We sat together in his room. He prescribed something for Mum to help her get through the funeral. She asked if he could give me something, too, but I refused. I did not want the sharp edges blurred. I had to feel every tear; I had to remember.

I have to remember for the rest of my life.

We sat in the front row at the crematorium. My four grandparents, all alive then, behind; Mum's brother and his family, and her sister with her husband. Richard's friends from school and from the Lizard. His ex-girlfriend, Vicky, came with her parents. A couple of his teachers. People my parents knew. A family from one of the caravans that had been staying with us every August since we'd come to Kynance.

But no Zoe.

The minister said nothing about Zoe or the baby. That was how my parents wanted it. Just that Richard had fallen from the Buttress, the rocks he loved.

I kept turning round, thinking Zoe would creep in at the back, late, sliding into a pew. At the end, we stood. Mum was shaking and gulping as the coffin slowly disappeared.

"*Stop!*" I nearly cried aloud. "*Zoe isn't here yet.*"

I didn't cry out; they didn't stop the coffin; Zoe never came.

Richard's friend shambles out of the surgery with a pale green prescription in his hand. This time he looks at me and nods, then looks away.

I can't think about Richard now.

That is the past, and I am here for the future. My memories are always there. I lock them away tightly and wait for my name to be called.

"Emily Knight." Dr Redfern stands in the doorway, gesturing me through.

If he doesn't refer me, I don't know what I'll do.

I haven't had to see him since I moved home last year. He welcomes me back to the Lizard, asks about Bath. It's only been a few months since I left, but sometimes I find it hard to believe that the city is still there, turning on its own axis. That when I wake in my turquoise room at Kynance, there are still buses grinding along the Upper

Bristol Road, taking people to work at the hospital, ambulances still howling, rain still sliding down the tiny window of my old office, another girl sitting at my desk with earphones jammed on her head.

He says something about his son, who is living in Australia, and his daughter in Birmingham. She was the bump his wife's hand lay on when we saw them in Helston that time.

Babies.

Everyone having babies, passing on their genes. Even Richard has passed on his genes.

But not you, Emily.

Go away, I tell Richard silently.

"I want to have a child," I begin.

What happened?

I have heard those two words so many times; heard them screamed at me, shouted at me, sobbed at me, whispered to me. I have heard them silently in my head.

You saw what happened.

Looking back, I fancy I sensed it coming that day, like the darkness of an eclipse. I could remember the words we three spat out in the kitchen, yet they seemed to have come from the mouths of others.

Zoe wanted to talk to you, I silently tell Richard. *She told you she was keeping the baby. You were going on at her to get rid of it. That's what you said. Zoe was so upset. You were horrible. She was crying. You slammed out of the house. You'd been drinking. You'd been drinking in Truro, you said. I tried to get you, one of you. You were painting. We ran to the Buttress. You were up there. Zoe asked you to come down. But you said, "Leave me alone," and then you slipped.*

I have been asked over and over what exactly did we say, what did Richard say? I never told my parents what he said about them – that they were not his real family. Richard was dead, Zoe had vanished, there was only me left. The police must have talked to Zoe at some time, but my parents never saw her again after that day.

You could have stopped it.

Yes. Maybe. I know I could have cooled things down between Richard and Zoe. If he hadn't been so inflamed, he might not have run away and, if he did, he might not have slipped. Afterwards, when I heard that monstrous foghorn, I would tremble, cry, howl with it. Once I fainted at its voice.

I step out of the surgery into sunlight. It was so much easier than I expected. I stumbled over the words at the beginning; the doctor asked me to slow down. He googled the fertility clinic and turned his screen round so we could both look at it, the website as familiar as my own hands.

"An excellent idea." That was what he said.

I skip between the parked cars on the green. Tourists are milling in front of the shops. I stop and watch them: a man in sunglasses carrying a boy on his shoulders; a woman pushing a pink baby in a pink buggy; a young girl with a hand to her back, arching her large bump forwards. They're all ahead of me, but I am catching up.

I stop and turn.

I'll take the coast path back home.

The sea glitters silver-blue, the horizon hazy. Across the bay, the Land's End peninsula is a mauve arc. As soon as I join the coast path, I can see the Buttress looming up ahead. Below me, gentle waves curl onto the sand and pebbles in Bishop's Cove. The ebbing tide has exposed slimy boulders and shards of dark rock under the cliff. I remember Richard leaping from rock to rock one day that last summer.

Today, kids are splashing in the shallows, and a dog is racing after a ball. I can hear raised voices, but not the words. No one on the beach is looking up to the glowering crag above.

167

They don't know its story.

I walk on, breathing in the garlic and bluebells, the brine and sea-weed. Sunlight fractures on the pale sea. Under the tramped-down soil and grit of the coast path, protruding lumps of rock jut up, worn smooth by generations of hiking boots. Over the scraggy hedge, I see the caravans, the roof of the clubhouse, and, further on, the chimney of our bungalow.

I branch off through the hazy bluebells. Bees rise from the flowers. A Red Admiral. I scramble up onto the Buttress.

Richard died when he hit the rocks. Not the rocks in Bishop's Cove that he so often explored, but unseen jagged teeth on the northern side of the crag. Rocks only seen from the sea. Rocks no one could reach from above.

Richard was dead, and we had no decisions to make about ventilators, life support, quality of life.

"Did he jump?" the police asked me. So did the paramedics.

He fell, he fell, he slipped, he was angry, not thinking.

I do not think Mum has ever come to the Buttress since then. In the days after, Dad would climb up and smoke, looking out over the bay as twilight fell, just as Richard did so often. Since I have been back, I come here often. Sometimes I don't think about Richard because I don't think about anything beyond the colours of the sky, the slapping of the waves like a watery heartbeat, the scent of the foliage, the taste of brine, the rough lichen under my fingers. I fill all my senses and simply breathe in and out.

And sometimes, rarely, I talk to Richard here. He loved this serpentine crag. He knew every crevice and angle. He loved the way the land fell away to the sea. He was here often in life, and this is where death stole him.

If he is anywhere now, it must be here.

"Rich," I say aloud. "I want to tell you something."

168

June 2012

We leave early. It is one of those cool pastel mornings, though maybe the gooseflesh on my arms is more to do with fear and excitement than the weather. Maybe it's the heady mix of past and future colliding.

Today I am going back to Bath. Mum is going to drive there, and I will drive back. We will be home by evening.

Dad comes outside to wave us off.

"Good luck," he says and hugs me. "Drive safely, both of you."

It's quiet at this time. No cars are moving in the caravan field; no residents seem to be up. The sky is a pale mauve-blue, and I think it will be hot later. I turn once to the Buttress, hazy beyond the far gate, and I imagine I can sense Richard standing there.

Mum guns the engine, and I get inside, the clinic letter *crackling* in the pocket of my jeans. I watch Dad in the wing mirror; as we turn left onto the main road, he goes back inside the bungalow.

This is my first appointment. Dr Redfern referred me straight away, as he promised. Only a few days after I saw him, the phone rang one morning. I was still in bed. I heard Mum speaking, then the bedroom door swung open, and she was there, holding the receiver out to me, mouthing *Bath* and, for half a second, I had no idea who in Bath was calling me.

It has not been a year since I was last there. It cannot have changed that much. But it will have, in subtle ways. We are going into the city before my appointment, and I know it will be different. I will no longer have keys to a flat in my pocket. I will no longer be struggling with Waitrose carrier bags of groceries, trying to shop for a week with no car. I will no longer feel I belong, but because I know the streets like the veins on my wrist, I won't be a tourist, either.

Mum stops for petrol in Helston. I hear the *scraping* of the petrol cap as she unscrews it, the *clunk* of the nozzle settling in the hole, then the *buzzing* rush of fuel. Numbers flash by on the screen.

I tug the letter out of my pocket and read it again. It confirms the appointment the secretary made with me on the phone. I check the date and time. The letter is getting scruffy. It arrived as a sheet of cream paper with two crisp folds, but now it's got bent, and one corner has torn, and there is even a smudge of blood on it from when I tore my nail too far down last night. I've kept that letter with me since it came, in my pocket, in my bag, beside my bed as I sleep.

I'll get a scrapbook, I decide, flattening the paper on my knees. *Or an album and put it in.*

I'll put everything in. Every appointment letter, every piece of paperwork I get. Every scan photograph. Whatever information I can get on the sperm donor. Everything I can find, and I will make a beautiful book for my child.

My child.

The words still don't sound like they should come from my mouth or be thought in my dreams.

Mum comes out of the shop, shoving the receipt into her bag. Off we go again, and I watch the petrol needle swing slowly upwards to the top of the tank. My clinic letter is still on my knees.

"I'm going to make an album for … the baby," I say and shake the letter. "All the letters and scans and everything. Put it all in a book, and then he or she will be able to see what happened and how much I wanted to do this."

170

"You won't be able to tell them much about the father, though. You won't know anything about him."

"I'll know something."

His colouring, height and weight, job, blood group. Less and more than I would find on a dating site profile.

"Not about what he's like as a person, what he enjoys on telly, what he eats, what he thinks."

"I don't know … I don't know how much more you can find out. But it doesn't matter. It'll be so loved. So wanted."

"I worried about Richard. That he would spend all his life wondering. I even thought his … other parents might spend their lives wondering, too. I didn't want him to look for them, but I knew he should."

"He'd have done it as soon as he was eighteen if it mattered to him that much."

"He was going to, though."

"Maybe."

"We didn't know much. I know they were very young. Sixteen or so."

Like Zoe.

"I think it must have been hard for them," Mum says. "I want to think it was hard for them. Not that they just ditched him. I think they were bullied into it. Like maybe Zoe was."

I jump as she echoes my silent words.

Zoe wasn't bullied into giving up her son. He lives with her, and her husband, and his little sister, and the new baby.

New baby.

That was in 1999. I don't say anything. I can't lie; I can't tell the truth. Instead, I drink water from the bottle by my feet, which is silly because we're not even at Truro, and my bladder is always treacherous, but I don't want to have to speak.

"I'm worried," Mum says, "in case it doesn't work."

She's said that a lot. She knows what it is like to want a child, what it's like to feel the hot rush of blood every month.

"I'll do everything I can. Stop drinking. Eat well."

"You need to take folic acid if you want to conceive."

"I am." I smile. "I have for months."

The yellow plastic pill box lives in the drawer by my bed. It was part of my secret, but now it can come out.

When living in Bath, I found it disorientating travelling between my two homes. I loved Bath, and I loved the Lizard. Even after Richard's death, I loved it. I woke in Bath before holidays back home, fluttering inside, knowing by evening I would be absorbed back into that landscape, under a mauve-black starry sky. Returning to Bath, I would cry as my parents stood waving on Truro platform; once the train had snaked over Brunel's bridge at Saltash, I put Cornwall behind me and looked onwards to my adopted city.

And now, today, I am returning to Bath once more.

I left the hospital in early December last year. I didn't have a leaving do because I hadn't ever joined. I didn't have presents because I didn't belong to anyone. No one felt loyalty to me. I simply typed whatever was sent to me with the help of a faded, dog-eared copy of the *British National Formulary*, a medical dictionary, and Google. On my last day, I didn't even have a desk to clear: no memories, no framed photos of family and pets, no pot plants. Not even a favourite mug; I used whatever I could find in the ward kitchen along the corridor where we were allowed to make drinks.

That afternoon, I came out of the hospital at five o'clock. The sky was a luminous ultramarine. Orange Belisha beacons flashed on the zebra crossings. Outside the main doors, the hospital Christmas tree glinted with tiny coloured bulbs: red, green, pink, blue. Cold colours. Winter colours. My breath clouded the air in front of me. I turned back to face the huge edifice: the glass doors leading to the atrium, where the café was now closed, and where the cleaners snaked black cables across the tiles. There were lit windows in the corridor above and three figures standing talking; one guy was gazing down to my upturned face. More windows on the floor above. A ward. Some boxes on the windowsill, something yellow, probably a sharps bin. Movement. The party of three was breaking up. The guys went left, the girl right. She was holding something: books or papers. She was in theatre blues. I turned my back and walked to the bus stop, the Christmas tree lights winking on the edges of my eyes.

And here I am at that hospital again today, but this time, I am with Mum and arriving, not departing, and it's a hot blue day. We park in one of the overspill car parks. We're early.

We've been into the city centre. Only very quickly. It was smelly with exhaust fumes, and my eyes felt gritty.

Was the air always this dirty?

I stomped along, neither belonging nor visiting, just as I knew I would. I saw faces in the crowds I knew by sight. A woman who'd lived a few doors along from one of my flats; a bloke in a suit I'd seen around town so many times; a Goth guy with long dyed black hair and eyebrow rings. But no one I knew, no one I had to speak to, just faces in a crowd. We went into Nero's by the Abbey. Mum had a coffee, I had an Earl Grey, and we shared a piece of lemon cake.

I get out of the car. The ground is dry and dusty. I show Mum where we have to go and think of those lunchtime walks I used to take, those walks that led me to this clinic and, ultimately, to this day.

The clinic is away from the rest of the hospital, down a hedged lane. The traffic sounds fade. There are a couple of birds scuffling on the path in front of us.

I have to get this right, I think over and over. *I have to say the right things. I want to bring a child into the world on my own. I cannot, must not, say anything stupid.*

The walled garden is riotous with lavender, foxgloves, and roses. Red admirals and whites drift up from the lavender and spiral away over the bright blooms.

When I open the glass doors again, I am not asking for a booklet; I am here to see a consultant.

His name is Mr Robin Gale. I know the name. I never typed for Gynae, but sometimes one of the other girls in my office did. She said she liked Mr Gale's letters: he was clear on the tape and always gave patients' details correctly. I may even have passed him on a corridor or stood behind him in the queue at the atrium café.

I have the letter in my pocket still, to bring me luck. I fill a beaker at the water dispenser and sit down on a squashy chair beside Mum. It is cooler in here. I look through the door to the garden beyond, to the bright sky and the dipping butterflies. There's no one else in the waiting room. A door opens at the back, and there's a nurse in blues with a clipboard in her hands.

"Emily Knight, please," she says.

We follow her through the door at the back into a narrow passage. She's asking about our journey. Mum says we made good time; the traffic really wasn't bad. The nurse opens a door for us and gestures us through.

Mr Gale stands behind his desk. I think I might have seen him around the hospital.

"Ms Knight." He offers his hand across the desk.

"Mr Gale," I say. "This is my mother, Cheryl."

He shakes Mum's hand, then we all three sit down. Him one side, us the other. He's in his fifties, I think. Thick grey hair, blue eyes. He's wearing a cobalt blue shirt. He has a wedding ring, a plain gold band.

174

"I have a letter here from Dr Redfern."

I follow his eyes to the sheet in front of him. Yes, I see my surgery's letterhead, about three short paragraphs of type, Dr Redfern's squiggle at the bottom.

"He says you used to work here. What department were you in?"

I'd mentioned it to Dr Redfern when I saw him, when I was explaining why I wanted to go to Bath for the treatment. I'd said I was a medical secretary in Bath. Not a bottom-grade typist in a tiny hot room.

"ENT and oral," I say.

"Ah." He smiles. "That's why I've not come across you before. When did you leave?"

"Just before Christmas."

"And you're back living with your parents now?"

"Yes," I say, and I wonder if it's a trick question.

Is it good or bad to be living with my parents?

I also wonder if Dr Redfern said anything about Richard in his letter.

How long does something like that stay relevant to a patient's history?

"Having a baby using donated sperm is a long journey," Mr Gale says. "I'm sure you realise that. Just as you realise there are no guarantees. Today I want to talk to you a bit about why you want to do this, what situation you're in, what your health is like, that kind of thing. I'd also like to do a quick ultrasound of your womb and ovaries to see what they look like. We'll talk about the options available to you, and you can ask me any questions you have. Then I can explain how we move forward from here. You don't have to make any decisions today."

"OK," I say.

He checks the letter. "You're thirty-six years old. You don't have any children. You've never been pregnant, then?"

"Never."

"But you have relationships with men?"

"I'm not seeing anyone at the moment. I want to do this first. But, yes, I have had relationships with men."

"You've not had any children with any of them. I know this is intrusive, but can you tell me why not?"

Because they were married, because they'd had their kids, because they'd had vasectomies, because they were alcoholics, because they refused to even consider it.

Because, I knew, I always knew, that having a baby with any one of them would have been the most stupid thing I could do, leaving me with a lifetime of pain, connected forever to a man who didn't want the child, but would still force himself into its life to spite me if nothing else.

"None of my boyfriends would have been suitable," I say at last, and I know Mum is reciting the same litany in her head that I have just sung. "A lot of them were older than me. They'd had families. I don't think I ever had a man who wanted to commit himself to me and a baby."

None of that is a lie. I suddenly understand I don't have anything to hide.

"Are you close to any children at the moment?" Mr Gale asks. "Other people's?"

"Not now. A bit when I was in Bath."

"No brothers or sisters with families?"

"No."

"You're an only child, then?" He turns to Mum. "So, this would be your first grandchild?"

"Yes," Mum says, and the moment has gone.

First biological grandchild, I correct silently.

176

"Oh yes," Mum says. I haven't heard the question. "I think it would be wonderful for Emily, for our family. I didn't know anything about this, but she showed me the booklet from the clinic. There's still a lot to learn, like choosing the donor. Emily says she would choose him, is that right?"

"Absolutely." Mr Gale writes on a sheet of paper and hands it to me. "This is the sperm bank we recommend. It's in Denmark. Have a look at the website in your own time, see what you think. There are others, in Britain and America, but the best sperm comes from Denmark."

"Why is it the best?" I ask.

"Because they have such thorough testing and investigating of the donors. Family medical history, character references, and so on. You'll see when you look. You can even see a photo of the donor as a child."

"But not as an adult?" Mum interjects.

"Not as an adult. But all their physical statistics are there, colouring, jobs, education, background."

I glance down at the paper. It's a website address for the sperm bank.

The sperm bank. This is really happening.

Mr Gale hasn't thrown me out of the door; he's given me the details of the sperm bank in Denmark. I didn't know the sperm would come from Denmark. Scandinavians are so good-looking. Tall, blond, blue-eyed.

Vikings.

"The first thing you need to consider is whether or not you'd want an open donor. An open donor means he is happy for the child to get in touch when they're eighteen. A closed donor isn't."

"I'd definitely want him to be open," I say.

"It's like being adopted," Mr Gale says, and I flinch because I said those words not so long ago.

I wonder if Mum remembers, too.

"What would Emily tell the child?" Mum asks. "Surely it would be awkward for a little one."

"It's not that rare these days," the consultant says. "When you consider the couples who need donated sperm, the lesbian families, as well as the single women … It's becoming much more commonplace."

"Perhaps not in Cornwall." I smile.

He laughs. "Perhaps not. There are societies for donor families, and I recommend everyone should join them. They can offer you a lot of advice about how to tell a child. Honesty is the best policy, I believe, being open from the start and telling the child how wanted they are."

"They are." I can almost feel a ghostly bundle in my arms.

My child. This is real. It's happening. It's happening to me, Emily Knight. I am going to be a mother.

"Before we would go ahead with any treatment, you would need to see one of our counsellors. This is compulsory. Everyone does it. It gives you a chance to talk about any worries you have about telling the child, and other people, how you will cope on your own, and so on. Then she will assess you and decide if she thinks you are a suitable person to be a single parent. Our decision to treat women is based on her assessment."

I nod because there's nothing else I can do. All kinds of people bring babies into the world – unwanted babies, unloved babies, babies conceived in brutality, abused and rejected – and are never judged.

But I will be.

I want a baby so much, and I will be judged by a stranger.

I look away for a minute, away from Mr Gale's face, and his papers, and his mobile phone lying on the desk, and I look at the square of blue beyond the smeary window. I can just see the reaching fingers of a tree's branches.

"I'm sorry?" I turn back to him.

"I know there's a lot to think about. We need to have a talk about the treatment options available. There are two ways of conceiving with donor sperm. Many single women go for a procedure called IUI, which is where you measure your ovulation, and the sperm is injected into the womb through a catheter on the right day. Do you know if you ovulate regularly?"

"I haven't tested it. My periods were always fairly regular, but I know that doesn't mean ovulation."

He writes something on his pad. "If you chose IUI, you would need to have your tubes X-rayed with a contrast dye, so we can check they're clear for the eggs to travel along. It is a painful procedure but necessary."

"Would that be done here?" Mum asks.

"Yes. As would the insemination."

"So, I would have to come up here as soon as I ovulate?"

"Yes," he says again. "I realise it's a long way to come. And you'd have to drop everything and come. Ovulation may not happen exactly when you think it will, so this probably isn't the best approach for you. Which brings me to the other option. IVF. We would stimulate your ovaries with drugs, so they produce lots of eggs, and then we'd collect them under sedation and fertilise them with the sperm. A few days later, you'd come back for the embryo transfer."

"Sedation?" I ask. "Not a proper anaesthetic?"

"No, just sedation. It's very effective. You won't remember anything. We go in through the vagina. No incisions. There'll be some pain afterwards, but you won't remember the egg collection itself."

Oh Jesus. I am a wimp.

Painful contrast X-rays, egg collection under sedation.

You want this, I say silently. *You want this so much. It may be painful, but it's transient. And the child is for life.*

179

I have drifted away again. Mum is asking about the costs. Mr Gale is saying something about IVF being considerably more expensive, but the results are much better.

"Emily, for you, I would consider the possibility of IVF. It is dearer, yes, but the success rates are higher. And for someone travelling from so far, it would be much easier. You would know when to take the drugs and when the egg collection and embryo transfer were to take place. OK, you might have to postpone the egg collection by a day or two if you hadn't produced enough follicles, but you would know pretty much what was happening. You would have to come to Bath for both of the procedures. The scans … we could try to get them done at your local hospital."

"What scans?"

"We need to do a couple of ultrasounds during the work-up stage to check the ovaries are responding properly to the drugs."

"Are these scans painful?" I ask without meaning to.

"No. These are just transvaginal ultrasounds. I'd like to do one today just to get a look at your insides. Very straightforward. Not painful. You do need an empty bladder, so would you like …?" He gestures towards the door.

I stand, and my legs feel wobbly. In my hand is the website for the sperm bank.

I am about to have an ultrasound.

Words wing through my head as I walk to the door.

Sperm, embryo, follicles, transfer, IVF, ultrasound, sedation, baby.

It's not a proper ladies, just a cubicle amongst the clinic rooms. As I squat, I hear voices in the corridor, the *slam* of a door. There are sanitary pads and a box of tissues on a nearby shelf.

The accessories to infertility.

I run the tap and squirt liquid soap on my hands. In books, characters look at their reflections in mirrors and acknowledge dark truths. I look at my own face in the glass.

This is the face of a mother.

It's like I'm in the wrong character's head. I never dared to believe this could be my story, my happy ending.

Mum and Mr Gale are talking about the cost of IVF. They break off as I shut the door behind me once more. The smell of the liquid soap on my skin reminds me of other days in the hospital. There's a bed behind a curtain. Mr Gale asks me to take off my boots, jeans and knickers.

"Would you like to see, too?" he asks Mum as I lie down on the paper sheet covering the bed.

"If that's OK." She stands at the foot of the bed.

Mr Gale fiddles with the scanner. There is a TV screen mounted on the wall above the bed. This is where I will see those dark, hidden parts of me.

Ovaries, fallopian tubes, womb. The names of distant stars, and as unknown.

The probe is cold when it slides in. Mr Gale moves it around. Images jump on the screen in grey and black. I glance at Mum, and she is staring at the monitor. My hands flap at the paper sheet over my hips. I turn my head again. Mr Gale is gazing at the screen, too.

"Your womb looks good," he says. Then, "Look, that's your right ovary."

The image crackles. I don't know how he can see anything in the blotches of dark and light. If I think about the probe inside, it hurts.

"It looks cystic," he says. "That's very common."

"Is it a problem?" I ask.

"It's often quite a good sign for IVF. You're likely to produce lots of follicles. All done."

Mr Gale slides the probe out, and now I can feel the cool jelly on my skin. The images on the screen die to darkness.

He hands me a box of tissues. "Have a wipe and come through."

I clean myself and pull on my jeans.

"IVF sounds like the better option," Mum says on the other side of the curtain. "Easier to plan from a long way away and a better chance."

"That's true, even though it is more expensive. Having said that, women can use up a lot of money on unsuccessful IUIs and then have to move to IVF after that."

We walk back through the waiting room, past the squashy chairs, the magazines, the water machine. I can feel a streak of jelly on my thigh. The website address is in my pocket with the first letter. Something else to keep for my album.

In the garden, the sunlight hits my face. I can smell lavender and roses, and underneath the flowers, the thick smell of city traffic on hot tarmac.

"I'm going to do it, aren't I?" I ask. "It's going to happen."

"It's going to happen." Mum jabs the keys at the car, and the locks spring open. "You just need to think which way you want to do it. I'd go for IVF if I were you."

"It's dearer."

"That doesn't matter. And you heard what he said. You could waste a lot of time with the other, and you'd have to keep coming up and down."

I'm not working now, but it would still be tiring and inconvenient, and surely that kind of stress would be a bad thing? I want this so much, but I am afraid, too.

"D'you want to go in and say hello to anyone?" Mum gestures to the electric doors leading into the hospital building. The doors by the labour ward that I walked out of at lunchtimes when I came to look through the windows of the Fertility Clinic.

"No."

I watch those doors a moment, remember cameos from the past: a man dementedly shoving coins into a vending machine, another guy shouting into a mobile about his wife's terrible labour and episiotomy, an older couple walking in with an **It's a Boy** helium balloon.

"I'll call Dad."

I check the signal bars on my phone and dial home.

Mum reaches into the car for a water bottle.

I scuff the dry ground while I wait for Dad to answer.

I drive home. Mum's car is a nice Golf.

But I should get a car of my own, I think.

I need a car, and I need a job and, above all, I need a baby.

As we leave Bath, we talk about what Mr Gale said. We think the same. IVF. Better chances, more exact. From somewhere comes the ghost of a conversation I had with Zoe that last year, before she became pregnant. I think it was something to do with RE. We were in my room talking about abortion and IVF, and she'd said maybe God didn't intend for some people to be parents, and I had thought she meant Mum and Dad. There we were, two girls, two naïve kids, throwing these words around, words that would become so powerful to us later.

Words we didn't even understand back then.

The A30 grumbles on through West Devon to the Cornish border. Mum's quiet. I glance at her. Like me, she's wearing sunglasses, but I can see she's sleeping. I turn on the radio for some noise above the *whooshing* of the wheels and the *throb* of the engine.

I am lucky.

I almost say it aloud. I am going to be a mother all by myself. I will not have to compromise over names, and bedtime rituals, and feeding times. I will not have interfering in-laws. My child won't see its parents arguing. I will not fear every day that my man will walk out, leaving me with a child who cries for its father. My child won't have to spend alternate holidays with its father and his new wife, and a bunch of stepbrothers and stepsisters, or worse, a new baby to take its place. And me. I won't have tricked anyone into fathering a child he didn't want. I won't have forced that man into a lifetime of financial and emotional commitment he didn't ask for. I won't be tied to a man who no longer wants me or our child. This is something for me.

Something strong, positive, powerful, overwhelming.

When I lived in Bath, I used several pregnancy tests. If my period didn't come at daybreak on the due day, I wondered, with fear and hope, if I might be pregnant, that a Durex had torn or the guy hadn't come out in time. I can recall those tiny white windows with no blue line showing life. Then I'd wrap up the wet sticks in tissue and shove them in the bin, relieved because it would have been a complete disaster if the line had swum into focus.

Tony, the Irish alcoholic; Jonny, who wanted me to have a threesome with him and his ex; Kevin, who I only met twice; Ryan, who was obsessed with computer games and *Lord of the Rings* figurines; Malcolm, who was married with teenage children; Steve, who was also married with teenage children, but didn't bother to tell me. I curl up inside like a salted slug when I think of the men I let touch me, sleep with me, share my life, even for just a few weeks. Those blank windows on the testing strips were a blessing.

Could it have been Richard, looking out for me from somewhere beyond the sky?

I am surprised that I never considered this before.

I don't get the letter from Mr Gale for another week. He reiterates what we spoke about and the options available. He asks me to go back to Dr Redfern and get some preliminary bloods taken. It is like a game. Every little move takes me closer towards the end, but the end is still a long way off.

Denmark.

I don't know much about Denmark. When I was little, I had a jigsaw of the countries of Europe, and Denmark was purple, a crumbly splatter of purple islands held together by a bright blue sea. I know my European countries by the colours of that jigsaw.

The Vikings came from Denmark. Denmark and Norway.

I know this because I lived on the northeast coast, where the word *Viking* is still uttered in a shocked hush. Richard and I spent much of our time on the vast pale sand of Aidan's Dunes, him investigating rock pools, me splashing in a warm lagoon that flooded up from the sea. Some days, when it was foggy, we couldn't see the craggy black Farne Islands; we couldn't see the giant red bulk of Bamburgh Castle. On those days, it was just us in a pocket of visibility, with sea mist all around. We would pretend we could hear the muffled *splash-splash* of approaching oars, that we could see the dragon head and the square red sail of a Viking longboat sliding out of the gloom, and we'd scoop up our shoes and run back to the dune grasses.

My child will be a half Viking.

Mum wanted me to look at the sperm bank's website straight away, but I kept the piece of paper safely in my bedside drawer and never typed that address on my laptop. It would be bad luck, a jinx, when there were still so many steps to take.

After a week or so, Mum stopped asking.

I'm on my own in the house. I pull the laptop onto my bed and turn it on. Then I slide open my drawer and take out the paper. Mr Gale used the back of a physiotherapy referral form. I unfold it. The Internet is ready. I type in the address and click on the link for a list of donors. The screen fills with names. Here they were all along, men who could have given me a child. I thought I would never find anyone, but here they were, across the North Sea, waiting for me.

They are code names, of course. Height and weight are given, and eye and hair colour. Jobs are there, and blood groups. Not age. And, on the far right-hand side, boxes are ticked or crossed for open or closed donors. I filter out the closed donors, and the list shrinks.

Do I choose a man who looks like me, who is like me? Or do I choose the sort of man I might pick for myself?

I laugh aloud at that. I would like my baby to look like me, if only a little like me.

I skim through the names, pausing over the blonds and redheads, those with blue eyes. If I click on a name, I can find out some more, but I have already seen another column of figures showing how many more women can pick these donors. I want to read about a blond, blue-eyed biochemist, but I don't click. It's too early. I've looked, I've seen how it works. That's all I need for now.

I know they're out there, these men, these Vikings.

July 2012

"I'd like to talk to you on your own."

"I'll wait here," Mum says, lowering herself back onto one of the soft chairs in the clinic waiting room.

At the doorway, I glance back at her, and she gives me a quick thumbs-up. Then I follow the counsellor into the warren of narrow passages and into a small room next door to the ladies I'd used last time.

There are more squashy chairs, a low table with a lime-green box of tissues on it. There's a dry-looking plant on the windowsill. In the back corner of the room are a washbasin and yellow sharps bin.

I sit down and face the woman opposite me. Her name is Doreen. She has my folder on her knee. I watch her skim through the letter Mr Gale sent me after my first appointment. She will have seen it before. I fold my hands on my lap.

This is the woman who decides. She's the fairy godmother and the wicked witch in one.

"Tell me why you want to do this," she begins.

I tell her …

"You live with your parents, I see. What do they feel about it?"

"They're delighted. They think it's a wonderful idea for me."

"I don't see anything on your file about your employment. What are you doing at the moment? How will you be able to look after a child and work?"

"We live at a caravan site. It's mostly residential now, but we still have a clubhouse with a bar. And we do meals. The locals use it. I'm going to take over from Dad as bar manager. It's the world I grew up in, the world I know. My parents are there, too. It will work out."

"What about boyfriends? Would you want to have romantic and sexual relationships with men in the future?"

"Of course. But not until after I've had my baby. The baby is number one right now. After that, well, yes, if I met someone I liked enough."

"How are you going to feel knowing that your child won't have a father? That they won't even know who he is and won't be able to contact him until they're eighteen?"

"Lots of children don't know their fathers. And sometimes, those that do find it more traumatic than if they didn't. I think a child needs love. It doesn't matter where that love comes from. It's having it that matters. I will love it so much. And I will tell it how wanted it is."

"It can be very difficult explaining about a donor-conceived child, both to the child and to friends and family. There are groups you can join and books written for the purpose of telling the children. Have you thought about this?"

"Mr Gale emphasised the importance of being honest from the start with the child, and I agree with that. As for other people, it's not something to brag about, neither is it something to hide. I don't think methods of conception need to be discussed, whatever they are. As for the child … I want it, and I shall love it, and I shall be a good mother. It's like being adopted."

"You have to consider the possibility that the treatment won't work. There would be other options available. Fostering, adoption. As a single woman, you wouldn't get a baby, but you could get an older child. You need to think about what happens if things don't go to plan."

"I know that. I will give it some thought."

"Would you have any regrets about using donor sperm?"

"No."

Mum's reading her paperback when I come out into the waiting room. Doreen made very few notes. She watched me when I was speaking; she nodded sometimes and laughed once with me; she showed me some books about telling children about their origins – they were illustrated by donor children. I gazed at the bright crayon drawings, and my throat swelled.

Women have done this. Women like me have done it, and it has worked, and their children have drawn pictures to help other children understand.

"Let's go," I say to Mum.

I drink from her water beaker while she packs away her book and finds the car keys. It's hot in the waiting room. A man is in the far corner reading the paper. A couple sits, knees together, hands entwined, on a sofa, whispering urgently. This shabby building in its tangled garden is a heady place of despair and dreams. It's a world of magic and alchemy, and I'm part of it.

It's part of me.

July 2012

Emily Knight is thirty-six years old and is currently living with her parents in Cornwall.

The family owns a caravan site, and this is where Emily plans to live for the foreseeable future and bring up her child. She will soon be taking over the role of bar manager, and this means her place of work will be close to home.

She is an only child and has never conceived with her previous boyfriends.

She has chosen to have treatment here in Bath because she lived in the city for some years and worked at the hospital as a medical secretary.

Emily's parents fully support her decision to conceive with donor sperm and are looking forward to becoming grandparents.

I talked to Emily about explaining her child's origins and told her that, should her treatment be unsuccessful, there were other options she could consider, such as fostering and adoption.

Emily does not want to dwell on the possibility of failure at this point. She tells me she would choose an open donor, so her child could contact him in the future.

Emily believes using donor sperm would be the most responsible way for her to become a mother.

I can see how much Emily wants the chance of a baby. She has researched the treatments and understands what lies ahead.

I support her decision to proceed with donor insemination.

It has taken ages to come. I had to ring the clinic to find out what had happened to Doreen's report. They said she had been ill, and then there was a delay with the typist.

It's my life, I wanted to shout. *It's my baby.*

And then, one day, without any warning, there it was, facing downwards on the mat, so I couldn't see the name or the postmark.

I scooped it up, turned it open, and I knew. I read it a second time. Read the typed letter from the secretary, telling me to ring the clinic to make another appointment with Mr Gale.

Donor insemination is not really like being adopted. If you are adopted, it's because your parents, for whatever reason, did not want to share their lives with you. If you're conceived with donor sperm, you could not be more wanted. You grow up not knowing your father, but there it ends. The same but very different.

Mum talks about Zoe a lot at the moment, about how Zoe's parents bullied her into giving up her baby, about how Richard's baby and mine would have been cousins.

Will be cousins, I amend to myself.

Mum asks me if I'd tried to find Zoe on Facebook or through mutual friends. She's asked me this before, of course. I do search for her sometimes, yes, I do, but I never find her because I don't know her name now. I suspect she has severed herself from everyone from school, as no one else knows where she is, either. Beth asked me once about Zoe, and I said I had never heard from her after that day and we had long ago stopped trying to find her.

This August will be twenty years without Richard.

'*Nearly a quarter of a century*,' Mum says.

Longer than he was alive.

I ring the clinic in Bath and ask for an appointment with Mr Gale. The secretary tells me he is away at the end of July and the beginning of August. She offers me a cancellation at the end of the month, and I am about to accept when I realise. It's that date.

Richard's anniversary.

"Mr Gale's away again in September," the secretary tells me. "He's on a course, then he's on leave."

I hesitate. "I can't do that day in August."

"You'll be looking at early October then," she says, and I hear the distant *tap-tap* of her fingers on the keyboard. "I've got a 9.15 on—"

"I'd prefer afternoon if possible. I'm coming from the Lizard."

She doesn't reply.

"The very end of Cornwall," I emphasise.

The end of the world, where the sun slips under the curve of the earth, leaving a bloody stain on the sky.

She gives me an afternoon appointment in October. It's a long way off, but it doesn't matter. I must let Mum have this August for Richard, then we can start looking forward to a new life, a new person to love.

August 2012

I receive a text. I don't get many. Since leaving Bath, I haven't talked to people much. I occasionally hear from friends, people I was at uni with, or people I worked with, but we have drifted apart like ice floes. A lot of them couldn't understand why I'd leave a city like Bath to come back to a caravan site at the Lizard. And they don't know about my plan, either.

Hi there, if you're still on this number, we'll be in Cornwall in a couple of weeks. We've got a cottage in Portreath. Do you fancy meeting up?

It's Malcolm. I deleted his number from my phone ages ago, but I recognise it. And I recognise his arrogance. I saw him around town quite a bit after we split up. Usually on his own. Once with a glamorous brunette – who wasn't his wife. He ignored me that day, like he did when I saw him with his family. Just before I left Bath, I saw him in Waterstone's, and I told him I was leaving town. He asked me for a drink, and I said no. I never imagined I would hear from him again.

Probably not a good idea. Enjoy your holiday.

Only after I send it do I realise what it sounds like – that it's not a good idea as I will go weak at the knees and faint with longing, and beat his chest to make him stay down here with me, while his wife and kids go home to Bath.

I can easily get away for a day. I could drive over to yours. Or we could get a Travelodge for a few hours. What do you reckon?

When Malcolm and I parted, it wasn't for the first time. Married men continually dump their girlfriends and then come back, time after time. That's how it goes. And each time he came back, I'd let him in again. When we finally parted, it came from me.

A Travelodge for a few hours? I smile. Not even the offer of a meal or day out.

I hesitate before responding. It could be one final madness before I start my treatment. I was fond of him once. Tall, broad, dark hair, blue eyes. We were introduced by a mutual friend at her party. Malcolm had come without his wife. He left with my number. Two evenings later, he was outside my flat in an Audi sports car. Half an hour after that, he was in my bed.

No.

I don't want madness. I don't want to go backwards. Malcolm belongs to those days in Bath and to the past. I have already started my plan, my journey, and I need no distractions along the way, especially ones that bring no happiness.

I turn the phone off.

It's evening, and I'm behind the bar with Dad. My parents have let the place get scruffy over the last few years. It needs to be decorated. Badly. But the shabby walls and chipped paint haven't put off the regulars. There's a crowd at the bar, the pool balls are *clacking* on the two tables, and some old guys from the Lizard are playing cards in the corner. Mum does a lot of the cooking these days, though we have two part-timers: a chef and a barman. We only do meals in the evenings now. I see a group of holidaymakers in the window; their table is cluttered with empty plates and screwed-up napkins. I lift the flap and go to clear the debris. My hands smell of beer, but it's a comforting smell, one I've grown up with.

As I walk back to the bar with the pile of empty plates, I glance around the room. Four card players chuckling; families squabbling; one of the pool players jeering at his friend; a couple, younger than me, cuddling together on a bench, sharing a packet of crisps.

I feel dizzy and dump the plates on the bar with a crack. I am lonely. I don't know anyone. I've lost touch with old friends, and I haven't made any new ones. Apart from my family and customers in the bar, I only speak to the checkout staff in Tesco, or the guy on the till at the petrol station when I fill up Mum's car. I need friends. Maybe even a man to share my life with. I suddenly realise that I hardly know how to go about meeting people.

A baby will help.

I'll meet other mothers in the hospital, at playgroups, and at school.

But I won't be like those other mothers.

Dad's looking at me strangely. I'm still standing by the bar flap, staring at the whizzing lights on the fruit machine. One of the greasy napkins slides off the stack of plates to the floor. I bend down to pick it up. It's smeared with tomato ketchup.

"You OK?" Dad mouths at me as I straighten.

I nod and gather the plates again.

Not like those other mothers.

But this is the end of the world. The rules don't apply here.

Richard will be forever nineteen. We don't know what he would look like if he were alive today. We can imagine. I picture him as muscular and greying, with sun-creases round his eyes from trekking in the Himalayas or from the blinding white light of the Arctic. I hardly ever look at photographs of him. Only after he'd gone did we realise we had so few, especially from the later years. There are pictures of him as a little boy: at a birthday party he had in Seahouses, on the dunes with me, carefully studying the Lego high street he was building on the living room floor. Then, after we moved to the Lizard, a few flat school photos, with blemished skin and smirks. And so few of us together.

When I think of Richard, I don't see his face or even his profile. I see a sort of three-quarter view, and his head is kind of muzzy, like I'm looking through a rain-washed window. It's the set of his shoulders, though, and his long legs that mark him out, and the mixture of arrogance and uncertainty that crackles in the air.

But his voice …

I can't recall his voice. I try to grasp it, to capture his vowels and speech pattern, but it's gone. And then sometimes, when I'm on the twilit cusp of sleep, or just concentrating on something like a difficult parking manoeuvre, or a fiendish Sudoku, I'll hear him. Sometimes so clearly that I start with a jump; sometimes just a breath in my ear. Boozy and slurred down the phone: *Hang on, there are the pips. Cheers, Em.* Cruel and spiteful, lashing out in the kitchen that dreadful afternoon: *I'm bored of it all. I'm bored of you.* And then, nearly always as I am just about to fall asleep, that ghost voice on the Buttress: *Leave me alone.* And that one seems to echo round my brain – *alone, alone, alone* – until I snap my eyes open and absorb the shapes and outlines of the bedroom and drink cold water to wash his voice from me. Why can't I remember the laughter, the jokes, the times we had fun? The times before Zoe.

It's the anniversary. Twenty years. I know Mum expects something to happen, expects me or Dad to do something, say something, but we don't know what, and there's nothing to do or say. At times like this, I wish Richard had a grave where we could gather in a tiny crescent and gaze at the name and date until our eyes fizzed and feed bright flowers – daffodils, roses, carnations – through the holes in the metal vase. Somewhere Richard was, somewhere to ground us. But after death, as in life, Richard soared away, and now he is nowhere. Just a shadowed figure and a voice in my head.

Dad and I close the bar after lunch. It's a hot day, a blue and gold day, with an ugly black frame.

"I don't know what I want," Mum says.

"Something to make it better," I say lamely.

"There isn't anything," Dad says. "We've just got to move on, look ahead. Concentrate on what Emily's going to do. Richard would want that."

"If only she'd had the baby," Mum says.

Dad looks confused for a second. He thinks she's talking about me.

"We should have had her stay here afterwards. Then she could have kept it."

Dad puts an arm round Mum and looks helplessly at me. "We couldn't do that, Cheryl. She was only sixteen. She had to sort it out with her own family."

The same tired words that achieve nothing.

I walk away to the sink and fill a glass under the tap. I concentrate on the rush of the water and the tangled garden beyond the window. I should have said something after the eclipse. It weighs on my chest, crushes my breath, this secret I guard.

Later, I walk out to the Buttress. I go alone. Mum would never come; Dad looked at me, and I shook my head. I saw Richard fall. They didn't. I haven't walked to the Buttress every anniversary. Sometimes I was in Bath. I didn't make it a pilgrimage to come back. I didn't want that date as the sun of my solar system, but it has been. Twenty years. Richard has been dead longer than he was alive. Surely that must be the tipping point, the time for change.

A couple of hikers have stopped by the Buttress. The man is gesturing at the rocks with his hand. The woman nods, says something. I hesitate at our gate. The high white sun is on my head. No clammy fog today; no tortured wail of the foghorn.

The walkers move on, smile at me as they pass.

They don't know. They don't have any idea.

They stride on towards Kynance. I trample through the dry bent grasses to the crag. On the rocks below, the waves curl and break with a soft *whoosh*. The horizon is bright and clean. The sun's too bright for me to see the tiny brushstroke of Wolf Rock Lighthouse, but I know exactly where it is. A dark boat moves towards the Channel.

"I have to let you go now, Rich. You've been free for twenty years. We have to be free too now." I glance behind me. I am alone. "I've seen your son." I am shocked that I have said this. "A long time ago. At the eclipse. It must have been the magic of the eclipse. I saw him. I saw Zoe, too. She seemed …" I trail off.

I was going to say *happy*, but that's not right. She looked stressed.

"She kept your son," I say instead. "She defied her parents. She didn't kill him or give him away. She kept him, and he's OK. He's a young man now. He'll be like you. So, you're still here."

I stop, embarrassed. Some crazy woman talking to a rock. Maybe this time next year, there will be someone else. They might still be inside me, growing, forming bones and organs, and hands and eyelashes.

Or they might be born.

It's only a year away. A lot can happen in a year.

"Goodbye, Rich."

I turn away from the Buttress. His voice.

Alone, alone, alone.

October 2012

Making a baby requires only two tiny cells. Making a baby requires a chunky navy padded bag of inhalers, ampoules, syringes, and needles. I turn round once more and see it sitting on the back seat. Baby Starter Kit. Contains everything you need to make a baby – except luck.

To the west, the falling sun slices red-gold through towering clouds. Mum's driving with sunglasses on. When the sky darkens, she shoves them onto her head, and a few moments later, she snaps them down as the sun pierces through again.

I saw Mr Gale again this afternoon. Just a flying visit to the clinic and then home again. I have my magic box of tricks on the back seat.

Mum came in with me to see Mr Gale. He had a trainee with him, a girl with a dark ponytail, stitting quiet and still in the corner. He asked me about my cycles and when I had last had a period. He scribbled the date on the neon orange Post-it block in front of him and then swivelled to check the calendar taped to the wall. Hospital issue: twelve months on a page, bank holidays in red, laminated.

Mum had a spiral-bound notebook on her knee. She wrote down the dates for me.

A nurse knocked and came in with the navy bag, like a doll's holiday hold-all.

I leaned in close to Mr Gale. "Will this work?" I asked him.

He was typing my notes on the computer keyboard. He stopped a moment. The cursor flickered.

"Yes," he said.

Doctors don't make promises. But he did.

The nasal spray turns off the reproductive system. In a couple of weeks, I have to have a scan, like the one Mr Gale did before, to see my ovaries are *quiet*. He says I can have this scan done in Cornwall. But I can't do this on my own. I now have to choose my donor, choose whose blood will mingle with mine in my baby's veins.

The nurse at the clinic told me the spray would be bitter in my throat, and it is. It's like I've snorted up cleaning fluid or something. I swallow, but I can't get rid of the taste. A squirt in each nostril morning and evening. As I slide the bottle back into its little cardboard box, I realise that I have hardly thought of Richard since I said goodbye to him on the Buttress.

I come home early from the bar. Mum wants to look at the sperm bank website with me. We sit side-by-side on my bed as I turn on the laptop. This time we will click on the profiles. We'll read about these guys who are willing to bring children into the world they'll never meet until adulthood. The list of names comes up.

"It's one of them," I say, and I hear the awe in my voice.

"What?" Mum asks.

I point at the screen. "It's one of them. My baby's father is there. I've just got to find him."

She's got her notebook again and turns to a clean page.

"Let's filter it to open donors and make a preliminary list," I say. "Then we can narrow it down."

I skim over some of the donors. Most of them are Danish or from somewhere else in Scandinavia, but there are Germans, Russians, and Mexicans.

I want a Viking.

Some of their jobs don't interest me. I reject a butcher, an IT guy, a personal trainer.

The blue-eyed biochemist is still listed. Mum writes down his codename. I click on other profiles: a teacher, doctor, graphic designer, two university students, a journalist, an engineer.

I want a Viking.

I want someone with similar colouring to me, so the baby will look like me. I would like him to share my blood group because that's easier, and I'm not that tall, so a tall donor would be good. And he's just got to appeal to me.

"OK," Mum says. "That's twelve. I think that's enough."

I take the paper from her and look at the names. Some jump out at me, my secret favourites. She's noted their heights and weights, their colouring and jobs.

"We'll each make a shortlist of three," I suggest.

I tear a page from her notebook and find a spare pen on my bedside table.

"It's like *The X Factor*," Mum says.

I glance up at her. "*The XY Factor.*"

The next morning, I bring my computer to the living room. My shortlist of three is in the pocket of my jeans.

"I don't know," Dad protests. "It's not my choice. I can't say."

"Please," I say. "Just look at these three guys."

"Only three?" he asks, relieved.

"Only three."

How strange – or was it? – that Mum and I both chose the same three donors for our shortlists. All Danish, two blonds, one auburn. The biochemist, the doctor, the journalist.

"I think I know," Mum says.

"I think I do, too." I sign into the sperm bank.

Dad looks vaguely queasy as though the screen is going to be flooded with sperm close-ups.

I don't read the profiles anymore. I think I know the details off by heart. The biochemist has blood group O, and I'm A. The journalist has green eyes and red hair, and I like the idea of those eyes, but he's just a bit shorter than I'd have liked. The doctor is blond, with blue eyes, he's tall and slim, and the same blood group as me. His codename is Rafe. Last night I went to sleep with the name *Rafe* whispering round my dreams.

Dad's got his glasses on. He's studying the screen.

"It's not up to me," he starts.

"Terry," Mum interrupts. "Of course it's not. It's completely up to Emily. It's just that we both came up with these three names, and we'd like to know what you think. Then Emily can order the sperm."

"I would like to know," I say.

"Is it coming here?" Dad asks.

"What?"

"The sperm?"

"No, no, it goes to the clinic."

I don't know which of the three Vikings Mum likes best. What if neither of them wants Rafe? What if Mum likes the idea of a green-eyed baby like Rich? What if Dad dismisses the blood group thing because he thinks biochemistry would be interesting?

It's my choice, I remind myself.

"OK," Dad says. "If you're pushing me for an answer, I'd say this one." He nods at the screen.

Mum swoops over his shoulder. "That's the one I like!"

"Who did you pick?" Dad asks me.

I stand behind them. Rafe's profile is on the screen. The cursor's winking steadily like the pulses of Tater Du lighthouse.

"Rafe," I say, and it's like all the adrenaline is flooding out of me.

He was there all along. My baby's father, my baby's donor.

My Viking.

His name is Rafe, and he has the XY Factor.

After only a few days, I no longer taste the spray in my throat, or I no longer notice it. I think of the grainy black and white images I saw of my womb and ovaries in Mr Gale's office that first time, and I wonder what is happening in there now, in that dark, secret, velvet-lined cavern. I don't feel ill or different, just excited and afraid now that the days are counting down to my egg collection and whatever lies beyond.

I have ordered Rafe's sperm. It will be flying from Denmark in a drinking straw. Only now that I have made my choice do I apply for further details about him. I wasn't going to at all. I would have his sperm, which was enough, but Mum said I should find out all I could for the baby. And I remembered the promise I'd made at the petrol station. I would make an album, a scrapbook, of everything I could for my child.

The first thing I asked for was a photograph of Rafe. The sperm bank doesn't show adult photos, but it will show baby ones. I click on the attachment and feel sick. I should have done this before choosing him. What if he looks awful? He might have become an awful-looking adult.

And then I'm looking into a pair of huge blue eyes. He has soft pale hair that falls long over his ears. He is wearing a Breton striped T-shirt and jeans. He is sitting on the floor, and one hand is reaching out for something – a toy? – that's not in the shot. He has even white teeth in a wide smile.

"He's beautiful," I say aloud and smile back at him.

I would be so happy to have a little boy like that. Or a girl with that same pale hair and dark blue eyes. I might not. My baby might have red hair and freckles like me. It might be a mixture of both of us. It might look like neither of us. It will be its own person.

I save Rafe's photo to my desktop. I'll print it out for the scrapbook later. Now I open up the huge document that contains all the extra information about him: his interests and hobbies, his plans for the future, his medical history, and his family. There are pages and pages of it. It's like a huge one-sided conversation. In five years, he would like to be married with his own children, he says; he hopes to become a neurology consultant; he likes reading, both fiction and non-fiction; he runs; he plays pool; he is trying to improve his cookery; he once tried to learn the sax but isn't musical; he doesn't own any pets at the moment; he likes fast cars; he doesn't smoke, but he likes the odd beer; he has travelled around Europe and has been to London; he speaks and writes fluent English.

There are pages of health charts showing who in his immediate family has any problems like dermatitis, cancer, diabetes, hypertension, and so on, their heights, weights, hair and eye colour, jobs. There are pages for him, his parents, two sisters, grandparents, three uncles, one aunt, and cousins.

I look away from the screen. All these people out there in Denmark. They will also be related to my baby. A whole family, a whole world.

Richard must have felt this, too.

My own eyes film over when I bring up the last page. It's a handwritten note from Rafe to whoever selects his sperm. His writing is a little unsteady, angular, scruffy. I can see it on a prescription pad or in a patient's notes.

Thank you for choosing me, it says. *I know how much you want a baby, and I know you will look after him or her so well. I wish you the best of luck.*

He's speaking to me from across the sea. He knows how much I want a child, and he wants it to happen for me. He knows I will love it. I may not know his real name. I may not know what he looks like, where he lives, but he knows this about me.

And still, I don't tell anyone.

Yes, there will be people who make judgements about me. Some of them will know me, some won't. I count off the people I know who have had children. Rachel moved back to Wales and had a boy and a girl, but I don't think their father is ever around these days. Sonia and Gary had a daughter soon after university, then they split up, then got together again, and had another girl, and now they're always breaking up and making up. Jane is divorced with a son. Beth has a large family, but one of her kids is ill. One of the girls I worked with in Bath has three children, each with a different father: one Jamaican, one Polish, one Greek. Malcolm's children are growing up knowing their father shags around and makes their mother cry. My old boyfriend Jamie seems to be doing OK with his family, but who really knows? I suppose there has to be someone doing what used to be normal for everyone. And then there's Zoe. She brought up her illegitimate son whilst married to someone else. Has she ever told her son, my nephew? Does he know his father's name was Richard Knight, and he was nineteen years old, and he fell to his death one clammy misty August afternoon? Perhaps he doesn't even know. Perhaps he never will.

My child will know everything.

He or she will know how much I wanted a baby of my own, how carefully I selected Rafe. One day they will be able to meet, my child and Rafe. They will have to wait eighteen long years, but when I analyse the sad, complicated lives my old friends have with their children and lovers, I know what I have done is better, is the best way to make a baby. We may not have my child's father around, but we will have no pain and no sadness and no betrayal and no threats.

We will have love.

Yet, still, those people will judge me. They will envy me, but they'll judge me. If I just picked up some oik in a bar to get me pregnant, they wouldn't judge me; if I had a tortured relationship that ended in tears and violence, and with me a jilted single mother, they wouldn't judge me. But they will because I had the balls to make a choice, to make the right choice, one that others would wish they had done.

I check the clock. It's time for my throat spray, then I'll be off to the clubhouse for the evening.

It is called a transvaginal baseline scan. I am in another waiting room, this time in the basement of the hospital in Truro. Several older guys are in here and drinking from large plastic beakers. Some drink water, and some drink a pale squash. There is a table in the corner with squash bottles and spare beakers. Lots of scans require a full bladder, but mine doesn't. Lots of scans are performed to see things that are happening inside, but mine is to ensure nothing's happening.

The radiographer calls me in, and I follow her down the corridor to the imaging room. There's paper on the bed and a screen on a bracket for me to look at. She sits at the computer and asks me the usual: name, address, date of birth. I tug off my boots, peel down my tights and knickers, and swing myself up on the bed. The room is warm, but my skin shivers suddenly. I don't look at the probe before the radiographer slides it in.

"So, you're having IVF?" the radiographer says, focusing on the black-and-white screen.

"Yes." I don't want to have to justify myself lying on this bed with the probe inside me.

"What I'm looking for is a thin lining to the womb. And I'll look at your ovaries, too, see what they're like."

I look at the ceiling, not the screen. There's a stain on one of the big square tiles. It looks like coffee, but it can't be.

Water perhaps.

There are voices on the corridor outside.

"Looking good." The radiographer slides the probe out. The jelly is cold and wet on my thighs. She hands me some hard paper towels to dry myself.

"What did you see?"

"The endometrium, that's the womb lining, measures 2.6 mm. That'll be fine. Your ovaries have some small follicles." She bangs on the computer keyboard. Over my head, the screen flickers with nothingness. "It says here I'm to give you a copy of the report, and you're going to phone your clinic with it. That right?"

"That's right."

My tights are twisted, and my feet feel cold and clammy inside them. I shove my boots on again.

"Here you are." She hands me a small white printout. "Good luck with it."

"Thank you," I say and start for the door, with a flutter in my chest.

When I was reading about IVF, researching the treatment and what happens to the body and so on, I found out you have to inject yourself. Or get someone else to inject you. I read accounts online of women fainting, husbands stabbing their wives' buttocks with needles, the *trauma* and *pain* and *indignity* of it all.

And now it's my turn. I don't have a husband to jab my arse. I'm injecting into my own thighs.

The padded navy bag is on the bed beside me. I have to do this first thing in the morning when I wake up. The injections must be at the same time every day. The nurse at Bath told me that yesterday when I rang up with my scan results. I read the printed slip word for word, and she told me I was ready to start injecting. Nearer and nearer to the egg collection. Those two words, those two soft sounds, still terrify me.

First, I break a tiny ampoule of water and draw it into the syringe. It's hard not to get air bubbles, but that doesn't matter because I'll be sucking it up again and again. The hormone drugs are a dry powder at the bottom of little phials. I stab the needle into the top of one and squirt out the water. Instantly the powder dissolves into a fizzy liquid. I suck the solution back into the syringe, then stab, squirt, and suck again and again. I have four phials to mix together this way. On the last one, I suck the grey-white liquid more slowly into the syringe. There are still a few tiny bubbles. I hold it up to my eyes: a slim syringe with this gritty mixture, this magic potion. I jab the needle swiftly into my thigh and press down. It's done. I withdraw the needle. There's a dot of blood to mark the injection site, but that's all. No pain, no swelling, no stinging, or blotchiness. It's an anti-climax.

The clinic has even provided me with a tiny sharps bin for the dirty needles. It's yellow with a slitted lid, a miniature version of the hospital ones. I shove the syringe, needle, and ampoules in it, and they *click* together at the bottom.

The nurse at Bath told me something else, too, yesterday. On the tenth day of injections, I need another scan. This time it's to see if the ovaries are responding properly to the drugs and producing lots of eggs. And this scan has to be done in Bath.

November 2012

It is just after six in the morning and dark and freezing cold on the platform at Truro railway station. Only a few other people are waiting. Some are slouching on benches, some are walking up and down, tapping phones. Our breath turns to white speech bubbles before our faces.

"You don't have to wait," I say to Mum.

"Of course I will."

She looks knackered. We left the Lizard just after five. Still the middle of the night. I can't take the car to Bath today as Mum needs it. I'm getting the train there and back in one day. Mum will collect me again tonight.

My wallet, keys, phone, and ticket are in a little leather bag against my hip. I have a rucksack on my back; at the bottom of it is a small cold bag with two turquoise ice blocks. If my ovaries are ready today, Friday, then my egg collection will be on Monday, and I have to collect a different injection, already cooled and prepared in a syringe, to detonate them. At home, it must go into the fridge until I use it.

There is a quiet murmur of traffic from the town. Someone's mobile rings down the platform. I'm shivery, and not just from the cold. The signal changes; the level crossing lights by the station flash amber, then red-red, red-red; the siren whines; the barriers judder down, pale in the darkness.

"Very best of luck." Mum gives me a quick hug. "Call me with any news."

Two headlamps swell as they creep closer, almost silently. Lit coaches, guys hunched over laptops. The train *hisses*. There's a door right by me. I follow a guy on with iPod buds in his ears. The coach is nearly empty. Mum's outside on the platform, giving me a thumbs-up. The doors *slam*, the *whistle* blows, the engine *roars*, and we are off, sliding out of the station, through the level crossing with its frantically flashing lights, and away to the rest of the world.

The train's packed by the time it gets to Westbury, where I get off. I step down onto the platform, my legs shaky and my throat dry as I have been snoozing on and off most of the way. When I lived in Bath, I often had to change at Westbury. It looks different now: much brighter, with flower pots, and the café is open. Before, I was usually there in the evening, waiting for a connection to Cornwall, the platform dark, cold, almost deserted, and vaguely sinister.

Today it's cold but busy, and I only have a few minutes before the Bath train arrives. It's a two-coach bone-shaker, and I stumble down next to a guy eating a blackened banana.

Bath looks beautiful as you approach it. By train or car, it doesn't matter. In sunshine, in rain, or in twilight. My heart contracts as I watch the pale gold buildings through the opposite window, over the heads of an old couple eating biscuits. I check my watch. I'll have time to walk through the city to the hospital.

As I step down from the train, I feel like I've come home, but that cannot be right.

Home is where the heart is.

Home is where my child will be. But my child will be made in Bath, so my heart will be forever here, too.

Another room, another bed, another probe. This time I am in a tiny windowless room. It's dark. I have undressed, and I know my feet and stripy socks are damp. I even apologise to the nurse for my feet.

"I'll just take some measurements," she says.

She *clicks*, and red lines appear on the screen. It seems like the probe has been inside me for hours. I feel sick watching the grey and black flickers, the red lines jabbing across my insides.

"There's your artery."

The nurse indicates a moving grey worm, and I turn away. I'm not squeamish about blood or injections or anything like that, but I'm tired and hungry and thirsty. I reckon my blood sugar has dropped through my boots – or, rather, through my socks.

At last, she pulls out the jellied probe. "OK, get yourself dressed, and come through to the room where you saw Doreen."

"What's the problem?" I ask.

"You can't talk about it half undressed. I'll see you in a moment."

She shuts the door behind her with a *click*. I'm standing alone and half-naked in a dark cupboard with a paper towel in one hand and my knickers in the other. The tiles are icy through my damp socks.

Something's wrong. Something's not working properly. Everything's been going so beautifully. It really is too good to be true.

I still feel sick, but it's no longer because of that wormy little artery or the stretching sensation of the probe. It's deeper than any of that.

The nurse is waiting in the counselling room. She's sitting where Doreen sat. The dismal plant is still on the windowsill. There are crumbs of soil on the sill. Maybe someone watered it, and they dribbled out. There's a box of tissues. Pink this time.

I crumple into the chair.

"It's nothing terrible," the nurse says and even smiles.

Why couldn't she have said that in the cupboard room?

211

"Your ovaries aren't quite ready for the egg collection. Mr Gale started you on a fairly low dose because you live a long way away, and he didn't want you to run into any problems. I've just had a quick word with him, and he wants you to up the dose for a few more days. You'll need another scan next Tuesday to see how things are going."

"So, no egg collection on Monday?"

"Not Monday, no. If we're lucky, maybe later next week."

"The scan … does it have to be here?"

"We would prefer it, but Mr Gale said he can arrange for it to be done in Truro as you have such a long way to come. Again, you'd need to get a report and read it to us over the phone."

"That's fine. I can do that. They will work, won't they? The ovaries?"

"They just need a bit more time."

I nod and think of those books Doreen showed me in this room. Books with pictures drawn by donor babies.

"Have you got a cold bag with you?

"Yes."

"I'll give you the next injection to take home. It must be kept in the fridge. On Tuesday, ring up with your scan results, and we'll tell you if you're ready to use it and exactly what time to use it. It's called an HCG triggering injection."

"Do I see Mr Gale today?"

"He's got other patients, but it'll be him doing your egg collection. Whenever that is."

The nurse leaves me alone for a few moments. When she returns with the syringe, it's in a dark blue sheath. I put it into the cold bag and tug the zip firmly.

This weekend, I feel ill on the increased dose. Not exactly sick, not exactly faint, or headachy, just awful. Chemicals and hormones are seething inside, so I might become a mother. It's a powerful word, *mother*. It suggests someone who has gone through hope and fear and pain to bring forth life.

I wonder if I'll feel stronger as a mother?

Right now, all I can think about is the egg collection. The two words whisper still in my head.

I won't be unconscious. I'll feel it.

I'll feel Mr Gale inserting a needle through the walls of my vagina. I'll feel every sting as he sucks out each egg.

It's only pain, I say silently to myself. Pain can be endured.

"*Both ovaries are enlarged and contain eight follicles,*" I read aloud.

I am ringing Bath from Mum's car in the hospital car park. It is lunchtime, and I have just had the scan. It was a different radiographer this time. A guy.

"*On the left, the largest follicles measure 26mm, 18mm, 17mm, and 16mm. On the right, the largest follicles measure 20mm, 17mm, 17mm, and 15mm. All remaining follicles are sub-centimetre.*"

The radiographer thought I should be ready to go.

The nurse mutters the figures I have just given her.

"Thursday," she says. "We'll do it on Thursday. Do you have a pen and paper? You need to write this down carefully."

Yes, I do have a pen and paper. They're on my knee.

I drop the scan results and pick up the pen. The mobile signal *fizzes*, and I catch my breath, but the line holds.

"You'll have the egg collection at 8.45 on Thursday morning," the nurse starts. "Tonight, you must use the HCG injection at 8.45 exactly. And tonight will be the last time you use the spray. Tomorrow you don't have any drugs. No spray, no injections."

I write this down; the letters are bumpy on my knee. I tell her I will call the clinic again once I am home to check I've got it right. I hang up the call.

In forty-eight hours, it'll be done. My eggs will have been taken and mixed with Rafe's sperm in the lab. Cells dividing, tiny lives forming. Maybe on that day, another woman in another clinic, here or in Denmark or somewhere else, is also having her eggs mixed with Rafe's sperm.

My child might have a donor twin.

The bedroom is on the second floor with sloping walls. There are two single beds with pale green and white covers. There is a radiator, but I am freezing. Shivering, terrified. I sit on the right-hand bed and listen to the traffic *sloshing* through the rain and the *hum* of the bathroom fan. There are voices from somewhere in the house.

The floor below?

Mum comes out of the bathroom.

The fan still *whirrs*.

"OK, let's have some food," she says and unzips the red-and-green patterned cooler bag.

Mum booked us into this bed and breakfast by the hospital. Otherwise, we would have had to drive up through the night to get to the clinic for eight tomorrow morning. I watch her unload paper plates, knives, forks, and beakers onto her bed. Cold chicken, a block of cheese, a Tupperware box of salad, bread rolls, Pepsi, fizzy water. There's a carrier bag leaning against the wall; through its flimsy plastic, I can see crisps and the purple wrappers of Dairy Milk. It's my last meal before the egg collection.

As I bang open a bag of crisps, I feel a sudden calm. I'm here in Bath, with its familiar soundtrack of traffic and ambulances and rain and shouting, and everything will be all right.

At the door to the lab, the nurse asks me to take off my slippers and walk along a red line on the floor. Mr Gale's standing by the bed in surgical blues. I can only see his eyes between his hat and mask. Behind him is a window hatch.

I stand on the red line, the floor clammy under my bare feet, and sign in again with my name and date of birth. It is cold, and I am only wearing a hospital gown. It's off-white, with a repeat pattern in mauve.

I turn away from the woman at the hatch and slide onto the bed. There are two more figures on either side of Mr Gale, masked and gowned, like plague doctors.

Where did they come from?

I never saw them come in.

And I can't be hallucinating. I haven't had any drugs yet.

Mr Gale takes my left hand and cannulates me quickly. I feel cold and exposed lying on the bed. Terrified and calm. His eyes meet mine.

"Here are the drugs to make you forget," he says. "Just go with it."

Beep beep beep beep.

It sounds like a blood pressure machine; there is a terrible pain deep inside me; I open my eyes.

It is a blood pressure machine. The numbers flash in red. There is a curtain pulled around my bed. A small locker. This is where I started. I am back on the ward. My clothes are in that locker.

The pain makes me gasp. I am wet and sticky. I try to sit up, but I cannot move because of the pain. I lie back, awkwardly on my left side, watch the blood pressure screen, and wonder what is happening to my little eggs.

The curtains *swish* behind me, and one of the nurses comes in.

"All done," she says. "All fine."

"I don't remember anything," I say.

I don't. It feels like I have had an anaesthetic, but without the wooziness, the disorientation, the headache.

"Mr Gale took seven eggs," she tells me.

"Seven?" I move too quickly, and pain sears me. I was hoping for more. "I was hoping for more," I say aloud.

"Seven's good. You only need one, don't you?"

She asks me to go to the ladies and then eat something. I sit, ever so slowly, and drop one leg and then another, over the edge. Someone's put my slippers down there. I can't reach them with my toes. I don't think I can drop down because of the pain.

I count to three in my head and slide off the bed. I almost stumble getting my feet into the slippers. My gown slaps wetly against my legs. When I turn round, I see a vast spray of blood on the sheet and more on the mauve patterned gown. I walk slowly, stiffly, out onto the ward, and blood slides out of me and drips in dark tears onto the lino.

When I have eaten – a sandwich, a banana, a small packet of crisps, and a Crunchie – and got dressed, the nurse tells me I can go. I fumble my phone out of my bag to ring Mum. My curtains are open now; opposite me, the curtains are closed around another bed, and I can hear low voices, a woman's and a man's, but I cannot hear what they are saying. There is no signal on the ward, so I *creak* to my feet once more and walk out towards the waiting room with its squashy chairs and water machine. Mum will be waiting at the guest house. She went back to get some breakfast while I had the egg collection. The owner knew I was having something done at the hospital and said Mum could sit in the lounge until I was ready to leave. She is only a few minutes away. Three signal bars appear in the waiting room, and I call her. The nurses will not let me leave the clinic alone.

I drop my rucksack onto a chair while I wait for Mum. I do not sit because it hurts too much. The waiting room is empty, but the radio plays on. I recognise the song, one from my days in Bath. At the desk, the receptionist gazes at her computer screen and then turns round to talk to someone behind her. In my rucksack, I have more drugs. This time it's tubes and tubes of gel I have to insert to make my womb friendly for the coming embryo. I have to start this evening. I don't think about how I can put anything in there right now.

It's a grey, washed-out November morning. It's not raining now, but it looks like it might have done, like it might again. I recall the hazy pastels of the summer garden, the butterflies, the blue sky. Making a baby takes time. The seasons turn. I grow older.

Mum's coming up the path through the garden, brushing the damp bushes with her folded pink umbrella. I hoist the rucksack onto my shoulder and stumble towards the glass doors.

"Give me that bag," she says when she sees me, "and take my arm."

I do. I don't think I have ever had to lean on anyone before, but we shuffle away together, down the damp path, her with her brolly and my rucksack, me hunched over, with every tiny footstep reverberating in the raw pain inside.

I lie on my bed and read the instructions a third time. I shake the tube of progesterone gel, so the contents fall into the tube. I slide the tube inside me. It is cold. It does not hurt as much as I feared. I squeeze the bulb, and the gel shoots out. When I withdraw the tube, it is stained with brown-red blood, but the bleeding has mostly stopped. I lie there a moment while the gel seeps into me, and I imagine a soft, dark lining growing in my womb, gentle as velvet, the colour of wine.

Now there is nothing for me to do but wait for the embryologist's phone call. It will be tomorrow morning at eight o'clock, I was told. Then I will know how many of my seven eggs have been successfully fertilised. I wonder what Rafe's doing right now. Denmark must be an hour or two ahead.

Perhaps he is on a late shift in the hospital ...

I imagine a profile and blond hair, lit by a desk lamp, as he writes in a patient's notes.

Or maybe he's in a bar somewhere, drinking with friends, other medics. Or maybe he's with a girl …

Whatever he's doing, he will not be thinking of me because he does not even know I exist. He doesn't know the desperate hopes I have for his tiny tadpole cells.

"For you." Mum's standing over me with the phone in her hand.

I glance at the clock with gritty eyes. Exactly eight o'clock.

"Miss Knight?"

"Hi, yes, it's me." My voice sounds cracked. I want to reach out for my water, but I have to have this conversation first.

The bed dips as Mum sits down by my feet and wraps her dressing gown tight around her. "It's Lesley, the embryologist at Bath."

"And?" I ask.

I wonder which one was Lesley.

Was she in theatre with me?

"You had seven eggs collected yesterday, and six have fertilised."

I give Mum a thumbs-up.

She exhales and grins.

"I think we're looking at next Tuesday for your transfer," Lesley says. "If things change, we'll call you, but let's say two-fifteen on Tuesday afternoon. We'll put in just the one embryo, and we can freeze the others, providing they're all doing OK."

I hang up the call, shout a silent *thank you* to Rafe, and turn to Mum.

I am in the counselling room again. Someone has cleaned up the spilt soil on the windowsill. The box of tissues is another lime green one. A woman in blues swishes in and *clicks* the door shut.

218

"Hello, I'm Lesley. We spoke on the phone a few days ago." She sits beside me. She's holding my notes and a small piece of paper. "This is your embryo. The one we're going to put in today. Would you like to see it?"

I nod, and she hands me the picture. Then she reaches behind her for the box of Kleenex and puts it where I can reach it.

It is only a small monochrome image. It looks like a perfect circle, with a fine, dark edge. Inside the circle are smudges of light and dark. It's like a planet.

No, a moon. A cratered moon.

Lesley points to the top right of the circle. She is saying something about it having started to send out a shoot, a tiny finger, ready to attach itself to my womb lining.

"There's another embryo very similar to this one," she tells me. "And a couple of others that are also doing well. So you'll have at least three frozen."

"I thought six were fertilised," I say at last.

"The other two … I'm not sure about them. They may not be suitable to freeze."

I cannot stop staring at the tiny moon in my hand. I want to draw it in charcoal and Indian ink. I want to paint it with a diameter of six feet. I want to see it, hold it. I reach out, like the tiny grasping shoot from my embryo, to the box of tissues and tug out a wad.

"Can I keep this?"

"Of course. It's yours."

The picture is mine. And so is the moon, the embryo. Mine.

All mine.

This time, the lab is dark, with a brighter square of light from the hatch. It does not look like the same room. The red line is still on the floor, dulled to a rusty blood colour in the half-light. The local radio plays quietly. I feel strangely relaxed, calm. It might be the Valium or whatever it was they gave me. Or it might be knowing that, in a few moments, a living, viable embryo will be in my womb.

It is the same nurse who did my scan ten days ago. She smiles at me. She looks friendlier, less dragon-like; even her features are softer in this room, this dark-red womb of a room.

"I'll talk you through what I'm doing," she says. "I'll be inserting a catheter through the cervix and then sending the embryo through it."

"I don't want to know," I tell her.

I'll feel it.

The nurse arranges my legs in the stirrups. I concentrate on my breathing.

I wish she would hurry up.

She washes her hands at the corner sink and asks about my journey and who is driving me home.

"Mum's in the waiting room," I tell her. "We're going straight home afterwards."

Because there will be nothing more I can do.

"The first thing I have to do is wash you inside."

I concentrate on the radio ads while she stretches me open like a tight neckline. I remember some of the companies from my days in Bath. Some of the commercials and jingles are the same; some are new.

I look at the ceiling. The tiles have a dark flecked pattern. I study this pattern. I breathe in and out. Something tickles me, deep in that dark core where I could not scratch it away if I even tried.

"Give me that," the nurse says quietly, and I realise she is speaking to someone at the hatch. I can't quite see who it is. It might be Lesley. "You said you didn't want to know, but I think you will want to know the embryo is going in right now."

Right now.

That tiny moon, that cluster of cells.

Suddenly my feet are free, and a paper cloth is draped over me. It is done.

It's done. It's done.

"Thank you," I whisper.

The nurse is tearing her apron behind her neck, folding it up and shoving it into the pedal bin. The bin closes with a hefty *clunk*.

I let my hand slide down to my abdomen.

Hold on, little one. Send out your shoot, your questing fingers, your hook. Find somewhere soft and warm and safe. Stay with me. I love you.

"You can go back to the ward and have a cup of tea now. One of the other nurses will go through what happens next and give you your pregnancy test to take away."

Back on the ward, I take off my gown and get dressed. My cubicle is diagonally opposite from where I lay before. I am next to the cubicle of quiet urgent whispers.

A young nurse brings me a tray of tea and a biscuit, one of those individually wrapped ones that are crunchy and taste of caramel. I pour the dark tea and unwrap the biscuit. I imagine all the muscles around my womb are tense, trying to hold it steady to stop the tiny embryo from falling out.

The young nurse comes back with papers. She sits on the bed beside me and tells me about the two-week wait.

In two weeks, I can take a pregnancy test. If I bleed before then, it doesn't necessarily mean a failure, and I should still take the test. If the test is negative, I can get another one and try again a few days later. It's very early for the hormones to show. Until then, I must avoid strenuous exercise.

I *crunch* the biscuit guiltily. That should not be a problem. I must avoid sex, too. That shouldn't be a problem, either.

And now, it is the only thing I think of, that tiny dot hiding deep inside. I think of it when I wake, when I pull beer in the bar, when I read in bed, all the time. I visualise it swelling and dividing, stronger and stronger. Each day I wake fearful of bleeding and slide my hand beneath my bottom, but my bedding remains dry. I go for short walks: they told me gentle exercise would be safe. I walk to the Lizard and look in the shop windows, mostly closed now for the winter. One day I walk to the Buttress, my head full of the tiny life I'm carrying, and it is just a rocky crag, nothing more and nothing less, and afterwards, I am both happy and sad with that.

Dad dances awkwardly round me. In the bar, he will not let me lift anything heavy. Women's health unnerves him. He is probably remembering the days before Richard, when he and Mum measured out each anxious month with her bleeding womb.

I wonder what Dad thought when Mum told him she was pregnant? Did he really believe it?

Perhaps only as she grew big with me inside her. I have never asked my parents about those days. I do not know if they were hoping for another baby after me or if they decided two was enough: one boy, one girl, one dark, one auburn, one adopted, one theirs.

Years ago, one of my favourite artists was Gustav Klimt. He painted a canvas called *Danae*. In the picture, the princess is lying curled on the floor of her tower prison, copper hair falling over her naked white shoulders, whilst between her legs, Zeus impregnates her with a shower of gold. I imagine sperm as tiny sparkles, more silver than gold, lighting up the dark tunnels of a woman's body. Conception should happen with a supersonic boom; instead, it is silent, slow even, where no eyes can follow.

It's magic, alchemy.

And then IVF. Fertilisation occurs under bright lights, outside the warm protection of the mother. It is watched and assessed. Man creates in the lab the same magic, the same alchemy.

Or is it not more magical, this fusion of egg and sperm, nature and science?

December 2012

I wake in the darkness. The duvet has slipped, and I am cold. My bladder throbs. There is no lightening of the sky in the gap between the curtains. I reach for the alarm clock, drop it, swear, and retrieve it from the floor as gooseflesh blossoms on my arm. It has just gone five o'clock, and today is the day.

As always, I feel under my body for blood. Nothing. I shake the duvet around and snuggle under it again. I cannot take the test just yet. I'm too scared.

I shut my eyes, but they snap open again. The ache in my bladder grows and swells. I do not think I will be able to go to sleep again, but if I get up now, I'll have to do it. It has to be done first thing, when the concentration of hormones is at its strongest.

I slide out of bed, and my teeth *chatter*. I stuff my arms into my bathrobe. The pregnancy test is on the dressing table. I pick it up as I leave the room. It's cold in the corridor. The overnight lamp glows with its weird yellow hue. I shut the bathroom door carefully and quietly.

I've used these kits before. Several times in Bath, in hope and in dread. I remember the first time I bought one, a long-ago summer's day in Helston, with a tearful Zoe waiting on the pavement outside Boots. I think of her in a bathroom I've never seen, watching the lines change and swim before her eyes.

I sit on the lavatory, with the wet white stick on a piece of tissue on the floor. I gaze round the room, looking at everything but that stick. I notice the marks on the mirror, the coloured bottles in the shower, the pale islands on Mum's towel where she once spilt some bleach on it.

I wipe myself and flush. I wash my hands, and still, I don't look down.

I clean my teeth. And then I pick up the frail little wand. There are two blue lines in the window. The control line is thicker and darker, but the second, paler, line is more beautiful.

It's a lifeline.

Mum comes into my room at six-thirty. She is expecting me to be asleep, but I am reading with the lamp on. She stops and looks at me, and I tug my mouth into a serious straight line. Then her eyes fall on the white stick, half wrapped in tissue, on the floor, and she swoops on it. Her cries wake Dad, and he comes blundering in with his receding hair spiky on his head. Mum's dragged me out of bed and is hugging me; Dad shoves her aside to hold me, too.

"Well done, well done," he says into my hair. "I'm so happy for you."

Mum gazes at those two blue lines. "Now there are four of us again."

I ring the clinic as soon as they open and tell them the news. The nurse tells me I need to go for a scan in Truro just before Christmas. The radiographer will need to find a heartbeat. It is overwhelming, that something that tiny would even have a heartbeat. I realise I know so little about the development of babies in the womb. I don't know when it will grow great vessels, bones, organs, limbs, tiny nails.

When does it become a boy or a girl?

225

This time it is like the telly. Cold jelly on my skin. If I could float up out of my body, I would look like all the actresses on telly who have ultrasounds. I would look down and see my pale legs covered with a paper cloth, my head turned on the thin pillow to look at the screen. All that is missing is the guy sitting beside me, leaning forwards to hold my hand and gaze up at the screen with me.

I'll have it like this, on my own, please.

Just me and my little moon.

"There, look," the radiographer says. A different one again, as I am now in the maternity department. "It's about the size of a baked bean now."

I look, but I cannot see anything. The screen is dark and fuzzy. And then, a tiny white dot.

"There, there," I say.

"That's the heartbeat. I'll print you a picture."

It flashes, so tiny and brave in the darkness. It's like Wolf Rock Lighthouse or the flickering of a marker buoy, rocking on the waves.

The screen blurs again, and my throat hurts, and I taste salt, and I realise I'm crying, and for the first time in my life, I think I may be crying with joy.

January 2013

Oranges. There are lots of different sorts. Huge loose ones rolling like planets; middle-sized ones trapped in packs of four; clementines, tangerines, satsumas, easy peelers; some with tiny leaves still attached to make them look Mediterranean and summery amongst the dismal Christmas decorations in Tesco. I put two nets of clementines in the trolley and two packs of bigger, tough-skinned oranges. I stick my finger through the net, rub one of the fruits, and inhale the sharp scent.

I move the trolley on to the potatoes, carrots, and parsnips before I can load up any more oranges. They are all I want to eat at the moment. They help with the nausea.

That smell in the cheese aisle ... That cold, cheesy smell.

I scratch the orange skin again and breathe in. I choose a packet of Brie for Dad. I cannot have Brie now. Nor salami. Nor pâté. And no alcohol. I have not been drinking since I started my IVF. I did not drink over Christmas. What I carry inside is far too precious. I don't mind serving beer and spirits in the bar. It is just something I am not doing at the moment.

Pasta, rice, tins of tomatoes, kitchen paper, bin bags ...

At last, I wheel the trolley into **Confectionery**. There they are, gold and shiny. I drop a four-pack of Crunchies on top of the tea bags. I don't even like Crunchies. I never have. But they remind me of that day, the day my child was conceived.

A loud voice on the tannoy; a guy slams his trolley into mine; a couple of packets fall by themselves to the floor under my wheels. I lean down to shove them back on the shelf, and as I straighten, I feel light-headed and queasy. The list blurs in my hand. Just a few more things.

"Oranges, oranges," I say it like a mantra as I unload the shopping on the conveyor belt and throw things into carrier bags.

As soon as I have pocketed my bank card and club card, I wheel the trolley over to the window and rip one of the bags of clementines with my nails. The net is rough and hurts my fingers, but the cool oval fruit feels wonderful in my hand. The pitted skin splits, and I shove in two segments together. Sweet flesh bursts open in my mouth. I hold the rest of the orange in one hand as I wheel the trolley to the car. I put the open bag of clementines on the passenger seat. I eat another. The sickness subsides. I reach into the back seat and pull one of the carrier bags forwards. It has a set of bodysuits with animals on them. I open the packet and shake one out. It's a little lion. My child's going to be a Leo. Its due date is August 8. The suit is so tiny. I fold it up again and put it into the packet.

So many things to get, and I don't know what I'm having.

Mum has dug out my old cot, but that is only the beginning. I still need a pram, high chair, car seat, clothes, toys, bath, soft towels, creams, and cosmetics.

Today I've made a start, though.

I fire up the ignition, and the radio shouts into the car. All around me is the bittersweet smell of oranges.

My first appointment with a midwife, and I am terrified. Over the years, just that word has made me shrivel inside with fear. Old hags with warty noses, whose idea of pain relief is a chunk of wood to bite on. Or, more likely, these days, bossy nurses ticking boxes on forms and telling you that an epidural will cause your baby to have three heads, and a Caesarean section will kill you, the baby, and everyone you have spoken to in the last fortnight.

The midwife does not come to the little surgery on the Lizard green, so I have to go into Mullion. I gather up all my IVF paperwork. I'm dreading talking to her about that, too. Thirty-six, nearly thirty-seven, no man, body clock ticking, *desperate, desperate, desperate.*

No.

I throw the file down onto the bed. My disloyalty shocks me. That little baked bean inside is the most amazing thing that has ever happened to me, the most amazing thing that will ever happen.

I am not desperate; I made a choice. I am not even that old. I am going to be a mother. I am powerful.

The phone rings. I hear Dad mumbling, saying something about "Yes, this afternoon would be fine, see you then."

"Do you want me to come?" Mum asks as I slip my coat on in the hall.

I think a moment, shake my head. "Not this time. I want to meet her on my own. I've got to talk to her. About the birth."

"Yes. Of course. You stick to it. You can choose nowadays. If she's difficult, you can always find someone else. Don't have a row, just stick with what you want. Your baby, your body, and all that."

"That was a guy interested in renting number fifteen. He's coming up later." Dad squeezes past me to the front door. "Good luck," he calls as he jogs outside.

Number fifteen is our empty caravan. It is a small one, at the far end of the field. Its end window looks straight to the Buttress.

It's a cool blue and white winter day. The moorland is brown and muted. Winter colours always make me want to paint again. The cold white skies, the mud and earth and skeletal twigs. I pass Mullion School on the left. The building has kept its original heart, but there are new bits, new doors and windows. I wonder if any of the teachers I had are still there.

Would they remember me? Would they remember Zoe? Would they remember what happened to Rich?

I feel a strange tug. I want to pull into the car park and walk down the slope to the entrance, which is probably not the entrance any longer. There comes a hazy vision of Zoe breaking down in front of Beth and Jane that day.

That day.

Results day. Richard's day.

Stop it, Knight.

The midwife's name is Tessa. She is about my age with shiny, dark hair in a bob. She's wearing pink jeans.

"So, this is your first baby?"

"Yes," I say. The room's hot. I slide my coat off. I watch her face. "I'm a single mother. I've used donor sperm. From Denmark."

Tessa grins at me. "That's really exciting. Did you have IVF or IUI?"

"IVF. It worked the first time."

I simply can't erase that pride I feel. Pride for myself, Rafe, my clinic, and my baby.

"You're so lucky. First go. You must be really healthy."

Isn't she going to scowl at me, say something about fatherless children growing up to be murderers? Isn't her face going to show her thoughts: No wonder she couldn't get a man looking like that.

She's not. She's asking me about the clinic and why I used Danish sperm rather than British, and suddenly I am telling her the whole story: how my boyfriends would have been useless fathers, how I moved back to Cornwall, how I had already decided I wanted to do it on my own. I tell her how I chose Rafe and how I have three frozen embryos. I tell her how scared I was and how happy I am now.

There are a lot of questions we have to go through. My medical history and what I know about the donor. She asks about my mother's experience of pregnancy, and I tell her I am an only child. I'm the only child my mother carried to term, so it is not a lie.

I am thawing fast. I like Tessa. I like her smile and her laugh. I like her attitude. There's just one thing.

"It's early days, but have you had any thoughts about the birth yet?" she asks.

"Yes. Can we talk about it now, please?"

Let's get it over with.

"Of course." Tessa waits, pen in hand.

"I want a Caesarean," I say.

I imagine my mouth hangs open about to gabble on: my terror, my overwhelming terror of birth and pain, my mother's millions of stitches after me, her haemorrhage.

"I'll need to refer you to a consultant, then," Tessa says.

I splutter.

"If you have a Caesarean, you need to see a consultant, that's all."

"Is … is that it?"

She looks confused.

I blush. "I wasn't expecting you to say that," I mumble at last. "I was expecting you to say, '*No, no, you can't have a Caesarean.*' I'm so frightened about … doing it any other way."

"A lot of ladies choose to do it," Tessa says. "Everyone's different. Some women are terrified about the thought of surgery. I don't have a problem with you having a Caesarean section. The obstetricians are very easy-going about it, too. I don't think you'll have any problems there. You're young and healthy. You have to do what's right for you and the baby. The consultant will give you a date for the birth. It'll be about a week before your due date, all being well."

I feel dizzy. I was expecting to be judged for being a single mother; I was expecting a fight about the Caesarean. But Tessa is lovely, and everything is going so well.

"It's just another way of giving birth," I hear myself say. "Like IVF is just another way of conceiving."

I walk out into the surgery car park with my green folder under my arm. I can hear the shouts of kids in the primary school playground over the road. It is lunchtime. I can sense the first questing finger of nausea coming on. I do not feel it on waking like I thought women did; mine comes on in the middle of the day. There are a couple of clementines on the passenger seat. Before I drive off, I eat one. The juice soothes my stomach like medicine.

My IVF worked the first time. I like my midwife. I can have a Caesarean with no arguments.

I grin to myself.

Everything is good.

As I roar up past the secondary school again, I see some dark figures kicking a football on the top field.

No, better than good.

I can almost believe that I might meet a decent man now. That is all that's missing.

"What happened with the guy?" I ask Dad later in the bar.

It is cold and dark; the bar is quiet. Mum has not had to cook anything yet. She is reading at a table by the heater. I have the local paper spread out on the bar and a biro in my hand.

"What guy?" he asks.

"The guy who wanted number fifteen."

232

"Oh, yes. He's taking it."

"What's he like?"

"Young. Early twenties, I think. He's working at the Lighthouse."

"The lighthouse?"

"The restaurant. He's a chef."

The Lighthouse is the restaurant at the Lizard. In recent years it has been renovated, re-named. It's been reviewed in the *Saturday Times*.

"He said he was renting a room off someone at the moment, but he gave me a deposit – in cash – and said he'll move in at the weekend."

I turn back to the motoring page. I need a car of my own. It's my birthday coming up. I circle an ad for a Ford Fiesta and one for a Getz. I would prefer an Audi TT, but sadly that is out of the question and probably not the sort of car for a new mother.

It's extraordinary that word, *mother*. I never thought it would apply to me. It seemed as unlikely to mean me as *man* or *dwarf* or *size 8*. I cannot feel anything inside me yet, no movement or fluttering, no swelling or hardness, but I know it's there, that tiny beacon flashing with each heartbeat, splitting and dividing and growing, becoming stronger each day. My constant companion.

A Vauxhall Corsa and a VW. I do not know anything about cars. I want something cheap and safe and not too ugly. I shove the paper at Dad and ask him to take a look.

I see the new bloke moving in on Sunday afternoon. Dad and I are going to Mullion to look at the Getz I had circled in the paper. Dad had rung up about it and spoken to the owner, asking all the stuff about miles per gallon, miles on the clock, MOT, and so on. It turned out the owner knew a friend of Dad's who had lived in one of our caravans for a while after his divorce. As we walk out towards Dad's car, a shabby red hatchback comes up the drive.

Dad waves.

I see the driver raise a hand.

"That's him." Dad zaps his keys at the car, and it *beeps* as the locks release.

"Who?" I ask.

"Number fifteen."

"What's his name?" I have heard it before but forgotten.

"Nathaniel Winter."

I do not think about Nathaniel Winter over the next few days. Dad and I both liked the Getz. I took it for a test drive round Mullion. It was silver and small, but there would be room for a baby seat in the back. It had recently been cleaned and valeted; it did not smell of dogs or cigarettes or those smelly hanging up things. It was fine, and I managed – nervously – to offer just under what the owner was asking.

A couple of days later, Mum suggests she and I take it up to Truro and do some baby shopping.

"A lot of the big things we can get online," she says. "Things like a buggy, a bath, a car seat, and a playpen, but we could start by having a look at them in the shops and making notes. We could get some more bodysuits, socks and mittens, blankets."

Isn't this too early? I ask myself. *My little one isn't safe yet. There's a long way to go.*

Then I open my bedside drawer, where I once kept my secret bottle of folic acid, and look at the small, curling photograph from that first scan. I remember the bright flash of the tiny heartbeat on the screen, but the picture is dark and grainy and, without the radiographer to guide me, I struggle to make out much. It must be a little bigger now. A little stronger. That frail reaching hook, like an eyelash, has taken a firm hold on my womb. I still use the progesterone gel each evening; I hope my little baked bean, my little moon, does not find that sudden squirt too cold.

I put the picture safely away. I must get used to my new car. And there are so many things I need to buy I should start immediately. The time will race by, and nearer the birth, the weather will be hot and heavy, and I will be hot and heavy, and everything must be ready.

It is mid-afternoon when we return with a boot full of shopping: newborn bodysuits and tiny white socks, scratch mittens, cot sheets, cellular blankets, half a dozen bottles and a steam steriliser, even nappy bags, shampoo, baby oil, and the first packet of nappies.

As I lock up the car, I glance down the caravan field. The sky is pewter and clotted with clouds. It's getting dark, and it's going to rain. I can see the small red car parked beside number fifteen at the end of the row. I jog up the path to say hello, introduce myself. There are no lights on in the caravan, no noise from the TV or radio. I knock on the door, but there is no answer. I cup my hands and squint into the living area. It's dark in there, but I can make out a jumper or jacket thrown down on the bench, a couple of books, some CDs, a pair of trainers on the floor.

He must be at work. He must walk there.

That was why I thought he must be in, because the car was there.

I peer quickly into the car, too – it's a Suzuki Swift – and see only an empty CD case on the passenger seat and a water bottle in the back. There are not any stickers or nodding dogs or dangly things.

I shrug. Mum must be wondering what I am doing. I run back to the house as the first cold raindrops fall.

It is Saturday night, and I am behind the bar. Dad's got a cold and is at home. Mum comes out of the kitchen with two plates of scampi and chips for a couple in the window seat. I have a bag of clementines with me just in case, but at the moment I'm feeling OK. There are a few of our regulars drinking beer and people from the caravans. A guy from the Lizard – someone Rich knew so many years ago – is playing pool with a giggling blonde. Through the square windowpanes, the night is dark. There is a white flare of light as a car comes down the drive – one of the residents heading out.

The front door opens, and a guy comes in. He is wearing a hoodie and jeans. He stands a moment, watching the pool game, or maybe the blonde bending over in skinny jeans, then he shoves back his hood and comes up to the bar. I have not seen him here before. He's very young with a straggly dark ponytail. Under the hoodie, he seems to be wearing about three layers. He asks for a lager. The cold froth spills on my hand as I place it on the bar. He hands me a fiver. He has long, thin fingers. I imagine he is meeting friends here and that he will take his drink to one of the tables; instead, he pulls along a bar stool. He glances round the bar, back to the pool table and the blonde, who is now drinking her vodka, at the scampi couple talking quietly together, at a group of three guys crowding over one mobile phone and swiping through photos.

It's horrible being first in a bar, especially one you do not know. I did it a few times in Bath. Steve – the one who forgot to tell me he was married – asked me to meet him in a pub in a part of Bath I didn't know. I walked there and arrived early and ordered a glass of red. I was the only girl there, and I sat at a wet, beery table on my own, shrinking into my coat, which I kept on in case I wanted to run away, and felt the eyes of all the drinkers on me. I must have been there nearly fifteen minutes before Steve turned up.

"You come far?" I ask the young bloke.

"Sorry?"

"Have you come far? I don't think I've seen you here before."

"Not far. I'm renting one of the caravans."

Of course. Number fifteen.

"Nathaniel?"

"Nate."

"I'm Emily. Is everything OK in the caravan? I hear you're working at the Lighthouse?"

"Yes," he says carefully.

"Are you new to the area?"

"I've been here since New Year." He drinks lager and avoids my eyes.

Rich's old friend comes to the bar for another round. I walk away from Nate Winter to get the drinks. I glance back once, and this time, he is looking at me.

"Can I have another?" Nate nods to his empty glass and fumbles in his pocket for change.

"Have you been to the Lighthouse?" he asks.

I'm surprised he's asked me anything.

"Many years ago. It was different then."

"You grew up here?"

"Since I was eleven. Tell me about the Lighthouse now. What's the food like?"

"It's good. The chef's really creative. He's designing a new menu for the season. A new range of fish dishes, more vegetarian stuff, and some really fab desserts."

For a moment, I sense a spark. A passion. I imagine this young man chopping herbs, tasting sauces, arranging delicate confections of berries and spun sugar.

Well, no.

He can only be the junior chef, the dogsbody, but he's a dogsbody with a vision.

"Have you been to Cornwall before?"

He hesitates. "Once when I was a kid. I don't remember much."

I can't place him. He's not from round here, but his voice doesn't give anything away.

He stands up to leave and fiddles with the zip of his hoodie.

I wipe up some spilt beer from the bar.

"You say you grew up here," he says in a rush. "Do you remember what happened at this caravan park?"

I stop wiping. The cloth is cold and wet under my hand.

"What happened?" I repeat.

"Yeah, there was a murder or something. Back in the nineties."

"There wasn't a murder," I say.

"Oh. It was something one of the waitresses said. I must have got it wrong. Night then."

He pulls on his hood and shambles away to the door. The automatic light comes on as he steps outside, and I can just see him walking away towards the caravan field. The light expires, and it's dark out once more. I am still holding the wet, beery cloth.

I rinse my hands. Suddenly I feel the need for an orange, and I start peeling one of the clementines roughly, angrily. He was talking about Rich. Something a waitress said. He could only have been a kid at the time. I shove in a segment of orange.

Shit.

He said he had come to Cornwall as a child; perhaps the waitress thing was a lie, and he was staying here with his family when Rich died. He might have seen the police and the ambulance, heard us all crying and shouting. Maybe his parents didn't explain what had happened, and he still thinks there was a murder that day.

I wonder if I should have said anything more.

It is a cold, dry afternoon. I wrap a scarf round my neck and set off down the drive. I only have to walk along the main road for a very short distance before I reach the first grey houses of the Lizard. The

238

village green is churned up with mud and scrubby grass. A few cars are parked there, despite the cold and the time of year. I walk on, past the green, the surgery, and the pub on my right. The gift shop is closed with blinds drawn; the café is open but empty. I wish I had brought gloves. I stuff my hands into my coat pockets. The coat is big on me as I have lost weight these early months.

Maybe it's the orange diet.

I see the sign hanging motionless from its pole. The depiction is not of the Lizard lighthouse with its twin towers but a tall, skinny, improbable structure. The restaurant is set back a little from the road, behind a paved terrace, bare except for a few ornamental trees in huge pots. I can see lights on inside the restaurant and just about make out a group of diners at a window table. Below the hanging sign, there is a menu on a clear-fronted board. **The Lighthouse** it says at the top, and there's the same skinny scribbled drawing of a tower.

Smoked salmon and fennel salad; langoustines in garlic; chicken with cream and tarragon; asparagus and lemon risotto; cannon of lamb with parsnip puree; mint and green tea sorbet; vanilla crème brûlée.

I think of Nathaniel Winter and wonder if he is in there right now and what he's doing. It is slightly different from the pizzas and chips we serve in the club.

The restaurant door opens, and two couples come out. One of the women is buttoning up her coat; one of the men is checking his phone.

I turn away and walk down the lane towards the lighthouse, the real lighthouse. The wind gulps at my face, and I taste the cold and the brine.

I have lived in stasis for so long, and now each day, my body is changing. I can see it in strange, subtle ways in the mirror. My skin is clearer, and my hair is growing. I am thinner.

Not for long, I think ruefully, not that it matters.

I wonder how it'll feel when I'm big and swollen in the July heat, when little feet stretch the skin of my stomach as they kick.

I cannot wait to find out.

On Sunday, I walk the other way, northwards along the coast path to Kynance. The sky and sea are grey, blurring imperceptibly on the horizon. Marbled white currents swirl over the underwater skerries. The offshore islands at Kynance look vast and black and uncompromising: the tall fang of Gull Rock, the squatting hulk of the Bishop, the sloping shoulders of Asparagus Island. On my right, the moorland stretches, brown and scrubby, to the main road.

I wonder what creatures live there foraging in the hard winter soil.

At Kynance, I turn round and head for home. My left ear stings with sudden warmth out of the wind. I walk fast because it is cold, and I am starting to feel queasy. It's the time of day, and probably the gaping drop to the ocean and the rise and dip of the steely breakers.

Someone is up on the Buttress. Standing where Rich stood.

Where Rich fell.

For a second, I want to cry out. It's a bloke in jeans and a hoodie. The gate to our caravan field is open. I always close it and check it; someone has come in or out since I went walking.

Instead of going into the field, I fasten the gate and start towards the Buttress. The guy jumps down from the crag to the muddy grass.

Yes, I was right. It's him. Nathaniel Winter.

I stop, suddenly embarrassed that I have caught him there. He stops, too, and watches me. There is a straggle of dark hair falling out of his hood. We stand there, both of us, before the rock. It can only be for a few seconds, but my brain hurts with memories. I forge through the grasses and half-dead twines of foliage until I'm standing in front of him.

"It wasn't a murder," I say.

240

He pushes the stray hair inside his hood and says nothing. He has grey eyes. Grey like the sea and the sky. Grey like rock. Hard. Flinty.

"It wasn't a murder," I repeat. "It was an accident." I gesture towards the Buttress. A squall of rain hits me in the eyes, and they sting. "It was my brother."

He says nothing.

"My older brother, Richard. He fell off this rock. He died. It wasn't a murder."

Nathaniel turns around, looking at the crag or the sea. I don't know why I am having this conversation with a stranger on the cliff while rain falls like cold tears.

"I think you should know because I really don't want anyone asking Mum about it. She gets very upset."

"Yes, of course," he says into the wide gape of the bay.

I'm cold and wet, and I want an orange. I don't know whether to walk away.

"It's raining. Let's go," he says at last, as if we had walked out to the Buttress together.

We don't speak until we reach his caravan.

"Are you working tonight?" I ask him.

"No. I don't do evenings at the moment."

"Do you fancy a game of pool then?"

"In the bar?" He nods towards the clubhouse.

"Well, yeah. If you'd like. I'll be there."

"All right. I'll see you later. He unlocks the door. "Emily."

I stamp off down the gravel path, noting, as I always do, the rainwashed colours: pink, white, black, gold, and silver.

He remembered my name.

And now he knows about Rich.

If I have a boy, do I call him Richard?

241

Mum has not said anything about this, but I am sure she would like it to be a middle name. I do have a list of names in my bedside drawer. Names for boys and names for girls. Names that I have always liked, and some that have just come to me.

The decision will be mine – like all the decisions. I will not have some husband wanting to call our daughter after his mother, or our son after a foreign footballer or anything ridiculous like that.

"I met Nathaniel on my walk today," I tell Dad behind the bar. "I asked if he wanted to come and play pool for a bit tonight."

"With you, you mean?"

"Yes, obviously me." I am stung that he thinks I have become so insular, so defensive, that no one wants to play pool with me. At least, that is how it feels.

"What did he say?"

"He said he would. I don't know if he will. I just felt sorry for him. He's only a young guy and new down here and doesn't know many people. I don't know why he'd want to live here, really."

Nathaniel seems so young and alone. Perhaps I see my own isolation mirrored in him.

"He must have his reasons."

"He said he only moved to Cornwall in the New Year," I say.

"He came for the job."

"Where did he come from?"

"Oh, uh, Worcester, Hereford, somewhere like that."

I move away from Dad to serve a man at the bar. He is one of the regulars from the Lizard. I have known him since we moved here. He and his first wife, then his second, and now the woman he's with tonight.

Why would a young chef take a job at the end of the world just like that and move into a chilly caravan on a cliff? A family row? A broken heart? Something or someone he wanted to escape from? Or was it simply that he thought it'd be the first step on the path to being another Rick Stein?

I hand over the change, and the customer takes his two drinks away.

I sip my own glass of water.

Dad at my elbow. "Here's your date for the evening. See what you can get out of him. He was really evasive with me."

"Still on for a game?" Nathaniel asks me.

"Definitely. Drink?"

"Half of Stella, please."

I lift up the bar flap and follow him, my water glass in my hand. He puts his beer on a free table, the one in the window, and chucks his hoodie onto the seat. He's wearing jeans, the same pair he wore on the cliff, and a long-sleeved black T-shirt. His hair's loose tonight. He whips the triangle off the light and racks the balls with a quick *clatter*.

"You can break," he says.

I choose a cue from the rack – the one with the scratched handle is the straightest, I know – and rub the dusty square of blue chalk over the tip. The dry chalk, the cue's worn shine, the tacky surface of a white ball handled too often. The same sensations, the same moves I've been dancing for years.

"Do you like it down here?" I ask, straightening up and glaring at the yellow I have carelessly left over a corner pocket.

"It's fine." He whacks the yellow in. He's left-handed.

Rafe is left-handed.

"I haven't seen much of anywhere. Just the restaurant, Tesco, not much else," he says.

"Had you been looking for work down here for a while?"

He's missed the next yellow.

"Yeah, for a while. I … needed to get away. I like being on my own. I'm not scared of going somewhere new. I don't know how long I'll stay. It depends on … stuff."

Yes, I was right. He wanted to escape. If he can mend the family rift, or get over the lost girl, or whatever it is, he'll probably disappear back to wherever.

"Where were you living?" I ask.

"The Lizard."

"I meant before."

"Oh. Near Worcester. You could have got that one in if you weren't talking."

I mutter into my drink as he sinks another yellow. He wins the frame; two of my reds are still on the baize.

"So, you grew up here at this holiday park, and, what, you never wanted to move, see anywhere else?" He racks the balls again.

"I did move away. I went to university in Bath. I came back last year."

"Isn't Bath more interesting than the Lizard?"

"It's different."

"And you're happy now you are back here?" He breaks off; the white rolls into the corner. He pulls a rueful face. The ball rumbles down to the hole at the baulk end. He scoops it out for me.

"Yeah," I say. "I am."

And at that moment, I almost tell him why. I almost tell him what I have not shared with anyone else.

It is three-thirty in the morning, and I am awake, sitting up in bed with my laptop buzzing quietly on my knees. Its screen is the only light in the room, and it's starting to make my eyes ache. I have been reading online articles about donor babies born to single women. For every happy photograph of a smiling mother cuddling a pink infant,

244

there are dark comments about fatherless children, the immorality of it, the destruction of the family, the cruelty of having a child who cannot know its roots.

What's wrong with these fucking people?

I shouldn't read this shit, I know that, and if I do, I should shrug off the ignorance and bigotry. Instead, I should gaze at the fluffy-haired babies in their mothers' arms and think, *That woman will be me.*

Perhaps they can't help it. Perhaps it really is something you can't understand unless it has happened to you, like watching your brother fall through the mist. One article says that donor babies will always know they were not conceived in love.

What? What the fuck?

My hand has gone to my womb. I can't feel anything, but I imagine the warmth of my love seeping through skin and muscle.

How many people are conceived in love? Lust maybe, drunkenness, apathy, anger, desperation, even dislike. But love?

I know exactly which babies are: the donor babies.

Yes, they're conceived in a laboratory, not in the crimson darkness of a woman's body, but they're still made of love. Two tiny cells of love.

I picture even the embryologists cheering on the little bundles as they grow. These are the wanted children, children of parents who would do anything to feel that love. Donor conception is the greatest act of love I can imagine.

An hour later, and I am still awake. The house is freezing. My hot-water bottle has gone cold and flaccid long ago. I kick it to the floor and find a pair of woolly socks. The curtains are half-open. I stand there, almost mesmerised by the cold. The roof of the garden shed sparkles with a frosting of ice.

Nathaniel Winter.

245

Dad's right: our guest doesn't give much away. We played two frames of pool. I won the second: Nathaniel said he let me. He does seem self-sufficient. Still, when I first moved to Bath, I was his age or younger. He just seems young because I am no longer young.

It was surely easier for me, though.

I was on a degree course where everyone was new, and we were all finding and discarding friends. Rachel was one of the first people I met on the first day. It must be so much harder when you move somewhere for a job, a job in a small place like the Lighthouse. A place at the end of the world.

How can Nathaniel meet people and make friends? I wonder.

Maybe he does not want to.

A few days later, he comes into the bar in the evening. I hand him half a Stella. He shrugs off his hoodie and hooks a bar stool with his foot.

"Are you going to be a chef?" I ask him. "Like, with your own restaurant? Is that the idea?"

"Yes. You have to start at the bottom, but that's the general idea."

"Mum did some catering training a long while ago. She does the meals here. Not like the Lighthouse stuff."

He grins and nods towards the blackboard. "I like scampi. I like pizza. I like burgers."

"Have you been to catering college or whatever it's called?"

"When I left school. I knew what I wanted to do. I'd been working in a café for a while by then. It pissed me off because I could already see what they were doing wrong, how they could make things better, but they weren't going to listen to a squirt of sixteen."

"There are loads of good restaurants in Cornwall. At least, I hear they're good. I hardly ever eat out. Maybe there'll be an opening somewhere. The Lighthouse or somewhere else."

"I don't know how long I'll be here."

I recall he said something similar before.

"You were lucky to get the Lighthouse job."

"Yeah. I'd finished at college, and I was working in a pub in Worcester but looking out to move."

"D'you miss home? Your family? I felt quite wobbly when I first moved to Bath. Even though I was at university, and we were all in the same boat."

"Families." He laughs. "They fuck you up, your families. Someone said that."

"Larkin," I tell him. "*They fuck you up, your mum and dad.*"

"That's it. Have yours?"

"What, fucked me up? God, no." I stop.

I do not have to ask: his have, and hence why he's on the run.

"Pool?" he asks.

I turn to Dad at the end of the bar.

"OK to play pool?"

"Sure." He grunts.

I whisk away Nathaniel's empty glass, smeared with cold lager froth, and help myself to three segments of clementine hidden behind the bar. When I get to the table, he has already racked up the colours and taken out the white.

"I won't let you win tonight," he says. Then, "You smell of oranges."

I do not see Nathaniel for a week or so. He does not come into the bar. I miss playing pool with him and talking about nothing. I have not learnt much about him or how his parents have fucked him up. He told me he is the oldest of three, but he didn't tell me the others' names or anything about them and swiftly changed the subject. He is good at that. If I pry too much or ask him something he doesn't want to explore, he simply starts talking about something else.

I hope I haven't upset him, this prickly young man.

"Have you been dumped?" Dad asks me one night.

A letter comes for me from the hospital. Well, it is not a letter as such; it's a computer printout, offering me an appointment with an obstetrician in early February. I write the time in my diary. It's the day after an appointment with Tessa, my midwife. And before that, I have a scan at the end of January. There are so many appointments to keep, so much involved in making a person.

I have walked in a circle: down the main road to the Lizard and back along the coast path, above Bishop's Cove to home. Already the afternoons are longer and lighter. I pass the Buttress, and then there is the gate to our field. Nathaniel's car is parked outside his caravan, as it almost always is. I *click* the gate shut and glance over to his windows. He is standing there in the grey half-light of the van, staring out towards the Buttress.

I wave, embarrassed, and start walking.

"Emily."

I stop and turn. "Hi."

He's standing on the top step of the caravan. His hair looks wet and ragged, like he has just had a shower. He's wearing bright red socks; no shoes.

I take a few steps towards him. "How are you? Not seen you for a while."

"Sorry. I've been tired."

"No worries."

"Tea?"

"What?"

"Cup of tea? I'm just having one."

"OK, thanks."

I haven't upset him, I think and am ridiculously pleased.

He stands aside for me in the doorway. The gas fire is on, with jumping blue-orange flames. He *snaps* on the lights.

"Sit yourself down." He gestures to the diamond-patterned settle in the big window.

I sit and notice the angle of the Buttress, how it's framed in the window.

This is what he looks out on every day.

"Here you go." He appears at my side with a mug of tea.

"Thanks, Nathaniel."

"Nate. Please. Nathaniel's just ridiculous."

"I think it's a nice name," I start.

If I hadn't met Nathaniel Winter, it might well be on my own list in the bedside drawer.

"Do you want me to shut the curtains?" he asks.

I do not understand. "Why?"

"Because of … the rock."

I smile and drink tea. It's too hot.

"It's fine," I tell him. "I see it every day. Long time ago, before Rich's accident, I painted it a lot, drew it. Different styles, different ways. I was just looking at it now and thinking I might have another go one day."

Nate slides onto the settle opposite me and picks up a mug from the table.

"What happened?"

"With Rich?"

"Yeah. Will you tell me?"

"It's not a secret. I only said what I did because of Mum."

Two hikers are striding down the gentle slope from the Buttress towards our gate. The man has a staff and bright rucksack.

"It was the day we got our GCSE results."

He fiddles with his watch.

"A friend had come back here with me. Her name was Zoe."

Nate's watching the hikers as they pass the gate.

"She was my friend and Richard's girlfriend. Sort of. They'd been having a thing over the summer. I wasn't that happy about it. I felt excluded. It pissed me off. Zoe was up here a lot, and I was left out. Anyway, she came here with me because she had to talk to Richard urgently. She was pregnant, you see, with his baby."

Nate flicks his grey eyes to my face, then away again.

"She was sixteen. He was nineteen. He was about to go away to university."

"What was he going to do? At uni?"

"Geology."

"Where was he going?"

"Exeter. Not far from us, but too far for Zoe. Her parents were … very religious."

Nate snorts.

"You laugh, but—"

"I'm not laughing."

"They were religious, and Zoe getting pregnant, well, it was the worst thing that could happen, so she didn't tell them. She thought they would make her give up the baby. They didn't believe in abortion, but they would have found her an embarrassment, as a single mother."

I stop. My hand has fallen to my abdomen once more.

Different people; different times.

"Zoe was trying to get Rich to marry her."

"He didn't want to?"

"No. He wanted to go to uni. I think she was just a bit of fun to him, but she loved him and thought he could be a way out from her family. So, she and I came up here. Richard had been drinking. He was in a foul mood. Zoe was getting desperate. She knew she would have to come clean about the baby, and she wanted to know that Rich would stand by her. But he didn't. He told her to have an abortion. It all got out of hand. He ran off. It was a foggy day. The foghorn was going. You won't have heard it. It's changed since then. It had a terrible noise. Zoe and I ran after him. He was on the Buttress. '*Leave me alone,*' he said. And then he'd gone, and it was just us screaming, and the foghorn, and beneath all that, just silence."

"He fell."

"He fell," I repeat. "He didn't jump. I saw it. I saw him fall."

"I'm sorry."

"It's OK." I realise I am holding my hot mug. I put it down with a hard *thunk*. Maybe I'm shaking. "I've told a few people before, but not here. Not with it, the Buttress, just there."

"It must have been terrible." Nate jumps up.

I watch him pacing up and down. Faded grey jeans, black hoodie with a red-and-purple design on the back, red socks, hair on his shoulders loose, damp.

"What happened to Zoe? Did she have the baby?"

"Yes," I say, startled by myself. Now I have to tell him how I know this. "Afterwards, Mum and I tried to get in touch with Zoe through her parents, but they wouldn't let us see her. They said there wouldn't be a baby in our lives, and we should forget it. We never heard anything. Then, in 1999, there was the eclipse, do you remember? You'd only have been young. The eclipse. Anyway, I was down here for it with some friends, and I saw her. Zoe. And the child. It was a boy, a little boy. She had a girl, too. She said she would write to me. She never did."

"Perhaps she didn't know what to say."

I shrug.

"Do you know for sure it was him? Richard's son?"

"He was the right age. The girl was too young."

"You've never told anyone he exists? Not even your parents?"

I shake my head. "I couldn't on the day. My friends were here. There was a big party. And then … what was the point? Zoe never wrote to me. Mum would've been heartbroken all over again."

"So, you have a nephew?"

"Not a full one. Rich was adopted. I wasn't, but he was, so we weren't blood relations. But yes, he's still my nephew, as far as I'm concerned."

I stand up, turn my back to the Buttress, and find my legs are wobbly.

"I should be going." I don't ask if he will come to the club tonight. I know he won't.

"I'm sorry about your brother."

Suddenly the walk through the field seems insurmountable. I am drained by my words, by my memories, by the past, and the present, and the future, the way they blur and chase each other.

"Are you OK?"

I jump at his hand on my arm. "Yes, yes. It's never easy talking about it. That last bit. About what happened at the eclipse."

"I won't say a word. I promise."

"My parents would never forgive me for not telling them."

"It's all right."

The nausea is sliding around in my guts again. I need an orange. I imagine the sharp scent rising from the split peel, but all I can smell is the gas fire and whatever shampoo Nate Winter has just used on his hair.

Mint maybe, or tea tree.

"Should I walk you back? I can get some shoes."

"Really. I'm fine."

"I feel guilty."

"Whatever for?"

"I asked you."

We stand there, the two of us in the small caravan, with the gas fire spitting.

He puts an arm round me. "Thank you for telling me."

His words fall somewhere into my hair, and I am shocked at how it feels to have his arm around me, to feel that intimacy with a man after so long. I don't know what to do.

Feebly I flutter a hand at his back, and I feel the red-and-purple pattern on his hoodie. It has a different texture, a harder, shiny texture. Then we have broken apart, and my hand is on the door latch. Cold air sucks in as I open the door. For a second, I think I might just throw up.

"I'll see you," he calls as I start away across the grass to the gravel path.

"See you," I echo, but I don't look back at him or the Buttress.

It is darker now in the falling light.

Nathaniel Winter has screwed up my sleeping. Before I met him and started playing pool with him, I was sleeping fine. It is now four in the morning, and I am in the kitchen with a jumper and furry robe over my T-shirt. I'm drinking tea and half-heartedly doing the Sudoku in the paper. I have put two fives in one of the three-by-three boxes, and I rub it out with the stubby grey eraser on the end of my pencil. I rub too hard; the flimsy paper tears.

"Shit," I say aloud.

The wall clock ticks on; the cooker clock's neon figures change.

I should never have told him about Richard. I should never, ever, have told him about seeing Zoe and her boy at the eclipse.

That is the secret I have held next to my heart all these years. I've kept it from my family, who should have known, and now I've told

some guy I hardly know just because we play pool sometimes and because—

I stop and drink the last of my tea and grimace because it's cold
and slimy. I *click* off the light and pad back down the chilly corridor
to my room.

Colours squeeze through the greys and browns and khakis of winter. When I look out into the back garden, there is a narcissus with
three or four bright heads, the colour of egg yolks. There are half-hid-
den snowdrops, white and green. Blue leaches into the pale sky. The
seasons are turning as my baby grows, and on the last day of January,
I go back to the hospital for a scan.

Mum comes with me this time. On the grainy screen, I see it. A curled-
up fish, a tadpole. Huge head, tiny folded legs, like frogs' legs. White
dashes mark its spine. It looks both human and alien.

Mum sniffs a bit and squeezes my hand.

The radiographer gives me another flimsy piece of paper. Two photographs: in the top one, I can clearly see the profile of the head; the
second shows the beautiful curve of the spine, like a chain of pearls.

February 2013

I am thirty-seven today. I do not feel it. When I look in the mirror these days, I notice there are feather lines round my eyes, but I don't think I look old. I don't think I will look that much older than the other mothers in the park or at the school gates. I rub olive oil over my abdomen every day. There is nothing to see yet, but if I lie on my front, I think I feel a hard marble low down in my pelvis.

My birthday is a Sunday, the night Nate often comes to the bar. I have not seen him since he asked me into his caravan. I've avoided that end of the field, the coast path, and the Buttress. He works day shifts at the restaurant, he told me. Early starts but home by mid-afternoon. I wonder what he does in that cold caravan.

Watch films maybe, listen to music, sleep.

One afternoon when I was taking some rubbish to the wheelie bins at the back of the club, I looked up the field, and his car had gone from its parking space.

My cards are on the mantelpiece – from Mum and Dad, a few family members on Mum's side, Rachel and her children in Wales, Sonia and Gary and their two.

I open up my Facebook, and there are messages from other people: secretaries I worked with in Bath, a girl who once lived in the flat below me, people from school, including Jane and Beth. I type **Nathaniel Winter** into the search. Nothing. **Nate Winter** then. I'm startled when an entry appears. There's a long photograph of a country landscape – I've no idea where, back where he's from probably – and a profile picture of him. It must have been taken a while ago because he looks so young. His hair is in a ponytail, so I cannot see how long it is. He is wearing a bright patterned T-shirt. It was taken outdoors somewhere: there's blue sky and part of a building. I can't see anything about him, any information or details of his friends because he has closed his profile. I hover my finger on the mouse pad.

No, I can't add him. I hardly know him.

Mum and Dad have gone to the club. They said I could stay at home, have a rest, watch a DVD, eat more of the gorgeous cake Mum has made.

Alone in the house, I am restless. I don't put my feet up. I don't watch a DVD. I do eat cake. I hear the *rumble* of wheels and see head-lamps as cars come up the drive to the bar. A couple of cars go the other way, leaving the site.

I clean my teeth and brush my hair. I wrap a green velvet scarf round my neck and check my pockets for the house key. It is cold and dark outside. I tilt my head to the stars. They are like hundreds of tiny embryos blinking and pulsing in a giant womb.

I hear the *crunch-crunch* of someone walking across the gravel in the caravan field. They are not carrying a torch. I stop where I am, in the car park, and wait.

"Hi," he says and walks towards me in the half-light from the bar.

"Hi," I say, and though it is an icy-cold night, I can suddenly smell the gas fire and the astringent fragrance of his shampoo again, feel the texture of his hoodie under my hand. The jolt of my heartbeat.

"How are you?" I ask lamely.

"Fine. You?"

"It's my birthday."

I don't know why I said that.

"Oh. Well, happy birthday, then. Why are you spending your birthday in a car park?"

I gesture to the club. "I was just going in. I was at home."

"Not out partying?"

"I don't have anyone to party with."

"You'll have to party with me. I'll let you win tonight."

Nate opens the door for me. Dad looks up from the bar where he's pulling a pint for someone. I see the surprise on his face – quickly subdued.

"What are you drinking?" Nate asks.

"Just fizzy water."

"It's your birthday."

"Yeah, but still, just fizzy water."

"Probably just as well – with your pool playing."

What am I going to tell you, little baby? That while you were growing from a baked bean to a frog, while your spine lengthened into that pearly chain, I was playing pool with a man more than ten years younger than me? Worse than that, how when I saw him coming out of the darkness, I felt something soar inside?

I rack the balls and hook the triangle back onto the light. I squat down to retrieve the cue ball. I don't look at Dad as I straighten. Nate is coming over with the drinks. I chalk my cue and break off. A yellow hovers in the jaws of a pocket, doesn't sink.

"That was silly," he says.

"I was playing pool before you were even thought of," I say.

He pots the yellow, straightens, chalks his cue. "I guess you probably were."

I drink water, waiting to see if he's going to ask me how old I am. He tries a plant into the middle pocket, misses. He doesn't ask.

"What did you get for your birthday?"

"A few bits and pieces. Books and stuff. Money for the car."

"What car you got?"

"The silver Getz."

"Sexy."

"Better than a Suzuki Slow, I mean Swift."

We are down to the black. It has ended up hard against the cushion, a foot or so from the white. Easy for a left-hander. He *whacks* it in.

"You said you'd let me win," I protest.

"That was before you were so rude about my car."

He hooks the cues in the rack and sprawls in the window seat. An image in my mind: Richard and Zoe playing pool, Richard standing behind her, holding the cue with her.

"Hey. Hello." Nate's waving his hand in front of my face.

I crumple on the settle beside him, my back to the window. Mum's behind the bar saying something to Dad. I watch them absently.

"You miss Richard on your birthday? And Christmas and that?"

"I think if he were alive now, he'd probably be living abroad somewhere, and I'd be lucky to get an email on my birthday."

"It's mine next month."

"Will you be going back to see your family?"

"I don't think so. I need a break. Like they say on Facebook, *it's complicated.*"

"What about your brother and sister?"

"I text them. I text Mum sometimes, too."

"Do they know where you are?"

"Vaguely."

"What about your dad? Is he around?"

He doesn't answer for a moment, then, "It's harder to talk to him."

I drink water again because I don't know what to say to that.

They fuck you up, your mum and dad. They were fucked up in their turn.

"Your Dad's giving me the evil eye."

"He is not." But I look at Dad, and he is watching us, puzzled and wary.

"D'you play crib?" Nate asks me.

"No. I'm not much good with cards."

"Come on. I'll teach you."

He jumps up and tugs on his hoodie. My scarf is an emerald splash on the bench. He hands it to me and then my coat. I stand, hardly realising what I am doing, and take them from him.

"Where are we going?"

He sighs. "My caravan. My house. My abode."

Outside again, and our breath clouds in the darkness. A helicopter is sweeping over with pulsing lights and a throbbing *whirr*. The gravel is noisy beneath our feet. As we pass the lit windows of the other caravans, we hear television sets, voices, and the sound of something heavy being dropped. There's a smell of garlic wafting from Nate's neighbour. I'm not sure if it makes me hungry or nauseous.

He unlocks his door, reaches in and puts on the lights. I follow him in. The curtains are drawn. There's a sliding pile of CDs on the settle where we sat. His phone is plugged in charging. He crouches down and lights the gas fire.

"Beer?" he asks. "Or I have a bottle of red. Australian."

"Not for me, thanks."

"Don't you drink at all?" He flicks the lid off a beer bottle, and it falls to the floor. Another bottle top on a faraway summer's day.

Richard.

I shake my head to clear the image.

"Emily?"

"Not at the moment," I say at last.

"OK."

"I'll have some water."

He runs a glass under the tap and puts the drinks on the narrow table.

I realise I am still standing, still wearing my coat. I slide it off and then my scarf.

Nate comes back with a pack of thumbed playing cards and a cribbage board.

"Who do you play with?" I ask as he shuffles the pack.

"No one now. I used to play with … my dad a bit. He taught me."

I struggle to understand what he's saying about boxes, and fifteens, and thirty-ones. We play with our cards open on the tabletop so he can show me what I should be doing, what I should be giving him, what I should keep for myself, why I should never lead with a five. I have my fingers spread on my cards, trying to add them up. I select two for his box, hand them to him.

"No, no, no," he says. "Think again."

Gently, he pushes my hands and the cards back, and I don't understand how something so tiny as the brush of his fingers can make me feel so suddenly light-headed and incapable, and I stare and stare at my cards until he rearranges them, and points out a flush of hearts.

It has gone eleven when I leave.

"I'd better go," I say. "You'll have to get up soon."

"I will," he says.

I fumble for my coat and scarf. I feel like I have been drinking, but I've only had water. The cards are scattered on the table; the pegs are where we left them in the board.

"Did you like playing?"

"Yes, but I still don't know what I'm doing."

"It'll come." He smiles. "Now I have someone to play with. I'm sorry it wasn't a great birthday party."

"It was lovely." I try to bite back the words too late.

He watches me as I fiddle with the tassel on my scarf. I am hungry. I need to eat. My blood sugar must be in my boots.

"Happy birthday, Emily," he says at the door.

I hurry through the empty car park and slip into the house before Mum and Dad get back from the club. I hang up my coat and run to the bathroom. Numbers chant in my head as I wash my hands: *ten and five is fifteen, so is seven and eight, so is six and nine.* Sometimes you can get to the same place by different routes. It is like IVF. The result is the same: a healthy baby. How it was made does not matter.

I know the usual perception of IVF is that it's a last chance desperate gamble, but it doesn't have to be. It can be a choice, a decision made and acted on swiftly.

Back in the kitchen, I find some bread and cheese and throw together some tomatoes and cucumber. Nate doesn't know about my baby. I cannot hide it forever.

When the hell should I tell him?

If I tell him, he will back off. If I do not, he'll find out as I grow bigger.

I hack off another chunk of cheese.

I like Nate Winter. I like him a lot.

And sometimes, like when I looked up across the colourful fan of cards to his grey eyes and straggly dark hair, and when he said "*Happy birthday, Emily,*" I could almost dare to believe that he might like me.

I'm thirty-seven and pregnant; he must be – *What? Twenty-two, three?*

"You're fucking crazy," I say angrily.

"Where did you disappear to?" Mum asks when they come in.

"Oh. I … We went to play cards."

"Cards?" Dad snorts. "When do you play cards?"

"He was teaching me crib. He used to play with his dad, and he misses it."

"I thought crib was for old farts, not young blokes," Mum says.

"He's the young bloke, and you're the old fart." Dad punches me on the shoulder as he passes.

Which is pretty much what I was thinking before they came in.

Of course I want to see him again. Pool, cards, whatever. It cannot come from me. It has to come from him.

Later in the week, I go to Tesco. I like the opportunity to get out alone. It is not that I am unhappy where I am, but just sometimes I need to get out into the world, listen in to other people's conversations, check out what they have in their trolleys, see what is happening away from the caravan site.

It's mid-afternoon when I get back. I park and open the boot. I take the first few bags into the hall and come out again. A car is *rumbling* down the track. It's red.

It's him.

He stops beside my Getz and winds down the window. "All right?"

"I've just been to Tesco." How redundant: I am hauling Tesco bags out of the boot.

"I'm going there now."

His hair looks limp, and his skin grubby. He must have just come home from work. It's the right time.

"D'you want to play cards again? See if you've remembered it?"

"Yes, I'd like to."

"How about this weekend, then? I'm not working. Come up sometime."

He revs, and the weary-looking Suzuki *trundles* on. I watch his brake lights flash, then die, and he turns left, and soon the noise of his car is swallowed up into white space.

262

I heave the next few bags indoors, reassured by the multipacks of oranges.

On Saturday lunchtime, Dad tells me to leave the club early. It is quiet, and we do not do food at midday. This idea of me becoming the bar manager is not really coming to fruition. We don't know what I will be able to do in the coming months. For now, we potter on as we have done.

Mum calls to me from the kitchen when I let myself in. I mumble a reply and go down to my room. I brush my hair and swipe on a film of lipstick. I want to look nice. I don't want to look like I have made any effort.

No, not this top, I think, and rip it off over my head.

When I take off my clothes, I always glance in the mirror. I don't look any different; there is just that little hard stone in my pelvis. Quickly, I pull on another top and brush my hair again.

Mum must be doing some tidying or cleaning as there are a lot of metallic *bangs* coming from the kitchen. Saucepans, bowls, and so on.

"I'm just popping out for a bit," I call, with my hand on the door latch.

I don't think she hears me. More *bangs*.

I hurry past the clubhouse. A couple of old guys from Cadgwith are getting into a car. I smile, wave, and carry on walking.

Nate's car is outside his caravan. I think I can hear the TV on inside. One glance over my shoulder; no one's looking. I *knock* three times. A moment later, the door opens.

"You came," he said.

"Is now OK?"

"Definitely."

As I close the narrow door behind me, he whisks a DVD out of the player.

"What are you watching?"

"Oh. Zombies. Not your sort of thing, I think."

"I like zombies."

"Cards today. Zombies some other time then." He opens the fridge and holds up a green bottle. "I got you this."

Fizzy water.

He pours me a glass. The tiny bubbles sparkle over the rim and fall on my skin.

We sit opposite each other, the cards and the board between us. He offers me the pack to cut. As I stare at the fan of cards in my hand, I wonder: *What is it about Nate Winter?*

I have never fancied a younger man before. They have usually been older than me. I don't know anything about him.

I like his hair, and I like his grey eyes, but why?

They are only hair and eyes.

Is it my hormones?

"Come on."

I jump and throw two cards face down. I hardly know what they are.

After the first game, he shuffles the cards. He looks out of the small window. You cannot see the Buttress from this angle, just the hedge that separates our field from the coast path, striding on to Kynance.

"I … er …" he starts. "I wondered if you'd like to do anything one day."

"Do anything?"

"Yeah, like go somewhere, do something. It's just that I don't really know anyone, and I never do anything except go to work and sleep and watch films."

"And play pool."

"And that. You'll know places and stuff, and I just wondered if you might like to. You might like a change of scene, too."

"That'd be great. What do you want to do?"

He is still shuffling those cards. I want to take them from him, hold his long, thin hands in mine.

"I don't know. Stuff. I haven't even been to Kynance."

"We could do that. Or go somewhere in the car. Of course. Let me know." I still don't like Kynance, but I would go with Nate.

"Your box." He shoves the cards at me.

Today, Tessa is wearing mauve corduroy trousers and a patterned shirt. She still does not look like a midwife. I give her my green folder of notes. Already it is looking a bit battered; the top corner has bent over.

"I'm seeing the obstetrician tomorrow," I tell her as she attaches the blood pressure cuff round my arm.

"That was quick. They might not give you a date tomorrow."

She lets the air out of the cuff and rips the Velcro apart with a *crack*.

"Ready to hear its heartbeat?"

I lie on the narrow bed, ease my jeans down, and check that little hard ball in my pelvis. As Tessa prepares the probe, I study the ceiling.

First the *sloshing* of my guts, then a steady *pulse*.

"That's your heart," Tessa says quietly.

I wait, suspended in this moment.

Like a high, tinny, radio whine comes the speeding heartbeat of my baby.

Twenty-four hours later, I am in the maternity waiting room at the hospital. I have the bent green folder on my knee. I open it and read Tessa's comments from yesterday once again. My blood pressure is fine; my urine clear. We heard the heartbeat. I close the folder.

I am the only single person sitting in the waiting room. There are three couples here.

Opposite me is a young dark-haired girl tapping on her phone. Her tattooed boyfriend has her green folder on his knees. The girl is very thin, and I cannot see a bump under her lumpy top.

Further along, is another couple: she is probably my age and must be about eight months now; he's older and has his hand on her swollen stomach; they whisper together.

The third pair is on my row of chairs. I sneak a look. They are both young, too. They're holding hands. The girl is visibly pregnant. The top of the green folder is sticking out of her woven shoulder bag.

A nurse appears and calls a name.

The whispering two stand and follow her, the guy with his hand on the girl's back. It makes me shiver.

I put my folder down on the spare chair next to me and raise my head high. I am proud to be here alone. I have seen articles online saying it is so brave to do this alone as it must be "terrifying."

They're wrong, they're wrong.

It is terrifying to contemplate having the child's father beside me throughout the pregnancy, reading my notes, feeling for kicks, putting his hand possessively on my back when we go to appointments, so everyone can see we are "together."

They're the brave ones, the girls doing it like that.

What I am doing is easy.

I am called in next. I see a registrar: a willowy blonde with a soft voice and tiny pearl earrings. She knows why I am here. She glances quickly through my file. I confirm that yes, this is a donor baby, and she does not flinch. I tell her I understand the risks of having a Caesarean section, but they are risks I'm more than happy to take. She says I will need to see a consultant nearer the time for the final decision and date, but she cannot see any reason why I cannot give birth the way I want. As I stand to leave, she tells me that I will be sent another appointment date later and can always change my mind between now and the birth.

I thank her. But I will not.

"Nate and I are going to Kynance on Saturday morning. Nate asked me to show him Kynance, so I said OK. I thought I might walk over to Kynance on Saturday morning. I'm just going for a walk. I may be some time."

This is ridiculous.

I stop practising the sentences in my head and walk out of my room to the kitchen. Mum and Dad are having a cup of tea before opening up for the evening.

"Tomorrow morning," I start, taking an orange from the fruit bowl.

"We're going to Tesco," Mum says. "We'll go early."

I fumble in the drawer for a knife and slice the orange in half. Juice seeps onto the plate. I cut each half in two. The scent rises around me.

"I'm going to Kynance tomorrow morning. With Nate Winter." I suck a segment of orange and do not look at my parents.

"Kynance?" Mum repeats. "Is that a good idea?"

"Does he know about the baby?" Dad asks.

"You know I'm not saying anything to people at the moment."

"Kynance is dangerous," Mum says. "You could slip. Anything could happen."

"I won't be on my own."

"Well, he won't be able to do anything, will he, if he doesn't know?"

"I'll tell him," I lie.

I throw away the orange skin. I will have to tell him one day. I cannot hide this forever. I know that.

Just a little longer.

"Would you go down the valley path?" Dad says. "Not the cliff?"

"Sure. Yes, we'll do that."

Dad walks out of the kitchen; I hear the bathroom door lock.

Mum picks up the empty mugs and brings them to the sink.

I am just standing there, with my sticky hands outstretched.

"What's going on with this guy?"

"Nothing. He doesn't have any other friends here. He moved down all on his own. We just ..." I shrug. "Get on well."

"How old is he?"

"I don't know. You don't ask people that."

"Emily."

"What?"

"This baby." Mum waves her hand towards my stomach. "It's what you've wanted for so long. You've worked hard to get it. It's the most important thing in your life, now and always."

"I know that." I rinse my hands at the sink.

"So don't do anything that could spoil things. Just take it easy."

"How can playing cards spoil things? How can going to Kynance spoil things? I'll be ever so careful."

"Please," Mum says and walks away.

They leave early in the morning. I shove my phone and a couple of clementines in my parka pocket. The zip closes easily. I suppose one day I will put on a pair of jeans I have not worn for a week or so, and they will not do up.

Nate unlocks the door when I knock. He's wearing a parka like mine, jeans, black Converse boots.

Not red, not like Richard's.

His hair is loose on his collar.

"Nearly ready," he says, standing back for me to enter.

The fire is off. It is cold. I stand, waiting while he finds his phone and goes to the bathroom. I notice the crib board and the box of cards are still on the table, pushed up against the wall. There is also a biro, a few receipts, and what looks like a blister pack of Nurofen.

"OK," he says behind me.

Out on the cliff, there is pale lemon sunlight. The sea is lazy, rolling slowly over the hidden reefs. I walk just ahead of him.

"At work …" I say. "… do they talk about Richard then?"

"What? At the Lighthouse? No, why would they? It was years ago."

"You said a waitress said there'd been a murder here."

"Oh. Yes, well, she's from Helston. I don't think she knows any-thing about it. I haven't said a word."

The path opens out into the scrubland by the car park. There are four or five cars. This is where I should say, "We'll go down the valley path," but I don't.

"This is the way down," I say instead, and we go through a gap in the stone wall towards the viewpoint.

He walks beside me, and I glance at him. His hair is blowing like mine. I must look a mess. He has his hands in the pockets of his parka. I put my hand in my pocket, and my fingers fold round the two small fruits there.

The *crunch* of gravel under our feet. The sudden cry of a seabird. The smell of salt and sulphur rising from the waves.

"That's pretty impressive," Nate says.

He has stopped walking and is tugging at his hair. Below us is the shiny strand of sand stretching to the offshore islands. The tide is ebb-ing, and it leaves a glaze between the jutting outcrops of serpentine. A few people are walking there. A couple of kids are running and churn-ing up the sand.

"We scattered his ashes here," I hear myself say.

"Where we are now?"

269

"No, on the beach, below the tideline."

He doesn't answer, but I feel him step nearer and put his arm round me once more. Something stings my eye – *A tear? The wind? A lost molecule of Richard?* – and I turn to face Nate.

"Emily," he says

"Nate."

"You're beautiful."

There, on the edge of the cliff, on the edge of the world, the edge of forever, he kisses me.

I wrap my arms round him and wind my fist into his hair. I want him. I want him so much. It overwhelms me.

"Jeez," he says as we stumble apart. He strokes the side of my face. His hand is cold. "I didn't know if I could do that or if you'd tell me to fuck off, but I ... I guess that was OK."

"It was OK," I say. "It was very OK."

He is taller than me. He stands behind me, with his bony chin on my shoulder and arms around me, holding me just where my child lies. We watch the slow surge and spray of the sea. He kisses my neck and my ear.

"Are we going to the beach, then?" I say at last.

I do not want to. I cannot walk that far. I don't care about the bloody beach.

"Are we?" he asks. "Or not?"

I free myself and turn to look at him. The wind sends my hair round my face. Through the bright strands, I watch his eyes, grey and cool as sea mist.

"Not," I say.

"Not," he repeats.

The world falls away into the ocean as we walk back along the cliff. We do not touch each other. Ahead, the Buttress rises, hard and dark, from the scrub. Nate swings open the gate into the field. For once, I hardly check the catch. There is no one around in the field. He shoves open the door into his caravan. I *slam* the door behind me, and only then does he touch me. He smoothes down my tangled hair. He runs a finger over my lips. He takes my hand, and together, we run through the tiny kitchen to his bedroom. He grabs at my parka, and as it falls to the floor, I just see the two clementines roll out onto the dark carpet.

After, I drag the duvet over myself. I am embarrassed at the dimples in my skin, the lines at the corners of my eyes.

"Don't," he says, gently peeling the quilt away. "I want to see you."

In a moment, my skin goes knobbly with the cold, and he covers me once more.

"Will you tell me about Richard?"

"Tell you what?" I ask, and the words taste thick in my mouth. I am still in the heat and fire that sparked between us.

"Not about his death. About him. What was he like? What did he look like?"

"He had dark hair. And green eyes. Real green eyes. He liked geology and sciences. He was a good driver. He got his test very young. He was capable. Good at doing stuff. Friendly. People liked him."

"Were you two close?"

"I think so."

Don't think about that last day when the elastic thread between us stretched and broke, when he said things that hurt, that still hurt.

"We were as close as any full brother and sister, yes."

"Did he try to find his parents? His real parents? I mean, his—"

"I know what you mean. It's OK. He was going to when he went away to uni. He was going a year later because he'd had a bad time with a girlfriend who dumped him. It really upset him."

"If she hadn't done that, and he'd gone away a year earlier—"

"Everything would be different."

Nate does not speak; he kisses me. The ghosts fade away again.

I gather my clothes from the floor. Fumble my jeans the right way round. Search for a sock. I feel Nate watching me, his eyes on my back. I turn round, and he smiles at me.

I lace my boots as he slides from the bed and pulls on his jeans. His hair is tousled from the wind and sex. He looks very young.

"Nate," I say slowly. "How old are you?"

"What does it matter?"

"Because of this. Because of what we've done today."

"Don't panic. I'm over sixteen."

I laugh in spite of myself, but I need to know. I have never asked him before.

"Please."

"How old do you think I am?" He throws himself back onto the bed and reaches out to me.

I catch his hands. "Twenty-something."

"OK."

"So, how old?"

"I don't think it matters. I really like you. You're beautiful, you're fun, you're interesting. So you're a bit older than me. So what?"

"I think it's more than a bit."

"If it matters that much to you, how old are you then?"

"Thirty-seven."

"No problem. Give me a kiss."

"I'll find out," I mumble into his mouth.

Reluctantly, I peel away from him.

"I must go. Where's my coat?"

"On the floor. Where you threw it." He jumps up and holds it aloft.

"I think you threw it."

I put the coat on and tap the pocket for the slim oblong of my phone.

"You certainly love oranges." Nate offers his palm to me: two clementines. The ones that had rolled out of my other pocket. I'd forgotten about them.

"Yes," I say.

"You often have an aroma of oranges. I've noticed. Is that why your hair's like that?"

"I find them restful," I improvise, and I know it sounds ridiculous before he laughs.

"I've never heard of oranges being restful. I'll have to work on a dessert. Restful Oranges Done Three Ways."

At the door, he holds me back. "Can I see you again?"

"Of course."

"I mean … like this."

"I know."

As I join the gravel track, I turn back. He is standing there in the doorway, a scruffy young man, wearing only jeans, waving at me. A scruffy young man who, to me, is gorgeous, wonderful, exciting. Nothing like I have ever known before.

But there's not just you to consider anymore.

The clubhouse is open for lunchtime drinking. I hurry past and on to the bungalow. When I open the door, I hear Mum's voice, and the receiver is missing from the hall phone. I tug off my boots and leave them by the door. They are a bit muddy, but there is no trace of sparkly sand crystals.

In the bathroom, I lock the door and exhale a huge deep breath from the depths of my lungs. I pull my hair round and sniff.

Mint maybe, or tea tree.

I wash and tidy myself and pad out into the hall. Mum's still talking. I might be thirty-seven and soon to be a mother, but I am terrified of walking into the kitchen and meeting her eyes and knowing she will know.

"Well, look, lots of good luck, and I'll ring you sometime next week."

Mum's winding up the conversation. I'm still standing in the hall when she comes out with the phone. It *beeps* smugly as she settles it on its cradle.

"That was Liz. She's seeing the cardiologist this week."

"Ah, right," I say. Mum's friend in Mullion.

"Did you have fun? Do you feel all right? You haven't overdone it?"

"I haven't overdone it," I mutter.

"Was it busy on the beach?"

"Yes, there were quite a few cars in the car park." This doesn't directly answer the question, but all I can smell is the mint-tea tree scent, and I am sure she must, too.

"What about Nate? What did he think of Kynance?"

"He thought it was impressive."

I remember the two small oranges and take them both out. I jab my nail into one. The peel slides off and the smell clouds around me, obliterating the other. I wasn't completely lying to Nate: I do find oranges restful.

Saturday afternoon. I want to get out. I need to get out. Mum and I ate lunch together in the kitchen. I found I was starving. She did not say anything more about Nate, but I felt she wanted to. Instead, I asked her about Liz and her heart problems and whether her daughter had finally ditched her husband.

Now, Dad is home from the club, and I have a few spare hours. Times like this, I wish I still lived in Bath. If I were in Bath, I could tramp the city streets for hours. I could lose myself in Victoria Park. I could wander along the river. I would be anonymous.

I scoop up my car keys and shout out to my parents that I am going for a drive.

I bump down the track and out onto the main road. I turn left, away from the Lizard. I don't know where I'm going. It does not matter.

What have I done?

I smile as I consider that.

Nate wouldn't tell me his age, but I never told him about my pregnancy. He wants to see me again. I want to see him. I desperately want to see him. Now this has happened, this sleight of hand that has changed everything, I want it again and again. But I cannot hide my growing baby from him.

But he'll run away if you tell him.

He said he was only going to be here a short while. He will disappear up-country again, and I'll never see him. I don't know what to do. I know myself. I know, as days go by, I get more and more tangled with men. I should turn around at the roundabout and drive straight back, find Nate and tell him about the baby. Before I get too hurt.

But at the roundabout, I drive on, past Culdrose, towards Helston. I don't know where; I just want to drive.

I wake early on Sunday. I have hardly slept. I tiptoe to the bathroom. Back in my room, I brush my hair and get dressed. I write a note for my parents in case they wake and leave it by the kettle:

Can't sleep. Gone for a walk.

Nate will be in bed. Asleep. It does not matter. I have to do this. I have kept too many secrets. This truth will always come out.

275

It has rained overnight. The grass and gravel are wet. The sky is heavy, pewter. Only a couple of caravans have lit windows. I reach Nate's caravan. Car outside. No lights inside. Bedroom curtains drawn. Dark blue curtains. I remember him swiping them closed yesterday, less than twenty-four hours ago. I knock on the door. Nothing happens. I knock again. It starts raining. I shove up my hood. I feel sick, and I have no oranges. I walk down to the bedroom window and rap on the pane. The curtain parts a couple of inches. He looks like he was about to swear but then grins at me and points towards the door.

"I've woken you," I say.

"It doesn't matter."

He is wearing boxer shorts and a T-shirt with a complicated design of skyscrapers. It looks a bit like a lino print I once did.

He shuts the door and flips down my hood.

"Nate, I need to talk to you about something," I say.

He stops, looks at me with those flinty eyes.

"What?" he asks warily.

"I … I should have told you yesterday, but I couldn't."

"You've got a boyfriend." He steps back from me.

"I haven't got a boyfriend. It's nothing like that."

"I'm fucking freezing. Let me put the fire on."

He crouches down, and the fire flares with a *whoosh*.

"Will you sit with me?" I ask.

I reach for his hand, and he follows me to the settle in the window. The curtains are drawn. I cannot see the Buttress, but I can hear the gentle drum of rain on the roof.

"What?" he says.

"I'm having a baby."

"A baby?"

"I'm about three months."

"Are you sure? You don't look like it."

"It doesn't show yet."

"So, whose is it? Is he someone here?"

"No one here."

He's sitting in a tense bundle. He looks upset, angry, something.

"I should have told you yesterday. It was just that what happened … I wanted that so much … I couldn't find the words. I'm sorry—"

"Who's the father?"

"There isn't a father. There's a donor."

As the fire warms the caravan and the sound of rain subsides, I tell him. I tell him about the clinic in Bath, and my lunchtime walks to look at it. I tell him about Mr Gale and the Danish sperm bank. I tell him about Rafe and the treatment I have had.

"Say something," I say. "I guess this means you don't want to … be with me anymore."

"You should have told me," he says at last. "You should have told me long before yesterday. I thought we were friends. You told me about Richard."

"Yes. I know."

"So, this guy, this donor, has nothing to do with you or the baby?"

"Nothing. I don't know his real name or where he lives. The baby can look for him when he or she is eighteen. He just won't be part of our lives. Except that, obviously, I shall have to tell the child and show them the stuff I have on him. A photo of him as a baby, his medical history, that sort of thing."

"You don't, like, fancy this guy? You weren't thinking about him yesterday?"

"No," I cry. "Of course I don't. Of course I wasn't." I pause to compose myself. "What are you thinking? What's going to happen?"

"You're going to have a baby. That's what's going to happen."

"What about you? What do you think?"

"It doesn't matter what I think. You were doing this before we met."

"You know what I mean."

"I just wish you'd told me. Trusted me."

"But you haven't told me everything. Like why you moved down here. Even how old you are."

"That's true."

"Nate."

"I think it's fine," he says, and I start to cry. "Have I said the wrong thing?"

I shake my head, and he puts his arm round me, and I can smell that scent, that intoxicating scent, and the stale smell of sleep on his skin. I turn my head, and his mouth is there on mine, and his free hand is searching for mine.

"It's a big thing to do," he says finally, rubbing my tears with his thumb. "But I'm cool with that. I don't want a baby of my own right now, but I like kids. I don't have a problem with it. As long as it's OK to ... you know ... Is it OK to have sex with a baby in there?"

"It is," I reassure him. "But I'll change. I'll get fatter and tired probably."

"It's not forever. Just a few months, right?"

He pushes aside my coat and fumbles with my top. His hand on my skin makes me jump.

"I can't feel anything."

"It's still tiny."

"You had me so scared then."

"I'm sorry." I am saying that a lot. "I just had to come and tell you and get it done. I was sure you'd say it was over."

"I'm not that shallow, Emily."

I'm about to apologise again, but I stop myself.

He wants you. He still wants you. You and your baby.

278

I throw my arms round him. I don't even know what I'm saying to him.

"Is this what the oranges are about?"

"They help if I feel sick."

"You must feel sick round me a lot then."

"In a good way."

"When is it due?"

"August. Will you be here then?"

"Of course."

"It's just you once said you might not be around for long, and I thought … I thought you might have gone."

"Yeah, but things are different now, aren't they?" He stands up and offers me his hand. "Aren't they?"

"Yes."

The bed is a rumpled mess. The quilt has gone lumpy; the pillows are flat. I don't care. He's much more careful, much more gentle today.

I wonder what the baby feels.

Happy, I hope, because I am happy.

I take Nate's hand and guide it to where the hard round ball is under my skin.

"You're amazing," he says.

The grass is still damp when I leave. The other residents are waking, moving around. One guy is taking rubbish to the bins. Another is getting into his car. Someone's cooking bacon.

I smell toast when I get home. Dad's in his dressing gown at the kitchen table drinking tea. Mum is spreading butter on a slice of toast. She then scoops out a spoonful of marmalade.

"Didn't you get wet?" Dad asks.

Mum looks at me, the marmalade spoon still in her hand.

"I don't think she walked that far, Terry," she says.

A *knock* on my bedroom door. It swings open. Mum, still in her dressing gown.

"I made you a tea," she says and puts it on the bedside cupboard.

"Thanks."

Through the open door, I can still smell the toast. It would make me feel sick if I were not already feeling sick because now Mum is closing the door. She sits beside me on the bed.

After that comment in the kitchen, I walked out. I did not say anything. I didn't confirm or deny her words. I just went. I heard Dad say, "*What d'you mean by that?*" and didn't catch Mum's reply.

"I'm not angry," she says at last.

"You are." I take the tea and drink. It is too hot.

"No. I'm just concerned. We don't know anything about this bloke."

"You don't," I say, replacing the mug with a heavy click. "But I do. I've talked to him a lot."

"How old is he?"

"Young," I snap.

"Your dad says he's about twenty-two."

"Something like that, I think. I did ask. He wouldn't say."

"Why wouldn't he say?"

"Shit, I don't know. I suppose he thought I'd be shocked."

"Are you shocked?"

"With him? No. With myself? Not really. He's nice. I like him. He's much better than those twats in Bath."

"That's not much of a compliment."

"He's nothing like any of them."

"What do you know about his background?"

Not a lot, I think. He doesn't talk about the past.

"He lived near Worcester," I say. "He went to catering college. He wants his own restaurant."

"What about his family?"

"He's the oldest. He has a sister called Lucy and a brother Josh. His mum works at a place for kids with disabilities. His dad's something in computers."

"You're going to have to tell him soon. About the baby."

"He knows."

That surprises her.

"What did he say?" she asks. "You told him about the donor?"

"I told him everything."

Yes, everything. Including things I haven't told you. Like what happened the day the sun turned black.

"And what did he say?"

"He said it was fine. No problem." At last, I turn to her. "Really. He thought it was a great idea."

"He probably doesn't understand what pregnancy's like."

"Meaning?"

"It's a massive upheaval for a woman's body. You won't know what you're going to feel like, especially near the end."

"That's a long way away. Why can't you be pleased? Why can't you be happy that I have found someone who likes me? Who's nice? You don't even know him."

"No, I don't."

"You don't know him, but you don't like him."

"It's not *don't like*. I can't explain it. There's something about him. He makes me uneasy."

"I don't see how someone can make you feel uneasy when you don't know them."

"I said I couldn't explain it."

I don't speak.

"I don't want you getting hurt," Mum says eventually. "Not now, when everything is going so well for you."

"How did you know? How did you know anything had happened with me and Nate?"

"Because you're always playing pool with him, playing cards with him. You met him yesterday, and when you came back, you were … shifty … embarrassed. You couldn't wait to get out in the car. And then, this morning. You've never gone walking at the crack of dawn in the rain. And again, you came back different."

"He makes me happy."

"I thought you were happy. You said you were. With the baby. That's what you've wanted for so long."

"I was happy. Very happy. I'm just a bit happier now."

"I think Dad's finished in the bathroom now." Mum stands up and wraps her dressing gown round her body. "Just be careful with that grandchild of mine."

That night, Nate comes into the bar. I am in the kitchen talking to Mum about a food order – "One burger without a bun, please, and the other with no chips" – and I do not realise he is there until I back out again.

"You look like you've seen a ghost," he says.

"I didn't expect you to come in," I say.

"Why not?"

I shrug. He sighs.

"Can I have a drink, please?"

Dad's not in the bar. Mum's in the kitchen doing the burgers. She will come out soon, though, and see Nate here.

"My parents know," I say.

"And?"

"And nothing."

"You've been doing a lot of explaining today. How many oranges have you had?"

We wander along the surf line in Bishop's Cove. The waves *suck* and *rattle* at the pebbles and butterfly shells. It is late afternoon, and a mauve-grey squall blurs the horizon. Further south towards the Lizard, a blonde girl strides over the sand with three black-and-white dogs running round her. Apart from them, we are alone.

"Did he fall into this cove?" Nate asks.

"The other side. There isn't a cove. Just rocks and sea."

The girl calls her dogs and slips leads onto their collars. They scamper up the track to the Lizard village.

I bend down, pick up a shell, rub the sand from it, and slip it into my pocket.

"Do you know anything about geology?"

"A bit."

Nate opens his hand. There are three small stones.

"Tremolite serpentine, banded gneiss, and I think that's schist," I say, touching each in turn.

I stop. I have a memory, an image on the edge of consciousness, of three similar rocks held in my palm. The day of the school trip. Walking with Zoe along the cliff path to our house. We stood on the Buttress. I glance up at its dark bulk. The squall is coming in.

"Emily?" Nate drops the stones into his pocket and pulls out a Twirl. "Go halves?"

He rips the purple wrapper and pulls out one slim finger of chocolate. I take it from him and bite, and there must still be sand on my skin because my teeth find gritty specks, like shell fragments in an omelette.

Rain splatters the backs of our heads as we walk back up the beach. The wind has risen, and the waves break louder and faster behind us.

283

"You once said things were complicated," I venture.

"What things?"

"At home. With your family. Why you needed some space from them."

He is walking ahead of me, along the narrow cliff track, so I cannot see his face. I lick the last of the sand and chocolate from my fingers.

"My mum and dad," he says.

They fucked you up? I almost ask, but don't.

"They're getting divorced. It came out of the blue last summer. It turned out Mum has been seeing some guy down the road from us. It all got toxic."

The path has widened by the Buttress. I reach for his hand. It is cold and damp in my cold, damp hand.

"I'm sorry to hear that."

"It happens all the time, doesn't it? But I didn't want to be there with all that."

"What about Lucy and Josh?"

"I think they're dealing with it better than me."

We are back through the gate and in the field. His caravan is cold, and I keep my damp coat on until the gas fire warms the living room. Nate makes tea and opens a packet of biscuits.

"Unless you'd prefer these?" he says, waving a string bag of clementines.

"You got those for me?"

"Of course," he says.

We go to Truro one Saturday afternoon in my car. I am aware of him looking at my profile as I drive. We wander round, looking in shop windows, neither of us knowing what – if anything – we want to buy. I watch the passers-by to see if their faces show horror or disgust.

"They're staring at us," I whisper to him.

"Good," he says and kisses me.

In the dark, we go to the Lizard lighthouse. It is the first time I have been in his car. He parks in the dirt car park on the cliff edge. There are ships out to sea, sparkling clusters of lights. Beside us, the bright flash of the lighthouse illuminates the spindly railings atop the abandoned second tower; on the horizon, Wolf Rock pulses its steady warning. It has been a long time since I've had sex in a car, and a Suzuki Swift is cramped. We laugh and cuddle, watching the lights of the night at the end of the world.

My parents have come to terms with it, at least. There was the same age difference between me and several of my boyfriends in Bath – I pointed out – just the other way round.

"But how old is he?" Mum keeps asking.

"Twenty-two," I say at last.

I don't want to say that I still don't know.

"Mum asked how old you were," I say to Nate as he racks up the pool balls. "I said twenty-two."

He *rattles* the balls in the triangle for a moment.

"Clever girl."

"I got it right? I was guessing."

"You got it right."

"Twenty-two." I chalk my cue. "So, you'll be twenty-three in March?"

"That is the number after twenty-two, yes."

He gestures for me to break off.

Now I add him on Facebook. I do not go on there often, and several days pass before I realise he has not accepted me.

"I never go on Facebook," he says when I ask him.

A day or so later, I look again, and he still hasn't accepted me. His page is still closed to me. I realise he is not going to accept me.

I search Facebook for his sister and brother. I find several Lucy Winters. Once I have discounted the ones in America, the ones who seem too old, the ones who say they are married, I am left with a couple of possibilities. A few moments later, I have found her, but like Nate, her profile is closed. As for Josh, I cannot find anyone who might be him.

When I was in Bath, if I added a new man to my Facebook and he didn't accept, it always turned out there was something he was not telling me or wasn't telling me straight. I wish, and wish, that Nate would just hit **Accept**, so I don't feel so unsettled, but a grown woman of thirty-seven, a woman with a baby on the way, cannot, *just cannot*, sob and plead with a young man to be friends on Facebook.

It's ridiculous. Laughable.

March 2013

Of course, I often wonder if Nate will get sick of me, but weeks pass, and he is still delighted to answer my knocks on the caravan door. Sometimes I sneak out in the early hours of the morning, creeping through the caravan field with a Maglite, under the dust of stars overhead. I always return before my parents wake. I think they know I go wandering at night, but they never say anything.

Nate has been to the house a couple of times, but I know he is not comfortable here. I think it is because of the age difference. One afternoon, he and Mum talked for a long while about pastry and baking, and I relaxed.

But, even so, I prefer to go to his caravan.

I am in the kitchen one morning, just talking to Mum about nothing, when I stop speaking suddenly. I have completely lost the thread of what I was saying because, low in my pelvis, is a tiny flutter, a ripple, an exhalation of movement.

"What is it?" Mum asks.

"I can feel it moving," I say.

I text Nate at work to tell him.

Wonderful xxx, he writes back later.

I am so lucky, I think. I have the two things I most wanted: a man and a baby. They did not come together, but they are both here now, with me.

I ask Nate if he would like to do something to celebrate his birthday, like going out for a meal, but he says he would rather just have fish and chips in the caravan, watch films, and play cards. I ask if anyone at work knows it is his birthday, and he says he does not think so. Then I ask about his family.

"Is this your first birthday away from home? I remember my first one in Bath. My parents sent my parcels up in a huge box. It felt weird opening them with friends watching and commenting."

Rachel, Sonia, Gary. The old gang. I should tell them about my baby now.

Should I tell them about Nate?

"Yes," he says.

"You haven't seen them for ages."

"We're in touch."

"Your mum will ring you on your birthday."

"Probably."

"What about your dad?"

"Maybe. Look, I don't like birthdays. Can we not talk about it, please?"

"Why don't you like birthdays?"

"I like other people's. It's just mine I don't like. I liked yours a lot. Didn't you?"

I smile, remembering. His ghostly figure in the car park, the *clack* of pool balls, vivid playing cards in the half-light.

Happy birthday, Emily.

Mum asks me if Nate would like a birthday cake. I say I do not know; he does not like birthdays.

"How can he not like birthdays at his age?" she retorts.

I shrug. I don't know. So many things about him that I don't know.

Perhaps something horrible happened on his birthday one year? Someone died or something?

I think about how willingly I told him about Richard and how I answered his questions, and I know he is not being fair to me. He must have a secret.

Has he been in gaol? What for? Drugs?

I don't think so.

Has he killed someone?

My mind races through these thoughts, but I think of Nate and his smile and spiky humour, and I cannot imagine him doing anything like that.

"He likes chocolate," I say at last.

"I'll make a chocolate one then," Mum says.

When we are in Tesco, I see birthday candles, and I pick up a couple: one shaped like a two, and one a three. They are white with sparkly bits. I drop them in the trolley. Mum returns with the bread she has been having sliced, but before she can see them, I whip them out and shove them back on the shelf. I don't want to remind him of the years between us.

We have had a lovely evening. I carried the birthday cake to his caravan without any candles, and he flushed with embarrassment and said it looked amazing and that obviously, I had not baked it.

We collected fish and chips in his car and ate them in front of the TV, with the curtains drawn and the gas fire hissing its blue flames.

Now it is nearly two in the morning. I think Nate has fallen asleep. I slide closer to him, feel the warmth of his long, lean body next to my skin. The baby flutters a moment, and I smile into the darkness. I want to curl round Nate and sleep here with him, but I am going to leave now. He has to get up so early; he should sleep quietly on his own. Reluctantly I sit up. Without the covers, it's cold. I dress as quickly as I can in the dark and lean over to kiss Nate goodbye. He half-opens his eyes, takes my hand.

"I love you," he mutters.

"You're asleep," I say.

At the bedroom door, I stop, gaze at him, his arm flung out on the rumpled quilt, the dark scribble of his hair on pale linen.

"I love you, too," I whisper.

Mum comes with me to my scan two days later. I am now twenty weeks.

Halfway there.

Mum drives, and I think.

Today I can find out the sex of my baby.

I still have not decided what to call it. The list is in the drawer beside my bed:

Aidan, Dominic, Roderick, Alistair, Richard, Nathaniel.

Lily, Isabel, Madeleine, Chloe, Lydia, Alexandra.

I'm not really sure. I had no idea this bit would be so hard.

"So, are you going to find out?" Mum asks me.

The jelly is cold on my abdomen. I move my head to see the screen. Grey, black, and white flickers. I see the head. It looks like a real human head now, outlined in white bone. The radiographer takes the measurements of leg length, head circumference, and waist.

It twiddles round and presents its long, knobbly spine. The vertebrae are so distinct that I feel I could reach out and run my finger down them on the monitor.

"Is everything all right?" I ask.

"Absolutely fine," the radiographer tells me. "Is there anything you want to ask me?"

Now. This is the moment. I can ask what I'm having.

I twist my head and look at Mum.

The future is suspended in a heartbeat.

"No," I say.

The radiographer hands me a wad of tissues to wipe the jelly from my skin.

"I thought you wanted to know," Mum says.

I know she is disappointed. I have had so much control in this pregnancy – choosing when to have treatment, picking a donor, requesting a Caesarean section – I suddenly want a risk. I want the unknown. Nate was the unknown, a risk I took.

"I'm sorry," I say to Mum. "I thought I wanted to know, but I want a surprise."

"Whatever it is, it'll be gorgeous," Mum says.

I take my strip of photographs from the radiographer, and we leave the tiny room.

"You can keep your secret," I tell the grainy image in my hand.

April 2013

The consultant obstetrician is slim and balding. His shirt sleeves are rolled up to the elbow. He has a soft voice with a faint Welsh lilt. He flicks through my green folder; it is now very battered, and the sticky name label on the front has almost fallen off. He checks the measurements taken at last month's scan and Tessa's latest notes. My blood pressure is still low. I have no signs of diabetes in my urine. The baby's heartbeat is clear and strong.

"Do you still want a Caesarean section?" he asks.

"Definitely."

"The due date is the eighth of August." He looks up at the laminated calendar on the wall. "That's a Thursday. I would want to schedule the section for thirty-nine weeks. How does the first of August sound?"

"That'd be great," I say.

"Let me just ring and check the list for that day. If it's full, we'll have to do it a day on either side."

He goes into a back room but leaves the door open. I watch him pick up a phone, dial a number, and wait, staring out the window.

I want the first of August. It's an excellent day.

Please let there be a vacancy on the list.

He starts talking.

"A lady for elective section.... first of August.... yes, good, great.... do that.... Emily Knight, hospital number.... hang on, I've got it here."

The first of August. My child's birthday. My little Viking, born in the heat of a Cornish summer.

May 2013

My shape is changing now. What was once a tiny marble in my pelvis has swelled and grown, and my stomach feels hard. I cannot get my skinny jeans on anymore. I am wearing long dresses – tie-dyed and patchwork – that fall over my bump and hide a lot of it. I bought some maternity jeans, but they are too loose and slide down, and there are no hoops for a belt, only an elasticated strip, so when I want trousers, I wear leggings. My skin is soft from the olive oil I apply twice a day. My hair is growing and is thicker, shinier, the colour returning. When I look at this new me in the mirror, I am surprised that I like what I see. I like my new shape, my rounded boobs, my growing bulge. I thought I would hate these feelings, but I love them. I love feeling my baby move and dive inside me.

I love knowing that I'm never alone.

The downsides: my gums bleed – and so does my nose – I have heartburn all the time, and I wake in the night with feet cramps that feel like fire.

I want to make a picture of all these things, the feelings they stir in me. The blood and the cramps, too. And Nate because he is all part of it. I just do not know where to start.

I thought Nate would have left me by now. I thought that, as I grew big, he would be repulsed. I think becoming a mother only reinforces the difference in our ages and experience, but he does not care.

He likes to run his hand over my bump and play with my new shiny hair. He thinks I will have a boy.

"If it's a boy, will you call it Richard?" he asks me one day.

"As a middle name," I say.

He smiles. "That would be really nice."

My world, my life, changes in a footstep.

It is a Sunday evening, and I am in the caravan with Nate. It's that heady time of the year in Cornwall, with twilight the colour of milky amethyst, the scent of bluebells and wild garlic on the air, warm sun by day, cool nights.

I lie on my side, as that is becoming the most comfortable position. I am staring at the dark-blue curtains and the narrow strip of lavender sky between them. Nate has his arm round me. He breathes softly into my neck. I can feel my eyelids drooping. The only sound is the tiny heartbeat of the alarm clock and the shouts of some kids outside somewhere. I'm happy, comfortable, and loved. I let my eyes close.

I'm vaguely aware of Nate peeling away from me. There is a cooler breath of air as the duvet moves. The bed *creaks*. He must be going to the bathroom or to get a drink. I hunch the duvet round my shoulders, suspended in that sleepy cavern.

Then, out of nowhere, he half-shouts, "Fuck, fuck, fuck."

I jump awake. "What the hell's going on?"

"Fuck," he says again. "Jesus."

He staggers back towards the bed. The caravan bedroom is tiny. He's hopping all lopsided. I cannot see his feet.

"What have you done?" I manage at last, sitting up and leaning over the bed.

"My toe." He slides down onto the bed. "Look at that. I think I'm going to throw up."

He lifts his foot. The little toe on his right foot is splayed outwards, pointing sideways. The skin is red.

"It's … it's sticking out. What did you hit it on?"

"The bed."

He faintly presses the toe back, but it springs outwards again.

"You might have dislocated it," I suggest. "Shall I have a look?"

"OK. No. OK."

Gently, I touch the toe. It feels soft, like it has no muscle structure, no bone. I push it back into alignment, and once more, it jumps back and points sideways.

"No more," he yelps. "Please. Don't touch it."

"It might be broken."

It does look horrible, sticking out at that unnatural angle. It felt so flaccid in my hand that it could have just fallen off into my fingers.

"It can't be. I just walked into the bed."

"It could be. Did you stub it?"

"I walked into the corner of the bed. My foot went on, and that toe … cracked back."

"Can you stand? Can you walk?"

He hobbles a few steps into the kitchen and back. "It's really painful."

"I think it's broken. You should get it looked at. Come on, I'll take you to A&E."

"Oh fuck, no, I don't need that."

"You might need time off work, so you do need to get it seen. Come on. We'll go now."

"It'll take forever." Nate lies down beside me, but I tug away from him.

"There's an A&E at Penzance. It's quicker there. Dad went straight in when we took him."

"What happened to him?"

"He fell and hit his head."

"Well, yes, obviously, they'd see him straight away. A toe will go to the back of the queue."

"That's the point. There was no queue. Come on." I throw his shirt at him.

He flaps it out and fumbles his arms into it. I unlace his Converse boot, so it's really loose; even so, he winces and swears as I ease his foot into it.

"You wait here," I say. "I'll bring my car up to you."

Am I being too bossy? I wonder as I hurry back to the house for my car keys. *Am I being too much like a mother?*

I shiver in the cool evening breeze. As I pass the clubhouse, I hear a snatch of music. The car park is full; it's busy inside. I should tell my parents what has happened, but if I do not move fast, Nate will change his mind and refuse to go. I will ring or text from the hospital.

He's sitting on the steps of his caravan when I bump slowly up the track. He opens the car door and gets in silently.

At least he's agreed to come, I think as I turn round and drive off.

I find a space to park in the small hospital car park. I am cold in a T-shirt and denim jacket. My hair is in a tangle at the back; I did not have time to brush it.

The hospital is quiet, the corridors empty. We walk slowly to A&E. The baby presses on my bladder.

"I'm going to the ladies while you sign in," I whisper and nudge Nate towards the reception hatch.

The waiting area for A and E is empty and lit with low lights. There are a couple of rows of chairs, a greasy-looking heap of magazines, and the usual posters on the walls: drugs, domestic violence, depression, sexual infections, give up smoking and alcohol.

I get to the ladies just in time. It is cold in here, too, and the lock on the cubicle door echoes hollowly. I squat and exhale in relief at the hot *whoosh* that leaves my body, and I wonder if this is what it feels like when your waters break.

When I get back to the waiting room, Nate is slouching in a chair, the laces trailing on his right boot. As soon as I sit beside him, a young woman in blues comes out from the back.

"Nathaniel Winter," she says, looking right at us, as we are the only people there.

She swipes aside blue paper curtains and gestures us into a cubicle. It's a tiny bit warmer here, and the lights are brighter. There are drifts of voices from behind other curtains and, once, laughter. A phone rings somewhere, ignored. The *sucking* sound of rubber-soled shoes on the floor. The same old hospital soundtrack.

"Someone will be with you shortly," the nurse says.

Nate swings his leg onto the bed and pulls off the shoe.

"That's a bit better," he says.

He is not wearing a sock. I look at the toe. It's still jabbing outwards. I wonder why something like a misplaced digit can make you feel so queasy.

The curtains part, and a tall, muscular woman comes in. She has dark hair screwed up in a scruffy bun and wears black-framed glasses.

"Hello there," she says, glancing at her papers. "I'm Dr Woods. Can you just confirm your name and date of birth?"

"Nathaniel Winter. Twentieth of March ... Ninety-three."

"OK, let's have a look at this toe. What happened?"

Ninety-three.

Ninety-three?

I look at Nate, but his head is bent over his foot. If he was born in ninety-three, it means that he wasn't twenty-three on his last birthday. He was twenty. He would have been nineteen when we first ...

My face burns hotly.

Nineteen.

Dr Woods straightens up. "There should be someone in X-ray right now. Come back here when you've had it done. Do you need a wheelchair, or can you walk?"

"I can walk." Nate flinches as he forces the boot back on.

Dr Woods swishes out through the curtains.

"X-ray, then," Nate says, standing unsteadily.

"She thinks it's broken?"

"Well, you heard her."

No, I didn't.

I was thinking about his date of birth. He gave me the day and month, just not the year. I knew there was something.

But why would he want to make out he was older? Because of me? Would I have slept with him if I had known he was nineteen?

Yes, I say silently.

"You OK?" he asks me as we arrive at X-ray.

I make myself look at him and smile. "I'm fine. I'm just worried about you."

I loiter in the corridor while he goes in for the X-ray. Suddenly, I remember my parents. I ring Dad in the clubhouse and tell him what has happened. My bladder is aching again. I will have to go back to the ladies before we leave.

Half an hour later, we're back in the same cubicle we were in before. A toddler or child is shouting somewhere. Rubber-soled shoes again. The phone, this time, is swiftly answered.

The curtains part, and Dr Woods comes back. She stands over Nate with her hands on her hips.

"OK, I've had a look at the X-rays," she says. "You have broken it. At the base of the toe."

"Should he strap it to the one next to it?" I ask.

299

"If it helps. But it won't make much difference. All you can do is let it heal by itself. I was concerned you might have damaged other bones in the foot, but luckily, they're all fine. Obviously, take some Nurofen. That should ease it a bit. And go easy on it."

"That's it, then?" he asks.

"That's it," she repeats.

It is dark. Nate is quiet on the drive home.

At last, he speaks. "Thank you for taking me."

I rest my left hand on his knee for a moment. "Of course I'd take you if you're hurt."

"I'm sorry it ruined the evening."

"It hasn't," I say, then, "Why didn't you tell me how old you were? I heard you give your date of birth. You said ninety-three. That means you were nineteen when we met. Twenty at your last birthday. Not twenty-three like you said."

"It's no big deal."

"I think it is."

I know I sound like I am whining, but I do think it's a big deal. If someone lies about one thing, they can lie about other things. I do not like the way my stomach is sliding about.

"I'm sorry."

"Why did you do it?"

"I didn't think you'd be interested if you knew I was nineteen."

In the dark, I flush.

Did he really lie because he wanted me so badly and thought I would ignore someone so young? Was it really desire for me?

That is what he says. I can either let this gnaw away at me or accept it and believe him.

"You're silly," I say lightly. "I don't care how old you are. I wouldn't have done anything any different."

300

He takes my hand, which is resting on the gear stick, lifts it to his mouth, and kisses the palm.

Deep inside, my baby flutters.

I drive straight to Nate's caravan and park beside his Swift. I help him up the steps. I make him a cup of tea and watch while he swallows a couple of Nurofen.

"You haven't got many of these." I *rattle* the packet at him. "I've got some at home. I'll bring them up for you."

At the door, I turn back to him. "Shall I ring the Lighthouse, leave a message, and say you're ill?"

"No, I'll go in."

"Do you think that's wise?"

Stop being so bossy, Knight. You are not his mother.

"I'll be fine."

"At least let me drive you down."

"It's the crack of dawn."

"I know. I don't mind. I'll go home and get the Nurofen, and then shall I stay here with you tonight?"

"That would be lovely." He smiles.

I leave the car where it is for the morning and walk down to the clubhouse. There are only a few cars outside now. Nearly chucking out time. I go inside. Mum and Dad are both behind the bar, talking to one of the regulars.

"How is he?" Mum asks.

I tell them that Nate has broken his toe and how I am going to stay at the caravan and drive him to work in the morning.

In my bedroom, I find the Nurofen in the bedside drawer. I throw together a bag with my toothbrush, hairbrush, clean socks, and so on.

When I go back out, one of the cars is leaving the club with a *crunch* of gravel from its wheels.

I want to be with Nate tonight. I don't want to be alone. If I'm alone, I will think too much, wonder too much. I knew he was hiding something, but his age? It's too small a thing, and yet a big thing.

I knock on the caravan door; it is open, and I step inside. Nate's idly flicking through the pack of cards. I take the tablets out of my bag and put them on the table.

"Shall I make us something to eat?" I ask.

"I'll help." He hobbles into the kitchen.

Nate wakes a lot in the night, swearing and cursing. The duvet is too heavy for his toe. I keep to the far side of the bed to give him space. At about three-thirty, I ask if he would like me to move into the tiny second bedroom where he keeps his clothes, but he tugs me back to him.

When the alarm shouts into the grey dawn, I am relieved. I have slept badly, too: Nate kept banging about, the baby was jumping, and now my brain is exhausted.

Nate shows me his toe. It is swollen and purple-black with bruising. There is bruising to the one next to it and under the foot.

He is slow in getting washed and dressed.

He takes more tablets.

I go into the bathroom and have a quick wash. When I come out, he is standing at the door, keys in hand.

Early mornings in May are like the twilights: that pearly sky, the scent of wild garlic, a sudden shiver of cool air.

It only takes a few moments to drive to the restaurant.

"See you later, beautiful," he says and leans in to kiss me goodbye.

A few more minutes, and I quietly let myself into the bungalow and pad down to my room.

I must have dozed off. I know it is mid-morning from the light and the feel of the house. I am lying on top of the covers, dressed except for my bare feet. The album has slipped to the floor.

I wonder if that's what woke me?

I reach down and pick it up. It's the album I am making about my pregnancy. I bought a big lever arch file, patterned with multi-coloured circles – because I thought they looked a tiny bit like an embryo – and a wad of clear envelopes. I have put every piece of correspondence from Bath into these envelopes: all my appointment letters, the photos from each scan, information about Rafe. One day, I will sit with my child next to me and show it to him or her.

A *beeping* noise. It's my phone. It's still in my bag, which is on the floor. I scramble off the bed and rummage through it – hairbrush, toothbrush, yesterday's socks – until I find the phone. It's almost out of battery. There is a new text from Nate.

I am anxious – *No, afraid.* I do not want to open it. I don't know what it's going to say, but I know I don't want to read it.

I sit down on the edge of the bed and tap the screen.

I'm a twat. Forgot my Nurofen. They're on the table. Any chance you could bring them down for me? You must have a spare key. I can meet you outside. Thanks xxx

That's all it is. He just forgot the tablets.

He's right, of course. We do have spare keys. I can collect the Nurofen and take them to the Lighthouse. I'm still tired, but I'm fractious, edgy, and I don't think I'll sleep again now.

I put the album away and text him back.

Meet you in half an hour. x

I unlock Nate's caravan. I see the silver-and-red boxes straight away. One the table, like he said. His box, and my box. I tip the foil blister packs out, put them together in one box, and throw the empty away.

I walk back to my car, the caravan key still in my pocket, and I drive down to the restaurant once more.

He is waiting for me. I have never seen him in his whites before, his hair screwed into a knobble. I pull in and park.

He opens the passenger door and scoops up the Nurofen from the empty seat.

"Thank you. It's so bloody painful."

"For Christ's sake, don't drop anything on it."

"We have steel toe-caps."

I wince at the thought of that puffy black toe forced into heavy boots.

"Don't walk home. I'll come for you."

"OK." He kisses me quickly and *slams* the door.

I drive home and park outside the bungalow. I drop my car keys into my pocket, and they *clink*. The caravan key is still in there.

I stop outside the house. This is another fork in my path, like last night in the car. I could go in and replace the spare key, have a bath, have something to eat, whatever, or turn around and walk up past the clubhouse, quiet and empty, and into the field of caravans.

And that is what I do.

I walk quickly. I do not want to be seen. Some of the residents know Nate is my boyfriend. I don't know what they think about the difference in our ages, but they will not think it is too strange that I am letting myself into his caravan again. But I know it's wrong, so I don't want to be seen.

I've never done this before. I've never checked up on a man. Never gone through emails or a mobile phone. Steve, one of the married men I slept with in Bath, left his phone charging in my kitchen once. I could have looked at it, but I didn't. An hour later, he came back for it, and I handed it over with a clean conscience.

Now, I close the caravan door behind me. I don't even know what I'm looking for. I feel hot and prickly, and I know that's guilt.

This is wrong.

I pick up books – horror fiction and cookery mostly. I open a few CD cases. I don't know *how* to do this. I don't know how you look for what you don't know. His laptop is on the floor, but I'm not touching that. I would need a password.

Just ignore it. If there's something, it'll be here.

I don't think the kitchen will hide much, but I open the few drawers and rattle the knives and forks around. He has a wooden block of expensive knives on the worktop; I lift that up to see if something is taped underneath. There's nowhere to hide anything in the bathroom, so I sidle carefully past the corner of the bed that broke Nate's toe. I open the tiny bedside drawer on his side: a couple of pens, his driving licence, the three stones he found in Bishop's Cove. On the other side, the bedside drawer is empty.

I go into the spare room. It's very small. There are twin beds, with hardly a gap between them. One is covered with his clothes: jeans, T-shirts, and hoodies tossed inside out. I nearly trip over a pair of trainers on the floor. On the other bed are some more books, a couple of clean towels, and an electrical cable for something. I sift through the stuff. Nothing.

Maybe I'm imagining it. Maybe it's just the hormones again. Maybe I'm looking for something that truly isn't here.

The cabinet between the beds. The surface is clear, except for an old Tesco receipt. I pull the drawer out with my eyes closed and then open my eyes. A brown A4 envelope. Fear surges through my chest.

This is it. Whatever his secret is, it's gotta be in here.

I take out the envelope. It *crackles* with papers. There's no writing on it; the flap has never been stuck down. I sit on the edge of one of the beds, amongst his abandoned clothes, and tip out the papers.

The first thing I see is Richard.

It's the front page of the West Briton from August 1992.

I stumble to my feet. Acid jumps up into my throat. I swallow saliva, crumple down again. I think I might throw up. The paper is yellowed and stiff in my hands. I unfold the whole page. There's Richard, a surly school photo; there's the Buttress. I have this same front page hidden away in the loft somewhere.

LIZARD MOURNS LOCAL TEENAGER, the headline shouts.

I start to read the print, the story I have read so many times before, the story only I could really write because I was the only one there.

Except for Zoe.

I don't read it all. I fold it up again. There is a handful of photographs. A family group.

"Jesus," I say aloud.

It's Zoe, a very pregnant Zoe, standing between two children: the little girl I saw her with and the boy, my nephew. The girl in the pink-and-green dress with the pink trainers; the boy in the coloured T-shirt. They are in the Lizard car park down by the lighthouse. The car park is full; other people are half in, half out of the shot. It's eclipse day. I look for myself, for Rachel, Sonia or Gary, but we are not there.

There are other photos: the man I saw, the older man, with the two children. Then the two children together leaning on the front of the car, the silver Ford. One of Zoe alone, hand on her bump.

I turn the photos over.

11th August 1999 Eclipse.

It's written on them all. The writing's more hurried, more sloppy, but I recognise it.

It's Zoe's writing.

There's just a piece of lined paper left. Nate's cramped left-handed script.

Richard Knight, Kynance Holiday Park, The Lizard, Cornwall

Parents – Cheryl, Terry
Sister – Emily

I stuff the whole lot into the envelope and run out of the bedroom. I don't even bother to check I have hidden my traces. I stumble down the track, the envelope hugged to my chest. I keep my head down. This time, I don't want anyone to see my tears.

I said I would collect Nate in the afternoon.

I don't want to.

I wonder if I am even physically capable of driving down to the Lizard.

I have spent the rest of the day in my room. I told Mum I had a migraine. I had not at that moment, but it came within the hour. I have taken Paracetamol, which has not helped.

At last, I stagger out of bed with my car keys in my hand. I haven't eaten, and I feel sick. It is a sunny afternoon, and I'm freezing.

As I drive to the Lighthouse, I pass a couple walking hand in hand.

I want to hold Nate's hand; I never want to touch him.

I keep the engine running until he comes out. He is hobbling and looks drawn.

"Hi," he says and gets into the car.

I let up the clutch and move off before he can reach for me.

"How's the toe?" I ask.

"Fucking awful. Maybe I should have stayed at home. How are you?"

"I'm tired," I say. It doesn't matter if I sound old. I'm tired, and I feel ill. "I've had a migraine all day."

"I'm sorry that you had a crap night, too."

"I'll be OK," I say as I turn into the drive. "I'll drop you off, then I'm going to bed. I'm not coming to the club tonight."

"Of course. You rest."

I stop by the Swift. He takes my chin in his hand and leans in to kiss me. I let his mouth graze mine. I don't know what else to do.

I go home. I have a warm bath. I make myself eat.

Mum frets: Do I need to see a doctor? I tell her no, it is just a migraine, and I am tired.

During the evening, Nate texts me to ask how I am. I do not reply until late. I say I am OK. I sign off as usual, with kisses. He writes back.

Don't get up to give me a lift tomorrow. I'm sure I can drive myself xxx

I put my phone away. I take the brown envelope out from under my bed. This time I only look at the photos. I look at my nephew.

The next day I am exhausted. I'm exhausted from sobbing quietly in my room, exhausted from batting away my parents' questions.

"You've fallen out with Nate," Mum says. "What's happened?"

"I haven't," I say. "I just don't feel well."

"Go and see the doctor."

"I'll be fine." It is an effort to keep my voice steady.

In the evening, Nate texts me to say hello. I write a bland reply. Soon after, he texts again.

Just went to the club. You weren't there. Would you like to meet up? xxx

I do not know what to do.

I can't tonight xxx

When Mum and Dad come back from the club, I'm in the living room, watching crap on TV. I'm not sure what I'm watching. I change channels a lot. People are talking, shouting, women with too much makeup on, cars exploding, men pointing guns, jarring laughter from a studio audience, a sweaty couple shagging in what looks like a hotel room. I switch it off.

"Nate came in looking for you," Dad says.

"He texted me," I say.

"He looked a bit glum. And his foot was bad. I think he wanted to see you."

Mum looks at me, raises her eyebrows.

"I'll see him tomorrow." I heave myself up off the sofa.

On Wednesday afternoon, I stand at the front window about the time when Nate should come back from work. A small red car goes by.

That's him.

I know he likes to shower off the heat and grime of the kitchen. Then I must see him.

I must.

I sit on the side of my bed watching the second hand tick round the face of my clock. I have the envelope on my knee. The pictures, the cuttings, they are not mine. I am returning them to him.

Suddenly my phone rings. It is a call. It's Nate. I answer it, and the migraine seems to crash behind my eyes like a handful of knives.

"Emily," he says, uncertainty in his voice. "Please come and see me. I know you've been avoiding me."

"I'll come now," I say.

I throw the phone on the bed and run out of the house before Mum realises I have gone. I hold the envelope close to my chest.

I look up as I approach his caravan. The door's open. He is standing there in the doorway: black jeans, black T-shirt, damp hair, grey eyes.

I stop at the bottom of the steps.

"You know," he says, and his voice seems broken.

I nod slowly.

"You took the pictures."

"I'm sorry." I hold the envelope to him.

Slowly, his fingers reach for it. "You should come in."

He stands back, and I follow him inside. He drops the envelope on the little table. The crib board and cards are still there. My chest aches with memories.

Happy birthday, Emily.

I must not cry.

We sit opposite each other. He looks at the table, out of the window, then at me.

"You know who I am," he says.

"My nephew."

"When you came for the Nurofen. You found my things."

"I shouldn't have done that. I just knew there was something. Please talk to me."

"What can I say?"

"That's why you lied about your age."

"You might have worked it out."

This is Richard's son, Zoe's son, my nephew, who I have thought of, dreamed of, for so long. He's here now, across this table, and for the last three months, he's been my lover.

"It's over, isn't it?" he asks.

I swallow. "It has to be."

"It doesn't. We're not blood relations. We're not really related at all. You and Richard weren't related."

"I know, I know, but … it's …"

"Emily, I …"

Auntie Em … now I know we're not in Kansas.

"Don't say it."

"I really like you. The last few months have been amazing. I love you."

"Why didn't you say? Why didn't you say it from the start? All those questions about Richard. Why didn't you tell us?" Now I am angry.

Why didn't he tell us?

"I don't know. I didn't know if I'd like my … family. I didn't know if I'd want to get to know you. Once I'd said it, I couldn't unsay it. I didn't know so many things. I didn't know how I would feel about you."

"I'm your auntie."

"You're not. Not by blood."

"Your mother is Zoe Cassidy."

"Zoe Winter. I don't know what she'll call herself if they get divorced."

"Who's your father?"

"He's called Phil Winter. I never knew he wasn't my father until last year when all this shit hit the fan. They told me they'd got married because I was on the way. They met at a church. In Penzance."

"Penzance?"

"My Aunt Amanda introduced them. It was a shotgun wedding because of me. That's true. But he wasn't my real father. Richard was."

"Zoe's mother … she said Zoe would be giving the baby up for adoption."

Nate shrugs. "No, she kept me."

"Yes, I knew that on the day of the eclipse."

His hand reaches out for the envelope.

"I was there!" I cry. "I saw Zoe – I told you – and her daughter. That's Lucy, yes? And then I saw her husband and the boy I knew was Richard's. And that was you. You were wearing a bright T-shirt."

I *slam* my hand down on the envelope. There is a spiky, hot ball swelling in my throat, and my eyes are stinging. I'm going to cry. I can't help it.

311

"I'm sorry. I don't remember you."

"Why would you? I was just some old woman your mother spoke to."

"I was only six."

"You knew I was your aunt, you knew I was desperate to find my nephew, but you didn't tell me."

"I didn't want you to be my aunt. I wanted you to be my girlfriend." He grabs my hand. "I still do. We can do this. We're not related."

I withdraw my hand. "I can't," I whisper.

My eyes are wet with starry tears, and when I look into his face, I see his are, too.

"Are Zoe's parents still at Gunwalloe?"

"Hell no. They've been in Hampshire for years. Grandma grew up there. She's on her own now. Grandpa died some years ago. Amanda went to Australia for a while. Nursing. She's in London now."

"You never, ever, knew about Richard until last summer?"

"Not a thing. I was really pissed off with them. They should have told me the truth."

"But you don't tell the truth!"

He shrugs.

"What's your dad like?" I ask after a brief pause.

"He's a good man. Yes. I thought he was my dad. Because of the church, you know, they had to get married because I was coming."

"Is your birthday the twentieth of March? I'm sure Zoe said you were conceived in July."

"I came early."

"Your grandparents knew about Richard."

"Yes, but they never said. We didn't have much to do with them when Grandpa was alive. Grandma's a bit easier now. We're not close. Nor are Lucy and Josh, because Mum isn't close to her. I knew they'd kicked off at her for getting pregnant, but what was the fuss if my parents were married quickly? I like Amanda, though. I talked to her a lot about all this. She suggested I could come and look for you all and where it happened."

"Why were you at the Lizard for the eclipse? I wouldn't have thought your dad would want to be anywhere near the Lizard."

"I don't know. I was only a kid. I don't remember much about it. I do remember the black sun and that, and I remember desperately wanting to piss."

"I was there with friends from university. You passed us in the car as we walked up to the Lizard."

"I don't remember."

"Zoe said she would write and explain. She never did."

"Do you want to talk to her again?"

I don't answer.

I don't know.

"I could ask her," Nate offers.

"I don't know. It's too much." I wipe my nose and eyes on the back of my hand.

"It turns out Mum was having an affair. I heard her shouting at Dad about how she'd only ever been with him for so long, and she was trapped, and how she'd never been able to be a teacher, which is what she wanted to be, and all this kind of stuff. Then he said that was a bloody lie because what about Richard Knight? Was she ever going to tell me the truth about my father? How Dad married her to save her name when she was expecting a dead man's child. I heard all that."

"Christ," I say, and this time, my fingers find his and interlock with them. "That must have been terrible."

"I texted Amanda. I asked her. She said I should talk to Mum. So I did. After that, I just wanted to get out. They'd lied to me all my life. They had no plans to tell me. I wanted to come down here. Amanda said it was a good idea to get some space. Mum went ape, but Amanda told her to let me go and find myself, or something like that. She said it wouldn't be too hard for me to find a job as a chef. She lent me money."

"Does Zoe know where you are?"

"Yes."

"She knows you live here? She doesn't know about us? You and me?"

"I thought you said there was no us? No, she doesn't."

"What does she know?"

"That I'm at the Lighthouse. If she wants to write to me, to write to me there because I'm staying with friends from work. I said I'd found the caravan site and been to the bar a few times and believed I'd met your dad. That's all. Nothing about you. I told her I probably wasn't going to declare myself anyway. 'No point any more people being hurt,' I said."

"So much hurt," I whisper. "So many years lost."

They fuck you up, your mum and dad. They were fucked up in their turn.

I stare out of the window at the slice of blue sky, the green-gold of the hedge. On the cliff beyond are banks of bluebells. Again, I cannot see the Buttress from this angle, but I can feel it, always there, a hulking giant.

Where it started and where it all ends.

"You weren't ever going to tell me?"

"I couldn't. I wanted to be with you. I didn't know what to do. I thought in the end, you know, it'd come out. I didn't know. But we're not related."

"It's more complicated than that."

"Do I look like him?"

"You're like him. Yes, I suppose you do. That day I saw you on the Buttress. When I told you it wasn't a murder. It was like I'd seen a ghost."

"That must have been horrible."

"It was unsettling. What did the waitress really say?"

"What waitress?"

"The waitress who said there'd been a murder."

"There wasn't a waitress. I mean, there are waitresses there, but I made that up. I knew it wasn't a murder. I guess it was unkind to say that."

I don't speak. I cannot be with him anymore, like we have. I know already that this is the hardest breakup I have ever had. I do love Nate.

I love him for who he is, and for who he isn't, and who I thought he was.

"I'm sorry for everything."

I nod, tears splashing on the table.

"Was he left-handed?"

I shake my head.

"I don't know where that comes from."

"One of Richard's biological parents?" I manage. "I don't know anything about them."

"I feel completely lost sometimes," Nate says. "Dad's family isn't mine, I don't know anything about Richard's family, and I won't ever, and I never knew about your family. I've missed out all round."

"So have my parents," I snap back. "They thought you'd gone forever. Mum never got over that. Then I saw you at the eclipse, and I knew you were alive, but I couldn't tell them, and Zoe never wrote, so it was just as well I didn't, and then you came, but you never said who you were. So, they have missed out, too."

"Are you going to tell them?"

"I don't see how the fuck I can."

"Never?"

"How can I?"

"What am I going to do?"

"I don't know."

"You mean it, don't you? It's over."

I want to say no, that I don't mean it, but I can't.

"I'm sorry," I say instead.

"I'll go home."

"Home?"

"Back to Mum. I can't stay here. Not now. I can't be near you and this place and everything. I did want to see your baby."

I put my hand over my mouth to hide the dreadful shape my lips are making.

"You can't just leave your job."

"I can."

"They won't give you a reference."

"I'll make up something. Family problems back home. I can't be here now, not if you're not …"

Another pause comes.

"When?" I finally ask.

"When will I go?"

"When will you go?"

"Tonight."

By the time I leave the caravan, my parents are in the club. I stagger, like I am drunk, down the path to our bungalow. The lights from the bar appear as fragmented shards to my eyes.

I lie on my bed and cry. I cry for what I have lost, what I thought I had, and what will never be. I cry for myself, for Nate, for Richard. I cry for the lost time.

For the years that make a lifetime, the heartbeats that change destiny.

I hear cars coming and going down the drive. I will not run to the front window to look. One will be Nate leaving. I know he will go. I believe him. I don't want to see the flash of a red car, hear its rumble vanish into nothing.

I cannot keep this to myself.

When I go to the bathroom and see my face in the mirror – bloody-veined eyes, blotchy skin, swollen lips – I know that lying will be harder than the truth. And worse. My parents deserve to know.

This is a night for truths.

I will not tell them about what happened at the eclipse. That will forever remain inside me. I imagine new blood vessels and muscles growing and stretching round that memory, covering it like tree roots around buried rocks.

I tell my parents when they return. Sometimes I can hardly get the words out.

Mum goes white, like she may faint.

Dad throws down glass after glass of whisky, grabs a torch, and *slams* out of the house.

Five minutes later, he is back.

"He's gone," he says.

And I cry again.

When we finally go to bed, it is almost dawn. Mum lies beside me in my bed.

At last, I sleep.

I wake, and the first thing I am aware of is that someone is there with me. It must be Nate. And then I feel the burning in my head, my raw eyes, the exhaustion and nausea that overwhelm me, and yesterday floods back like seawater that has been sucked away down the beach and now returns in a deeper, darker swell.

Days and nights pass. Hazy, one into the other. I sleep sometimes; often, I do not. I force down food for the baby. Mum goes to the doctor and gets a prescription for Diazepam.

If it were not for my baby, I think I might just crumble into nothingness.

At last, if I concentrate only on my breathing – *In, out, in, out* – I can hold the tears back. It is time to tell some of my old friends about my baby. Rachel, Gary and Sonia – who I keep seeing in my mind under a midnight morning sky.

I log into Facebook to write to them.

Zoe Winter.

That is why I could not find her. I did not know her name. I could search for her now.

Facebook opens. I glance down at my notifications.

One from the previous day:

Nate Winter has accepted your friend request.

EPILOGUE

August 1, 2013

Warmth.

A sensation of thick, warm liquid drains down from my spine into my bottom. Someone is crouched on the floor in front of me, sliding thick DVT socks over my feet. The feeling of warmth intensifies. I am turned onto the bed, my legs lifted up. They are so heavy now that I could not raise them myself. Now I have to turn my head to see Mum. I smile at her in her theatre blues, paper hat and borrowed clogs. She has her phone ready to take photos.

There is a ring of faces above my feet. I feel nothing except the overwhelming weight of my own limbs. The anaesthetist sprays me with something, prods me. Can I feel that? Or that? What about this? No, I tell him, then wonder should I have said *yes*, because I no longer know what I can or cannot feel. There seems to be no border between sensations. A green screen goes up in front of my face.

I look at the clock on the wall. It's just gone one in the afternoon.

The theatre is a big, spare room. Behind me is a long window, and I know it is hot and sunny outside. The radio is on, but the sound has been turned down, so it's hard to catch the song underneath the voices and noises.

It's the middle of the day, on the first of August, the high heat of summer, and in moments, I am going to hold my baby.

My little Viking.

I do not know when the surgeons start, when they draw that thin red line with a knife. Gradually, I feel movement inside me but no pain. Through the screen, an elbow jabs towards my face. The anaesthetist hovers beside Mum, looking over the screen.

"Any moment now," he says.

This is real. It's really happening. I'm having a baby.

Suddenly, out of nowhere, comes a deep roar.

I gasp.

That's him – or her.

"What is it?" I ask.

"Don't you know?" the midwife asks, surprised. "It's a little girl."

Someone asks Mum if she wants to cut the cord.

"No, no, I couldn't," she says.

Someone else is loosening my gown. And there she is wrapped in a blanket: a screwed-up red face, damp auburn fluff, still bloody, pink pixie ears, and long elegant hands, not the hands of a baby. She stretches out one of those long, thin hands and starts picking at the ECG lead on my chest.

"Does she have a name yet?" the midwife asks.

Night. Low lights. We are in a four-bed ward, in a corner that would look onto the corridor if the window panel had not been covered. There is a chair for visitors – one chair, for the *father*, of course – and a sink that I cannot wash in because I am not allowed off the bed yet. And then there is her crib, her clear-topped box pushed up against my bed. She is sleeping on her back, her little arms over her head, her legs in a diamond. Mum went home in the afternoon and came back with Dad, bringing a set of pink newborn rompers and a pink bunny. My little girl is now wearing a suit patterned with tiny rosebuds. The bunny is nestled up next to her. I feel tears when I see that bunny and those roses.

320

And now we are alone again.

It is only eleven o'clock, but they have turned off the lights. There are three other new mothers in this ward, but I have not seen them or spoken to them because all our curtains have been kept closed.

It's just the two of us, in our own little corner.

I am hot, and the wound throbs. I wish I could get up for a walk. Next time a nurse comes in, I will ask if I can go up and down the corridor. My phone is on the bed cover. I have texted everyone who knows.

All except one.

My daughter's name is Leona. She was born under the sign of Leo. She's a Viking. She has amber hair and the darkest midnight blue eyes I have seen. It's a lion's name.

I am a lioness, and she is my cub.

I reach into her box and lay my hand on her tummy, which rises and falls so softly. Twelve hours ago, she was still inside my womb, still in the dark and the warmth and the safety, with the metronome of my heartbeat to soothe her.

I withdraw my hand and reach for my phone. His number is still there, of course.

My little girl was born today at 1.23pm. Her name is Leona. We are both well and are going home tomorrow x

It's sent. I put my hand back into the crib. The movement tugs my wound, and I flinch. Leona does not open her eyes, but her fingers curl round mine. A flood of love surges through me. We started our journey alone, just her and me, and now we've found the end of our rainbow alone, together.

How it was meant to be.

I see the screen flash a second before the beep.

Huge congratulations. Can I see a picture, please? Look after yourselves x

I turn off the phone and slide it into my bag. I will send a picture of Leona to her cousin tomorrow or the day after.

I fall asleep in the half-light, with one hand resting on her chest. Our first night together. I will only ever have one first night with my first child. A once-in-a-lifetime moment.

Like a total eclipse of the sun over the end of the world.

Acknowledgements

A huge thanks to my family for all the support and belief they have shown in me over the years. To my mother Caroline, my daughters Raphael and Aelfrida, and those who did not live long enough to see this book in print: my father Chris, and my grandparents Sylvia and Alfred. I love you all enormously.

I would also like to thank Sarah Hembrow and Lara Colrain of Vulpine Press for believing in me and my stories and for all your help and advice. I appreciate everything you have done.

Lucinda Hart grew up in Cornwall and has been writing fiction since the age of three. She has a BA in Fine Art and Creative Writing and a MA in Creative Writing, both from Bath Spa University. The themes in Lucinda's books are often of great relevance to her. Place is also important; she uses her favourite locations in novels and hopes they will interest the reader as much as they have inspired her. She lives in Cornwall with her two daughters.

Printed in Great Britain
by Amazon

25298818R00189